MW01377474

Matthew's Discovery

BY
DONNA MCGEE

the Peppertree Press
Sarasota, Florida

For information regarding permission,
call 941-922-2662 or contact us at our website:
www.peppertreepublishing.com or write to:
the Peppertree Press, LLC.
Attention: Publisher
1269 First Street, Suite 7
Sarasota, Florida 34236

ISBN: 978-1-61493-179-9

Library of Congress Number: 2013941452

Printed in the U.S.A.

Printed October 2013

Matt Moo...

For the breath of inspiration, you will always be to me...
And to whom I dedicate this book.

Acknowledgements

Michelle, for believing in me, Joe for the patience and love you never tire of and to my supportive family and friends...
Thank you, I love you all dearly.

Chapter One

It was a sweltering July night, and Dr. Paul Nomrahaufa was soaking in his third cool bath of the day. He was used to stifling temperatures, being an archaeologist, but his hometown of Siwa, Egypt, was experiencing the worst heat wave in history. To make matters worse, drought-like conditions were growing in this city, known for its flourishing oasis. He started to doze off in the small tub when he heard banging at his front door.

"Dr. Nomrahaufa . . . Dr. Nomrahaufa!" a frantic woman's voice called. *BANG . . . BANG . . . BANG . . . . "PAUL . . . please!"* she urgently cried out, pounding on the door again.

He jumped into his pants, raced down the hallway to the front door, and flung it open. There stood Teadora, his brother's widow, in her nightclothes, holding her chest. The heavy-set woman reeked of smoke and could barely catch her breath. Paul saw terror in her black eyes. His thin body began to tremble, and his face turned white, matching the strip of gray in his black hair.

"It's . . . it's . . . . Come quickly . . . the twins . . . ." But Teadora was too winded to speak. She grabbed his hand and pulled him through the front door in his bare feet, and they ran up a dirt road leading to his son's house.

"Nathani, do you ever think about Mommy?"

"Of course I do, Ankhi. I miss her every day, and Poppy too."

"You know, sometimes when Auntie Teadora wears her perfume, I look around to see if Mommy is here. That sweet smell of jasmine makes me think about her so much."

"Ankhi, it's late; go to sleep. I'm tired, and we must get up early tomorrow for our lessons."

"Will Grandfather be home soon? I don't like him being gone for so long. Why does he disappear like that—does he not like us?"

"Ankhi, Grandfather's work at the pyramid is very important, and he must be there when the weather is not so hot. He's told you many times he doesn't like being away from us, but it's what he must do. And don't be silly; of course Grandfather loves us. What is with all these questions? Is something troubling you, brother?"

"No, not really. It's just that sometimes I think about a lot of things. Tonight I was thinking about the . . . the fire. It's been five years, Nathani, and I still don't understand how Poppy was able to save us but not himself and Mommy." And his sweet, gentle voice gave way to sobbing.

"Oh, brother, do not cry," Nathani said as he left his bed. "I do not know what happened that night, but at least we have each other. Listen, do you remember what Mommy always told us?"

Ankhi looked up at his mirror image and shook his head as tears streamed slowly down his tanned face. His brother's sympathetic blue eyes and silky black hair shined in the dark room from the stars' gentle reflection in the night sky. Ankhi sensed the comfort his brother offered and wiped his runny nose on the sleeve of his nightshirt.

"Well, she always said that no matter how dark a day may be, there is still light upon us. We must never forget our blessings, especially how good Grandfather has been to us. Now please, go to sleep," he said in a soothing tone while tucking him in.

Nathani climbed back into his bed, pulled the soft covers up around his neck, and closed his eyes.

"Psst, brother, are you asleep?" Ankhi whispered a few moments later.

"No . . . what is it *now?*" he sighed deeply.

"I have a secret to tell you."

"Can it wait until the morning?" Nathani replied calmly, trying not to lose his patience.

"Only if you want it to," Ankhi giggled.

"Yes, brother . . . I will wait until the morning. . . . *Now good night!*"

The next morning after their lessons, the boys found a note from Auntie Teadora telling them Grandfather would be home the next day and that she had gone to the market and would return soon. Ankhi then took his reluctant brother's hand and led him to their grandfather's study.

"*Ankhi, you know* we are not to be in here unless we are invited. *Have you lost your mind?*"

"But don't you want to know about my secret?"

"Well, yes . . . but we have been in here a million times. What could you possibly have a secret about?" he muttered while curiously looking around the familiar dark room with its shelved walls full of old books and dangling cobwebs. Even the green heavy ornate drapes were still drawn over the windows, reeking of musty mildew and Grandfather's cigar smoke he'd grown accustomed to in the last five years. Nothing seemed out of the ordinary or new. He knew every inch of this room, and there wasn't anything unusual amongst all of his grandfather's clutter.

Ankhi trotted proudly to the middle of the room. He turned around and stood on a large blue and gold tapestry rug their grandfather treasured. He began to tap his foot on the floor while a derisive grin grew on his face.

"Okay, brother, I give up! *What* is your *big secret?*"

Ankhi snickered, and it only seemed to frustrate Nathani more. Noting his brother's impatience, Ankhi pulled back the corner of the carpet, revealing a shiny brass handle lying in a groove of the wood floor. Ankhi boldly pulled the brass handle and opened a hidden door. He plopped down on his belly and stuck his head in the hole, and then half of his body disappeared inside the wood floor. He spread his legs wide apart, and his toes turned cherry red as he pushed them into the floor to anchor himself. A moment later, he popped up, struggling with a gold and silver chest. On the front, the lid had several symbols made with cut pieces of purple amethyst. Nathani recognized the first two. One was a squiggly line, and the other an elaborate carved bird. From the little he knows about hieroglyphics, he gathered it to be the initials A.N. But the third was a symbol that looked like a man squatting, and the fourth had missing stones. It wasn't anything he could decipher.

"What is this marvelous trunk you have found?" Nathani said, with his eyes so big his brother laughed.

"I'm not sure," he answered, shrugging his shoulders. "I have not yet opened it, and thought we could discover what's inside together."

Being the sensible one, as always, Nathani knew they shouldn't be in there nosing around in Grandfather's things. But his curiosity at that moment was bigger than his common sense. He became mesmerized with the shiny chest and knelt next to his brother. A strange tingling sensation warmed his body, and his small hands began to shake. Slowly he lifted the lid, and a gentle voice began to speak.

Your blood will bring forth the heir, the one we wait for,
shall be born in less of two hundred years. Her mark he
shall bear will set her free, a life imprisoned no more to
be. You must search the dark halls and dig on your knees,
for treasures you will find from long lost family.
Gather them carefully they will be of great need, the heir
will use them accordingly. Be not foolish of certain riches
you find, for they must be held until his time. You will
know which ones so heed, it is in writing for you to see.

"Brother," Ankhi uttered, "what is wrong with you? You are quiet. . . . Are you not amazed with this treasure?"

Nathani turned toward him as he shuttered from a chill and rubbed his arms.

"Ankhi, did . . . did you just hear that?"

"Hear what?" he asked, looking at him strangely.

"You did not hear someone speak just now?"

"No. Should I have? Are you sick with a fever, Nathani?"

"No . . . no, brother. I guess it was just my imagination," he assured him. Then he raised his hand and felt his forehead. He didn't seem to have a fever, and he was almost positive her voice was not his imagination.

"Well, you do not look sick, brother. *Come on,* let's see what treasures we have found," Ankhi insisted excitedly.

The boys pawed carefully through the items in the chest. There were numerous papyrus scrolls; solid gold objects that looked like mummies and dragonflies, beautiful crafted gold jewelry, and colorful gems in all sizes filled the box. At the very bottom were two books, with the same worn symbols as the chest. Nathani knew the chest must have belonged to someone very important, but who? And where did his grandfather get it from?

The boys heard the back door to the kitchen slam and knew Auntie was home. Quickly they closed the chest and placed it back under the floor. They lowered the door quietly, pulled the rug back to its position, and ran on tiptoes to their bedroom. They sat on their beds, out of breath, frightened, and grateful that Auntie did not catch them snooping.

"Ankhi . . . you . . . must . . . promise me," and he swallowed, catching his breath, "to *never* again snoop around in Grandfather's things. I am too young to have a heart attack!"

"Do not worry about me," Ankhi laughed. "We are *both* too young for that to happen. I will not do it again, brother; I promise. Now come, let's go see what Auntie got from the store. Maybe she brought us that delicious chocolate we love."

"You go ahead . . . . I have something to do and will be there in a minute."

"Okay, but if she bought chocolate, I do not promise there will be some left for you."

As Ankhi closed the bedroom door, Nathani shook his head. He thought about how his brother never seemed to take anything seriously, and sometimes it really annoyed him. They were twins but nothing alike except for their looks. Nathani sometimes resented that too. But he loved his brother dearly, even though he was a pest, or, as Grandfather put it, an imp with great curiosity!

He reached under his bed for the red diary Grandfather gave him last year. It's where he writes down all his deepest thoughts and feelings when Ankhi isn't around. His grandfather told him many times in private that he was special and the diary would one day help him understand that. As he began to pen the words from the mysterious voice, he wondered if what happened today was what his grandfather meant. After all, he was the one who heard the voice, not Ankhi. He thought about telling Grandfather about today but knew he couldn't. They broke the rules about being in the study without permission, and he didn't want to disappoint his grandfather with their naughty behavior. So Nathani just wrote it all in his diary.

The next day, their grandfather, Paul Nomrahaufa, returned home from the pyramid with many wonderful treasures. There were numerous colorful velvet bags and jeweled boxes of all sizes. Auntie, Ankhi, and Nathani helped him and two workers unload the camels and put all the marvelous treasures into his office. When they were finished, he asked everyone to leave except Nathani. Ankhi wasn't happy that his brother got to stay with Grandfather and all the treasures, but Auntie persuaded him with his favorite chocolate after Paul gave her a long, strange stare that Nathani had caught from the corner of his eye. Nathani's stomach began to roll around, making him feel sick as he wondered if his grandfather somehow knew what they had done. Nathani watched nervously as Paul walked around his desk and sat down. He looked exhausted. The last four months of work at the pyramid had been very productive, but he hadn't slept well, and it was apparent, even to Nathani.

"Grandfather, are you not well?"

"Oh, I am very well, Grandson," he replied with a slight grin. "Come here," he said with a wave of his hand, and Nathani obeyed. He lifted him up and sat him on his desk directly in front of him. Nathani began to fidget and rub his hands together nervously.

"Is . . . is something wrong, Grandfather?"

"No . . . not really, although I must say I didn't expect this day to come quite so soon."

"This *day*, Grandfather, what do you mean?" he asked, wringing his hands tightly together.

"Relax, Nathani, you are not in any trouble, my dear boy," he said with an assuring chuckle as he pulled his sweaty hands apart. "But I do know what you and your inquisitive brother did," he whispered amusingly while patting his grandson's knee.

"But how, Grandfather, how . . . did you know?"

"Ah . . . that is what we are to talk about, Nathani, and our discussion must stay between us. I want you to promise me that you will not speak of anything to Ankhi. He is not ready to know what I am to tell you. Besides, what I have to say concerns you . . . ."

"Me . . . . Grandfather . . . . What about *me?"* Nathani asked as his blue eyes widened.

Paul leaned back in his chair and tilted his gray balding head to one side. He stared up at the ceiling, then over to one of the bookshelves, and let out a sigh. Leaning forward, he reached for the top drawer to his desk and pulled out one of his cigars. Nathani watched as he snipped off a chunk on one end with a fancy silver clipper, then placed the large brown cigar between his lips and lit it with a wooden match. He sucked in deeply as the lit end glowed bright red and until gray smoke billowed from his mouth. Then Paul got up from his chair, and with his hands clasped behind his back and cigar hanging from the corner of his mouth, he began to slowly pace the office floor.

"Grandfather ... why ... why is it that I am special and not Ankhi?"

Paul continued to pace, and Nathani thought he was ignoring him. However, he was taking in his grandson's question with great thought and after a few moments sat back down at the desk. He took his cigar and tapped its long gray ash off onto the edge of a crystal ashtray. Then, leaning back into his chair, he placed the cigar in the corner of his mouth.

"Nathani, do you know what Bawii has told me?"

"You mean my teacher Bawii?"

"Yes."

"No."

"Bawii told me that although you are only eleven years old, you possess the intelligence of a much older student. He has also said that you will be able to go to college much sooner than I anticipated."

"Really . . . but what about Ankhi? He is smart too."

"Yes, yes, he is smart, but he doesn't take his studies quite as seriously as you do, and I know that is just his nature. Besides all that, he isn't . . . well, as gifted as you. Let's just say that he's like your father and you are like me."

"What exactly am I like you about, Grandfather?"

"There is something *very special* we share. When you and your brother discovered that chest under the floor, did anything . . . well, did something unusual happen?"

"Yes . . . . It . . . well, a voice spoke to me. It told me about an heir and that I was going to find family treasures and writings about this. Do you *know* of this voice, Grandfather, and what it all means?"

"Yes, Nathani, I too have heard the voice, and it has told me many things. As far as my understanding, the work we do in the pyramid will one day benefit a very important heir. But to be honest, I haven't figured out yet what he must do and why. All I know is that you *must* listen to this voice when it speaks, and do as it says. My father, who also heard it, had different ideas, and he died a horrible death."

"I'm sorry to hear that of your father, but why us, Grandfather, and not Ankhi and Poppy?"

"This I cannot answer. I can only guess that the voice chooses who for its own reason, and that is all we need to know for now."

Nathani sat quietly, looking down at his hands while he tapped his fingers together in some sort of rhythm. Paul re-lit his cigar and puffed at it vigilantly, all the while staring at him. There surely was more to tell him, but he felt for the time being he had said enough.

Nathani stopped his tapping and looked up. "I know you are not telling me everything, Grandfather, so I am going to ask you a question, and I hope you will be truthful. Why is it that I know you have more to tell me, and why do I know sometimes what someone is thinking before they even speak it? Is this the gift you have told me about?"

"Yes, my dear boy. You have a great sense of perception, and as far as I can tell, it is much greater than anyone in our family has ever had. You are not frightened by it, are you?"

"No, I don't think so. Should I be?"

"Oh, no . . . absolutely not!"

"Grandfather, I have but one more question. Who or what is this voice?"

Paul slowly pulled the cigar from his mouth and tapped its ashes into the crystal dish. His face, lined with age, seemed to relax, and he began to grin. He looked down momentarily, shook his head, then inhaled deeply. As he exhaled, he looked up and into Nathani's inquisitive eyes.

"I believe it is a soul. The *guardian* of the pyramid and the heir it speaks of will be the only one to discover who she truly is. And until that day comes, I know in my heart that we, and those who come after us, must continue work there. It is our family legacy."

"Is that why you work at the pyramid . . . because the voice told you to?"

"Oh, no . . . no, my dear boy," he chuckled as he assured him. I am an archaeologist first, who enjoys digging up the past. I worked for many years before it spoke to me. For me, archaeology isn't about what I must find inside the pyramid; it's what I discover about the things I find. This voice, Nathani, it . . . it does not speak all the time. As a matter of fact, I have only heard it a dozen times or so. But I can always feel its presence. The only time it has made itself known is when I've discovered something important for this heir."

"I'm not quite sure I understand that, Grandfather."

"You will, and soon too! When I go out next time, you will be coming with me. It's high time you see what your future holds."

"Oh, I am so happy to hear that!" And he leaned forward and gave Paul a big hug.

"I will be a great archaeologist, just like you!" Then he sat up and looked him straight into his eyes.

"But . . . but what about the . . .," and Nathani paled.

"What is it, Nathani? What troubles you?"

"The . . . the bad voice that's there, Grandfather."

"Ahh . . . you have sensed that as well."

"Yes, and . . . well, it frightens me."

"And so it should. It is very evil. You must understand that there is good and bad in everyone and everything in this world. However, it is up to you to keep it all in balance. I have seen what this evil can do to a weak man's soul and how greed can destroy the very best of a person. It is what happened to my father. My advice to you is simple. Avoid its serpent tongue with its temptations and false promises of riches. You are already wealthy and will continue to be so. You have nothing to gain from it . . . nothing at all!"

"So what is its purpose, Grandfather? What does it want?"

"Honestly, I'm not sure, but I believe it has something, if not all, to do with the heir."

"He must be pretty important, wouldn't you say so?"

"Yes, I suppose he is. But I don't think we should focus our lives or the work at the pyramid around him."

"Ankhi, will he work there too?"

"Well, I would hope so. You both will soon go to school in Europe and learn all you can about being an archaeologist and how to read hieroglyphics. Then it will be up to him what he decides to do with that knowledge. But you and one day your son, then his son, and so forth, will continue the work at the pyramid. It is your destiny Nathani, as well as theirs. Now, I think we have discussed enough of this matter, don't you? Let's go see what Teadora has made for supper. It smells like she has made quite a feast, and I am very hungry."

And so the work continued at the pyramid, generation after generation, and the Nomrahaufa legacy continued to grow. However, in nearly two hundred years of their digging, no one was ever able to reach the royal tombs. That is . . . until recently.

Chapter Two

Sol Nipuk yawned and let out a painful groan as he stretched his long arms from his sleeping bag.

"Ah, good, you are up, Dr. Nipuk. Do you wish something to eat?"

"Just some coffee would be nice, and two aspirins, please, Jobi. This stone floor I'm afraid has reminded me of my age," he replied, then smiled at the cook. "Oh, Jobi, make sure someone gets that pump fixed for the air mattresses. You never know when we may have to spend another night here. These ancient stones are cruel to an old man's body."

"Never mind what they do to old men. . . . *We all* suffer today," Jobi replied seriously.

Then he burst out laughing, and Sol watched Jobi's protruding belly bounce under his soiled denim shirt while he poured his coffee from a dented silver thermos.

Sol and his workers had been forced to stay in the pyramid overnight. An unexpected khamsin had blown in during the afternoon, making it impossible for them to leave safely. But here on the edge of the White Desert, and throughout this barren region in Egypt, these violent sandstorms are common in the spring. They can be just as unpredictable and surmountable as the winter nor'easters in upstate New York.

Dr. Sol Nipuk is the leading Egyptologist at this pyramid and well-known in the archaeological world. He looks quite intimidating at six feet, four inches tall, but those who know him describe him as a gentle spirit of a man, with a wonderful sense of humor. His vast knowledge of ancient Egypt is remarkable, and his older workers swear that when you look into his dark blue eyes, you will see a reincarnated man, with a soul of Egypt's past.

Sol drained the last few drops of coffee from his cup, then reached inside his green canvas backpack and pulled out his daily journal. After folding his sleeping bag, he went down a narrow ascending passageway that led to a large oval chamber.

He picked up his worn-out whisk broom and gave several swipes to a large, smooth, flat stone sitting in the middle of the room. He then took the broom to himself and brushed powdery grit off his baggy blue jeans and white cotton shirt before sitting down. This is where Sol sits most days and writes in his journal. He believes ancient scribes sat on this very stone while they worked to fill this space with its magnificent hieroglyphics four thousand years ago.

As he flipped through the gritty book, he blew away the sand that found its way deep between the bound pages. "April 2, 2008," he wrote as his pen skipped over a few specks of dirt.

"Time comes and goes. . . . It surely waits for no one," he said aloud while scratching his head of thick silvery hair.

The chamber is brightly lit and just twenty-five feet from the entrance of the pyramid. Sol calls it the welcome room, but it's his quiet place and a reminder of where he started fifty years ago as a young boy in the archaeological world. The tawny colored, pinkish limestone walls reveal intricate hieroglyphics and stunning, colorful crafted pictographs that have weathered thousands of years. These are life stories carved within these stones, and they tell a great living history of a place once called **Rhondra.**

Rhondra was a small city that flourished during the Middle Kingdom in ancient Egypt. Its location is in a strange, but beautiful, area near the westerly edge of the White Desert. The ominous, grand shapes found in this desert, a once filled seabed, make an unusual background to the only pyramid found in this isolated area. The sunsets are breathtaking as the chalky landscape seems to float on rivers of dark liquid gold, while the odd forms take on brilliant colors of the settling sun's pink sky. At night, especially during a full moon, people swear the eerie shapes move and strange voices rise above the hushed, cool desert. There are many stories about the White Desert, but the old-timers say, "If you sincerely listen with your heart, you will hear the truth of the desert."

According to the pyramid's hieroglyphics and pictographs, Rhondra was a self-sufficient city. Plenty of fresh water was available, and its inhabitants farmed a rich land for vegetation and livestock. The people who settled in this peaceful city were from all over Egypt. There were no slaves in this melting pot, and everyone led a purposeful and prosperous life.

Around 1940 BC, Prince Methus became Rhondra's ruler. He was the sole heir of King Mattaheus, a smart, noble warrior, who built Rhondra during a turbulent time in Egypt. But he prevailed, and as their bloody wars began to die down, word circulated of a new Pharaoh from Thebes who would bring diplomatic unity to the region. Upon hearing this, King Mattaheus sent word he would meet with him and soon leave his city with a small army to offer the new Pharaoh his help in attaining peace. He knew who he was; Mattaheus had fought alongside him in several battles before, and they had become good friends.

However, there was a greedy, evil king from the South, who wanted control of Rhondra, and when word got to him about Mattaheus's trip, he planned an attack. He deeply desired Rhondra, for it was rich in resources, and he was determined to have it and the wealth that would empower him.

On the eve of the first day of spring, on the way to Thebes, King Mattaheus and his army underwent a brutal attack, outside of the city of Fayyum. The king and his men were tortured with unspeakable acts through the night and then beheaded. After sunrise, the heathens tossed their headless, bloody bodies into a deep ravine, set them on fire, and left them smoldering to ashes.

When word got to the new Pharaoh of King Mattaheus's demise, he immediately took his army and hunted down this monstrous king, destroying him and his city before they attempted to take over Rhondra. He told his men that there would be no barbaric leaders during his rule, for it would be impossible to have peace in the land with those who held such practices.

While on his way back to Thebes, the Pharaoh came upon the bloody site where King Mattaheus and his men were murdered. They searched for bodies, finding only their charred bones and surprisingly a single ring he recognized as the king's. The Pharaoh decided to take the ring to Methus. He regretfully relayed what happened and how sorry he was to lose such a great friend and noble warrior. He told Methus the way to honor his father would be to rule Rhondra fairly, maintain the peace he fought so bravely to attain, and continue to be an ally to those who were once his enemies.

So Methus, at only thirteen, became king of Rhondra. Though young, he seemed to settle in as a good ruler right away. The elders and scribes said it was because King Mattaheus began his son's royal training and education when he was just three years old. He was taught about war and strategic fighting, and that a true ruler was no one unless the people of your kingdom believed and trusted in you. He learned that you had to earn people's respect; it was never a given, regardless of what title you held in life. Above all, never was he to trust a fool, nor be the fool, or take for granted what nature graciously offers. Just as the earth and its creatures are tended and nurtured to bring a great harvest, so should you treat the people of your kingdom. So Methus lived by his father's words and ruled a flourishing city.

When he was seventeen, he married Oonaphelia, a beautiful woman with baby blue eyes and long golden hair, who came from a city north of Rhondra. She was a devoted wife with extreme kindness toward others. Oonaphelia was an exceptionally gifted woman, who befriended all creatures and was said to have possessed great powers of intuition. With such a queen by his side, Rhondra grew to be one of the most beautiful and cohesive cities in Egypt.

Many years later, parts of Egypt suffered terrible droughts, and a horrible, flesh-eating plague broke out, consuming thousands of people. The king and queen were vigilant and kept their citizens safely behind the city walls, but to no avail; several families in Rhondra suffered great losses to this menacing disease. Sadly, King Methus and his sons were no exception, leaving Queen Oonaphelia with a young daughter to raise and a grand city to rule. But two years later, Egypt was thriving again, and so was Rhondra.

Then unexplainable things began to happen in her city. The Rhondronians would wake up to find their livestock missing and fields of thriving crops demolished. Even with the queen's guards set up around the city walls, no one could explain what was happening. There were rumors that a curse had fallen on Rhondra, and stories began circulating about large creatures seen flying over the night skies. Although the queen vowed to protect her city and people, many Rhondronians were too frightened to stay and fled their homes.

Hieroglyphics that could have explained to Sol what happened are unreadable. There are only bits and pieces of information about Rhondra's fall on its ancient yellowed walls. And he has a hard time understanding why anyone would have destroyed them. After all, the scribes were so meticulous about giving such full and vivid details of its history that not much of this makes sense to him. What brought her into ruin is just as puzzling, though, as the many mysterious events Sol and others have experienced there. With numerous unexplainable deaths, cave-ins, and loved ones' bizarre behaviors during his time at this pyramid, deep inside him, Sol believes whatever destroyed Rhondra is somehow connected to all the horrible things that have happened. However, he has never told anyone about this. But he has hopes one day he will be able to solve this mystery.

Sol finished yesterday's entries in his journal and patted his work boots into the soft gold sand that made its way into the pyramid from yesterday's sandstorm. He arched his achy back as he stood and gave it a few good rubs with his rough hands. He looked around the room, contemplating a painful conversation he needed to have with someone he cares for very deeply. He shook his head, did a few stretches to loosen his stiff muscles, then stuffed his journal into his backpack, picked up his phone, and headed out to the pyramid's entrance, where it met the heat of the day and bright, glaring sun. He slid his dark sunglasses on and looked around outside.

Inside a big white tent, he spotted the red hat with a faded yellow bandana tied around it. It was Rahga, the head engineer of safety operations. He was running through an emergency drill with the many men who work at the pyramid when he saw Sol wave to him. He knows what Sol must do today, and his heart is heavy for him. Although Rahga is an extremely muscular, tough-looking man, he owns the heart of a lamb. His dark brown eyes are kind, yet his face is stern and rugged with a bushy dark beard. The thick lines above his nose reveal his unrelenting worry of the what-ifs and dangers of the pyramid. Nevertheless, that's his job, what he lives for, and who Rahga is.

"Have they eaten yet?" Sol asked.

"Yes, they were up early and eager to clean yesterday's mess," Rahga replied amusingly.

"Ahh, it's good to see your sense of humor this morning," Sol said with a hearty chuckle.

"Have you made your call yet?" Rahga asked gently.

"No, but I am getting ready to. Make sure all the men have eaten well and drunk enough water before they go back in, okay?"

"Yes, father," he replied in a child's voice.

Sol shook his head, smiling, amused by Rahga's dry humor, and waved him back to the tent so he could continue his work. Rahga went to the men, and Sol walked to his vehicle to ensure he would have good phone reception. He reluctantly reached his callous hand down into the leg of his pants pocket and pulled out his phone.

"Well, who . . . in the world . . . ?"

Wrestling around in her warm covers, she pawed around for the nightstand and pulled down the chain on the antique lamp.

"Yes . . . this is Pearle."

"Pearle, thank goodness I got you. It is I, Sol."

"Sol?"

"Yes . . . Sol Nipuk," he replied bewildered.

"Oh, Sol, I am sooo s-sor-ry," she said with a yawn. "What do you mean, thank goodness you got me? It's 4 *a.m.* here; where *else* would I be?"

"Ah, my dear," he responded with a hearty laugh, "you know I have no concept of time."

"Yes, yes, I do," she laughed out loud and quickly covered her mouth as she sat up against her cushioned headboard.

"So, how are you, Pearle? How is Florida? Gosh, we have not

spoken in months! I bet the weather is nice there. Oh, have you finished renovating that marvelous structure yet?"

He continued to ramble on with small talk and his known quirkiness, without taking a breath, while Pearle's thoughts shifted to her childhood. She recalled the two men she adored most: Sol and, more importantly, her father. Their images . . . her childhood . . . embedded in her memories. *Sol*, she thought . . . *hmm . . . how much you looked like dad.* It was unbelievable how often they were mistaken for brothers. Handsome, tall, and neither of them ever seem to care about their unkempt curly black hair. *Oh, and those ridiculous straw hats*, she thought, laughing to herself, *with those ugly, sweaty bandanas tied around their heads—what were they thinking?!* And even though a child then, she admired their deep devotion to archaeology. It was as immeasurable as their friendship. Pearle chuckled again and shook her head, thinking about how they would always find something to laugh about, no matter how bad their day was. They just had this uncanny way of bringing humor to their difficult and, at times, dangerous work. However, she knows Sol uses his humor to mask unpleasant truths.

Pearle, now more awake, realized something was wrong. Sol has never called her at this hour, and his casual, drawn-out conversation was uncharacteristic of him. She rubbed her wide blue eyes and slid her slender tan legs from under the warm covers. She reached over to the nightstand and picked up a silver hair barrette he gave her on her thirteenth birthday. Pearle squeezed the cell phone between her head and shoulders, and continued to listen while taking her long black hair and securing it on top of her head with a snap of the barrette. She leaned forward and planted her elbows on her bare legs, and exhaled slowly with another yawn, then let out a sigh.

"Sol, I've known you for over forty years. You didn't call me at this hour to discuss the weather or the construction of my home. Are you okay? Has something happened?"

A long, eerie silence filled the phone, and it frightened her.

"Sol . . . . Are you still there?"

"Yes," he replied hoarsely. "I . . . ahem . . . I have much to discuss . . . but more importantly, I want you to come to Egypt."

"Oh?"

"Pearle . . . it concerns . . . ." But his voice faded.

"Well, what is it?" she asked impatiently, switching the phone to her other ear.

He began to pace nervously, and the hot sand crunched loudly under his boots. Sweat began to pour down his dirty face, and perspiration soaked his cotton shirt. What Sol was going to tell her next made him feel sick.

"I have uncovered something. . . . It is of much importance . . . to you and your family."

"Good grief, Sol, what is it?"

Breathing heavily, he exhaled and replied, "We have exposed several new tombs."

"This is wonderful news, but why do you sound so troubled?"

"There is something else. . . . I have found something that belonged to . . . to Oona."

"Something of . . . of Oona's . . . did you just say, *Oona's?*"

"Yesss . . .," his dry voice hissed.

Her stomach churned as her heart pounded. She tightened her grip on the phone and stood straight up.

"Well . . . what is it? What have you found?"

"I am not sure. I mean, I *know* what it is; I just do not understand how this could be!"

"Sol," she said exasperated. "Have you been drinking, because you are not making any sense. *Please* . . . just tell me already!"

He closed his eyes and took a deep breath. There was no easy way to do this, so he proceeded to tell her what he found inside one of the newly discovered tombs. When he finished, Sol pulled his sweaty, fisted hand out of his pants pocket and sank to his knees, relieved. Several moments passed with an uncomfortable silence between them, and he began to walk around in a circle as he waited for her to speak.

"Sss . . . Sol . . . this is impossible. It's been eight years, and finding that there . . . . Are you sure it's Oona's?"

"Absolutely. Who else better to know than I?" he snapped. Then quickly he closed his eyes, regretting he answered her that way.

"It just can't be; you *must* be mistaken!" she insisted.

"Pearle, look, I'm sorry, but there is no mistake," he sighed while looking down as he kicked hard at a mound of sand.

"Was there . . . anything . . . else?"

"No . . . nothing."

"Will it be safe until I get there?"

"Of course. Our security is the best and without one incident in *forty years* at this pyramid, and you know that," he snapped again. "My dear, you act as if this is the first time we have encountered something peculiar here. There are countless mysteries involving this pyramid, or have you forgotten?"

"No . . . no, I haven't. All right, I will be there as soon as possible."

"I have waited years to hear you say that, Pearle. It will be good to have you back here again. It's been . . . ."

"Listen, Sol," she sharply interrupted. "I'm not coming to stay any great length of time. It's just to see what we have discussed. You know I can't do that. I have Matthew to consider now, and I wouldn't. But . . . well . . . I could bring him along. . . ."

Sol laughed, "You mean you would be a nervous wreck leaving your grandson at home."

"You're a funny guy . . . but you do know me well, my friend."

"Look, Pearle, I'll make all the arrangements for your visit. I'm sure there's plenty on your mind right now. Besides, I'd like to do this for you, okay?"

"That would be great, Sol. Thanks."

"Oh, don't be silly; it is my pleasure. All right, then, it's settled. We shall talk soon."

She closed the phone with a gentle snap, then with a shaky hand removed her barrette and got back under the cool covers. Lying there in the darkness, she combed over every word Sol said. Common sense told her it all seemed impossible. He could be mistaken . . . couldn't he? She rolled over and closed her eyes, but all she thought about was the marble headstone that read:

Oona Almondative, Loving Daughter, Mother and Wife

Chapter Three

"What's up, Nana?"

"Oh, morning, Matthew. Not much, just making breakfast," Pearle replied with a gapping yawn.

"Where's our Italian dumpling?"

"Oh, my God, you just did not call her that," she said gruffly with a slight smirk.

Matthew put his head down and laughed.

"Come on, Nana, you know I was only kidding around. Seriously, where is Annabelle, sleeping in?"

"As if," she snorted. "You know she's always up at five like clockwork. She had an early doctor's appointment this morning."

"Is she okay?"

"Oh, yeah . . . she just went for a checkup."

Annabelle is their live-in housekeeper and has been with Pearle for the last fifteen years. She's an important part of their family, and Matthew loves her like a second grandmother. Barely five feet tall with short red hair, she's quite feisty for a fifty-nine-year-old woman who's twenty pounds overweight. But her nurturing nature and optimistic attitude make her so easy to love, and as far as Pearle and Matthew are concerned, there is no better cook in the world than their Annabelle!

"Hey, were you up late playing video games again?" Pearle asked while staring at him with one eyebrow in the air.

"Uh . . . no," he said, shaking his head.

"Really," she said in disbelief. "Well, those blue eyes and the road maps they have this morning say different."

"No, honest, I came down last night like always and made a sandwich about eight thirty, studied awhile for my history quiz, then conked out my usual time, nine thirty . . . maybe ten. But I did have some really weird dreams all night. Maybe it was that peanut butter and jelly sandwich I ate," he said, shrugging his athletic shoulders as he turned around.

"They were totally freaky," he said in a lower tone, as if talking to himself. He then shook his messy head of black curly hair, as if to blow off the thoughts of his dreams, and grabbed a carton of orange juice from the refrigerator.

"Oh, Nana, I almost forgot. You may want to call a plumber."

"Oh, is the toilet stopped up?"

"No, it's working fine, but there was a *really* bad smell in my room last night. It *reeked like poop*. . . . It was so gross I thought I'd barf!"

"Well, that's odd. I'll call the plumber later and have him come out and take a look."

He plopped down in his favorite seat at the marble breakfast bar and poured himself some OJ while trying not to spill any on his white collared school shirt he hated wearing. If he had a choice for the school dress code, it would be shorts and a tee shirt, with his comfy neon green flip-flops. As he watched his grandmother preparing breakfast, he wondered why she was still in her fuzzy pink bathrobe. *She never came downstairs in the morning not dressed—well . . . hardly ever,* he thought.

"Hey, Nana . . . you feeling okay today?"

"Yes, I'm fine, just tired."

"Is something wrong, then?" he asked while drumming the countertop lightly with his fingertips, as he does every morning.

"No, silly," she laughed as she poured herself another cup of coffee.

"So what gives . . . because you don't look fine to me . . . ?"

"Well, you can blame it on Mr. Nipuk," she said with a laugh. "Sol called me at four this morning, and I've been up ever since."

"Really, what for?" he asked, frowning.

"Well, he wants me to go to Egypt," she replied with a squeak to her voice.

"Wow . . . . Really, but why call at that hour?"

"Before I answer that, I'd like to know if you want to go with me."

"*What!* No way. . . . Are you for real?" he said, jerking to a stand and almost knocking over his juice.

"Yes, I'm for real! So do you want to go?"

"Well, *duh!* Hellooo . . . . Of course I do! So does this mean I'll finally get to see the Ruins of Philae? Oh . . . oh, and can we go to the Coptic, and what about the Alexandria and Luxor Museum? Holy crapola, I must be dreaming!"

Pearle laughed, "I assure you, you're not dreaming, and yes, we can try to visit all those places."

He sat down slowly, leaned back into the thick padding of the stool with the biggest grin, and inhaled the cinnamon aroma coming from the griddle. But as happy as he was, his guts were nagging at him. Something else was going on.

"Nana, are you sure that's what has you preoccupied this morning, this trip to Egypt?"

He watched as her shoulders rose as if she were going to take a deep breath. Instead, she casually picked up a large silver spatula next to the stovetop and turned over the French toast.

With her back to him, she cleared her throat and replied, "I'm not sure what you mean, Matt."

"Well, has something else happened?"

She was dumbstruck! She *couldn't* tell him the real reason she had to go, not yet. Pearle needed a second to think. Slowly, she reached over to the sizzling bacon, and gave it a nonchalant poke with a fork and decided it was ready.

"I hope you're hungry this morning, and as for this trip, yes, something wonderful has happened. Sol has discovered some new tombs; that is why I, well why *we*, are going," she replied nervously. She turned, faced him with a forced smile, and put his plate on the counter. But Matthew isn't stupid, far from it. Pearle swears he's twelve going on forty! She watched him as he carefully scanned her face. His big blue eyes were so squinted that he had deep grooves in his forehead like a dried-out prune.

"Oh, please, would you stop worrying and looking at me like that?" she giggled. "You don't want wrinkles on that incredibly handsome face of yours. I just have a million things on my mind right now, that's all." And she grabbed her coffee mug and sat down next to him.

"You're not fibbing, are you?"

"Good Lord, child, would you stop overanalyzing me?" she

said as she gently grabbed a handful of his thick hair and gave it a squeeze. "You need a haircut, mister! And it wouldn't hurt to run a comb through that mess either! You're just like your grandfather was, always dressed neatly but never worrying about that head of hair!" She shook her head and thought about other boys his age. *They just never seem to sweat the small stuff. . . .*

He gave her one of his big cheesy smiles, showing off his perfect brilliant white teeth, then grabbed the bottle of maple syrup and drenched his French toast with it.

"Okay, finish your breakfast, and would you please take human bites?!" she ordered as she drank the last of her coffee. "For heaven's sake, you act as if you haven't eaten in a week! Oh, which reminds me, there's plenty more in the warmer for the bottomless pit, I mean Daniel," she said with a funny gurgle to her voice, which made Matthew laugh so hard he almost choked.

"Oh, gee, the dogs are barking; must be him! I'm going to get dressed." And Pearle zipped out of the kitchen. The dogs, Zatu and Bella, are beautiful purebred German shepherds. Although Zatu is eight years old, if it wasn't for his black face, you probably couldn't tell him apart from Bella, who is still going through her puppy stage at two. They can be quite the rambunctious pair, but Matthew and Pearle absolutely adore them.

"Hey, Matt, what's for breakfast? *I'm starved!*"

Matthew laughed, "So what else is new? You are *always* hungry, Dan! There's more in the warmer," he said as he motioned with his head. "Hurry and get yourself a plate. We have a lot to discuss about the team this morning."

Daniel carelessly dropped his book bag in the middle of the kitchen, just as he usually does, and headed for the stove. Matthew shook his head, wondering if Daniel ever thought about anything other than food. For the last seven years that they have been best friends, Dan has always come to school with a supply of cookies, or some snack, stashed in his pants pocket. He's never without sustenance, and that's probably why he's growing like a weed. He's already five foot ten, nearly two inches taller than Matthew. But Dan's dad is six foot three, and he not only has his father's bone structure; he looks just like him, with brown eyes, dirty blond hair, and long, lanky arms and legs. However, Matthew doesn't care about their height difference, because he has a more muscular build and is always taunting Dan about his spaghetti arms and legs.

Daniel bounced down on the stool next to Matthew, poured a ton of syrup on his six pieces of French toast, and dug in.

"I thought you said you were hungry," Matthew joked, watching him pack a fork so full of food that he wondered if he'd fit it all into his mouth.

"Oh, please, Mr. Piranha, like you should talk."

Then Matthew grinned to himself and called out, "Bottomless pit!"

"Oh, yeah," Daniel responded, "well you're a . . . a . . . hungry hippo!"

"Piranha!"

"Garbage disposal!"

"So, did you come up with any master plan for today's practice, captain?" Dan asked, still laughing, as he shoved the heaping pile of food in his mouth.

"I thought maybe *you* would have for a change, co-captain!"

"Ya know, I get enough sarcasm from my father," Daniel said nastily after his remark seemed to strike a nerve this morning. "Look, Matt, I am not good with coming up with brilliant ideas like you. Besides, you are a leader. I am a follower. That's just the way it is with us. If you think I'm not good enough for the swim team, then get someone else! It isn't like I don't contribute anything. After all, you know I'm one of the fastest swimmers on the team, and occasionally I *do* come up with some helpful ideas for us."

"Well, what crawled up your butt this morning, a 747? Good grief, Dan, I was only kidding around. . . . Geez! What is your problem, dude?"

"What do you think? It's my father again!" he replied, disgusted, as his face twisted to one side as if he ate a lemon. "Seems he got himself a new girlfriend, but that isn't the worst of it. She's *ten* years younger than him . . . and . . . well, it's disgusting! He acts like, 'Look at me; I'm Mr. Cool' when he's around her, but he's totally clueless to the jerk he's being. I just don't want to be around either one of them anymore!"

"So don't, then. Tell your mom."

"I thought about that, but I don't want to start world war four between my parents, ya know? They are finally able to have a civilized conversation without it turning into a big old screaming match. And for them, that's a freakin' miracle in itself. I just do what I have to in keeping the peace, especially so my mom doesn't get upset."

"Well, maybe it's time to tell your dad flat out how you feel."

"Yeah, right, that would go over **reallll** well with him. All I'll get is his sarcasm and the usual crap of how immature I am and **blah, blah, blah, blee, blee, blee.** Been there, done that, buddy! Face it, he's just an idiot, and the best thing my mom ever did was divorce him. Well, anyway, let's just figure out what we're doing with the team. With this big meet coming up, I don't have time to stress over him. So . . . what's going on with you? Did I miss anything exciting this weekend?"

"Dan, guess where I'm going?"

Pearle couldn't help overhearing the boys talking about Daniel's father. She's good friends with his mom and sympathizes, knowing what a pompous idiot his father is. Then she listened to how excited Matthew was about going to Egypt. She smiled to herself, recalling the day she told her daughter Oona about her first trip there. *Funny,* she thought, *he reacted just like she did.* It was hard for her not to think about Oona when it came to Matthew. He looks just like her, with big blue eyes, deep-set dimples, and the curliest ebony-colored hair. He definitely has her brilliant, analytical mind, and his eyes playfully reveal the wonderful kindness she possessed. He's a constant reminder of the beautiful daughter she lost, but also a treasured gift that she left behind.

As she entered her bedroom, a flood of memories overcame her. She began to feel sick to her stomach. She sat on the edge of the bed and lowered her head between her legs. Pearle's head whirled, and she tasted bile making its way up the back of her throat. She grabbed her trash can and lost her morning coffee. Feeling better, she stood up and glanced over at a yellowed newspaper clipping on her dresser.

"Local woman still missing, police and volunteers continue to search area."

Pearle stared at the article, then picked up the silver picture frame next to it. It holds the last picture taken of Oona by the pool with Matthew, who had just turned three and was kneeling on his mother's shoulders. She remembers that day well as she manages a small smile. They both were laughing so hard that she was losing her patience and almost didn't take that shot. As Pearle looked closer at the photo, she was amazed that in all these years, she has never noticed how Matthew scrunches up his nose just like his mom when she smiled. How she ached to hear Oona's contagious laughter again. But the grief she carries around reminds her she never will. She gently placed the frame back on the dresser, kissed her fingertips, and gently touched Oona's face in the photo, then went out on her balcony.

Pearle deeply inhaled the morning's sweetness of gardenias below her. She was glad the landscapers persuaded her to put them in, along with bright apricot floribunda bushes. They planted them along the perimeter of the house and a paved path that leads down to the lake and guesthouse. The biggest undertaking for the landscapers was the acre of land they cleared of ugly overgrown brush at the back of the house. What emerged was a beautiful and peaceful view of the brackish lake with all its colorful lotus flowers that runs through the property. The one thing Pearle wouldn't change was a long patch of muhly grass by the lake. It was Oona's favorite place to be, and Matthew has always been fascinated with it. He says that when it's windy out, the silky, wispy tops sway gently like the hula dancers he saw in Maui once. But what he loves the most is watching the sunset there in the fall, when the muhly grass color is incredibly brilliant, and how it reflects a fiery, purple, reddish haze on the dark water. He simply describes it as "awesome!"

Her newly remodeled European-Spanish-style home is over four thousand square feet, and although large, it's unpretentious. It has warmth with rich earthy colors, and every room is inviting and comforting. However, you will find Pearle is eclectic in her decorating with the numerous Egyptian relics amongst most rooms. She thinks she got her decorating style from her dad, as their home in Egypt was quite similar and almost as large. She grew up privileged there, in a very wealthy family, but her father taught her about being humble at an early age. And Pearle has never let her money make her who she is. Her hard work and dad's teachings are what molded Pearle into the woman she is today.

Her father was not only a well-educated archaeologist, but also a philanthropist. And although she never attended any special college, like he wanted her to, she had the best archaeologist in Egypt school her. She was Sol's protégé growing up, and before that, she learned much from her father and grandfather. No formal institution could have taught her what she experienced hands-on from three of the most brilliant Egyptologists in the business, and her work and accomplishments proved that.

At one point, though, she almost went to college, but her life took a different turn at the age of seventeen, when she married a fellow archaeologist, Paul Sherapha. Paul was from a prestigious Egyptian family that was renowned for its archaeological work, just as Pearle's relatives. He was dedicated to his profession and was determined to make a name for himself early in his career. Paul and Pearle worked together every day, and no matter what treasures they found, he always told her she was cherished more than anything there was on earth.

Sadly, though, a week before their second anniversary, Paul died in a tragic accident. Shortly after his death, Pearle found out she was pregnant with their daughter, Oona. Heartbroken, she left her work in Egypt and went to live in Florida. They had a vacation home there. Paul had given it to her as a wedding present. The place had good memories, and she knew it would be the right place to heal and grow their daughter.

When Oona was four, Pearle decided to go back to Egypt and work with Sol again, determined to get on with life. Oona and her work kept her very busy. She was completely devoted to both. For years, Sol watched Pearle bury her sorrows while she dug up history and raised her beautiful daughter. As Oona grew, so did Sol's attachment to her. She was like a daughter to him and eventually became Oona's mentor, just as he'd been to Pearle.

When Oona finally went off to college, Pearle decided to cut back on her work and spend more time in Florida. This is when Pearle found out how wealthy she really was.

Years ago, her in-laws had insisted she invest half of the life insurance money their son had left her. Being a very strong-willed woman, Pearle decided to invest the entire amount into what she thought best for her and Oona's future. Besides, Pearle didn't need the money at the time. When her dad died, she received a structured, but partial, amount of her inheritances that made her very well off. Her father also willed a large portion of investments and part of his estate to Sol so that he could continue the important work at the pyramid. He made Sol promise him that no one but him, Pearle, and only surviving heirs would ever take over the dig site. He also bequeathed a very large legacy that Pearle received on her twenty-fifth birthday.

So after Pearle hired a law firm in Florida to get her legal and financial affairs in order, they discovered that between several investments and her large legacy, Pearle was worth a staggering five hundred million!

Her legacy contains an abundant amount of gold, Egyptian relics, and a collection of some of the rarest gems and jewelry in the world. There are numerous crates of artifacts, and they are stored in a secured wing she had built during the renovation. Amongst these magnificent treasures were five rare, jeweled medallions. Pearle got one on her thirteenth birthday, as did other heirs upon reaching that age. But like her legacy, it carries dark secrets from the past.

One day while visiting her ill great-grandfather, he discussed the importance of the legacy she would acquire and how she was to protect it, like many generations before her did. He cautioned, though, telling her it held many mysteries. She was only ten years old at the time, and to her, he spoke of the past seemingly in riddles. The information was vague, but one part of their conversation does stand out in her memory and quite clearly. It was when he told her about the medallions and that they were the greatest part of her legacy.

Then, he took her hand into his and told her to remember this
. . . . *The first female heir will be spared . . . a second will come home to the throne.*

Sadly, those were his last words as his breath disappeared from his ailing body. She had no clue what he meant, but something about it bothered her.

Several weeks later, Pearle decided to talk with her father about what her great-grandpa told her. She watched as his handsome bronzed face stiffened, especially when she repeated the part of the first female heir. But he insisted it was nothing but a foolish old man talking nonsense and she was to forget about it. Regardless of what he said, she knew he wasn't telling her the truth, and wondered why. Seeing him so upset, she decided it was best to drop the subject for the time being and perhaps bring it up another day. However, that day never came. Pearle's father died a year later.

Chapter Four

"Hey, Daniel, we missed you during the weekend," Pearle said while pouring herself another cup of coffee. "Where were you? Did you do anything exciting?"

Looking up, Daniel had a mouthful, but managed to get out, "Morning, Eeal!"

That's what it sounded like, but she knew what he meant and laughed.

"Great grub, Pearle. Thanks," he said after he swallowed. "I spent the weekend with Dad and his new girlfriend, reluctantly, mind you! Anyway, we went fishing down to the jetties and had lunch at my favorite restaurant on the beach. We didn't catch anything except for some seaweed, and Dad got a nasty sunburn! Pearle, you should have seen him! He looked like a walking beet by the time we left to go home. You know, I don't get it; he's a doctor and always telling me to put on sunscreen! Parents," he added sarcastically.

"Oh, Daniel," Pearle scolded, "parents aren't perfect, you know!"

"Yeah, right!" Daniel responded sourly. "Tell that to my Mr. Know It All father!"

"Well, other than the sunburn, it sounds like you and your dad had a great time."

"It was boring, well, except for lunch," he added, rubbing his stomach. "*You know,* I would have rather been here with you and Matt."

"We missed you too," and she went over and gave him a big hug.

"I guess Annabelle left without feeding the dogs, but usually she leaves me a note letting me know," Matthew said, looking around the kitchen for one.

"Then you better hurry and feed them. And write a note telling her they were fed. We need to get going soon, or you two will be late for school."

"Hey, Daniel," Matthew yelled out from the pantry, "would you give me a hand?"

"Sure, hang on," Daniel replied as he dumped his dirty plate in the dishwasher.

"Okay, Matt, what do you want me to do?" he asked while drying his hands on his clean pressed khaki pants.

"Good Lord," Matthew responded, "we do have towels for that, you know, Dan! You are such a slob!"

"Oh, shut up, Mr. Neat Freak; it's only water."

"Whatever," Matthew said, rolling his eyes. "Can you get fresh water for Bella and Zatu while I get their food?"

"Sure, and anything for the hairy Twinkie?"

"Oh, no way dude, that is just so wrong," Matthew laughed. "She's a teddy bear hamster, Dan, not a freaking dessert!"

"Okay, you two," Pearle yelled from the kitchen, shaking her head, listening to the two boys carry on. "Let's get going if you're done."

"Sure, Nana, just a sec. I need to get my book bag from my room. I'll meet you in the car," Matthew yelled as he took the steps two by two to his room. He opened the closet to get his book bag out and got a whiff of that horrible odor he smelled last night. *Maybe it's dog poop on my shoes*, he thought, but he checked them out, and they were clean. Then a frightening chill shot up his neck, into his head. His eyes began to water, and goose pimples popped up all over him. As the hair on his neck stood up, he swore someone was behind him. With a quick, reluctant jerk, he turned around.

"Nothing but the wall, Matt," he said to himself, relieved. He looked up at the air duct in the closet and figured his grandmother must have the air conditioner on sixty because of her hot flashes, and he laughed to himself. He knew he was letting his imagination get to him. He closed the door and stood there for a moment. But still, something wasn't right. His guts were gnawing at him, and he felt uncomfortable. Then . . . he sensed something bad, something evil was in the room. He became petrified and could hardly move.

BEEP . . . BEEP . . . BEEP. "AUGGGGH!" he screamed as he jumped nearly five feet into the air.

"No more peanut butter and jelly for you!" he yelled to himself as he raced out of his room and down the stairs.

"Okay, Nana," Matt said, winded. "Let's go!"

Pearle glanced up into the rearview mirror as she was backing out of the driveway and saw Daniel looking ridiculously glum.

"Hey, I just had a crazy idea," Pearle said as she winked at Matthew. "Would you like to go with us?"

Daniel turned his head and shot Pearle a wild cockeyed look.

"Would I like to go? YES!" he squealed. "But do you think Mom will let me?"

"I don't see why not. After all, she has let you travel with us before."

"Yeah, but we are talking about going *way out* of the country here. You know how she gets, Pearle, all spastic," and he began shaking his hands and head trying to imitate his mom freaking out.

"Well," Pearle snickered, "I'm not sure she is going to get that dramatic! I was thinking about calling her, but if you think she is going to have a hard time letting you go, I can stop by your house to perhaps . . . persuade her in person," Pearle replied, wiggling her eyebrows.

"That's a great idea," he said while he began to unbuckle his seat belt.

"Daniel, while I appreciate your happiness and enthusiasm, would you *please* get back into your seat belt?!" she urged.

Pearle quickly glanced over at Matthew when she heard a click.

"Listen, you two, if those seat belts aren't back on in *five seconds,* no one is going anywhere! I don't want to be pulled over for lapse of judgment in all this excitement! If the police stop us," Pearle warned, "I will . . . ."

"Well," Daniel quickly shot back smartly, "no prob, that is, if Detective Greene is around!"

Pearle looked back at him with his devilish, crooked smile and then over at Matthew. Her cheeks turned blazing red! Matthew turned around and gave his friend an icy stare. He usually tolerates his best friend's humor, but at that moment, he found him insulting and immature.

Daniel got the message and realized he had crossed the line of kidding around. He looked up cowardly at Pearle as she peered at him in the rearview mirror. She knew by the flush in his cheeks and pathetic look on his face that he was sorry. She gave him a slight smile as if to say she forgave him. But Daniel sat quietly for the rest of the ride to school, sulking from Matthew's scolding glance.

"So, Nana, when are we going?" Matthew asked as he leaned over the seat to give her a hug good-bye.

"I should hear from Sol in a day or so with all the arrangements. Which reminds me that I will have to call and tell him about Daniel, if his mom says he can go. Okay, you two, I'll see you at three." She focused her thoughts to her next task, pulled out of the school's parking lot, and turned right, heading north.

"Well, hello, Pearle. Nice to see you," the plump, friendly officer said at the front desk. "You want to see Detective Greene?"

"Yes, he is expecting me. Why are you up front today, Sergeant Higgins? Aren't you supposed to be in the back pushing paperwork?" she said playfully.

"Yeah, I usually am, but we're a little shorthanded this week. There seems to be a nasty stomach bug going around."

"Well, I hope you will be able to avoid it, sergeant."

"Ahh . . . been there, done that," he laughed, revealing his chipped front tooth. "I'll let him know you're here, Pearle. Have a seat in the waiting room."

"Hello, stranger," said the detective as he entered the waiting room a few moments later.

Pearle looked up at the six-foot-four good-looking detective and felt her face flush. Robert Greene's hazel eyes were bright this morning, and she noticed his golden brown hair seemed shorter than usual. As always, he looked meticulous in a starched baby blue dress shirt and perfectly creased khaki pants. She inhaled deeply and caught a whiff of his favorite aftershave, Old Spice. He was delighted to see her and that she was wearing the black silk top he gave her for her birthday last year. He had wondered if she really did like it or if she would even wear it. As she stood up, a slight wisp of air gave off the sweet scent of her Chanel No. 5 perfume, and he sniffed it discreetly with a smile.

"Come on, Pearle, let's go to my office, where we can talk."

"They really did do a nice job fixing this old place up, Robert," she said as she sat down, feeling the soft, puffy padding on the armrest of his new chair while noticing her feet could barely touch the new beige Berber carpet.

"Yeah, I like it, and besides, I needed the extra space, so it worked out pretty good. Okay, Pearle," he said, shaking his head and grinning, "let's talk about that phone call you got last night. Oh, listen, uh, if you have time," he stumbled, "would you like to have lunch with me today? We both have been so busy lately, and I have missed seeing you the last few weeks."

"Sure, that sounds wonderful," she replied.

"All right," he said, leaning back in his chair and crossing his arms. "So, tell me what's going on."

"Well, like I told you, Sol called, and he asked if I had all of Oona's personal jewelry. I told him I thought so . . . and that is when he said he found Oona's medallion."

"Okay . . . but I'm a little confused here, Pearle. What does this medallion have to do with her case?"

"Robert . . . Oona was wearing that medallion the day she disappeared."

"Are you sure, Pearle?"

"Yes, she had it on that morning at breakfast. Oona wore her medallion almost every day, even against my protest. She swore it had some sort of good karma or something like that."

"So how can Sol be certain this medallion is hers; I mean, couldn't he be mistaken?"

"He's not, Robert. Oona's medallion was one of five from my family's legacy. Besides, I have legal and historical documentation that these are the only recorded medallions in history of their kind. Oh, and I almost forgot, Sol also said the medallion's chain is missing from it."

"What kind of chain?" Robert asked eagerly.

"It's a thick gold chain with a distinct pattern and . . . well, it's somewhat hard to explain, Robert, but if you can come by the house tonight, I would be glad to show you the others. They all were made with identical chains."

"That would probably be a good idea, and would you mind if I took a couple of pictures?"

"Of course not, but may I ask why?"

"Oh, just an idea . . . that's all. . . . Okay, so what else did he have to say?"

She told him about the new tombs and as much of the conversation that she could remember and then her decision to go to Egypt.

"You know, Robert, if you wouldn't mind, instead of lunch, how about coming for dinner tonight? There are a million things I still have to do today, and it would be nice to spend some time with you before we leave."

"Oh . . . how soon will that be?"

"I'm not sure yet, but we can go into details later, that is, if you will accept my dinner invitation."

"Of course, dinner sounds great, and besides, there are a few more things that I'd like to discuss with you concerning Oona's case, if you wouldn't mind doing that tonight also."

"No, not at all," she said as she slid herself from the chair and stood. "How about 7:30. Is that a good time for you?"

"Sounds good to me."

"Oh, Robert, I do have one favor to ask of you."

"Sure, what is it?"

"Can we wait until Matthew has gone to bed before discussing the rest of this? I . . . I haven't told him about Oona's medallion being found. He was so excited this morning about the trip, I just don't . . . well, I just didn't want to upset him."

"That's not a problem, and besides, I agree with not telling him anything, not yet, anyway."

"Thanks, Robert," she replied and put her head down.

"What's wrong, Pearle?" But she didn't answer him.

"Hey, look at me," he said as he picked up her chin and looked into her eyes. "I understand you being upset. Sol's phone call last night was like dropping a bomb on you. However, if this information comes with some merit, we may have a good lead on this case. I promised you a long time ago that I wouldn't rest until I solved Oona's case, and I meant it. Hey, I've got an idea. How would you feel about me accompanying you to Egypt?"

"Really, Robert, I think that's a wonderful idea," she said with a big smile.

"Great, then we can discuss that tonight, but in the meantime, I have to get busy with another case here. So you go finish your errands, and try not to worry about anything. I'll see you about seven-thirty."

"Okay," she replied, and gave him a kiss on the cheek before leaving.

Robert closed his office door and began to pace, his usual ritual when he thinks. He was very disturbed with the information Pearle just gave him, and he had hoped she didn't see that in him. He frowned, spinning his mental wheels, trying to recall all the angles he dismissed over the years concerning Oona's disappearance, only to now have them all on the table again. "Damn, what have I missed?"

The phone rang at Sergeant Higgins's desk.

"Yes, DG, what can I do for you?" he said with his dry wit.

"Okay, smarty-pants, I need you to call down to records and ask them to gather all of the case files on Oona Almondative."

"Hey, what's up?" he asked eagerly.

"We will discuss that after you bring those files to my office."

"Wow, that's a lot of paperwork, sir!"

"It sure is, Officer Higgins," he snapped.

"Yes, sir, I'll get on it right away."

"Thank you, and get someone to cover the desk. I'm going to need you for the rest of the afternoon."

"Me?"

"Yes, you, unless you have changed your mind about becoming a detective," Robert snorted.

"*No, sir.* I am completely yours. I'll try to find someone to cover me, and I'll have those files to you ASAP!"

"Good," Robert replied. "Oh, and hold all my calls. Diane's still out running errands at the courthouse, and I have to go down to Criminalistics to check on another case."

"Yes, sir!" And he hung up wondering what it was that had prompted him to examine this old case again. What was found never did prove to be of any significance. *Well, something is up*, he thought to himself. *DG wouldn't go to all this trouble otherwise.*

Robert Greene is highly respected by his department, and no one ever questions his decisions or authority. After all, he was the go-to man while with the FBI for its difficult missing person cases. He is fondly referred to as DG, and anyone who calls him DG never means any disrespect, none whatsoever, and Robert knows that.

Pearle was now on her way to see her best friend, Dr. Denise Fuscilli, Daniel's mom. When she arrived at their home, Denise was outside planting flowers in her baggy shorts and oversized tee shirt. It was hard for Pearle to imagine this adorable freckle-faced woman, who didn't look a day over twenty, as a prominent doctor.

"Hi, Denise!" she called as she scaled the steps to the large front patio and gave her a hug. "Those are beautiful geraniums!"

"My therapy," she said with a grin. "Takes my mind off the office."

"So how is the practice going?"

"Everything is going wonderful. Having my own practice is better than I thought it would be," she said while carefully tapping the dirt around the last new flower. "You know, I am glad you stopped by. Have you got time for some coffee?"

"Absolutely, kiddo. Besides, when have you known me to refuse a cup," she answered as they went inside.

"Pearle, there is a big medical conference coming up, and I have been asked to give a presentation on a new method for treating pain I'm using. My patients are having wonderful results, and it has been just . . . well, overwhelming!"

"Wow, Denise, this is great news! No wonder you keep so busy!"

"Well, we both have been busy, and I've been meaning to call you and ask a big favor. Would it be too much of an imposition if Daniel stayed with you and Matt for about ten days while I am gone?"

"Well, that all depends . . . if you won't object to me taking him to Egypt."

"Wow, Egypt. Is it safe, Pearle?"

"I think so, and if it will make you feel any better, Robert may be accompanying us."

"Oh, really, that's wonderful," she replied. Then she and Pearle sat down with their coffee and began chatting.

When Pearle glanced down at her watch, she couldn't believe what time it was.

"Holy cow, we've been gabbing for two hours! I better get going and finish what I started doing today. So you're comfortable with Daniel going?" Pearle asked as she put her cup in the sink.

"Yes, of course I am. Especially since Robert will be going. Besides, Daniel would never forgive me if I made him spend ten days with his shallow father and the new girlfriend!"

Pearle laughed and added, "Yeah, I couldn't see that scenario playing out too well. All right, then, since I have your blessing to take your son, I will be off! I'll talk to you tomorrow, and thanks for the coffee," Pearle said as she opened the door.

"Anytime; you know that," Denise replied, giving her a hug.

Driving back to her home, finished with most of her running around, Pearle went over the rest of her mental to-do list. Passports, dinner, call Sol. *Hmm*, she thought, and chuckled to herself, *I wonder what time it is in Egypt.*

Chapter Five

"Well, well, look who it is, guys, Mr. Pretty Boy Swim Team Captain and his towel boy!"

"Ooh, boy, here we go," Daniel said, cringing and gritting his teeth.

They were used to Charlie Dixon, aka Crash, the school bully, and his verbal taunts. Crash has been bullying them and others in the school for years. However, recently, Detective Greene started educating students how to deal with bullies and violence.

"Okay, Daniel, let's try that new technique Greene offered last week. You ready?"

"Are you sure, Matt?" he replied hesitantly as they both turned around.

"Hey, Charlie, what's up? How's it going?"

He crinkled up his face like a dried olive and gawked at them menacingly. None of the kids at school called him Charlie, and *nobody*, other than his goons, talked to him!

"You ready for that quiz Mr. Haram will probably give us today in history class?" Matthew asked.

"My morning was going great until I saw you two jerks and your ugly faces, and who cares about Haram and his dumb test!"

"Well, sorry to hear you feel like that. Good luck on the quiz. See you in class!" Then Matt and Daniel closed their lockers and went into their homeroom.

"Holy crap, Matt, I think he was actually shocked at how we handled that! What am I saying? I'm surprised he didn't stuff us into our lockers after we said, 'Hey, Charlie.'"

"You know, Dan, it isn't going to get better right away, and it might even get worse. So you better watch your back, okay?"

"Sure, Matt," and he started to laugh and told him he had Detective Greene's number on speed dial in his phone.

"No way; do you really?"

"Yep, sure do. This Crash guy is bad news! I am so sick and tired of his bullying crap all these years. He is trouble with a big T. It sure would be worth it, though, if I could just land one punch and knock that punk out!"

"He's not worth the trouble, Dan; you know that. Besides, what would that prove? You would be expelled, and he'd just have another reason for him and his idiot friends to beat on someone, and that someone would probably be you, dorko!"

"Well, they never seem to need a reason any other time, now do they? If that idiot or his goons ever put one hand on me, it is on like Donkey Kong!"

"Oh, my Lord, you are lame, Daniel; you do know that, don't you?"

Daniel just rolled his eyes back at him, and they quickly took their seats as the bell rang.

"Okay, class, quiet down. Let's get attendance done, and then I'm going to give you the dates for all final exams next month," Mr. Haram announced as he walked into the classroom. "There is no reason why any of you should fail these tests. The school is offering you the opportunity to succeed. The rest is up to you students. Remember, you only get out of something what you put into it!"

Mr. Abe Haram, their homeroom monitor, is also most of the students' history teacher. His peers consider him a pleasant man, and for the most part, his students think he is a cool teacher. He's shorter than most of them, and he doesn't mind his five-foot, two-inch height. He thinks it makes him less intimidating to them and easier to reach. Abe has two passions. One is teaching, and the other is eating, especially Italian food. His expanded waistline, which he tries to ignore, is a constant reminder of the diet he should be on.

"All right, everyone, you have fifteen minutes before the bell and your first class. I suggest you use the time wisely! You know, for some of you, whose dog had a late-night snack and ate your homework, or maybe study for the pop quiz we might have in history class today," he said while wiggling his thick bushy eyebrows and getting a few giggles from the students. "Everyone, please open your books, not your mouth, for the remaining time here. Thank you, class!"

Mr. Haram is not only Matthew's teacher, but also a friend of the family. He's known Pearle and Matthew since he started dating Annabelle several years ago. Before he came to America with a master's degree for teaching history, he worked with several museums and their curators in translating ancient Egyptian hieroglyphics. When Pearle met him, she was excited to hear about his work and since has shared many long hours discussing and debating the mysterious language of the ancient Egyptians.

The bell rang, and Matthew quickly went to tell him about his trip to Egypt. He was eager to hear all about Matthew's plans and suggested they have lunch together. He agreed and went to his first class with Daniel.

It was finally noon, and after a confrontation he had with Crash during swim class, Matthew was looking forward to lunch.

"Hey, over here," Mr. Haram called from the lunch line. Let's sit outside. It's such a nice day, and with summer almost upon us, I do so enjoy these cooler days before the blistering heat makes it impossible to enjoy the fresh air."

"Sure," Matthew replied. "You know, Mr. Haram, I hate the summers here. I don't know what I'd do without our pool. Daniel and I practically live in it all summer to escape the boiling heat and humidity." *Hmm* . . . . "Even Annabelle enjoys soaking in it," he said with a cheesy smile.

"How is she, Matthew? You know I have been so busy lately, I have not had any time to call or see her."

"She's doing good," Matthew said as he took a big bite of his turkey sandwich.

"Maybe I better give her a call tomorrow before she never speaks to me again," he said, shaking his head, seemingly amused. "So . . . let's talk about your trip to Egypt. Are you going for vacation?"

"Well, yeah, but it's really because Nana has to see her friend, Sol, and some new tombs he's discovered. But she figured with spring break coming up and all, I might as well go too. Oh, and Daniel might be going also!"

"That sounds great! Okay, so tell me, will you be staying in Alexandria?"

"I think that's where Nana said, or maybe with Sol, since he is closer to the pyramid. But how would you know that?"

"Oh, my dear boy, that city is not only beautiful and historic, but the best place to stay, in my opinion. While you are there, you must go to the Alexandria National Museum. It is more modern, and you'll love the Pharaohs exhibit. It spans the three important periods of the Old, Middle, and New Kingdoms. I'm sure you will find it very interesting . . . especially with all the studying you have done with Pearle about ancient Egypt. There are thousands of years of history there, Matthew. As a matter of fact, there are a few displays that I contributed to in my old days.

"Yeah, Nana mentioned that your work and ability to translate the old writings is pretty impressive!"

"Did she now? . . . Well, coming from Pearle, that is a compliment indeed! Okay, so tell me what you know about Alexandria."

"I know the Pharaoh's lighthouse was nearly all destroyed around 300 BC, but what was left of it they have made into a small museum. There was a library with important historical information, but it burnt to the ground. Oh, and there is a pink granite column from the acropolis Serapus. Didn't Cleopatra rule there, as many famous rulers did? Isn't her kingdom underwater there, Mr. Haram?"

"Well," he replied with a chuckle at Matthew's enthusiasm, "it depends on who you ask. There are many stories about Cleopatra, her reign, and the exact location where she once was queen. She was an intriguing and very clever woman. Ahh . . . such a shame she killed herself. . . ."

"Why would someone so smart kill herself, Mr. Haram?"

"Well, if you ask me, sometimes people are too smart for their own good, but she killed herself because of love."

"How stupid is that? . . . All that power, and you go and waste it. She was an idiot, then, Mr. Haram," he said presumptuously, chewing the last of his sandwich.

"You know, they say she was related to Alexander the great."

"I think I read that somewhere, but not sure where or even when. This stuff is pretty cool, though, isn't it?"

"Ah . . . if only all my students shared your enthusiasm, Matthew. It would make my job not only easy, but much more enjoyable! You know, you would be amazed who is related to whom in this world. It's not . . . this world, that is . . . all that big as people think," Abe commented with his voice fading.

"Is something wrong?"

"Oh, no . . . no, my dear boy, never mind an old man and his thoughts," he said, assuring Matthew.

Then Abe whispered, *"Mehwet . . . Mewet."*

Matthew knows he has heard that wording before, he is almost sure of it! *Hmm*, he thought to himself, *I think it's . . . mother, mother . . . maybe not . . . .* His Arabic is good, but being preoccupied with Mr. Haram's odd mood, he didn't think much of it. Then, from the corner of his eye, he watched Abe shake his head as if to shake whatever thoughts he had out of his mind.

"All right, young man, let's finish our lunch and see what else I can tell you that will make your trip more enjoyable!"

During the rest of their lunch, he filled Matthew in on the best places to go and times to visit . . . even where the best restaurants were.

"Oh, when did you say you were leaving?"

"I didn't, Mr. Haram, and I have no idea. Sol is making all our arrangements. But we should know in a day or so."

"Well, I just want to make sure you have all the necessary work you will need to study for the exams coming up. Please let me know as soon as you can of your departure date."

"Will do, and thanks for all the information you shared," Matthew said as he picked up his lunch tray. "See you later in class. Bye."

"You are very welcome, Matthew. . . . See you soon."

Abe Haram watched him run across the courtyard to his next class. He reminded Abe that children grow up in spite of all the bad things that can happen in their lives. Abe personally knew this to be true. He never knew his real mother. It made him think about his home in Egypt, his father, and the woman who was like a mother to him. He wondered if he would have grown up different, or just the same, had he known his real mom.

Abe took his plastic fork and picked through his wiggly square chunk of red Jell-O, taking out the sliced peaches. He hated peaches. They gave him a rash. *I should have taken the chocolate cake,* he thought. Then he thought about how he resented what his real mother had done and the things he felt cheated out of in his life. He thought long and hard of his plan and if it was wise at all. Then, feeling the agonizing pain in his heart, he assured himself it was. Abe picked up his cardboard tray and noticed the large pink stained peach slices lying in the red fluid that was once his Jell-O, and tossed it all into the trash.

Chapter Six

"Pearle looked at the clock on her nightstand. It was 7:15. Robert would be arriving soon, and she quickly finished dressing. Matthew and Annabelle were setting the table and laughing about Pearle being unusually nervous that Robert was coming for dinner. Matthew asked her why his grandmother was being that way. She told him that it was probably because Pearle is finally realizing she is in love with Robert. And who knows, maybe she was going to tell him tonight.

"Well, I knew that a long time ago," Matthew said as a matter of fact.

"Yeah, me too," she replied, "but those two needed to see it themselves."

"Oh, that must be Robert," she said, hearing the door chimes. "Matt, go and get the door, and I'll finish here."

"Hey, Detective Greene, come on in!"

"Hello, Matthew. Nice to see you again!"

"Yeah, great to see you too, sir," Matthew said as he closed the front door.

"Oh, you can call me Robert. No formalities between us, okay?"

"All right, sir, I mean Robert," he said, smiling, as he led him into the living room.

"Matt, how are things going at school?"

"Actually, I'm glad you brought that up; I have to tell you about Crash . . . I mean Charlie Dixon, and what happened today. You are gonna freak out when I tell you!"

"Oh, did he give you a hard time?"

He told Robert about a confrontation he had with Crash during their swim class and how they ended up talking. Crash had actually apologized, in his own way, and by the end of class, Matthew had invited him over on Saturday so they could work on his breaststroke.

"Can you believe I didn't get the crap beat out of me? I mean, I was scared, Robert, but I just had to tell him how I felt. Everybody at school is so over him and his tough act."

"I had a nice conversation with Charlie last month after an incident, and I think that was a real wake-up call for him. He knows if he steps out of line just one more time, his life won't look too pretty behind metal bars."

"You know, Robert, he said something today that really bothered me."

"Really, what was it?"

"Well, he said, 'You don't know me, or my life.' I just know there is something wrong. . . . I felt it, Robert, in my gut. I mean, Charlie has done some pretty mean things to me over the years, but I feel sorry for him."

"He doesn't need pity, Matthew, just the right friends, and I think Saturday is going to be a great start for Charlie to go in the right direction."

Matthew became very quiet, and Robert stared at him for a minute.

"You wanna tell me what's wrong? Is there something bothering you about Charlie?"

Matthew looked up and straight into his eyes. The expression on Matthew's face was daunting, and Robert suddenly felt uncomfortable.

"Robert, can I talk to you about something private, and would you promise to keep it just between us?"

"Absolutely, you and I can discuss anything, and it won't go any further, I promise."

"Have you ever just known something, and it turned out to be true?"

"Yes, but that happens to everyone. It's usually good instincts or coincidence. Why? What's troubling you?"

"It's been happening a lot the last few months. Ya know . . . like I get this feeling in my stomach, and I can sense things, and I know before something happens that it is going to, but I don't know why."

"Can you give me an example?"

"You sure I'm not going to freak you out or anything?"

Robert laughed, "I think I'll be okay. Why don't you just tell me what's going on."

"Okay, a good one was this morning with Nana. I know she isn't telling me everything about why we are going to Egypt, and I sense it has something to do with Mom. Another thing is Crash. I could practically feel his father's fist beating him when he and I were talking today. It isn't like I can read people's minds, ya know, Robert . . . it's just a feeling I get in myself, and these things are just there. And it doesn't happen with everybody I'm with; it's kinda random like. Now this one might really freak you out, but just sitting here with you, I know that you want to ask Nana to marry you. Which, by the way, I have to tell ya, I think is about time! Stuff like that has been happening, and to make it worse, I'm having these really weird nightmares. I don't remember much about them, just that I'm running around inside a pyramid, and there is something . . . well . . . someone in there with me. At first, I just thought it was my snacking too late, but once I got to thinking about all this, everything started around the same time. You've got to promise me that you won't say anything to my grandmother. You know what a worrywart she is, and I couldn't handle her freaking out! She still thinks I'm five years old and is always trying to fix anything that goes wrong in my life. I wish she would just start treating me like a grown person and not some immature kid, Robert."

Matthew exhaled as if he released a hundred pounds off his chest and leaned back into the sofa. Robert was overwhelmed, especially about asking Pearle to marry him. He couldn't understand that because he had just decided on that after she left his office this morning, and nobody else knew that.

Matthew leaned forward and said, "I'm a weirdo, ain't I?"

"No, you're not," Robert replied with an assuring smile as he stood up and began to pace in front of the sofa. "Matthew, have you ever heard of intuition, and having a sixth sense?"

"Yes, as a matter of fact, Nana once told me when we were looking at some old photos that my grandfather had it. She also said something about our family was gifted with it, but I didn't think much about it at the time. Do you think that's what I have, Robert, intuition, and I'm not some sort of *freakazoid?*"

"Well, that's a new term I've never heard before, but no, I'm sure you aren't," he chuckled to himself. "It's extraordinary and not too common, but there are people who have that gift. I have never met anyone who is gifted like you, and to tell you the truth, I find it very interesting . . . not freakish. However, maybe you should speak with Pearle about this. I mean, she probably would know more about this than I apparently do. And you know, Matt, she might even be able to help you make sense out of all this so you would feel more comfortable about it and, as you say, not a freakazoid."

"Nah, I don't think so, not yet, anyway. So promise me you won't say a word to her, okay?"

"You have my word, but promise me that you will consider telling her. This isn't a small imaginable thing happening in your life; it's for real. And from what you've told me, you seem a little frightened. You need to talk to someone who understands what's going on, and the sooner the better. You want to be treated like a grown-up, then you have to start making decisions like one. But I will not say a thing to her, and when you are ready, I'd be more than happy to sit in on that conversation."

"That's a great idea, and thanks for understanding, because if Nana knew . . . ."

"Knew what?" Pearle interrupted as she entered the room.

Matthew looked up in absolute shock at Robert and became speechless.

"Well, hello, Pearle. We were just talking guy things," Robert quickly replied, with a sly wink to Matthew.

"Really, well I'm glad to see you two are having a good time," Pearle replied.

The room became quiet, and he caught himself staring at her when Matthew loudly cleared his throat.

"Ahem . . . I think I'll go into the kitchen and see if Annabelle needs any help," he said, snickering.

"Hey, wait up, Matt," Robert said as he pulled a bottle of Pearle's favorite red wine from a bag and set it aside. "Would you put this white wine I brought for dinner in the fridge so it doesn't get warm?"

"Sure can," he replied, looking at Robert. "I'll leave you two kids alone and let you know when dinner is ready."

Robert busted out laughing, and Pearle turned as red as could be.

"I'll take a glass of that wine now, Robert."

He poured them both a glass and sat down next to her.

"Is everything all right with Matthew?"

"Well, I believe so, but he's growing up, Pearle, and starting to go through a lot of emotional changes. He isn't that little boy who just tragically lost his mother and needs protecting all the time. I think once you realize that, Matthew might open up to you about things he feels that you won't, or can't, understand. He's a smart kid and a damn good one. You've done a fine job raising him, Pearle."

"Well, I guess you aren't going to tell me what you two talked about, but I just want to know if he is okay."

"If he wasn't, you know I'd tell you. For the time being, don't say anything. Let him come to you when he's ready to talk about the conversation we had tonight."

She agreed, and they were on their second glass of wine when Matthew entered the room and announced that it was time to eat.

"Great," Robert replied, "I am starving! You know, I never did get out for lunch today."

"Well, hopefully the dinner Annabelle has prepared will make up for it."

"It sure does smell delicious. What has she made?" he asked, inhaling the mouthwatering aromas coming from the kitchen.

"Ask Matthew; he helped Annabelle in preparing it."

"Wow, you cook too?" Robert asked, looking surprised. "You are a very talented young man!"

"He is learning," Annabelle quickly responded as she gave a hug to Robert.

"So tell me, Matt, what will we be feasting on this evening?"

Matthew took his linen napkin off the table and put it over his arm. He proceeded to tell Robert the menu as if he were a *garçon* in a French restaurant. Everyone broke into laughter as he tried out his French and embellished his accent to make his presentation more authentic. Their laughter continued through dinner, and Pearle realized that it's been a long time since they've done this. She thought about Oona too and how much she would have approved of Robert.

"That had to be the best veal I've ever eaten! Annabelle . . . Matthew, you really outdid yourselves."

"Robert, if you think dinner was great, wait until you taste the cheesecake," Matthew quipped as he cleaned off the dinner plates.

After dinner, Matthew went up to bed, and Pearle and Robert were in the living room talking about the trip.

"So tell me, Pearle, how did you make out this afternoon? Did you get all your errands done?"

"Yes, I did, Robert, and thank goodness; what a day it has been. The kids' passports are done, and all the other little errands I had to do I think I did," she laughed. "How about you—is your passport current?"

"Yes, I checked on it this afternoon. I am good to go!"

"That's wonderful. One less thing to worry about!"

"Pearle, I have to give the department a week's notice before leaving and an approximate date of my return. Have you gotten any tentative dates yet for the trip?"

"No, not yet, but we should know something by Monday. That's when I should hear from Sol."

"So tell me some more about this Sol of yours. He sounds like a very influential man in Egypt."

"Well, he is, Robert. His notableness in Egypt as one of the best Egyptologists has earned him a respectable political standing there. He's also very wealthy and belongs to many prestigious organizations in the archaeological world, and he's a bit of a philanthropist too. The Archaeological Society made him an honorary member many years ago. He has worked with many well-known and respected people in the society and contributed to some of the biggest finds in history."

"He almost sounds too good to be true."

"Well, he is a rare gem, and I find it a privilege to call him my friend and colleague. The intelligence of this man and his knowledge of Egypt's history would blow your mind, Robert! Yet he is so sweet and has the best sense of humor! That man could make you laugh in a scorching 120-degree cave with scorpions crawling all over it. Other than my dad, he is the most human person I have ever known."

"Sol sounds like a remarkable man. . . . Is he married?"

"No, he's not, Robert. Ya know, it's funny, because I asked him why he never married, and he told me years ago that his true love is the earth he digs and the ancient hieroglyphics he reads and translates. He said it was not humanly possible or fair to love two things like that at the same time."

"Sounds like quite the gentleman, if you ask me, and a man who knows what he wanted out of life. Ah . . . Pearle, I'd like to talk with you about something," he said, feeling a bit awkward.

"Sure, Robert, what is it?" she asked as she nervously gulped a big swallow of coffee.

He began the conversation, admitting his love for her, and Pearle told him that she felt the same. They both agreed that their long-term dating relationship had given them the opportunity to become good friends and really get to know each other, but he said he'd like to take it further. He began to lean forward to give her a kiss when he heard someone.

"Ahem . . . I am very sorry to interrupt you two, but I am pooped and would like to know if you need anything else before I turn in for my beauty sleep."

"Oh, Annabelle, ah . . . we were ah . . . ," Pearle stuttered.

"Listen, you two, I am a big girl. I know what was going on, and to tell you the truth, it's about time! Mamma mia, you two have tiptoe through the beautiful tulips too much," Annabelle said through her broken English.

Robert and Pearle blushed and started laughing.

"You know, Annabelle, if you wouldn't mind, could you put on a fresh pot of coffee for us? Robert and I have to go over a few things, and we will be up for a while."

"Sure, that's a why I asked. Ahh . . . Robert, would you like another piece of cheesecake perhaps?" Annabelle asked mischievously.

"You know, I think I would, thank you."

"Make that two," Pearle said, and Annabelle went off to the kitchen humming "That's Amore."

"She's something else," Pearle said, shaking her head, amused.

"Well," he said after he gave her the kiss he wanted to, "we can finish our conversation later. Right now we better get to the other reason I'm here."

"Yeah, I think that's a good idea too. Let's go get that coffee and get started, then."

They settled back in the living room with their coffee and cheesecake. Robert then pulled out his briefcase and took out several files.

"Good grief, detective, what's all that paperwork?"

"I brought most of my files on Oona so I wouldn't forget anything. If you are tired, Pearle, maybe we should do this another time."

"Oh, absolutely not. I made sure I got a nap in this afternoon. So where do we start?"

"Well, after reviewing Oona's file today, I'd like to ask you some more personal things about Sol. But I hope you aren't going to get upset by them. . . ."

"Of course not," she answered with an assuring smile.

"All right, Pearle, how long have you known Sol Nipuk?"

"Since I was a young girl, about forty . . . forty-five years now."

"Okay, so give me a little bit more personal history about him and how you guys met."

"Sol started working with my grandfather when he was about eight years old, give or take a few years. Then after granddad passed, my dad became his mentor, and they worked together all the time. It wasn't until after my mom died that I really got to know Sol. I was always with my dad after she passed. I had no other living relative, I mean besides my father."

"Then when Daddy died, Sol took care of me. It was one of my father's last wishes to him that he become my legal guardian. This is why Sol and I are so close."

"You never told me this before, Pearle. It must have been tough on you."

"Nah, it wasn't so bad. I mean, I missed Daddy terribly, but Sol was great, and his sense of humor really made things easier for me when I was growing up. Besides, it wasn't as if I was going to be living with a stranger, and Daddy willed our home to Sol. That made things even more comfortable for me. We were always like brother and sister, and we have maintained that relationship all these years. I owe a lot to him, especially my career. He was an amazing teacher, Robert. I have never met anyone like him; I don't think I ever will."

"Pearle, this dig site, what is that?"

"Robert . . . that dig site is a pyramid and thousands of years ago was surrounded by a beautiful city. However, it's quite small compared to all the famous pyramids that border the Nile River, but as far as I'm concerned, just as important. My father's family, generation after generation, dedicated their entire life work to it. What I discovered many years ago led me to believe that there is a connection to my father's ancestors. It has always been a mystery to me, why only *my* ancestors ever dug there. There was so much to be done there, but after Oona, I, well, I just didn't want to be there anymore, and besides, I had Matthew to consider."

"Pearle, does Sol only work at this site, and is he working by himself? Excuse my ignorance, but I have no earthly idea about these things," he mused.

"Well, he'll consult on different dig sites when asked, but Robert, he's been working on this site for most of his life and will probably till the day he dies. As far as having help, yes, you need a lot of skilled workers . . . otherwise, it would be an impossible endeavor."

"Do you know these people he employs, Pearle?"

"Yes. Besides being half of the benefactor for the work there, I spent about thirty years of my life at that place, so I am very familiar with most of them. Well, at least the ones that were there eight years ago."

"So let's see if I got this all down right. This site has been a family operation for many, many years. You stated in this old report that you have about seventy crates that contain valuable antiques-relics from your relatives you have inherited. That the day Oona disappeared, nothing was disturbed or taken, to the best of your knowledge."

"Yes, that's all correct."

"Also stated here is that some of these items have come from this pyramid, and Oona researched items that were possibly from other sources. So is it possible to find out where and whom an item originally came from, Pearle?"

"Robert, that is what archaeology is all about. Although I must admit, not every answer is that easy to come by."

"Do you have a master list to indicate whom and where your items are from?"

"All that information should be in Oona's paperwork. Her specific job was to itemize, catalog, and inventory every item in each crate. She had worked for years doing that, Robert. You have to remember, sometimes not every item can be pinpointed to its exact origin. The reason is that some of those relics are extremely rare, and some are one-of-a-kind . . . besides being thousands of years old. We have a difficult time in finding origins because records of earlier discoveries just aren't available to us. I'd like to believe they exist, but where they are is another question. I can only assume they came from the pyramid, but they could be from another source too."

"I guess you were correct in saying this is complicated, Pearle. . . . I had no idea."

"Robert, I would imagine it is similar to your police work. Sorting through all the evidence of a crime, deciding what's important, what's not. You try not to miss a crucial clue, but it's basically the same concept."

"Oh, before I go on, don't forget that I have to get a picture of the medallions."

"I won't forget, Robert."

"All right, Pearle, I want to discuss some possibilities about Oona's case with you. You have to understand that with her medallion showing up in Egypt, it has raised several questions and some old theories to her disappearance."

"I'm anxious to hear what you think is going on here, Robert, and why."

"We are getting to that . . . I just have a few more questions. How long had you lived at this location before Oona disappeared?"

"It wasn't long, Robert. I would have to say about a year."

"Before you had the secure room built, where did you house the crates?"

"Remember that big building in the back of the house? That's where we kept them.

"Yes, I do, sorry, should have looked further in my notes here. It says also that you had a top-notch security system with surveillance cameras everywhere. You never had any break-ins or any problems with that building, did you, Pearle?"

"No, no problems at all, Robert."

"Were there any problems at your last residence?"

"No, nothing," she assured him.

"Well, that's about all I need to ask you for now," Robert said as he set his briefcase to the side. "How about a heat-up on the coffee, Pearle?" he asked, holding his empty cup.

"Absolutely. Annabelle has this whole thermal pot here for us," Pearle replied as she began pouring a fresh cup for him.

"Thanks, Pearle."

He sat back into the overstuffed cushion, and she sat across from him, curled up, with her elbows resting on some fluffy pillows. As she stared intently at him, he knew she was eager to hear what he had to say. He sipped his coffee and smiled, then placed his cup on the mahogany table and cleared his throat.

"Oona disappeared almost eight years ago, and you claim she was wearing a medallion. You get a call last night from Sol, and he informs you that he has found this medallion in Egypt, at your dig site. Don't you find that bizarre?"

"Yes, Robert, of course I do."

"Second, what would Oona have to do with this dig site? Other than the obvious, what would her connection be to it? Third, if this had been a kidnapping, we would have received a ransom demand. You are very wealthy, and a kidnapping would have made more sense in this case. Especially since we found nothing of her person and no evidence of her remains. The only thing we found of Oona's was her footprints that were by the lake and deep fingernail scratches close to the water's edge. Forensic results showed that her footprints were only a few hours old, and the one fingernail in the deep scratches we discovered matched the DNA from hairs we removed from Oona's hairbrush. That physical evidence only proved Oona was at the lake and there was an apparent struggle. However, we found no one else's footprints or any other evidence suggesting abduction. It's like she just disappeared into the lake.

"Now, Oona had no life insurance. We even checked to see if someone may have taken a policy out on her. We came up with nothing, zip, nada! It is a complete mystery, her disappearance, Pearle. Then, of course, we looked at all the obvious things . . . but she had no known enemies, and her husband at the time had an airtight alibi. I double-checked it myself.

"As for Annabelle, she was the last person in this house to see her. She stated that Oona came in the kitchen about 12:40 p.m. that day to get lunch and had a small leather bag with her. When she finished lunch, she told Annabelle she was going to take Zatu for a walk and that she would be back in a little while. She left the house about 1:15, and that was the last time anyone saw Oona.

"Annabelle claims she was curious about the leather bag Oona had, and when she asked her about it, Oona told her it was the last part of some inventory she was working on, but didn't elaborate as to exactly what it was or why she had it with her. We checked out Annabelle's story, and it all fit except for the leather bag, since that wasn't found either. Your gardener was just finishing up for the day, and he stated he saw Oona and Zatu heading toward the lake about 1:20. He noticed the time because he was writing in his logbook. We checked that log, and indeed he had written what he planted that day here and the time he spent on the job. We then investigated the gardener further to make sure he had left your place. We found that he went to a discount garden center to purchase some supplies, and our detectives confirmed this. They examined the garden store's security camera recording, and his presence was confirmed during that time he said he was there. Plus, Annabelle claimed she saw him leave about 1:25 p.m. You had taken Matthew for a haircut and then went shopping. Your story checked out also. You arrived home about three-thirty that afternoon. By four, you went looking for her. Oona was not at the lake, but Zatu was. You found him lying at the water's edge and claim he didn't want to leave. You stated that he was acting oddly and seemed lethargic. Oh, and you said his fur was wet. After finding Zatu in his condition, you became very concerned and realized something was wrong. After checking the storage building, you didn't see anything out of place, and not finding her, you thought maybe she might have gone out. Her car though, was still in the garage. You waited a while longer, thinking maybe she left with a friend and would return shortly. You knew this was not her regular behavior and that she would never go somewhere without telling anyone where she would be. At 4:25 p.m., you called the station.

"I have to ask you a question you may not like, Pearle, but was Sol in the U.S. at the time of Oona's disappearance?"

"No, he wasn't, Robert. I spoke to him later that night, and he became terribly upset. As I told you before, he loved Oona like a daughter; he was just as devastated as I was about what happened. He insisted about coming here, but I told him it wasn't necessary. However, he showed up the next day and stayed with us for about two months. I know you are doing your job, Robert, and you are great at it, but as I know the beat of my heart, Sol would never have done anything to Oona. Besides, if he had anything to do with Oona's disappearance, why would he call me about finding her medallion? I'm no detective, but doesn't that strike you as odd?"

"*Odd* is an understatement with this case," he said with a snort. "Well, I am going to check the airlines and some other things. There's a line through his name in my mind, but to be crossed off my list, I have to be 100 percent sure. You understand, don't you?"

"Of course I do, Robert. You do whatever you feel is necessary. I trust you completely. Listen, I'm gonna get some cream for my coffee. Do you need anything?"

"No, Pearle, thanks; I am good."

He leaned back into the couch and put his hands up over his head to stretch. His mind seemed to go blank. He leaned forward and put his face into his hands.

"Robert, are you all right?"

"Oh, yes, I'm fine. Sorry, I didn't hear you come back. Did you get your cream?"

"No, I decided before I got to the kitchen that I wasn't going to drink any more coffee."

"Well, it's getting late, Pearle. Let's get those pictures taken, and then we will be done for the evening."

"Okay, get your camera, and follow me."

"You know, Pearle, back in my notes, you stated Oona was working on something. What was she doing, if you can recall?"

"She was cataloging the last few crates and their items."

"Did you ever find out exactly what she was cataloging? This report says you weren't sure at the time."

"Actually, I didn't, but we can find out. No one had ever asked about it again, and to be honest, I forgot about it. All we need to do is check Oona's inventory list from that day. But what would that have to do with all this?"

"The leather bag, Pearle!"

"You're not telling me something, are you?" she said while leading him up the stairs to her bedroom.

"Let's just say there is a lot more information to add to this case. I will tell you this, though: Something is definitely not right here. In all my years of doing this work, I have never run into so many obstacles and dead ends on a case. Just so much doesn't make sense to me."

"Robert, tell me something I don't know!"

"So, Pearle, what are we doing in your bedroom?"

"Oh, there's an entrance to the wing downstairs from here in my closet. I didn't want to go through the downstairs entrance and take a chance of waking Annabelle."

She opened her closet and brought him to the back of it.

"Geez, Pearle, your closet is as big as my bedroom!"

"Wow, nice security system you have here, lady!"

"Well, it better be; it cost me a fortune," she said as she bent over slightly to scan her eye.

The wall of the closet disappeared to reveal a solid metal door.

She then put her hand to the scanner, and that prompted the heavy door to slide open. They both passed the door and stood on a landing. Pearle turned her head and inhaled, then inhaled quickly two more times.

"You smell that, Robert?" she asked, sniffing the air again.

"Ah . . . I smell fresh paint, if that is what you are talking about."

"Hmm . . . I could swear I caught a scent of perfume or cologne."

Again, she took a whiff. . . . "I don't smell it anymore . . . strange," she said, and then started down the stairs.

"You said there is another entrance to this room, Pearle?"

"Yes, it is off the room where the animals stay, next to Annabelle's room."

"Does she have access to it?"

"Yes, and so does Matthew, but no one else."

"Who moved the crates in here from the storage building, Pearle?"

"I hired a company that the museum recommended. I couldn't trust just any moving company to come in here and move all these valuables. Besides, they were the company I used when we relocated here."

"Did you have them sign confidentiality papers, Pearle?"

"Yes, of course I did. Why do you ask?"

"Just making sure you protected yourself. You can't trust anyone anymore in this world."

"I know; that's why I had every one of the crates covered. Annabelle and I worked for weeks doing the tedious job. We covered them in dark cloths and then wrapped them in heavy tape so nothing would be exposed."

"That makes me very happy to hear you took that extra precaution. Good job, Pearle!"

"Well, thank you, detective, but I am not a complete idiot, you know!"

"Did I say that? Good grief, woman, you need a nap," he said, chuckling.

"Yeah, I'm just a bit tired; sorry," and she gently squeezed his hand.

When they reached the bottom of the stairs, Pearle stopped so quickly that Robert almost knocked her over.

"Pearle, what is it?"

"Oh, my God, Robert," she gasped. "Look," she instructed him, pointing to the security system on the wall. "The other door is open!"

Entry Point Accessed *** Unusual Extended Time
**** Door AJAR****
**** Door AJAR****

Robert acted instinctively and pulled his gun from his shoulder holster under his jacket.

"Stay close," he whispered. "This place is enormous, Pearle. I need you to show me where the other door is."

She instructed his moves as she followed close behind, clutching the hem of his jacket tightly.

"I don't understand, Robert," she whispered nervously. "If the door was open here, the lights should have been on when we came in upstairs."

When they got to the other entrance door, Pearle let out a gasp.

"Oh, my God, Robert . . . it's Zatu!"

Zatu was lying lifeless inside the door's entrance. Robert pulled his cell phone out and called the police station. She heard him relay a 10-94 and 10, something else on his phone. She was kneeling over Zatu in tears, and Robert's voice was a distant murmur. She began to check Zatu to see if he was breathing, but was shaking so bad she couldn't tell if he had a heartbeat or not. Robert, still on the phone, bent down and put his ear to Zatu's chest.

"He's breathing, Pearle, and other officers will be here with a veterinarian any minute. We're in luck. Dr. Hadwick was at the station checking on one of our K-9 dogs that got hurt tonight."

"He's our vet too, Robert!" she said with a nervous shrill.

"Pearle, stay with Zatu. I'll check out the rest of the room. If you hear anything, just yell, okay?"

"*Matthew* . . . we need to check Matthew!" Pearle said with horror in her voice!

"Please . . . Pearle, calm down! Other officers are on their way, and we will go through the entire house," he assured her.

What seemed like an eternity to her was only a couple of minutes, and suddenly blue and bright red flashing lights approached the property.

"Pearle, go to the door and let the officers in; then come right back here. Do you understand me?"

"Ye . . . yes, Robert, I will be right back," she replied with a shaky voice.

When she reached the back door, it was open. She felt every hair on the back of her neck stand up and a panic that chilled her spine! The officers rushed to the door, and Pearle told them about it being open. Detective Brian Kelly arrived behind the first patrol car. He gave directives to several officers to secure the property and then asked Pearle to lead him and the vet to Detective Greene.

"Robert," she yelled, exasperated, "the back door was opened!"

More cars arrived, and there were so many lights flashing that they lit up the entire area like a Fourth of July fireworks display! Annabelle came out of her room yelling for Pearle in a complete state of panic!

"Annabelle, I am here," she called to her from the secured room.

"Are you okay? What happened? Oye mamma mia, what's a going on, Robert?"

"Annabelle, did you hear anything tonight after you went to bed?" Robert asked.

"No, no, nothing!"

"Annabelle, stay here with Pearle. I'm going with these officers to check the rest of the house."

"Oh, no . . . I'm going too, Robert!" Pearle said as she darted out in front of him and sprinted toward the stairs to Matthew's room.

Chapter Seven

"Yes, Dr. Hadwick, okay.... Great, they will be so relieved! I will relay the message, and Doc, thank you very much for pulling an all-nighter. Zatu means the world to them."

"You're welcome, Detective Greene. I love happy endings too, you know!"

"Oh, Doc, how long will it be before we get a toxicology report?"

"I should have it to you by the end of next week if the lab is not too busy."

"Again, Dr. Hadwick, thanks for everything you did for Zatu."

"No problem. Oh, and listen, tell Pearle she may be able to pick him up in a day or two. I will call you, though, and let you know how he is coming along. He was through an awful ordeal, and I won't release him until he's been stable for at least twenty-four hours."

"Absolutely, you do whatever you feel is necessary. We know he's in good hands."

Robert hung up glad to have some good news to give Pearle when she and Matthew woke up. He yawned, realizing he hasn't slept in nearly twenty-four hours, and went to Pearle's living room to lie down on the couch. With the forensics finished and the Criminalistics crew gone, he felt comfortable dozing for just a few minutes, knowing there was an officer patrolling the area.

He looked at his watch, 5:08 a.m., and that was the last thing he remembered.

"Detective, yoo-hoo, detective," the gentle voice repeated.

Robert opened his eyes, and Pearle was standing over him with a big mug of hot coffee.

"Mornin'," he said, rubbing his eyes, with a big yawn. Then he swallowed, tasting the bitterness on his tongue from last night's coffee.

"What time is it?" he asked as he sat up.

"It is a little past ten," she replied, and handed him the steaming brew.

"Wow, guess I was more tired than I thought. Where's Matthew?"

"He's still asleep. He had a very restless night, and I am a little concerned, Robert. He was having terrible nightmares and speaking in what seemed to be ancient Arabic. Some of the things he was saying . . . just didn't make any sense to me."

"Oh, anything in particular?" he asked, scratching his scruffy, unshaven face and sipping the hot coffee.

"To be honest, some of the language he used sounded like a spell or a curse of some sort. He mentioned *ushabtis*."

"What the heck is that?"

"Ushabtis are small Egyptian carvings made of wood, wax, or stone, and were shaped in the image of a deceased person, usually royalty, and it was customary for them to be placed in the person's tomb. Some believe they were used for black magic; others say they were to be used to do the manual labor of the deceased in their afterlife."

"Really . . . it was pretty intense around here last night. Matthew told me he's brushing up on his language skills for Egypt, so maybe it's just a combination of everything in the last few days, you know."

"You're probably right, and it definitely was a little crazy here last night. Well, anyway, Annabelle is making brunch. Are you hungry?" she asked.

"I'm a guy who's always hungry," he said with a hearty laugh.

"Okay, and if you want to shower, you can use the guest bathroom upstairs. I see the sergeant brought you some clean clothes, so go ahead. I think anything you would require is up there. Annabelle made sure of that this morning."

"She's a sweetheart; remind me to thank her when I come down, will you?"

"Sure, and take that coffee with you. I'll put a fresh pot up while you are showering."

"Thanks, Pearle. I can only imagine what I must smell like."

"Now that you mention it . . . . Oh, I am only kidding, Robert! I'll see you when you're done," and she kissed his cheek and turned to go to the kitchen.

"Pearle," he called softly to her from the steps, "I love you!"

"Yeah . . . yeah, that's only because I offered you a shower and a good, hot meal," she said, laughing.

"Oh, she's a funny one," he said as he turned and went up the stairs.

As he showered, he reflected back on last night. Forensics found nothing disturbed or apparently stolen. Nothing about last night makes sense . . . a crime with no crime . . . . *How redundant!* he thought. He reached up and adjusted the showerhead to high. The pulsating hot water felt good against his tense, aching neck.

"What the hell am I missing here? . . . Okay . . . go over this one more time. This was a highly orchestrated crime. . . . Whoever did this put a lot of thought into it. . . . They had knowledge of Pearle's sophisticated security system, to perpetrate what appears to be a perfect crime! But what's the crime . . . B&E (breaking and entering)? Nah . . . can't be.

"Think, Robert, think. . . . How could I have overlooked that?! Pearle has to do a physical inventory! It is the only way to be sure. She didn't go through everything thoroughly last night. There has to be something missing. No one would go through all this trouble and not take squat!"

"Great meal, Annabelle. Thank you," Robert said as he got up from the table.

"You are very welcome, but are you sure you have had enough?"

"Oh, yes. I'm so full I could go back to sleep," he said with a yawn, patting his full belly.

"Pearle, we really need to talk now; Detective Kelly is probably on his way over."

"Sure, Robert, whatever we need to do," Pearle said as she led the way into the living room.

"Morning, guys."

"Well, look who it is! How ya doing, Matthew?" asked Robert.

"I'm good, just tired. These freaky nightmares are getting to be a real pain in the butt. Hey, did you guys eat?"

"Yes, we did. Would you like to talk about the nightmares?" Robert asked.

"Nah . . . I'm good. I'm gonna grab some grub." And off he went to the kitchen.

Detective Kelly arrived and was filled in on the condition of Zatu.

"This could have been much worse, Pearle. I am so happy Zatu is going to be okay."

"Thank you, Brian. Can I get you a cup of coffee or anything else to drink?"

"You know, Pearle, I would love a cup of coffee if you wouldn't mind."

"I'll get it, Pearle. Black, Brian?"

"Yeah, thanks."

"All right, detectives, where do you want to start?" Pearle asked eagerly as Robert gave Brian his coffee.

"Let's start with the alarm system, Pearle. I need to know what company put it in and the date it was installed."

"That file is in the office. Would you like me to get that for you?"

"Yes, and Pearle . . . I am going to need a list of every company that was involved with your renovation. Is that going to be a big headache for you?"

"Not at all, Brian. I've got a whole file with every single person who had anything to do with the remodeling. I'll fetch it all for you and be back in a few minutes."

"Robert, how's she doing after last night?"

"Good, so far as I can tell."

"She seems like a tough lady, Robert, and sure has had her share of troubles."

"That she has, but I'm hoping we will be able to get to the bottom of this mess. I have a feeling we are going to find out a lot more than any of us ever imagined."

"Oh, what do you mean?"

"Well, I got to thinking about last night. It seems like the perfect crime was pulled off. However, besides poisoning the dog, what was the crime, breaking and entering? It has to be more than that. I want Pearle to do a complete inventory of her belongings downstairs. No one would go through all the trouble of breaking into this place, undetected, and then leave empty-handed. I am also convinced that whoever was here . . . knows Pearle on a personal level, don't you think so?"

"You are absolutely right, Robert. It wasn't some botched robbery gone bad. It was a highly thought-out plan. That is why I have asked her for the names of everyone involved with the renovation. Anyone who was in this house, especially the security company, is a suspect. I was going to suggest the inventory thing to her also, but glad you are already on it."

"I haven't told her yet. I will, though, as soon as she . . . ."

"I'm back," Pearle announced as she entered the room.

"Brian, here is all the contractors' information, and I included the company that did the landscaping. I believe every person who was in this house is in those files."

"This is wonderful, Pearle. I'll take all this paperwork with me and get the information I need, then return it in a few days. Is that okay with you?"

"Sure, I don't see a problem. Do you, Robert?"

"No, not at all, Pearle. It is all standard procedure, and besides, Detective Kelly is much better with paperwork than I am!"

They all started to laugh as Matthew came in to join them.

"Hey, I am glad you are here, Matthew," Detective Kelly said. "Come here and sit with us."

"Oh, what's up?"

"I need to ask you some questions about last night, that is, of course, if you are up to it."

"Sure, whatever you need to ask, go for it!"

"Okay, Matthew," Brian laughed, "tell me what you can remember after you went to your room last night."

"Well, I went up to my room after dinner. I had some major reading to do for English class. Bella came up with me, but you know, Zatu didn't. Come to think of it . . . that was kinda strange."

"Why do you say that?" Robert asked.

"Usually when I go up to bed, both dogs come with me, right Nana?" Matt asked as he looked over at Pearle.

"Yes, they are your little entourage every night," she laughed.

"Okay, so once you were upstairs, did you notice anything

different or hear something that was out of the ordinary?"

Matthew thought about Brian's question for a minute.

"Well, I'm not sure if it's a big deal or not, but I did notice the spotlights come on a few times."

"Spotlights . . . . Can you tell what time that was?"

"Ah, let's see, I went up about nine or so, right, Robert?"

"Yes, I believe it was about that time," he answered.

"I took a quick shower first and then played with Hunter."

"Who is Hunter?" Brian asked.

"Oh, he's my hamster! He's nocturnal, and I let him out of his cage every night for like a half hour or so, and he rolls around in his exercise ball. Then I usually feed him and clean his cage."

"So did you do all that stuff with Hunter last night?"

"Yeah, and now that I think about it, he wasn't out too long because it was getting late, and I had that studying to do."

"Okay, do you remember what time this was?"

"Yes, I do. I looked at the clock, and it was half past nine. That's when I put him back in his cage. Oh, and that is when I first noticed the spotlight go on."

"Great. Now, do you remember what time it was when it came on again?"

"Yes, after I was in bed reading, oh . . . for maybe about twenty minutes or so, I caught the light again from the corner of my eye."

"Did you think that was out of the ordinary?" Robert asked.

"Well, it doesn't happen that often, if that's what you mean."

"Matthew, it's really important for you to tell me what time it was when you last saw the light come on."

"I would have to say it was around eleven, but not much past it because when I looked at the clock a little while after that, it was eleven fifteen. That's when I turned my light out and Bella climbed in bed with me. That's all I remember, till you and Nana came in my room last night with the police. Oh, wait a minute, I just remembered something. Not sure if it's important, but I was almost asleep, and Bella started whining. Then she started scratching at the windowsill and growling."

"Has she done this before?"

"No, she hardly ever growls. She's a gentle dog, even-tempered and always happy. It seemed to take me forever to get her calm and come back to bed. I thought maybe there was a raccoon or skunk out there, and I looked out the window but didn't see anything. Eventually, though, she did stop. That was 11:35 and when I looked at the clock for the last time. Then I fell asleep, with her head resting on my leg."

"Wow," Brian said. "What a night for you. I just need to ask you one more thing: Do you remember the dogs acting funny or different during the night before you went to bed?"

"Well, Zatu seemed a little antsy."

"What do you mean?" Pearle asked.

"She was pacing back and forth and whining when I went to put the wine in the cooler Robert had brought over. Remember, Nana, you had asked me to do that before dinner. So I figured she had to go, and I let her out."

"Does anyone recall what time that was?" asked Brian.

"Guessing, I would have to say about five to eight . . . ," Robert said, looking at Pearle.

"I would say that is about right because I came downstairs about 7:45, and I remember looking at the clock on my dresser when I left my room."

"Now, does anybody remember what time or if they had let Zatu back in after Matthew put him out?"

"Gosh," Pearle said, looking at Matthew, then Robert, "I didn't let him in. Did one of you guys?"

Both of them shook their heads no.

"We'll have to ask Annabelle if she let him in, because now that I think about it, I don't recall seeing him until," she hesitated, "well, until I . . . ."

Brian cleared his throat.

"Matthew, I want to thank you for all your help," Brian said as he stood and shook his hand.

"Sure, and if I remember anything else, I'll let Robert know."

"That would be terrific. Thanks!"

"You're welcome, sir. Now, if it's all right with you guys, I think I'll go snooze for a bit. Hey, Nana, where's Bella?"

"She should be around here somewhere, unless Annabelle let her out."

"I'm gonna go see where she is. I hate to say this, but I'd sure feel better with her upstairs with me."

"I don't blame you for feeling like that after last night, but you are very safe," Robert said, assuring him as he rose from the couch.

"Come on, Matt, I'll help you find her! I'll be back in just a minute, Pearle."

"Robert," Brian interrupted, "I am going to ask Pearle some questions about the contractors."

"Sure, go ahead and start. I should only be gone a few minutes."

"All right, Pearle, so the paperwork you gave me contains names and contact numbers of all the contractors you have had here, correct?"

"Yes, from the builders to the air-conditioning company and landscapers."

"What about the movers you hired from the museum? Robert mentioned that you had used them before?"

"Yes, I did, and their information is there too."

"Good, then if you don't mind, I'd like to ask you some other questions."

"Sure, Brian, but shouldn't we wait for Robert to get back?"

"That's fine with me. May I use your restroom, Pearle?"

"Of course; it's down the hall, second door to your left."

"Thanks, and maybe you can check on Robert to see what is taking him so long."

As Brian washed his hands, he checked himself in the large antique mirror. He has put on a little weight lately and is very uncomfortable about it.

"Ah . . . time to hit the gym again," he muttered in disgust as he grabbed a thick chunk of his stomach hanging over his slacks while shaking his head. He buttoned his jacket, smoothed his short blond hair with his damp palms, straightened his tie, and checked his teeth for food as he smiled widely. *Not too bad, buddy,* he said to himself as he eyed himself up and down, left to right. He dried his hands, turned the light out, and headed back to the living room.

Pearle went to the kitchen and found Annabelle making homemade spaghetti sauce.

"Oh, you got me drooling; it smells so good in here, Annabelle! What's for dinner?"

"Spaghetti and meatballs," she announced while stirring her big pot of homemade sauce with a large wooden spoon. "Matthew said he was craving it! I'm making him his favorite chocolate cake too, but no tell him, okay?"

"No problem," she said, amused. "I won't say a word . . . promise," she said as she put her right hand up as if she were under oath.

"Did Robert and Matthew go outside, Annabelle?"

"Yes, they said they were looking for Bella, and I told them I let her out so she could do her business. Geez, I thought they would have been back by now, though," she said as she glanced out the window.

"Maybe I better see if I can find them. If Detective Kelly comes looking for me, tell him I went to get the boys."

"Sure, I see if maybe he wants to eat a little something, no?"

"Yes, Annabelle, thank you. I didn't even think to ask him that."

"Whoa . . . Nana," Matthew said as he nearly ran into her as she was opening the door. "Robert needs Brian, and he wants some *Ziploc* bags too!"

"Slow down, Matthew. Is everything okay? Where is Bella?"

"She's okay and with Robert. Come on, he said to hurry!"

"Hey . . . what's all the excitement about?" Brian asked as he got to the kitchen.

"Robert said he needs you to get your case and follow me!"

"Nana, did you get those bags? Oh, I almost forgot . . . he said if you have an empty bucket to bring it too."

Brian looked at Pearle as she grabbed the blue mop bucket, and they all darted out the door. They found Robert standing over a pile of vomit and quickly covered their noses.

"Good grief!" Pearle exclaimed. "What is that *awful* stench?"

"That, my dear, is evidence," he said with a smile. "Bella was sniffing it when we found her, and I'd bet anything this is what Zatu left here last night. Brian, have you got any gloves for me in that magic bag of tricks of yours?"

"Sure do, wouldn't leave home without them! It looks like undigested steak to me; is it, Robert?"

"Yeah, I think so. Well, thank goodness Zatu rid himself of this, or we wouldn't have had such a happy ending with him."

"I agree. . . . Does it have anything else that you can see?" Brian asked, pressing a large handkerchief to his nose.

Robert looked up, then over at Brian, and began to laugh.

"Feeling queasy this morning, detective?"

Brian didn't answer, though. He just shot Robert a pathetic pale look, because he is used to being ribbed about his sensitive stomach.

"Hey, Pearle, did Zatu eat any steak yesterday?"

"No, he doesn't get table food."

"Brian, go about twenty feet to your left there, and be careful. I haven't had a chance to really look the area over yet. Something caught my eye, just not sure what it was, if anything. I was trying to keep Bella from possibly getting into this pile of yuck."

"Well, well," Pearle heard Brian echo. "Robert, we had better get the crew back."

"Already put the call in," Robert assured him.

"Matthew, do me a favor, and please take Bella inside and get her some water. I just want to make sure she didn't get into any of this stuff here, okay?"

"Sure, Robert! Bella . . . ," Matthew called, and both of them headed back to the house.

"Pearle, there's no reason for you to stand out here either. Why don't you go back to the house too."

"Ah, Robert, I see something shiny over there. . . . I am going to take a look."

"No, Pearle," he insisted. "Please stay where you are. I don't want us to contaminate the area more than it has been."

Brian came over to Pearle just as Robert did.

"Okay, Pearle, point to where you see this shining object."

"There," she said, and pointed about thirty feet away from Matthew's bedroom window. "Can you see it?"

"Yes, yes, I can," Robert said, squinting his eyes.

Just as he said that, the Criminalistics crew arrived.

"Where is Addy?" Robert asked, annoyed.

"Sergeant Foxx is on her way, sir," one of the officers replied.

"Let me know when she arrives," Robert growled.

Sergeant Addy Foxx is in charge of the Criminalistics team. She has been with the department for seven years and is one of the best Criminalistics technicians in the state. The sergeant's five-foot, eleven-inch presence adds to her overwhelming, chubby, but muscular, build, and dull, stringy strawberry blonde hair and prominent overbite. Her peers say she isn't much to look at, but the entire police department respects her and the impeccable work she does.

Brian and Robert were discussing the area they wanted roped off when Addy drove up in the department's new crime scene van. She parked next to a squad car and joined the rest of her team. Robert filled her and the crew in on what they found. When he finished, he took her to the side to talk with her privately.

"I am disappointed with the way things went last night. Brian and I found several items out here that were overlooked and shouldn't have been!" Raising his voice, he added, "Addy, what's the problem?"

"I'm sorry, sir; I thought we thoroughly combed the area last night. Then, soothing him, "Don't worry, Detective Green, I will personally make sure every inch is inspected; I promise."

"We will see, sergeant. Now get your crew to rope off about one hundred or so yards south from here. Then go approximately one hundred yards west that way with tape. That blue bucket out there is over a pile of dog vomit. Make sure you collect every bit of it. Oh, and do not forget photos and the area surrounding it."

"Sir, no disrespect intended, but I do know how to manage a crime scene," she said while giving him a peevish sneer.

Robert's face reddened, then scrunched up in disgust as he held back undignified words that wanted to roll off his tongue.

"Really . . . . If you have any questions or a problem, come and get me," Robert scoffed coldly. "Addy, no sloppy job today," he added sarcastically as he walked away and headed toward Pearle.

"*Gee, I wonder who crawled up his butt today,*" Addy said to herself. She pulled out her camera and began to plan how she was going to cover the large crime scene. Then she quietly said, *"Just another miserable day in paradise, Addy Foxx, and one more hard-working dollar for dear ole Uncle Sam. There has got to be a better way!"*

"Pearle, I am going to ask that you return to the house now and walk back on the same path that you came on. Oh, and make sure no one comes out of the house for a while. I want my crew to do a thorough search with no interruptions."

"Absolutely, Robert, no one will interfere with your investigation."

"Thanks, Pearle," he replied, and then got back to directing the crime scene crew as she carefully walked back to the house.

"Hey, Robert, you done with that puke? If so, come over here for a minute."

"What's up, Brian?" he asked as he snapped the blue rubbery gloves off his hands.

"Now, what do you suppose that could be?" Brian asked, standing closer to where Pearle said she saw something earlier.

"I'm not sure, but let's go have a look. Huh . . . the plot thickens," Robert said.

"Okay, I'll bite, what plot thickens?"

"What you are looking at, detective, is Pearle's medallion, which, by the way, is worth a fortune. Now tell me, why would anyone drop something so valuable, Brian? Oh, and look here; how nice of them," he said sarcastically, pointing to a boot print.

"Addy," Robert yelled out, "I got a print here. Bring your kit."

"Be right there, sir," she hollered back.

Addy did perimeter measurements, then took a series of pictures of the location, medallion, and boot print. She then proceeded to recover the boot print with a plaster of paris impression.

"Anything else you want done, sir, in this perimeter?" she asked Robert.

"Well, yes, Addy. What is up with you? You're acting like you never been on a crime scene this large before."

"Sorry, sir, I think I am coming down with the flu. I've been feeling like crap for a couple of days now."

"Why didn't you say something? Geez, Addy, the way things

were going here it was like you were intentionally doing a bad job on this case. You are one of the best Criminalistics I've ever worked with. Your investigation has been totally out of character for you!"

"I do apologize. Usually I can work through anything, but this creeping crud that is going around the station is kicking my butt."

"Do you think you can get through today?"

"Yes, sir, I sure can. Don't worry, this area will be searched completely."

"Listen, Addy, I'm sorry if I came down too hard on you, but there cannot be any negligence on our part in this investigation, you understand? Remember, when one of us screws up, it reflects on the whole damn department."

"I sure do. You don't have to say anything else, detective."

"Addy, don't bag the medallion yet. I am going to get Pearle so we can have her identify it."

"Yes, sir. I have to wait anyway,; the boot print is still setting up."

Robert walked away and went to the house. He found Pearle dozing on the couch.

"Hey, Pearle," he said as he sat on the end of the couch.

"Robert, hey to you, are you all done out there?" she asked sleepily.

"No. As a matter of fact, I hate to bother you, but I need you to come back outside with me."

"Oh," she said, sitting up.

"It will only take a couple of minutes."

"Sure, let me get my shoes. Is anything wrong?"

"No, I just need you to identify something."

"What is it, Robert?" she asked.

"I probably couldn't describe it properly. I'd rather you see it for yourself."

"All right, Robert, I'm ready to go."

As she followed behind Robert, she saw the yellow *DO NOT CROSS POLICE LINE* tape, covering an extensive area of the property. They went to the spot where Addy was with the boot print and medallion.

"Officer Foxx, I'd like you to meet Pearle Sherapha."

"Nice to meet you," Addy said as she shook Pearle's hand with a very firm grip.

"Same here, officer," Pearle replied, blinking while looking up at the tall woman as the sun blinded her.

Addy stepped to the side, and Pearle let out a gasp.

"Robert . . . that's *my* medallion!"

"I thought so, Pearle, but we had to have you identify it. So you are positive it is yours?"

"Absolutely. I can tell by that new clasp. I had it put on last year. I am so creeped out," Pearle said as a chill shot through her and made her shudder.

Brian had joined them and looked at how frightened Pearle was. He was convinced of his suspicions about the break-in and knew what she had to do.

"Look, Pearle," Brian began, "so much has happened since last night, and I understand you're upset, but we need you to see if anything else was taken. Although the initial search showed nothing disturbed, whoever broke into your home had a reason for doing so. . . . They didn't break in for nothing! Apparently, they knew what they were looking for. There must be more items missing. You couldn't possibly know exactly what was taken from the quick look we did last night. You have to do a complete inventory of all your valuables, Pearle."

"I agree with Brian. Pearle, you need to do an inventory of your items like we spoke about this morning, and the sooner the better."

"Yes, Robert, I sure do. . . . I just don't even know where to start. Do you realize all the crates there are, plus the dozens of drawers?"

"Hey, Robert," Brian interrupted. "I have an idea. Things out here are going along smoothly. Why don't you give Pearle a hand? If anything comes up, I can handle it."

"It's not you I'm worried about, Brian," Robert replied, looking over the crime scene.

"Look, you're the boss. It's your job to worry," he said with a slight chuckle to his voice.

"Robert, it would be great if I could get your help. We could get through the stuff much quicker with two people. That is . . . if you wouldn't mind," Pearle added.

"Of course, I wouldn't, Pearle. All right, Brian, you're in charge, then, but you know where I am."

"Yes, I do."

"Pearle, we have to take this medallion in with the rest of the evidence and process it."

"Oh, I can't take it back with me?" she asked.

"No, I'm sorry. It's evidence, and we need to dust it for prints," Robert added.

"Well, you will be careful with it . . . won't you?"

"Ms. Sherapha, I promise you, I will personally make sure the utmost care and security is upheld with your medallion," Addy said, assuring Pearle as she was kneeling on the ground with her back to her.

"Well, I hope so, Officer Foxx, because that medallion is thousands of years old and worth several million dollars!"

Addy swallowed hard and tried not to choke on her words.

"Before I process it for prints, I'll contact Mr. Peters in Tallahassee. He specializes in the handling of valuable antiques. You'll have your medallion back with no harm done to it, I promise," Addy assured her.

"Thank you, officer. That medallion is a family heirloom, and it is priceless to me."

"You don't have to thank me, Ms. Sherapha; it's my job," Addy said as she bagged the medallion and continued her work.

"Brian, I am going back to the house. If you need me, just call."

He gave him an assuring nod, and Robert left reluctantly with Pearle.

Chapter Eight

"So Robert, when will we finish up with the questioning again?"

"Probably tomorrow. Brian said he wouldn't mind coming by in the afternoon."

"Then I better tell Matthew to call that boy from school he invited over and tell him they will have to make it another day."

"Yeah, that's right. Crash was coming over to work on some things for the swim team."

"I'm sure he'll understand. Besides, Matthew isn't feeling that great. He says he has a bad headache. Annabelle went to pick up a prescription that Denise called in for him. Hopefully that will help.

"He probably just needs a good night's sleep, Pearle. By the way, did you speak to him about those nightmares like you said you were going to do?"

"No, I haven't, Robert, but I will after dinner."

"Well, we might as well get at this. Now, I hope you have an inventory list of everything, Pearle."

"Of course I do. The one with my personal items is in my desk. I'll be right back." And Pearle whisked out of the room.

Okay, I got it; let's get going." And she headed upstairs, with Robert right behind her.

"Where do you keep the stuff on that list, Pearle?"

"Over here," she said, pointing to a fake front on a dresser. "I guess, though, it wasn't such a great idea after all."

"Why?"

"Well, that's where my medallion was, Robert."

"Wait!" he yelled as she walked toward the dresser.

"What is it, Robert?" she said, startled, turning toward him.

"Good grief, Pearle, we didn't dust for prints up here. We had no reason to. Don't touch anything; I have to get someone in here from the team. Your bedroom is now a crime scene too, I'm afraid," he said as he pulled his cell phone from his coat pocket.

"Hey, Brian, it's me. I need a team here at the house. Can you spare two people?"

"Sure, Robert. What's up?"

"Pearle's medallion was taken from her bedroom, and you know what this means."

"Whoever the SOB was that broke in last night knew where it was! This is getting to sound more personal, don't you think, Robert?"

"Yep, and that's what's worrying me."

"Hang on a sec, Robert. Marconey, Michaels . . . leave that for Addy. I got something else you need to take care of right away. Detective Greene needs you at the house right away. Hey, Marconey, don't you need your kit? All right, Robert, they are on their way."

"Thanks, Brian. How is everything going out there?"

"We are almost done, maybe another hour or so."

"Sounds great. I'll speak to you later, then," and Robert hung up.

"Pearle, would you go downstairs and bring the two officers up when they arrive? I want to look around before they get here."

"Of course. I'll bring them up as soon as they come."

"Hello, Ms. Sherapha, it's Officer Michaels from Criminalistics."

"Sam, how are you?" she said while opening the door. "Come on in."

"I'm good, Pearle, thank you. This is Officer Sol Marconey. Detective Kelly said Detective Greene sent for us. Oh, before I forget, how is Zatu doing? I heard about what happened this morning when I came on duty. Is he going to be okay?"

"Yes, Dr. Hadwick said he'll make a full recovery. By the way, how is that adorable Akita doing? It's Pepper, right? I haven't seen you guys in a while. I think the last time was at the dog beach, wasn't it?"

"Yeah, it was, about two months ago. Pepper is fine, still a puppy and chewing on everything. He really had a good time playing with Zatu that day. Well, I'm glad Zatu is going to be all right. He really is a great dog. Okay, so before I have my head chewed off," he laughed, "where is Detective Greene at, Pearle?"

"This way," she said with a slight giggle as she led the two officers upstairs to Robert.

"Gentlemen, did you bring your gear bags?"

"Yes, sir, they are right outside the door."

"Pearle, before you go downstairs, did you notice anything unusual or out of place in here?"

"No, Robert, no drawers were open, and everything seemed to be just like I left it when I went downstairs last night."

"Ms. Sherapha, what have you moved or touched in here since the break-in, and has anyone else been in here?" asked Marconey.

"The only thing I recall touching was this dresser here for my undergarments and the closet to get my outfit for today. Otherwise, I didn't even sleep in here. . . . I slept in Matthew's room last night. I will check, but I don't think Annabelle has been in here today."

"Thank you, Pearle," Officer Michaels said. "We will have to dust everything from the closet into this room, so we may be a while, and there will be a bit of a mess to clean up."

"Sam, don't worry about that. . . . You do whatever it is you have to, for however long it takes. I'll put some coffee on, and if you want anything at all, just let me know, fellows, okay?"

"Thank you, Pearle," Sam replied, and with that, she went downstairs to the kitchen.

"Pearle, how do you know that officer?" Annabelle asked, being her nosey self.

"Oh, Sam is who Oona got Zatu from. He bred shepherds for a while and had a dog training school before joining the police force. Sam trained many of the K-9 dogs for the department. Oona took Zatu to his obedience classes. He really was very good at what he did. Such a shame he doesn't do it anymore, though."

"Oh, what happened?"

"It is a sad story, Annabelle. All I know is that there was a bad storm one night, and I guess lightning struck the kennels he kept his dogs in, and a horrible fire ensued. He wasn't home at the time, and he blames himself for losing all his dogs that night. Ya know, I think he had a thing for Oona. He was always calling her and making excuses that he was just checking to see how Zatu was coming along after they finished his advanced obedience class."

"Oh, my God, that is such a horrible thing to happen! Oye mamma mia, he must be carrying around so much guilt. He seems like such a nice man too."

"He is, Annabelle; that's what makes it even harder to understand. Sam really loved his dogs and took excellent care of them. I guess it was just a freak accident."

Pearle went and stood by the kitchen sink and just stared aimlessly outside. Annabelle knew she was thinking about Oona.

Almost two hours had gone by since Marconey and Michaels showed up. Pearle and Annabelle were sitting in the kitchen, drinking a new batch of sun tea that Annabelle had experimented with and going over their grocery list.

"Well, ladies, I guess we are done upstairs."

"That was quicker than I thought it would be, Robert. Did they find anything?" Pearle asked.

"They did pick up a few prints, so we might get lucky. Then again, they could just be one of yours or Annabelle's." Either way, we'll find out. Hey, Pearle, got any coffee? I'm running on low here," he said, yawning.

Robert sat hunched over, stirring his coffee while staring blankly at the table.

"A shiny penny for those thoughts, detective," Pearle whispered across the table.

"Sorry, Pearle, just contemplating," he replied dryly. Then he drained the last bit of coffee in his cup and stood up, stretching his arms toward the ceiling. "I am ready when you are."

When they completed the inventory in Pearle's bedroom, noting only her medallion was taken, they decided to move on to the secured room and continue their work.

"Gee, Pearle, this room looks like I just walked into a bank vault!"

"I wanted to keep the jewelry and gems separate from the bigger stuff. Besides, that's how Oona inventoried everything."

"Yeah, Pearle, we need the inventory list to start this."

"That's what I'm after; it's down here," she said, pulling out a large rectangular drawer with some effort. "Ah, here we go," and she handed Robert a large red file.

"So should we start here, then go to the crates, Pearle?"

"Yes, we might as well."

"I guess I'll hold the list and check off items as we go along. . . . Is that okay with you?"

"Absolutely, Robert. It will take less time that way."

Robert sat down and started to leaf through the pages of the inventory list. Pearle looked up and saw a weird expression on his face. "Something wrong, Robert?"

"Ah . . . Pearle . . . there seems to be some pages torn off. . . . Page three is totally missing, and so are several in the back. Here, take a look," he said as he handed her the list.

Pearle scanned the list carefully, then turned it over.

"That's weird. Nothing is on the back of the last page except an odd dirty design I can't quite make out."

"Here, let me see that," Robert said, reaching for it.

"Well, I'll be . . . that isn't a design . . . it is a shoe print. Oona must have stepped on it at some point . . . hmm . . . but you said she was petite like you."

"She was, Robert, why?"

"Pearle, whoever made this print is about a size nine or ten wide, and they are not petite!"

"Really, how can you tell that?"

"It's my job, silly," he replied with a smirk, amused by her question. "So what about those missing pages—any idea why they are gone or what was on them?"

"No, I have absolutely no idea at all. To be honest, when I put all this stuff in here, I never really looked at this list. I just put everything away."

Robert stood up, and as he towered over Pearle, he reached into his khaki pants pocket. He pulled out a pair of blue gloves and put them on.

"I have a feeling that whoever was in here last night may have taken those missing pages and possibly what was on them, Pearle. I'm going to take a few pictures of the shoe print, and then I will have to dust this list for fingerprints. If I am correct in my suspicions, there was more than one person involved with the break-in."

"Oh, what makes you say that?"

"Because, we found a boot print outside next to your medallion and now this different print on the back of your inventory list, which looks pretty fresh to me. Look here," he said as he rubbed some of the dirt outside of the print. "Let's get this inventory going, Pearle. We need to find out if anything was taken."

An hour and a half later, they sat in silence. She was shocked to find out that the other three medallions were missing, along with numerous pieces of jewelry.

"Pearle, I have to ask you something. Who knew about these medallions?"

Her dry lips seemed sealed; then, very slowly, they peeled away from each other as she began to speak.

"Ah, let me see . . . Matthew, Annabelle, Sol, and myself," she said softly. "Only Matthew and I knew where they were kept, though, Robert."

"All right," he replied, and gave her a gentle smile.

"Guess we ought to get the rest of this done, Robert." And she walked out of the room to where the crates were.

They worked with no real conversation except speaking of the items and checking them off as they went along. The silence was getting unnerving to Robert, and so was her somber mood.

"So, Pearle, tell me, have you ever ridden a camel?"

She turned toward him with a half smile. "Yes, of course I have, why?"

"Well, would you be willing to give me a lesson while we are in Egypt?" he said with a chuckle.

"I'm not sure if you want me to teach you. After all, you know what they say about woman drivers."

"Sure I do," he replied with a wide grin.

But she just shrugged her shoulders.

"Is that a yes?"

"Of course, Robert, but I have to warn you; camels can be pretty nasty."

"I bet it'll be a riot, Pearle; I'm sure you'll get a good laugh out of it!"

"Come to think of it," she giggled, "that probably would be quite the site." And the grim expression on her face was gone.

"Hey, I just remembered something. A couple of days before she disappeared, Oona said she found something in my great-grandfather's crate and wanted to discuss it with me. She said it would interest me very much, and I recall her saying something like, 'Mom, there are some weird things about our family that I just don't understand!'"

"That *is* strange, Pearle. Did you ever find out what she was referring to?"

"No, never got the chance to," she said with her voice fading. "You know, with everything that's been going on and with Sol's phone call . . . we need to find that crate. It shouldn't be too hard. After all, she cataloged by date, then by family member. All we have to do is find that inventory list for that day."

"Hey, guys, thought I'd come down to give you a hand. That headache finally went away, and I feel pretty good now," Matthew said as he pushed up his sleeves and sat down.

Pearle stood up and said, "Glad the headache is gone; you know, your mom was about the same age when she started to get migraines. But they seem to go away in a couple of years."

"Oh, God, Nana, don't tell me I'm going to have more of them."

"I'm sorry, I can't tell you that, but if it's any consolation, there are medicines today to control them."

"Oh, well, I guess it is what it is. So, what do you want me to do?"

"Well," she said while bending backward, stretching her back, "you can help by taking stuff out of the crate, and Robert will mark it off the list as we tell him what it is."

Pearle turned, looking at how many crates were left to do, when her attention was drawn to a particular one in the distance.

"What ya see, Nana?"

"I'm not sure, but I am going to find out. Robert, would you go to the wall over there and turn that lifting contraption on?"

"Sure. What's up, Pearle?"

"I want to remove that crate that is sitting atop the one draped in purple. Can you see it, Robert, back there?" she asked, pointing the way. "By the way, do you know how to work that machine?"

"Sure, I've run a few machines in my life. . . . I can handle this."

Robert removed the top crate; then Pearle and Matthew moved in for a closer look.

"This is the crate Oona was working on," she said as she removed the purple draping. "It has my great-grandfather's name on it and a question mark. She told me she put that there to remind herself to ask me about an item she couldn't figure out. Annabelle must have covered this by herself when we were getting ready for the movers. Otherwise, I would have thought about it then."

"Wow, Nana, mom was working on this crate?" Matthew asked softly while running his hands along the crate.

"Yes, Matt, your mom worked on all these crates. She worked for years on this inventory for me."

"I don't ever remember this old crate, though," she said, scratching her head.

"Robert, do me a favor, and see if you can move this crate to where there is some more light. I need to have a better look at it."

"Sure, Pearle. Hey, Matthew, give me a hand, would ya?"

Robert and Matthew were nearly out of breath, wrestling with the crate. They were just a few more inches from where Pearle wanted it when there was a loud, explosive POP, followed by the sound of crashing metal against the concrete floor. An entire side of the crate blew out, and nearly all its contents went spilling in every direction onto the floor.

"Oh, my God, Pearle, I am so sorry I didn't see that side," Robert said, horrified.

"Oh, goodness, Robert, how were you to know? Besides, that crate is older than the three of us put together, and then some!"

"Holy cow, Nana, look at all this stuff," Matthew called out from another room as he scanned the floor covered in the crates' contents.

"Matthew, just gather the stuff, and bring it here, okay? Hey, Robert, look at this," she said, pointing to a broken lock on the crate.

"Well, now we know why the side blew out. I'll bag this lock and see if we can get a print."

Pearle just shook her head and began sorting through the remaining items in the crate.

"We have a problem," Robert announced as he flipped through the pages of the inventory list. "It seems half the page for this crate's inventory was torn out too."

"You've got to be kidding me!" Pearle said, throwing her hands up in the air.

"No . . . I wish," Robert said, shrugging his shoulders. "Do you have any idea what should be in this crate?"

"Good Lord, I sure don't. Like I said before, Oona was working on this, and to be honest, Robert, I don't remember this crate."

"Maybe Oona made a second copy. There must be a backup disc! I don't think she would have gone through all this trouble without doing that. Don't you agree, Pearle?"

"Probably, but I don't have her computer anymore. I wouldn't even know where else to look for something like that, Robert. I went through all her files and never saw a second list. You know what? Let's just sort through everything we have here and make a new list. Then I will recheck her paperwork to see if maybe I overlooked a copy. There really isn't much else I can do."

Meanwhile, as Robert and Pearle continued doing inventory, Matthew was discovering something of his own. When the crate's side exploded, a large leather bag made its way into the next room. It was lying next to a crate in a dimly lit corner. Matthew was busy gathering items when he abruptly stopped in front of some scrolls and several colorful bags. He bent over to pick up one of the bags and began to feel a funny tingling feeling over his entire body. Strangely, everything seemed to silence. He heard nothing except the internal sound of the air he inhaled and exhaled and the beating of his heart. His eyes were wide as he looked around the room. He didn't understand what was happening. Then, from the corner of his eye, he glimpsed a purple pulsating light in the next room.

"What the . . . ?" He stepped carefully over the scrolls, and as he neared the light, he saw it was coming from inside the leather bag, and squatted down next to it. And through the eerie silence, a sweet, unfamiliar voice began to speak:

Do not fear dear Heir, my voice brings a message as you stand near.
This bag you see glows of me. Gather the scrolls and bright bags amongst
your treasures. Put them together with mine in this larger leather.
Keep them safely and do not speak of what I requested of thee,
for soon you shall meet my ally then one day me.

"Hey, Matthew, how are you making out over there?" Pearle yelled out.

Matthew fell back onto the floor and shook his head. The light was gone from the bag, and for a second he thought maybe he imagined what he heard. But he knew differently, and for some strange reason, he also knew he had to do what the voice asked of him.

"Ah . . . goo . . . good, Nana. I'm almost done. . . . Be there in a sec," he yelled back as he peered around the room. Matthew picked up the items he was instructed to and put them in a leather bag, then hid it behind a large cardboard box so no one could see it. Then he finished gathering the rest of the stuff and loaded it in another big bag to take to Pearle.

"You gotta see all this stuff, guys," he yelled out.

"Well . . . bring it here, and let me see!"

"I'm trying, but this bag is . . . **way** heavy!"

"Whoa, hold on, Matthew! Let me help you with that!"

"Thanks, Robert. . . . This must weigh a hundred pounds," Matthew said.

"I'm not sure you are too far off in your estimate! This bag really is heavy," Robert said as he struggled attempting to lift it to his shoulder.

"Just drag it, then, fellows," Pearle called out. "I don't need either one of you hurting yourselves!"

"No arguments from us," they yelled back, and then carefully dragged the leather bag over to where Pearle was sitting.

"Matthew, would you please do me a favor? Go tell Annabelle

that we will probably be ready for dinner in about an hour or so."

"Sure, no problem, but please wait for me before you go through that bag, okay?"

"We will, and would you bring us some water?"

"Yep, be back in a few minutes," Matthew said as he raced out the door.

"Hey, Pearle, I never asked before, but what ever happened to Matthew's father?"

"Ahh . . . Anthony Almondative," she said with a curl to her lip. "The last time I spoke with him was about six, maybe seven years ago when he signed the custody papers for Matthew."

"He was a big-shot neurosurgeon, right?"

"Yes, and last I knew, he was teaching at one of the universities in Vienna. You know, Robert, I just don't get it! How can a father not want to be with his child, or, for that fact, at least know how he is doing?"

"Does he ever ask about his father?"

"No, not really. Matthew was only three when Anthony left, so he doesn't remember much of him."

"What's the story on Oona and him, anyway?"

"Well, they met in Europe when Oona was in college. She said it was love at first sight! He was quite the charmer and very good-looking. They eloped after a short romance, and Matthew was born ten months later! But she moved back here to the States with me in her fifth month of pregnancy. They were having problems, and she couldn't handle the stress of all the arguments anymore. So anyway, Anthony showed up a week after Matthew was born. They planned to build a home here, and they worked, or I should say *she* worked, on their problems, but things never got any better between them. Personally, I thought he was an arrogant bastard, and I definitely did not like the way she let him treat her."

"Anyway, after Oona disappeared, I honestly think that's when Anthony realized how much he loved her and couldn't accept what happened. His attorney sent me a letter last year that informed me he had set up a trust fund for Matthew. I wanted to send a note back saying thanks, but no thanks," she said, looking disgusted.

"Oh, is he wealthy, Pearle?"

"Yes, he is, Robert, extremely wealthy! He comes from a very prestigious family in Italy, a long line of famous neurosurgeons. Matthew, his children, and their children will never have to worry about money between the both of us."

"Does Matthew know this?"

"Yes, he does . . . why?"

"Well, you would never know it! He doesn't act like a snobby rich kid. I tell ya, Pearle, some kids today are so self-absorbed. It's hard to believe how shallow they have become. It's nice to see that Matthew has his head screwed on right. He is more together than most eighteen-year-olds I know! You have done a good job raising him."

"Thank you, Robert, but I raised him just as I did Oona. She never acted like a spoiled rich kid either. She was always respectful and never expected anything handed to her, and that's the way I am trying to grow Matthew. I truly believe that kids are a result of their environment, if you know what I mean. It isn't necessarily their financial status or where they come from, but how their parents set the example. And yes, I do know of some great parents and their kids are just who they are. But I see it mostly as monkey see, monkey do, ya know? To add to that, though, I do know some really good kids from bad situations."

"Hey, did I ever tell you that Matthew has an extremely high IQ?"

"No, I don't think you have."

"Do you know he can translate hieroglyphics, and can speak three languages too?"

"Can he? Wow, how long has he been able to do that?"

"Gosh, I started teaching him when he was three. He seemed to pick up other languages naturally, just as he did with swimming," she said proudly. "My Oona was a great swimmer too," she added. "It really is amazing that he has so many of her talents."

"Hey . . . are you talking about me?" Matthew said as he appeared with two cold water bottles.

"Why, yes, sir, we sure are!"

"Did you give Annabelle my message?"

"Oh, yeah, she said no problem. She hadn't put on the pasta yet because she was talking to Abe."

"Who is Abe?" Robert asked nonchalantly.

"Oh, he's my teacher at school and Annabelle's longtime boy-friend!" Matthew piped.

"Really . . . you never mentioned him before, Pearle," Robert said, sounding perturbed.

"Gosh, I guess I never really had any reason to. I figured Annabelle would have brought him up in her questioning. Why, what's wrong, Robert? You look upset."

"Well, with everything that has happened here, why on earth would you not mention him?" he said heatedly! "He has been here, I am assuming, and everyone *is* a suspect that has been in your home. I thought you understood that from all the discussions we have had!"

"I'm sorry. I guess I just forgot about Abe," Pearle responded back, sounding annoyed.

She felt like she was being interrogated by him and did not like it one bit. He knew by the fire in her eyes that she was infuriated with him! Robert took a deep breath and shook his head.

"Pearle, listen, it's just that I have to stay vigilant and be kept aware of anyone associated with you and the family. I didn't mean to lose my temper; I apologize."

"You're right, Robert," she said calmly. "I guess with everything that's happened, I didn't see it that way and should have. Why don't we call it a day here and just go relax. I think we all could use that."

"But Nana, I wanted to see what other stuff was inside that sack I found!"

"Matthew, we will, tomorrow. It's been a long day, and I just want to eat and then relax tonight. Listen, you can come down after dinner and start to go through it if you want. Just don't mix it up with the inventory I've done. Otherwise, we will return to 'Matthew's discovery' after breakfast!"

"Now that's pretty cool, Nana," Matthew said, with a big cheesy grin.

"I thought you would like that!" she smirked. "Okay, guys," Pearle said, prodding them out of the room. "Let's get out of here for now and go get something to eat."

Chapter Nine

"Good morning, Annabelle."

"Ah, buon giorno to you! How'd you sleep a last night . . . good?"

"Yes, I think I just passed out from pure exhaustion!" Pearle replied with a gaping yawn. "The last thing I remember is Robert calling and checking in on us from his office."

"He went to work last night?"

"Yes, he wanted to make sure all the evidence that was collected was processed correctly and that he had a complete list of it before he went home. Besides, with spending all day here yesterday and not being at the station, there were a lot of things he had to check on."

"Oh, mamma mia, Pearle; I forgot to tell you. Denise called last night to see how you doing. I told her everyone was doing just fine, and you would call her today. That was okay, wasn't it?"

"Yes, Annabelle, and thank you. I forgot about calling her back last night. I'll give her a buzz in a little while."

"Hey, where's Matthew? Has he been down for breakfast yet?"

"Yes, and he say he was feeling hungry like bear! He ate a good breakfast and then said he was going to shower and be in his room doing work Daniel dropped off from school."

"Is there any coffee?"

"Sure, I just made a pot for you."

"Ah . . . Annabelle, I don't know what Matthew and I would do without you."

"Hah, I not know what I do without the two of you! God truly blessed me with this family. I can no imagine my life without you both in it."

"Annabelle, the feeling is mutual!"

"Okay, no more this mushy stuff. . . . What would you like me to make for dinner tonight?"

"Hum," Pearle sighed, as she mulled over Annabelle's request.

"Oh . . . I know, a roasted chicken with all the trimmings, and your scrumptious apple crisp for dessert would be perfect!"

"Consider it done," Annabelle replied, sashaying her way to the freezer. "You think Robert will be here for dinner too?" she asked with her head in the freezer.

"I'm hoping so," Pearle answered as she poured herself another cup of coffee.

Matthew was coming down the stairs when the doorbell rang.

"I'll get it, guys!" he yelled as he raced to the door.

"Morning, Robert. You're here early. Come on in!"

"Thanks, Matthew. How are you today?"

"Great! Well, except for some more weird nightmares. Must have been that extra piece of chocolate cake I ate! The girls warned me not to have it, but it was so good, wasn't it, Robert?"

"Yes, it was. Hey, Matthew, I have a surprise for you."

"You do," he said, widening his eyes.

"What kind of surprise?" asked a voice behind them.

"Good morning, Pearle!"

"Morning. . . . So, what's this surprise you have?"

"Well, let's go outside and see," he said with a devilish grin.

"Zatu!" Matthew yelled.

"Oh, Robert, you brought him home," Pearle cried out.

"I thought you both would like that," he said, contently grinning, as Pearle and Matthew hugged Zatu.

"I knew you would like the rest of the family home."

"But how did you manage this? I thought Dr. Hadwick said he had to stay until Monday," Matthew asked, looking away, trying to hide his teary eyes.

"Well, when I called over to his office this morning, he said Zatu was ready to go."

Zatu licked Pearle and Matthew so eagerly that Robert thought he would take their skin off. He tried to swallow, but felt an emotional lump growing in his throat. It was humbling to see the love they had for Zatu. But he was even more humbled when Matthew ran up to him and gave him a hug.

"So . . . ," Robert barely managed to get out as he choked up. "I . . . ahem, I guess you're happy to see Zatu, Matthew?"

Matthew didn't say a word. . . . He just nodded.

"Matt, why don't you take Zatu inside and let Annabelle see him!"

"Good idea, Nana; she's gonna freak when she sees her big guy!"

"Annabelle! Annabelle," Matthew yelled as he and Zatu raced toward the kitchen. "Look who's home!"

"Oh, my Zatu!" she exclaimed.

Then Zatu stood on his hind legs, towering over her, as he began licking her as if she were a pork chop!

"It's a so nice to have my big boy a back home again! Aye, mamma mia, we have got to do something about your breath, though. Whew, it smells like you ate doodie! Come, Matthew, let's a get Zatu his teeth brushed, and then we find out if the doctor wants him on special diet."

"Come on, Zatu, hold still; we have to brush your teeth!" Matthew urged. "Ugh, yuck, you have got the grossest breath I have ever smelled there, buddy," he said as Zatu started licking his face again!

"Well, gang, how's the homecoming going?" Pearle inquired as she and Robert entered the kitchen.

"It's going good. We almost done cleaning Mr. Doodie Breath's teeth here!" Annabelle said, laughing.

"Oh, Robert, did the doctor say Zatu is on any special diet?"

"No, he said he could have his regular food, and that we were just to watch him for any diarrhea or vomiting."

"Oh, yuck, that's gross! I think I'm gonna toss my cookies," Matthew said, wincing. "Well, that's as good as I can get his teeth. Nana, I am going to take him out to find Bella! She is going to be so excited when she sees him. I'll be back in a few minutes."

"Hang on, Matt," Robert yelled out the door. "Do me a favor, and try to stay away from the taped-off area if you can."

Matthew turned around, with Zatu pulling him eagerly the other way. He gave Robert a thumb up and then took off running to look for Bella.

Robert leaned against the kitchen counter and folded his arms, and as he stood there, Pearle noticed a slight upturn to the corners of his mouth.

"They really are amazing, pets, that is. The joy they bring you is beyond comforting. Funny," he laughed, "I think sometimes I prefer them to humans. In my opinion, there is nothing more trustworthy or faithful than man's best friend," Robert said as he turned around and looked out the window. Pearle wasn't sure, but thought she saw tears in his eyes.

"I had a dog once. . . Snickers, a beautiful black retriever. She came from a top breeder who supplied K-9s for my father's sheriff department. She was my best friend when I was a kid. We truly grew up together. I swear that dog was my shadow. Kind of the way Zatu is with Matt. And sooo loving and even-tempered, although Dad had her trained to protect the family. Now that I think about it," he laughed, "during the winters, she hated to sleep on the cold wood floors we had. She would wait until I fell asleep and then crawl in my bed ever so quietly, and when I woke up in the morning, she would be under the damn covers with me. Can you imagine that? It broke my heart when she died. . . . I swore back then I would never own another dog and go through that heartache again."

"Oh, I am sorry to hear that, Robert. What happened?"

"She was killed," he said, looking quite pathetic. "Gosh, it was a long time ago, but I can remember every single detail of that awful day. I was home alone, and my parents were at work. I think I was about a year older than Matthew is now. Anyway, this guy, who we found out later was a convicted child molester, broke into our house and tried to abduct me. Snickers had gotten ahold of him and was biting the crap out of him, tearing real good into him. It was during that time I managed to call my dad, and as luck would have it, he was patrolling an area near our neighborhood. Dad and his backup got there just as this sicko was trying to drag me out of the house. She saved my life, Pearle. I will never forget that day and what she sacrificed for me."

"Oh, my God, Robert. That is awful! How . . . well . . . how . . . how did she die?"

"The sick bastard hit her in the head several times with a baseball bat. She was alive when Dad arrived, but by the time we got her to the vet . . . well . . . Snickers was gone. So needless to say, after that day, I decided to become a cop and make sure twisted people like that ended up behind bars."

Pearle was flabbergasted! She was speechless and appalled by what happened to his dog, and more so that Robert had to witness such a tragic, cruel event.

Annabelle was in the laundry room and overheard Robert's story. She was leaning over the washer with a towel to her face so they did not hear her weep. She blew her nose into the towel and then threw it into the washer, disgusted and angry, thinking how anyone could do that to an animal! She strolled back into the kitchen with red eyes and her cheeks flush. Pearle just shook her head at her, and they both gave each other a sympathetic look.

"Hey, here comes Matt with Bella and Zatu. He looks so happy, Robert!"

"Hi, guys. I found Bella down by the lake. She was acting weird, Nana," Matt said in a matter-of-fact way.

"What happened?" Robert interrupted.

"I don't know. She was like going into the water and barking, then backed out, like something was scaring her! Zatu went over too and barked for a while. There must have been a big fish because it made a really *big* splash. Then they ran away from the lake! That's how I finally got them to come with me."

"Well, maybe there's a big fish in there, and they wanted dinner," Robert said with a laugh.

"They don't like fish, Robert," Matthew said as he ushered the dogs out of the kitchen and to his room.

"Do you have any idea what's in there . . . I mean the type of fish, Pearle?"

"I have absolutely no idea at all, Robert," she said as if she were amused. "I know there are turtles, and occasionally you will see a gator, but as for the fish, beats me! You're more than welcome to go stick a fish pole out there and see what bites."

"Do me a favor, Pearle; please keep Matthew away from the lake for a while."

"Oh," she said, looking at him strangely.

"We are going to search the lake again, Pearle."

"Really . . . what for?"

"That's what Brian and I are going to talk to you about when he gets here."

"What time did you say he was coming, Robert?"

"When I spoke to him this morning, he said around ten, but would call us when he was on his way."

"Well, it's nine. Are you hungry, Robert?" Annabelle asked.

"I sure am! I haven't eaten since dinner last night!"

"Okay, I make you breakfast. It be ready in ten minute."

Robert was taking the last sip of his coffee when the doorbell rang.

"It must be Brian," Robert said as he rose from his seat. "Thank you, Annabelle. That was delicious! Pearle, it sounds like Brian; are you ready?"

"Morning, guys, and before I forget, here is your medallion," he said while handing Pearle a small brown envelope he removed from his shirt pocket after they settled into the living room.

"Was there anything on it?"

"I don't know. It was processed, but I haven't got that information yet. Oh, and here's your file of paperwork. We copied the information we needed and will get in touch with everyone for questioning."

"Okay, Brian, so where are we in this investigation?" Pearle asked.

"So far, we have no real suspects. We will finish all the questioning with everyone concerned here today, which reminds me, is Annabelle available for some questioning?"

"I believe so. Why?"

"Robert mentioned Abe Haram to me last night and his involvement with her and the family. Pearle, you understand that anyone connected to this family will have to be questioned."

"Yes, Brian, it was made *very* clear yesterday," she said while gazing over at Robert, with her eyebrows raised and her jaw crooked to one side. "You do whatever is necessary. I am sure Annabelle will help any way she can. As for Abe, I'm not sure what he could possibly have to do with all this. After all, we are good friends, and he is very fond of Annabelle and Matthew!"

"Like I said, Pearle, it is just procedure, that's all. Okay, then, ahh . . . let's see my list . . . yeah, here we go. Robert tells me you are going to have more cameras installed and a new security system put in?"

"Yes, I have a new company coming out in a few days. I don't want to worry about anything while I am gone."

"You also hired a private security company for the nighttime?"

"Yes."

"Robert, have you discussed any of our plans yet?"

"Not in detail, but I've mentioned it."

"Pearle, Robert and I have agreed that we need to do another search of the lake. This medallion, I mean Oona's medallion that has turned up in Egypt, don't you find it quite odd being you claim she had it on the day she disappeared?"

"Yes, it's . . . well, it seems impossible, Brian!"

"That's what we think. So tomorrow we have arranged for our divers to come out and some excavating to be done. The equipment that is available today is much more advanced than what we used eight years ago. We are hoping that this new technology will give us something more than what the first search produced. The conditions our divers had that week were less than optimal. It was raining, and the water was very turbid, although, I will say, it was an exhaustive search. Since all the evidence we collected proves Oona went into that lake and didn't come out, we feel there has to be something that was overlooked due to those conditions. She just didn't go in there and disappear! We found nothing to the contrary of her leaving the lake, nor did we find any other evidence to indicate someone else was in the area. Well . . . you know the story, Pearle."

"So let me ask you, Brian, what do *you* think happened to Oona?" she said in a barely audible voice.

He looked at Robert, then back at her as he scratched the palm of his hand.

"In all honesty, Pearle," and he let out a loud exhale, "I think a gator got her. It's the most logical explanation and the only one I see feasible at this point. But, on the other hand," he began as he stood and paced, "if this medallion in Egypt does turn out to be Oona's and you are sure she was wearing it the day she disappeared, then we have a whole new scenario to consider. Not to mention, how did it get there? or who put it there and why? That medallion is worth a fortune. . . . Why leave it in a pyramid? If this medallion is truly Oona's, I believe someone had to have access to the tomb before Sol got in there the day he discovered it. There are logical explanations to all this, but we have not found them yet and won't until we do this new search and that medallion in Egypt is examined by you, Pearle. We could go through many scenarios and theories here, but I refuse to do that before we do our job of gathering facts and solid evidence to prove what happened to Oona. As it stands now, all we have are assumptions, based on what we think happened, according to the evidence collected eight years ago."

"I understand, so go ahead and dig, or do whatever it is you think is necessary."

"Thank you, Pearle. I was hoping you would be okay with this."

"Why wouldn't I be, Brian?" she remarked, seemingly annoyed.

"Well . . . it's just that . . . it has to be very difficult going through this again, Pearle. And we want you to know we understand that."

"Your concern is appreciated, detective. Thank you. So . . . is there anything else you fellows need from me at the moment?"

Robert looked oddly at Brian, then back at Pearle.

"No, I think we are caught up with everything for today. Will I be able to speak with Annabelle now?" Brian asked politely.

"Yes. I'll go get her," Pearle said stiffly as she rose from the couch and left the room in an icy manner.

"What's wrong with her, Robert?"

"I don't know, Brian. Maybe she is just stressed out from the last few days."

"Robert, do you think Pearle and Sol could be mistaken about this medallion being Oona's? I mean, if you look at this realistically and put everything in perspective, how does a medallion show up in Egypt eight years after the victim wearing it disappeared in a lake here? To complicate matters, it's found in a recently discovered tomb that is four thousand years old!"

"I wish I had an answer to your questions. However, I think the bigger question is why is it there, and where is Oona?"

"This case is one for the books, Robert. . . . You do realize that, don't you?"

"Yes, I do, Brian, but whatever it is, we will find out one way or the other what is going on here and what happened to Oona Almondative. That I do know!"

"From your lips to God's ears, Robert!"

"Annabelle, there you are! Thanks so much for giving us your time. We know how busy you are!"

"Oh, no problem, detectives," Annabelle said as she bounced into the living room. "Whatever I can do to help, it's my pleasure."

"All right, I guess what I need to ask you about is your relationship with Mr. Abe Haram," Brian said as he took out his notes from her prior questioning. "Annabelle, why didn't you mention him during our conversation the other night?"

"Oh, I don't know; I guess I didn't think about him or why he would have anything to do with this."

"Well, I had asked you a specific question, and that was if you were involved with anyone, and if so, had they been in the house?"

"I'm so sorry, Brian. I was a little upset that night, and I no mean to omit anything you ask or answer untruthful! I hope you know that."

"Sure, Annabelle. It's understandable with all that was going on that night. Could you tell me now about Mr. Haram?"

"Sure, sure, anything I know, you know!"

"Great. Okay, tell me when and how you met Mr. Haram."

"Ah, let's see. I meet him at the school, when I go to learn better English, about seven years ago. After class, we talk a little bit, and he seems like a nice guy. So then, we made coffee date for next week after class. We've been seeing each other on and off all this time. For a while, we got pretty serious, and he ask if I want to get married, but I tell him no! Three a times he ask; he very stubborn man."

"Oh, stubborn, what do you mean, Annabelle?" Robert asked.

"Well, you think a man after two times would get message that woman no wants to get married, but this man keep asking; I don't understand!"

"Has he gotten angry about your refusal?"

"No, I wouldn't say that, but he look like he not happy about it either," she chuckled.

"Has Mr. Haram ever asked you about things around here?"

"Like a what?"

"Oh, you know, like anything about the security system, what Pearle has of value in her home, when and if someone may not be home. Just anything, Annabelle, that maybe at the time seemed like a harmless question, but if you thought about it now, it doesn't seem right to you."

Annabelle didn't say anything for a few minutes. She sat there thinking about what the detective had asked and seemed like she was concentrating.

"While you're thinking about that question, let me ask you something else. When did you last speak to him?"

"Oh, last night, when he call."

"Could you tell me what you spoke about?"

"Sure, he ask how I was and apologized for not being in touch more, but he has been a very busy with the two schools and getting ready for final exams."

"What else did he say?"

"That he spoke to Matthew at school the other day, and they had a very nice lunch together."

"Does he and Matthew do that often, have lunch together?"

"I don't know about that, but he and Matthew are pretty friendly. He thinks the world of that boy."

"What makes you say that?"

"Well, whenever I see him, he always asks how Matthew is and Pearle. He seems to be very caring man, as far as I have seen."

"Did he say what he and Matthew spoke about at lunch?"

"Yes, he said that Matthew told him he was going to Egypt and was very excited about the trip. Matthew was wondering if he had any suggestions of places he should visit while there."

"Anything else?"

"No, not really, except he ask if I was going, and I told him I didn't think so, because someone had to stay here and take care of the family animals. Pearle would never put them in cages and have strangers take care of them!"

"Annabelle, did you tell him about what happened here the other night?"

"Yes, I did! I told him how upset I was and very angry about what happened to Zatu!"

"What did he say to you about everything?"

"He was very upset, and seemed terribly concerned. That was other reason why he say he called because Matthew was no in school Friday."

"Can you remember anything else about the conversation, Annabelle? Please, it's important," Brian stressed.

"I'm sorry, but may I ask question, detective?"

"Sure, Annabelle, anything. . . . What is it?"

"Why you want to know so much about Abe? You think maybe he have something to do with all this crazy stuff that happened?"

Robert looked at Brian, and they both hesitated a minute before answering.

"Annabelle, anybody who knows this family and this home is a suspect. We are convinced that it wasn't a stranger who just decided to break in here and rob the place."

"What make you say that, detective?" she asked with sincerity.

"We really can't disclose any more information than what we have told you, Annabelle, but if you think about what was done and how, doesn't it make sense to you that whoever is responsible knew what they were doing?"

"Of course; I no stupid woman, detective!" she said with her head held high and eyes glaring.

"I didn't mean to offend you, Annabelle, and I am sorry if I did," Brian quickly replied.

"Look, I may not speak good English, detectives, but I am not an idiot! I go to college in my country, and I do very well for a woman!"

"Oh, what did you major in?" Robert asked innocently.

"Major, what you mean, Robert?" she asked, still agitated.

"What did you study, Annabelle?"

"Oh, I study chemistry and geology. I have a BA degree in geology, Robert. I like science, but my true love turned out to be cooking! Can you imagine that?" she said, sounding even surprised herself. "I decided to go on to study with best chefs in world at cooking school! You know you have to be invited to go to such prestigious school," she added.

"Well, from my own experience, you certainly did very well in school, Annabelle!" Robert replied.

"Thank you, and I work very hard in school! Not many women make it to graduate; you compete with many great chefs who are men."

"So what made you come to America, and how did you end up working for Pearle?" Robert asked.

"Ah, this good story of my life," she said as she beamed, happy to talk about it.

"Famous Chef Mr. Josephi came to Italy and taught our class for two months and had offered me a job. Anyway, I tell him yes, and after I finish school in spring, I come here to America and work for him at his restaurant in Sarasota. I learn a so much from that man in six years. Mr. Josephi not only great chef, but good-hearted person! Then one day I had car accident and hurt my back; it made my life change," she said sadly.

"Oh, gosh, I'm sorry to hear that, Annabelle. So what happened to your job?"

"Mr. Josephi was so good to me, but I could not stand ten to twelve hours like I use to, so I had to leave that job. Lucky me, shortly, I see ad in newspaper for experienced chef, private home. Ms. Pearle hire me same day I come to see her. I have been with her for fifteen years now! I not only have great job doing what I love, but Pearle and Matthew are my family! I love them both very much, detective! I am a very lucky woman."

"Do you have family, Annabelle?"

"Yes, I have one brother in Italy, but I don't hear from him much."

"Oh, why is that?" Robert asked.

"He become a priest and now acts like he better than me. He and I not always get along when we were younger. I do get cards from him on holidays, and he never forgets my birthday. I send to him too, but we no close the way brother and sister should be. It was his choice, not a mine!"

"That's too bad, Annabelle. Sorry to hear that," Robert replied.

"So you have no other relatives here in America?"

"No, I don't think so. Why?"

"I was just wondering, that's all," Robert said.

"Okay, let's get back to Abe," Brian said. "Did anything else come to mind that would be important for us to know about Abe?"

"I can't think of anything right now, but if I do, I will tell Robert right away," she assured him.

"Thank you, Annabelle. We do appreciate all of your help today."

"It's no problem, detective. We are going to find out who did this to us, yes?"

"Yes, Annabelle, we will," Robert said, assuring her.

"Good. Now I go make coffee for everyone and get coffee cake I make this morning."

"So, what do you think, Robert?" Brian asked as he shifted closer to him.

"What I have been told about Abe Haram from Pearle and what Annabelle has added, he seems like a great guy, but . . . ."

"Yes, go on . . . . What's the *but* about, Robert?"

"I don't know. I just have this gut feeling about him. It's nothing that was said exactly to say differently, but something doesn't feel right, Brian. Have you ever just had a hunch about someone who seems so innocent, and it not turn out that way?"

"Half of my cases have ended that way, Robert.

"You know in our line of work that instincts are what we have to rely on regardless of what we have been told."

"I know, Brian, and we are going to have to ask Pearle some more questions about Abe." "Robert, didn't that kind of hit you strange, the interest he has in Matthew?"

"*Yes!* That's one of the things bothering me the most, for some reason, but I am so glad you said that. It could just be that he truly likes the kid. But being Matthew is like a son to me, and my relationship with Pearle, I wasn't sure if it was just a personal thing. You know what I mean?"

"Look, Robert, let's face it; this case *is* personal for you. But I know that will not have any bearing on your professional judgment. You have been doing this too long, and if anything, you will be more scrupulous! We really don't have any solid leads, any definite suspects, and now with this medallion showing up in Egypt, Robert, this case has gotten very complicated!"

"Ha," Robert laughed sarcastically. "Complicated is an understatement! But for now, I guess we need to concentrate on the questioning left to do and the search of the lake again. Once we get all that done and put everything together, maybe then we will see something that was missed. Oh, by the way, did you bring those reports from the original search we did on the lake?"

"Yeah, well, I think I did. Hang on, and let me check my briefcase. Yep . . . here they are. What did you say you needed them for, anyway?"

"I was down at the lake the other day, and something seemed different to me, and I can't quite put my finger on it, Brian. Did you bring the photos too?"

"They should be in the back of the file."

"Yes, they are. Guess I just didn't take my time going through all this stuff. Sorry, Brian."

"I'm back," Annabelle announced as she came from the kitchen with the coffee and cake she promised the two detectives.

"Oh, good. Brian, I know you will enjoy the cake! Annabelle is a fantastic baker!" Robert said, boasting as he was rising from the couch with his hands full of the file he was reading.

"Oh, nuts!" Robert groaned as he dropped the file and watched the papers scatter all over the living room floor!

"Ah, no problem; I help you," Annabelle said as she put the tray on the coffee table and knelt on the floor to help.

Brian was pouring himself some coffee and ribbing Robert about his clumsiness when he noticed Annabelle sitting on the floor, reading one of the papers from the report. Robert looked up as Brian made a vocal with his throat as to clear it and nodded toward Annabelle.

"Hey, Annabelle, what's got your attention there?"

"Robert, this can't be right," she said, staring at the paperwork.

"What are you talking about?"

"Well, I know a lot about minerals and geological material from Florida, but this is no nothing from here."

"Oh," Robert said. . . .

"Here, look . . . see this? This is not from around here. You sure they didn't make a mistake on report?" she asked.

"Annabelle, get off the floor, and come sit up here. Please explain to me and Brian exactly what it is you are seeing and disagreeing with."

"What makes you so sure it is wrong?" Brian asked.

"Well, remember I tell you I study in college chemistry and geology?"

"Yes, but what does that have to do with the report?"

"I study more than four years rock and mineral formations from all around the world. Trust me, this type of mineral is no here in Florida, and look at this; you only find this in . . . ."

She hesitated for so long that Robert was becoming impatient.

"Robert, may I look at rest of file, and do you have pictures too?"

"Ahhh . . . Yesss . . . ."

"Good, give me, because I think we have even bigger mystery, detectives," she said as she began sifting through all the papers, and put them in some kind of order with the pictures.

Robert and Brian were flabbergasted and just sat there as she worked diligently, mumbling in Italian.

"What's going on here?" Pearle said as she entered the living room.

"I think we may have come across a real professional here, Pearle," Robert boasted as he pointed to Annabelle.

"Annabelle claims she has found discrepancies in our report from the lake."

"Is this true, Annabelle?" Pearle asked.

"Yes . . . I see several errors in the analysis that make no sense to me. Maybe it's just a typing error. Just give me some time, and then I can better tell what is wrong, okay?"

"Sure, the detectives seem very interested in what you have found, and I am interested too. Annabelle, take your time."

"Pearle, may I see you in the kitchen for a moment?" Robert asked.

"Sure, you can help put the groceries away that Matt and I brought home," she said, smiling.

"What's up, Robert?" she asked while emptying the grocery bags.

"Brian and I have some concerns about a particular person, and what I have to speak to you about has got to say strictly confidential, and that means not discussing this with anyone but Brian or me!"

"Oh, you sound pretty intense, Robert. What's going on?"

"Put that cold stuff in the fridge, Pearle, and come sit down. I have some questions I need to ask you concerning . . . Abe Haram."

"Abe?"

"Look, Pearle, there isn't any solid evidence about any individual, but there are too many things about Abe that make him a suspect. I probably shouldn't have said anything yet to you; however, being it involves Matthew, I felt better informing you of my suspicions right away."

"Matthew," she replied with a wild look in her eyes.

He sat her down and calmly explained why he felt Abe Haram was a suspect.

"Robert, I am having a hard time with this. . . . Abe is a sweetheart!"

"I told you, Pearle, it's just like I said. . . . He does know this family and that you have many valuables here."

"Did Matthew tell you he had lunch with Abe the other day, the night of the break-in?"

"No, he didn't. . . . Why?

"I'm just asking, that's all."

"They are very friendly, Robert, and he has known Matthew for several years, even before he was his student. Now that I think about it, Abe has known about several things in my home for years. He's even seen several of my artifacts, and we have had lengthy conversations about our profession. Why all of a sudden would he want to take something from me now, when he had many opportunities to do so in the past?"

"Did he know about the other medallions, Pearle?"

"I never told him about them, if that's what you mean."

Robert sensed someone behind them and turned around.

"Matthew, ahh . . . . How long have you been standing there?"

"Not too long, sir, but I did hear what you said to Nana about Abe. I have to agree with her. Abe has always been very nice to me. Why would you think he has something to do with the break-in?"

"Matthew, I really can't go into too much detail about everything, and we are not sure about much with this case as it is. There are too many things that only Abe knows about your home, and that is why he's a suspect. . . . Do you understand that, Matt?"

"Yes, Robert, I do."

"Matthew, you have to promise me that you will not discuss this with anyone. Everything you have heard and what we have talked about is between us, and Brian only . . . okay?"

"Sure, Robert."

"Great, and thanks for being so grown-up about this."

"Geez, I am not a child, you know!"

"No, you aren't, Matthew, and I sometimes forget that; I'm sorry. It's just that it can be difficult hearing things that aren't very nice about someone you know and trust."

"Yeah, it is, Robert. Especially about Abe and that he might be the one who poisoned Zatu. But I've learned you really don't know people as much as you think you do."

"Well, we can talk more later . . . oh, and Pearle, don't forget about the excavation tomorrow. They will be here around 8 a.m."

"Excavation, Robert? What's going on?" Matthew asked as he took a seat next to him.

Robert looked at Pearle, and he knew by the horror in her eyes she had not yet discussed with Matthew why the department was coming out to the lake.

"Pearle, I think you need to be honest here and tell him what is going on," Robert said as he gently grasped her hand.

"This has to do with Mom, doesn't it, Nana?"

"Yes, it does, Matt."

"Nana, I know a lot more than you think I do," he said, looking directly into her eyes.

"Would you like me to leave you two alone for a while?" asked Robert.

"If it's okay with you, Nana, I would like Robert to stay."

"I'd like that too," Pearle said as she shifted in her seat.

"Gosh, Robert, I just don't know where to start."

"Matthew, how much do you honestly know about your mom's disappearance?" Robert asked.

"Nana, please don't be upset with me, but I have overheard a lot of things said about Mom's disappearance over the years."

"Oh, honey, I'm not upset with you. I'm upset with myself."

"But why, Nana?"

"I guess all these years, I tried to protect you. In the interim, I forgot how you were feeling about your mom's disappearance. That wasn't fair of me, and I'm sorry, Matt."

"Look, Nana, I know Mom disappeared eight years ago by the lake, and her body was never found . . . am I correct?"

"Yes, Matthew," Robert said.

"Okay, so if you searched the lake already for Mom but didn't find her or much evidence, why search again?"

"Well, the first search was thorough, but the conditions during that time were not good. And since we have more sophisticated equipment than eight years ago, I believe if anything is there, we will find it. Plus . . . with some new information, we feel it's the right thing to do at this time."

"Oh . . . what new information?"

"Your mom was wearing a piece of jewelry that day, and the department believes we may have overlooked it, so that is why we are going in there again."

"You mean her medallion?"

"Yes, but how'd you know?"

"Like, duh, guys," Matthew responded, "every picture I have seen of Mom she always had it on, so I just figured that's what it had to be." Then Matthew gave him a long, uncomfortable stare, and Robert felt like he was looking into his soul.

"Robert," Brian interrupted, "I need to see you when you get a chance."

"Ah . . . yeah, be right there," Robert answered as he looked away from Matthew's odd stare. "Listen, we can continue this conversation after Brian leaves, okay?" he said as he walked away from the table. Then he stopped and turned to look at Matthew. "Hey, is everything okay?"

"Yeah . . . yeah, all is good. Thanks, Robert; it's really good to have you around."

"Matthew, you two are like family to me, and anything I can do for either one of you, I will. And don't either one of you ever forget that," he warned with a smile, pointing his finger at them as he walked backward out of the kitchen.

"You better sit down for this one, DG!"

"Oh, God, now I'm really worried," Robert said with a crooked smile. "All right, let me have it."

"I contacted that new geology professor we use at the bureau and discussed Annabelle's findings. Robert, he agrees with her. This guy was real nice and said to send him this old report with fresh samples, and he'd be more than happy to help us out."

"Annabelle, I want to thank you for the immense help you have been to us today," Robert said. "You do realize, though, that all this information we discussed is strictly confidential, and you're not to discuss it with anyone."

"Of course I do, Robert. You don't have to worry about Annabelle. As Matthew say, my lips are sealed!"

"Good," he said with a chuckle.

"Well, if you don't need me anymore, I got to check on dinner."

As Robert watched Annabelle leave the room, he began to pace back and forth. His head was spinning. He took a deep breath and sat down.

"Well, detective, I'm all ears; let's have the rest!"

Brian related what Annabelle found wrong in the old report, and what the geology professor had to say about it. Robert could tell by the expression on Brian's face that he was feeling the frustration of the day too.

"Ya know, Brian, there are many strange things in this world, and I surely have seen my share, but to be honest with you, this is like some wild nightmare I can't wake up from! And talk about nightmares, I can't wait to see the look on the chief's face when we present all this! He is going to have a conniption about this erroneous geological report!"

"Well, just let me know when you are going to do this, because I'll make sure I'm out on a call or something!"

"Ah, Brian, you, and I do stress, *you*, will be with me when the crap hits the fan in his office!"

"Thanks, Robert, and all this time, I thought we were friends!"

Both men were laughing when Pearle and Matthew came into the living room.

"Sounds like things are going well."

"Not exactly, Pearle. As a matter of fact, things have gotten more complicated!"

Chapter Ten

Zatu was with Matthew in his bedroom, sprawled out in his usual spot on the bed. Matthew was lying on the floor, chin resting on his hands, in deep thought as he watched Hunter rolling around in his exercise ball. He usually looked forward to this nightly ritual with his hamster, but not tonight. His mind was on "Matthew's discovery." Zatu sensed something about Matthew tonight and ambled off the bed to lie next to him. Matthew rolled over, and Zatu rested his head on Matthew's chest. As he rubbed his soft fur, he thought how lucky he was that Zatu had survived being poisoned the other night, and sat up to hug him. Other than his grandmother, Zatu is the only other connection he still has to his mother. But Zatu knows that . . . and many other things. He remembers that day at the lake when Oona disappeared. He saw what happened to her, and the horror of that day still torments him.

On that day, Oona was almost finished with her inventory job. She was doing some research on a strange, but beautiful, gold relic she had come across a few days earlier. Zatu was being his rambunctious self and wouldn't let her concentrate, so she decided it was time for lunch. She told him after lunch, she would take him down to the lake so he could expend his energy. He was nearly a year old, and although trained well, he was still a puppy with inexhaustible energy. Oona took the item she was researching with her. She thought maybe with the natural sunlight, she could read the hieroglyphics on it better. She put it into its leather bag and took her notes with her to lunch.

"Hi, Annabelle. Where's Mom and Matthew?"

"Hello, Oona! Mom took him for a haircut and then to do some shopping."

"I swear, Annabelle, she is the only one who can get him to sit still for a haircut!"

"Huh," she chuckled. "I think it because she bribes him!"

"Knowing Mom, you're probably right! What's for lunch today? I'm starving," she said as she scanned the inside of the refrigerator.

"How does a turkey club sandwich and homemade french fries sound?"

"Ooh, sounds delish, Annabelle!"

"What's that bag you got there?" she asked.

"This . . . ?" she said, waving it in the air. "A piece of beautiful, but puzzling, inventory."

Annabelle couldn't help but stare at her. If anything was beautiful, it was Oona. She was a spitting image of her mother and very athletic. She swam every morning at six for an hour and every afternoon with Pearle and Matthew. Other than her work, Matthew was her life, and she lived every day knowing the blessing he was to her. Her husband, Anthony, traveled a lot. She was never upset about it either, due to their strained relationship. On this particular day, he was in Vienna giving a seminar about open brain surgery for epilepsy. He had mastered a new procedure that was very successful on patients whose epilepsy couldn't be controlled with medication. He was due back in a week.

"Annabelle, lunch was great. I'm going to take Zatu for a walk and see if I can burn off some of that obnoxious energy he has so I can finish my work. We'll be down at the lake. Oh, listen, if Mom gets back before me, please tell her where I am and not to forget I have to talk to her, okay?" Those were her last words as she left with Zatu.

It was a beautiful day! The pale yellow sun was bursting with brightness, and the sky was so clear you could see forever! When Zatu and Oona got to the lake, she couldn't help but take in the beauty all the scenery afforded. The lake was calm, like a blue crystal sheet of glass. The lily pads and flowers meekly bowed with the gentle breeze. The muhly grass moved ever so slightly, as if it were waving. It was a serene and peaceful setting, just what Oona was wanting. But Zatu . . . well, had other ideas.

He was wound tight, racing around and letting loose! *Just what he needed,* she thought, *to expend all his puppy energy.* Oona had recently taught him how to jump up and catch a Frisbee. He seemed to catch on quickly, and practicing this seemed to exhaust him, for at least a few hours, anyway.

Oona tossed out the Frisbee a little higher than usual, but Zatu leapt incredibly high and caught it. He turned around and came bounding at her as she was picking up a treat she dropped.

As she stood, Zatu jumped up and caught his large paw on her gold chain. As if in slow motion, when her chain snapped, the medallion flung off and gyrated up into the air. Then, it slowly reversed direction and tumbled down toward the lake. It made a landing on a large lily pad close to shore, with a loud PLOP!

"Zatu!" she scolded sharply. "Well, you're lucky, Mr. Reckless, that my medallion didn't go into the lake!" All Oona could think of at that moment was her mother's constant nagging about not wearing her medallion all the time.

"Well, you better pray, Zatu, that there aren't any gators in there," she said hotly while rolling up the cuffs of her jeans. As she stepped into the lake, she realized the leather bag was hanging from her wrist. "Oh, Zatu, look at all this trouble you caused," she said aloud while struggling to remove it. And before she could take her next breath, the lake started to rise, and the water began to churn. Zatu leaped up as the ground beneath him grumbled. The lake erupted violently, strewing bubbles of dirty green foam and yellow scum into the air. The bubbles were getting bigger, and Oona noticed it was quickly becoming very dark outside. She felt her feet sinking rapidly into the slimy, gooshy bottom of the lake.

"Zatu! Zatu!" she screamed.

He made a flying leap into the lake and grabbed her arm with his powerful jaws. Suddenly, she felt the bottom disappear from her feet, and under the water she went. The lake's gritty earth churned violently on her body! Her skin felt like it was on fire as the lake battered her with rocks and dirt. With brute force, Zatu brought her to the surface. She gasped, filling her lungs with air! Zatu pulled her with resolve toward the shore! Yank! Down again Oona went, and Zatu with her, his jaw still clenched tightly around her forearm. This time his jaws bit down harder, struggling against an unknown force, to lift her toward the surface. She knew Zatu wouldn't let her go; *he couldn't,* she thought! She tried to swim upward as her leg muscles burned from the effort she exerted, but something . . . someone . . . had ahold of her. Pulling . . . pulling her down deeper and deeper into the blackness. Panicked, she kicked like mad with every bit of strength she had, and suddenly, her legs were free. They both emerged splashing frantically, coughing, and gasping for air! Zatu towed her quickly toward the shore. They were almost there, just a few more feet to go. She felt the bottom against her back; Zatu's paw touched the ground. *They did it. . . . They were going to be okay!* Then two cloaked arms shot up from the filthy, foaming rage and pulled them both under again. Quickly, it grew darker, and her eardrums throbbed in searing pain as they descended deeper into the turbulent lake. Oona tried in desperation to see what had ahold of her, but the water was turbid; dirt was whirling madly around, stinging her eyes every time she desperately attempted to open them. It was getting colder, and she grew weak in her battle. Zatu felt Oona go limp and slip from his jaws as she succumbed to the cruel, unknown force of the lake.

He awoke hours later with his head pounding, lying at the edge of the lake. Although he was weak and his jaws throbbed, he stood and looked around for his Oona. Not seeing her, he made a mad dash into the lake and dove down until he felt like his lungs would burst! But after several attempts and reeling from exhaustion, he realized she was gone. Oona was nowhere to be found. He tried to save her. He remembers his jaws around her arm . . . relentlessly pulling her toward him, afraid he would hurt her, his grip so strong! She yelled his name; she pleaded for his strength to save her. "Zatu, please help me! Pull, Zatu, pull!"

Heartbroken and exhausted, his shaking body collapsed in the dirt. He whimpered loudly; it was a sorrowful, pathetic cry. But no one was there. No one could hear Zatu's heart breaking.

The lake had returned to its calmness, and the sun basked in its orange glow amongst the blue sky. The muhly grass swayed to the gentle rhythm of the breeze that blew. Zatu's love and devotion should have been enough to save her, but the evil the lake possessed was stronger . . . more determined . . . to have what it desired! There was nothing anybody could have done to save

Oona that day. But what saved him? How did he come to be at the edge of the lake? He could only recall Oona's desperate cries for help and his struggle to save her. Would she ever know the shame and tremendous guilt Zatu feels for his dreadful defeat . . . ?

Eight years later, he sits in the same spot when he goes down to the lake with Matthew. He doesn't know the caution he is guarded with by Zatu. If only this brave, devoted pet could expose the danger, and secret horrors he witnessed about the evil that broke his heart, taking his devoted master away. If only . . . .

Matthew went to his closet where he put the leather bag from his discovery. He knew he should be in bed, but he had to see what was inside. Something urged at him, and it wasn't curiosity. He began thinking about that strange feeling he got when he was in the secured room. . . . Whose voice did he hear? He thought about his nightmares and heightened sense of awareness he had lately. *Maybe I need a CAT scan,* he thought. *Yeah . . . that's it; maybe I have a brain tumor. I know I've read that these things happen to people when things go wrong in their brain.* However, something told him everything was real. *But how could it be?* he thought. His mind wrestled with a compelling force he could not explain. However, with all the analytical thinking he did, he wasn't coming up with any commonsense answers, and he was worried.

He decided to open the bag, and saw nothing. *How could this be? It had weight, and he felt many objects in it!* Frustrated, he turned it upside down and gave it a good shake, and a purple sack fell out onto the bed. *"What in the world?"* he said, astounded. The bag started moving, and Matthew jumped back. Zatu growled and sniffed the bag. Then, as if it were nothing, he picked it up ever so gently in his jaws and gave it to Matthew. He took it from Zatu carefully, untied the braided golden rope that held it closed, and placed it gently on the bed. Slowly, a wrinkled purple head began to emerge, followed by three orange bouncing eyes. Matthew was so stunned, he stood there with his mouth open and watched as the rest of this purple thing struggled to get out of the bag.

"Well, are you just going to stand there catching flies, or you going to help me get out of this contraption?" the purple creature squealed! "I won't break. . . . Just give it a tug," he instructed, pointing to the end of the bag. "That's it . . . good . . . one . . . more . . . ."

"Whew, thought I'd never get out of there," it said, lying on the bed, stretching. "Ahhh, this feels so good," he said as it stood on its tail end. He wiggled over to Matthew and held out a tiny hand with four stubby fingers.

"I'm Oopi, and who might you be?"

"Well, I . . . I am . . . Mat . . . Matthew," he stuttered.

"And who might this large hair ball be?" he asked, looking at Zatu.

"That's my dog, Zatu," Matthew uttered, still in disbelief.

"Well, what's wrong with you, boy? Haven't you ever seen a purple three-eyed worm before?" he asked, seemingly insulted.

"Ah, no . . . , no, I haven't, Oo . . . Oopi!"

"Well, now you have!" he replied abruptly.

"But . . . how can . . . ? What . . . what . . . are you?"

"I, sir, am a Phule, from Rhondra."

"Rhondra?"

"Yes, Rhondra. . . . It's my home in Egypt."

"Oh, good grief," Matthew said as he collapsed down on the floor.

"Have ye got any food for a hungry fellow, young man? It's been a long time since I have had a decent meal, you know!"

"Oh, ah, what would you like?" Matthew asked.

"How about something fresh, crispy, and green?" he said, rubbing his two small hands together.

"Okay, I'll . . . ah . . . I'll go down to the kitchen and get you something from the fridge."

"Kitchen, fridge, what in all of Egypt are those?" he asked, standing with his hands on his torso.

"The kitchen is where we cook and keep our food. The fridge is short for a refrigerator, where we put food that is perishable and to keep things cold." *Why am I explaining this to a worm?* he thought to himself, shaking his head.

"Then let's hurry to this kitchen. . . . I'm famished and need to eat right now!"

Matthew almost laughed, but held it back.

"Oopi . . . how long have you been in that bag?"

"Oh, let me think, three, maybe four?"

"Three or four years you haven't eaten? No wonder you are so hungry. I'm surprised you're even alive," Matthew said in disbelief.

"No, no, nooo . . . dear boy. . . . Three to four *thousand* years!"

"What?" and Matthew stopped dead in his tracks!

"You heard me, boy; let's go eat!" Oopi said impatiently.

"Can't be. That is absolutely *impossible* for anything to live that long, especially without food!"

"Really . . . well, did you ever think it was possible you would see a large purple three-eyed, good-looking, talking worm?"

"No, but . . . ."

"Well, then, no buts . . . . See me, feed me!" he ordered.

Matthew put Oopi on his shoulder and snuck quietly downstairs, then into the kitchen.

"Good, no one is up; it's safe," he whispered.

When Matthew opened the refrigerator, Oopi started to bounce up and down and clap his little hands!

"Oh, yummy, yummy, yummy, I'm gonna fill my tummy," he chanted happily. "Oh, my, my, my, look at all those delicious things!" And Oopi jumped from Matt's shoulder, landing with a soft thump into a bowl of grapes.

Matthew heard someone coming, freaked out, and closed the refrigerator door quickly with Oopi inside.

"Matthew, oh, I thought I heard someone. What you still doing up?" Annabelle asked with a big yawn.

"Oh . . . I . . . ah . . . . Yeah . . . I . . . just got a little hungry and came down for a snack, that's all."

"You okay, Matt? You seem . . . a little nervous, no?"

"Oh, Annabelle, of course not; I'm fine . . . ," he said with a nervous chuckle.

"You sure?" she answered, looking at him oddly as her eyebrows twitched.

"Sure, I'm sure. I'm just gonna . . . worm around here and find something tasty, then head back to my room," he said with a small grin on his face.

"All right, I go back to sleep. Good night. See you in the morning."

"Night, Annabelle. Sleep well," he said as he watched her leave. He waited until he heard her door close and quickly yanked opened the refrigerator door. There Oopi was, wrapped in several lettuce leaves, leaning against a bunch of green grapes as if they were an inflatable sofa, chewing on some broccoli.

"Well, you look comfortable," Matthew said, chuckling softly.

"Do you always shut your guest in this fridge? By the way, it's cold in here, and did you know it gets dark when you close the door, young man?" Oopi said, munching on a juicy grape.

"Sorry, someone came into the kitchen! Oh, yuck, Oopi. How can you eat that gross stuff?"

"What do you mean . . . gross?" he asked with his mouth full of broccoli and grapes.

"It means disgusting, terrible!"

"Oh, dear boy, no, no, no . . . . It's more like fantastic and delicious!" Oopi replied, still stuffing his tiny wrinkly face.

"Do you want something to drink, Oopi?"

"No, I don't require fluids," he said with a burrrp . . . phaaa!

Matthew snickered at the funny burp he let out, then opened a drawer below him and took out a couple of pieces of cheese.

"Ooh . . . what's that?" Oopi asked curiously, rubbing his hand over the plastic wrapping.

"It is cheese for Zatu; that's his favorite snack!"

"Oh, my, I have never seen cheese like that before. Well, I am stuffed. . . . Should we get back to your room? I am sure you must have questions for me, young man."

Matthew lifted the now plump purple worm to his shoulder and headed back upstairs to his room.

"Zatu, I brought you something," he announced, waving the slices of cheese in the air. In a flash, the dog bounced off the bed and headed for them. Oopi looked down and focused on Zatu's large white teeth.

"Oh . . . oh, my, I . . . I would not want to fall in his direction when he was hungry," Oopi said, swallowing hard with a shudder. "He **is** a big guy and . . . uh . . . Matthew, he . . . ahem . . . he doesn't like worms or anything like that, does he?" Oopi asked with a quiver in his voice.

"Not that I know of," Matthew said with a laugh.

"Whew, glad to hear that, young man. Glad to hear that indeed!"

"Go on, then . . . give him that cheese before he changes his mind!" Oopi urged. "Oh, bless the gods . . . . My, my . . . he doesn't chew his food . . . just swallows," Oopi said in disbelief, shaking his head with his hand on his cheek.

Matthew was cracking up now!

"I'm glad you find my concern of that giant hair ball with those humongous, sharp fangs so humorous!"

"Oh, he won't hurt you. Besides, if he was going to bite you, he already would have! He likes you; I can tell," Matt said, assuring the panicked worm.

"Glad to hear that, but I best keep my eyes open when around him!" he said, batting his eyes, unconvinced of his safety.

"All right, Matthew, let's get down to things. We have a lot of information to cover before I take my nap. Do you know anything about what you have in your possession and why?"

"Not really, well, except for you. I do not understand how it is even possible that I can be talking to a worm . . . a purple one with three eyes yet!" he said.

"Umm, ahem . . . let me see if I can explain," he said in a logical tone, clearing his throat. Oopi inched his way up to Matthew's chest and sat, rubbing his bulging belly contently. "My job, which I will say *is* of *great importance* to you, and amongst many things I must do, I will be extremely essential to you one day for your survival."

"Survival . . . . Oopi, what are you talking about?" he asked, scrunching his face up at the worm.

"Oh, dear, you have not read the book yet, have you?" he said, scratching his soft, wrinkly head.

"Er . . . what book?"

"The book, silly!" he exclaimed as he wiggled up higher on

Matthew's chest, waving his little purple hands.

"Listen, I'm sorry, but I have no idea what book you are talking about! Can you give me a clue here and help me out?"

"I see we have a problem, but no need to worry at the moment," Oopi said as if talking to himself. "We must get some rest and then begin this conversation. We both need our rest. . . . Yes, indeed we do. But I must tell you a few things about me that you must never forget. Otherwise . . . I will be of no use to you. First, I always sleep in my pouch. . . . **I MUST** eat every time I awake, and when I must bring light to a situation, you need always to have the leather necklace I carry in my bag around your neck. Now, if I forgot anything, I will remember it tomorrow." Oopi stood on his tail, yawned, and stretched his little chubby arms way out.

"You know, I am so tired that what you just told me makes no sense at all . . . here you go," he said while yawning himself as he put Oopi back into his little leather bag. "Do you want me to close it up?"

"Yes, and put me back into the larger sack, please." As Matthew put the bag into the closet, he could already hear his new little friend snoring.

"There's a snoring worm from Egypt . . . in my room! Zatu, am I dreaming? No one is ever going to believe this!" he said to himself. *What am I talking about? . . . I don't even believe it!*

What is a chubby purple talking worm with three eyes here to help me with, and WHY? Help me with what? he wondered, sitting on the edge of his bed, looking totally baffled. Then he recalled the voice that came from the bag. "Hmm . . . I wonder," he said aloud while getting into bed. "Zatu, I either need that CAT scan, or our family tree had some nuts on it!"

He rolled over and turned out the light, hoping not to be haunted with nightmares tonight. Instead, his thoughts turned to Oopi. Luckily, sleep overcame him quickly, and Zatu snuggled next to him to do the same.

But his dreams came, and they stormed his mind. He saw stone walls and marble pillars with hieroglyphics. He seemed to walk endlessly through musty dark hallways with ornate arches. He detected an odor, peppermint mixed with a strong perfume.

A small halo of light was shining. It was coming from him, but he wasn't carrying a light. . . . His hands were empty and sweaty. Another room, it was dark, he was able to look out to other connecting rooms that were enormous, and they seemed endless. He was seeing things like a picture slide show, room after room. Abruptly he came to a dead end with an acrid odor. His stomach churned. A sudden gust of wind erupted, chilling him to the bone. The room was icy, and he felt someone behind him. He was too afraid to turn around; something told him not to. He began to run. His footsteps echoed off the ancient stained, marbled walls. Matthew came to a dead end and froze. Someone was still behind him. Quickly he jerked around and saw an eerie cloaked figure hovering in the corner. It was dressed in a brilliant blue and ebony-trimmed robe. An oversized flowing hood covered its face. He carefully eyed the floating shape that neared him, and his heart felt like it was in his throat. Matthew cringed when it got close enough that he could see a grossly decayed bald woman beneath the dark hood. She slowly revealed her boney, oversized hands and long orange and brown curled fingernails. She smiled deviously at him, exposing her wrinkled, decayed mouth. He wanted to escape her morbid presence, but his shaking legs would not budge. As she came closer, her breath emitted a sickening, sweet, rotting vapor, and Matthew began to gag. Red and green deceitful eyes glared intensely at him from under her hood. As petrified as he was, he managed to yell out with a trembling voice and ask her name. An icy, forceful wind whisked around him, and her dry, cracked lips whispered crisply, *"Escursia."*

"Who are you, Escursia, and what do you want from me?" he demanded!

"It is not what I want, my dear; it is her wishhh I ssssseek," she answered with a harsh, evil hiss.

"Whose wish, Escursia?" he yelled at her. But no answer came from her rotten orifice.

"Speak whose name calls you to me!" he yelled, this time at the top of his lungs. A strong, raging wind exploded violently throughout the room. Dreadful howling and deafening screeching made Matthew drop to his knees, cringing and holding his

ears. Her morbid odor reeked through his nostrils and lay heavily on his tongue. Sandy debris blew everywhere. He turned quickly and faced the wall to protect himself, but the small stones stung him like thousands of bee stings, and his flesh burned.

"*STOOOPPPP . . . STOP!*" he screamed.

A moment later, silence came, and when he turned, Escursia was gone. Only her rancid foulness remained. The silence chilled his bones. He got up and started to run. He didn't know where to go; he just ran. Matthew called her name: "Escursia . . . Escursia . . . show yourself!" he yelled, demanding her presence. But his calls to her were empty echoes, bouncing off limestone walls. Out of breath, he stopped to rest. The halo of light that guided him was fading. Matthew began to panic . . . as his fear of the dark seized him! He lifted his heavy feet and raced down the gloomy, darkening hallways. His heart was beating so fast, his eyes began to throb. He felt his fear taking over. . . . He could hardly breathe now as the small light disappeared! His feet pounded harder the faster he went, and the vibrations through the vacant corridors grew louder . . . almost deafening. . . . He kept running and running and running. . . .

Chapter Eleven

"Morning, Annabelle. Do we have anything for a headache?"

"Matthew, what's a wrong—you no feel good today?"

"I'm fine, just didn't sleep well and woke up with a bad headache."

"Well, here," she said as she gave him a plate of freshly made waffles and bacon. "Maybe after you have something to eat, you feel better."

"I'm really *not* hungry," he said, pushing the plate away abruptly. "I *just* want something to drink and some headache medicine," he answered with his head in his hands.

"Good morning, everyone," Pearle sang as she entered the kitchen, smiling.

"I'm afraid Matthew is not feeling well, Pearle."

"Oh, what's wrong?" she said, as she went over and felt his head for a temperature.

"Nana, **I just** have a headache . . . **that's all**," he said coldly.

Pearle looked at Annabelle. They were shocked! He never spoke to his grandmother that way.

"Matthew, what is it? What's wrong?"

"It's called a *headache*, Nana!" he replied sarcastically.

"Apparently, you must not have slept well either. I'll get you something for that headache, and in the meantime, you can adjust that attitude!" Pearle said as she went to the medicine cabinet.

"It's no nice to speak to your Nana that way, Matthew."

"Oh, geez, now a third degree. . . . I don't need this right now!"

"Young man! What is your problem this morning?" Pearle screeched when she overheard his nasty reply to Annabelle.

"Here, take these, and go back to bed!" Pearle ordered, looking at him in disbelief.

"I didn't mean it," he mumbled after he swallowed the pills.

"Well, go get some sleep. I'll call the school and tell them you will be home today."

"Oh, can you call Dan and ask him to come over after school and bring whatever work I missed?"

She gave him a nod, motioning him to go to his room.

Matthew looked down at his uneaten waffles and felt nauseated. He looked up at his grandmother, who was watching him, and she thought he was about to cry. But he didn't say a word as he got up and went to his room. Matthew crawled back into bed and was thinking about his nasty mood. *What is wrong with me, and what did I just do?* He rolled over, pulled the covers over his head, and quickly went to sleep.

It was nearly noon when Matthew awoke to the sound of machinery in the backyard. He went to his window and saw Robert with a bunch of officers and some other people walking toward the lake. He was feeling better and decided to get dressed and go downstairs.

"Annabelle . . . I'm sorry about this morning."

"I know you are. You feeling better?"

"Yes . . . much."

"Well, are you hungry?"

"I'm starving, Annabelle!" After he said that, he realized he had totally forgotten about Oopi! While Annabelle was in the pantry, Matthew quickly grabbed some grapes and broccoli from the refrigerator and put them down his shirt.

"I'll be right back, Annabelle," and he ran off to his room.

He locked the door behind him and took the leather bags out of his closet. He opened the smaller bag he had put Oopi in last night and turned it upside down on his bed. Oopi popped his head out and yawned.

"Greetings to you, Matthew," he said as he wiggled his way out of the bag and onto the bed. Oopi took a deep breath in and stretched his little arms up over his head. "Hmm . . . is that fresh greens I smell?" he said, inhaling while rubbing his purple tummy.

"Yes!"

"Well, where is it? I smell it, but don't see it!"

"Oh, yeah," Matthew laughed, and he reached down into his shirt and retrieved the grapes and broccoli.

"Oh . . . yummy, yummy, yummy, some loving for my tummy,"

Oopi chanted as he crawled eagerly toward Matthew.

"Listen, Oopi, I've got some things to do. I am going to leave you here for a while, but I will be back."

Oopi's body became erect, making him taller, and his three eyes scanned the room.

"What are you looking for?"

"The hairy beast, of course. . . . You know . . . the one with those big teeth, who doesn't chew his food," he said.

"You mean Zatu?"

"Yes, I do believe that's what you called him last night."

"No worries; he's downstairs."

"Well, then, I will eat this wondrous feast you have brought me and wait for your return." Oopi put the grapes under one arm and the broccoli under the other, then pulled the food over to Matthew's pillow and used his tail to make a comfortable dent in it. He heard Matthew laughing and looked up.

"Comfortable, are we?" Matthew asked, snickering.

"As a matter of fact, I am," Oopi said sarcastically.

"Anything else I can get you . . . maybe today's newspaper?"

"Glad to see your sense of humor this morning, my boy," he snapped. "We will see later who has a sense of humor," Oopi said under his breath as he watched him leave the room.

"How are you feeling, Matthew?"

"Much better, Nana. How are things going outside with Robert?"

"He's coming for lunch, and you can ask him that yourself, okay? Oh, Matthew, before I forget, Sol called this morning. We'll be leaving Thursday morning."

"Wow . . . that was quick! I didn't think we would leave that soon. This is great!"

"Are you sure you are up to going? You had me pretty concerned this morning."

"Nana, I didn't sleep well, and I think I had a migraine headache. I felt so sick, and I really thought I was coming down with the flu! Not to worry, though; I feel terrific now!"

"I'm glad to hear that, but I am going to keep you home to-morrow too. I just want to make sure you aren't coming down with anything. I called the school, and they are getting homework together for you and Daniel. Denise left this morning for her con-ference, so I have to pick Daniel up from school and get his stuff from the house. Dan was worried about Popcorn, so I told him he could bring her here, and Annabelle would take care of her while we were gone. So looks like you're gonna have a roomy to-night! Daniel can have the bedroom next to yours, and I figured to make it easier for Annabelle, you can put Popcorn's cage next to Hunter's."

"Sounds like a plan to me, Nana," Matthew said, all excited.

"As for what to pack, try to narrow it down to one suitcase, if you can. Of course, you have your carry-on to hold all your video games, music players, and whatever else you want to bring. I know they will show movies on the flight, but I'm sure having those gadgets of yours will help pass the time. It will probably be a six- to seven-hour flight. If we forget to pack something, or come to need anything, we can always buy it."

"Sounds like you thought of everything, Nana. What time do we leave Thursday?"

"I'm not sure, but our tickets will be delivered today, and then I can let you know."

"What about Robert—is he going with us?"

"I'm not sure yet."

"Nana, what's wrong?"

"Nothing, silly. . . . Why?"

"I can sense something is wrong today. Is it what happened this morning when I mouthed off?"

"Good Lord, no; I know you too long to know you didn't mean it," she laughed.

"It's about Mom, isn't it? You're worried about them . . . about them finding her."

"I'd be lying if I told you differently. . . ."

"Nana . . . promise not to laugh?"

"About what?" she asked.

"For some strange reason, I ... I ... think mom is still alive. I can't explain it. . . . It's . . . just something I have felt for a while."

"Maybe it's just wishful thinking, Matt," she said as she walked away.

"Anybody home?" asked a voice from the back door. Matthew knew it was Robert, and ran to the door.

"Well, it all depends on who you are looking for, officer."

"I'm looking for a very pretty lady who told me to come to lunch."

"Oh, you *really must be hungry!*" Matthew said as he opened the door. Robert picked him up over his shoulder and carried him into the kitchen. He put him down and exhaled dramatically.

"I'm not that heavy, geez!" he said.

"Must be getting old, then," Robert said with a laugh. "Feeling better, Matt?"

"Yes, lots. . . . Hey, can I go down to the lake with you?"

"Well . . . I preferred you didn't. There are so many people down there now, and with all that heavy equipment, I'd really feel more comfortable if you stayed here."

"Ah, man, I was hoping to watch you guys."

"It's really not all that exciting."

"Well, maybe for you, Robert, cause you're used to stuff like this."

"Could be, but like I said, it's much safer here than down there."

"Guess I'll go see what I'm going to pack for the trip, then. Oh . . . are you coming with us Thursday?"

"It all depends on today. If it's not Thursday, it'll probably be Monday."

"Well, I hope you can. I'll keep my fingers crossed."

"Thanks; I will too. I'm really excited about going! Your grandmother even promised to teach me how to ride a camel!"

"Oh, boy, this *is* going to be a good trip! I can't wait to see that."

"I just might surprise you, young man!"

"We'll see," Matthew said, giggling aloud.

"You ready for lunch, Robert?"

"Yes, Pearle, I'm starved! I slept in and didn't have time for breakfast or my second cup of coffee this morning!"

"Matthew, you ready for some lunch too?"

"No, I just ate. I'm gonna go upstairs and see what I'm going to pack for the trip. Nana, should I pack summer clothes?"

"I would pack a mixture of summer and a few warm pieces. Like I said, if we need anything, we can always go buy it. By the way, don't forget your hiking boots; you will need them for the pyramid."

"Oh, yeah, I almost forgot about taking them. All right, I'll be in my room," he said, and left Pearle and Robert in the kitchen. He was hoping Oopi had finished eating and was ready to talk. Matthew went into his room and locked the door behind him.

"There you are!" Oopi snorted.

"Did you enjoy your food?"

"As a matter of fact I did!"

"Good, then can we have that conversation we started last night? I sure do have a lot of questions for you."

"Yes, yes, I'm sure you do. However, before we start, I . . . ahem . . . ," Oopi cleared his throat, "there is someone I'd like to introduce you to."

"Oh?"

"Fetch my bag," Oopi ordered as he stood with his belly bulging and gurgling. "Ahh . . . maybe you ought to stand back just a bit there, son," he said, waving his tiny hand and stubby fingers in the air like a conductor.

Oopi stuck his head in the bag and began to whisper. A few minutes passed, and Matthew was growing impatient. Finally, Oopi stood up with his eyes floundering around in the air, and he proudly crossed his arms on top of his belly. Matthew then heard what sounded like something fluttering inside the bag. POOF . . . out from the bag popped a purple flying figure. It zipped back and forth across the room, made several quick circles in the air, then gently floated down beside Oopi on the bed. It was then that Matthew realized he had fallen back onto the floor. His face froze as he gawked in disbelief.

"Amora, I'd like you to meet Matthew. He is the heir I was speaking of and whom you will serve."

Matthew was speechless and stared at the beautiful creature, who wasn't more than four inches long. Her arms and legs were human-like, and her face was delicate and radiated a sweet innocence. She had a long, shiny gold tail and marvelous luminous, transparent purple wings. Amora's dark eyes were precious and reflected a sincere innocence. They were large bulging orbs, a deeper color of purple than her wings. When she blinked, her long black wispy lashes floated effortlessly up and down.

"It is with honor I meet you, Matthew," she said softly, with a bow of her tiny head. "I hope to serve you well."

"I . . . I um . . . ahem . . . ," Matthew stumbled. "Nice to meet you . . . Amora," he said in a whisper.

"You do not have to whisper at me," she giggled sweetly. "Please speak as you normally do."

Then she slowly flew off the bed, hovered in front of him, and bowed her head again.

"What's with all this bowing?"

"You are of more than an ordinary boy, do you not know this? You carry the prophesied mark and are whom we have waited for to serve."

Matthew looked at Oopi oddly, then back at Amora.

"Amora, he does not know yet the importance of himself nor what lies ahead."

"Well, we shall tell, then," she replied.

"Matthew," called a voice from the hall.

"Oh, no, Oopi, it's my grandmother. She will want to come in here!"

"Then let her," he answered calmly.

"Are you nuts?" Matthew said furiously as his heart began to pound. "Oh, sure, just let her in, and how do I explain you two, huh?"

"You won't have to. Let her in; trust me. There will be no problem."

Matthew turned around, flush in the face, and started for the door. He felt his legs begin to shake as he grabbed the knob; then, taking a deep breath, he slid the bolt across the door.

"What's with the locked door?" Pearle asked, eyeing him up and down and peering curiously into his room.

"Oh, I . . . I must have accidentally done that, Nana. Huh . . . silly me! Not like I haven't done it before," he said with a nervous laugh. "Sorry. . . . So . . . what's up?"

"Well, I was just wondering how you were making out with the packing, but I see no suitcase out."

"Oh . . . ah . . . yeah . . . I was just ah . . . just chilling. I figured I could do it later."

He nearly turned blue holding his breath, waiting for her to say something any second about Oopi and Amora. He exhaled and began to pull on his earlobe, then switched to his bushy eyebrow. He always does this when he is nervous, and when Pearle noticed, she shot him a wild-eyed look.

"Are you sure you are feeling okay, Matthew?"

"Why, ye . . . yess," he stuttered. "Wha . . . why?"

"Well, you seem like you're a nervous wreck." Then she shot him the dreaded high-eyebrow look.

"Me, nervous? Nah, I . . . I was just almost falling asleep. You just caught me off guard, that's all, Nana . . . . Nothing to worry about, really."

"Really," she said, raising her perfectly shaped brow higher. All right, if you say so. But you would tell me if anything was wrong, right?"

"Nana, of course I would. I swear, everything is copasetic! You know us kids . . . we can get weird sometimes. That's what makes us kids! I'm just so psyched about the trip," he said, trying to change the subject.

"Yeah, I'm pretty excited too. I really am looking forward to seeing Sol again. Since everything is okay with you, I'm gonna run to the store. Do you need anything?"

"Maybe some snacks for me and Daniel. Otherwise, I can't think of anything."

"Would you get some rest, then? Because you're freaking your grandmother out with all your excitement," she said, laughing.

"I will. Have fun shopping," he yelled out to her as he watched her disappear down the stairs. He closed his door, slid down it until he hit the floor, and looked over, aggravated, at Oopi.

"I have never lied to my grandmother, and I feel *terrible!*"

"That's what makes you purehearted," Amora replied gently, then turned to Oopi and asked, "She is the first female . . . isn't she?"

"Yes, my dear . . . she is."

"So . . . ."

He just shook his head this time while letting out a mournful sigh.

"Okay, you two, why didn't my grandmother see you?"

"Well," Oopi replied, "no one can see what you don't want them to."

"Because I *didn't* want Nana to see you, she couldn't? So does that mean if I *do* want someone to see you, they will?"

"Yes, depending on the person and situation," Amora replied.

"And what is this about the first female I heard you say after my grandmother left?"

"Matthew, do you remember when I asked you if you read a book last night?"

"Yes, but I told you, I didn't know what you were talking about," he said, raising his voice.

"Well, that book explains many things about why we are here. Without it, I'm afraid we are all useless to each other," Oopi said with a long exhale.

"You . . . can't . . . tell me what this is all about without *a book?*"

"I'm afraid not," Amora replied sadly.

"So . . . how do we get this book? Where is it?"

"That's the problem. It should have been in the bag! We have no idea where it is," Oopi said.

"What does it look like?" Matthew asked.

"It is bound in brown leather," she eagerly began. "The face bears your mark and the amulet."

"Soooo . . . I'm looking for a brown leather book with . . . ? Amora, what is this mark and amulet?"

"Remove your shirt, Matthew."

"Huh?"

"You heard her, boy; take off your shirt!" Oopi snorted.

Matthew jumped off the bed and slipped his tee shirt over his head. Amora flew up and around to his back.

"Come see into the looking glass. Good; now turn," she said with a waving motion of her hands, and pointed to the birthmark on his left shoulder.

"Wow, I've never really looked at it before. I mean, I've always been kidded about it in swim class, but I never paid much attention to it. So what does this mark mean, Amora?"

"It's the mark of a royal heir!"

"Me, a royal heir? You've got to be kidding me!"

"Yes, you are of royal blood, twice set," Amora said as she stroked his cheek gently with her tiny hand. Matthew backed away from her.

"Okay, now you are scaring me! How can I be of royal blood?" he said as he put his tee shirt back on. And what do you mean, twice set?"

"Amora," Oopi said, "this is going to be difficult. Yes . . . oh, yes, indeed. But I must figure this out!" He wiggled back and forth on the bed, scratching his head. He was talking to himself out loud when he came to a sudden halt. "Matthew, where was it that you found me?"

"In a crate downstairs. . . . My grandmother has tons of them down there with all kinds of stuff from Egypt!"

"Ahh . . . home," Oopi said, looking at Amora with his eyes expressing joy.

"Matthew, you must take us to these things you call crates! The book must be somewhere amongst them. Amora, I need you to try and remember Zara's words when you were with her last."

"I do not remember; forgive me," she yawned. "But I may be able to recall later. I must sleep," she said with another yawn.

"Yes, yes, of course you must! Maybe your dreams will help you."

"Let's not talk about dreams!" Matthew added sarcastically.

Oopi looked at Amora, then peered intently at Matthew. "Dreams, Matthew . . . what kind of dreams?"

"Nightmares, Oopi, with a gross-looking, putrid-smelling woman called . . . Escursia."

"Oh, no, no . . . this is not good. . . . No, not good at all," Oopi said, throwing his purple hands in the air as his eyes popped straight up and seemed to freeze.

Apparent from their reaction, Matthew knew Escursia was bad news. Amora was stricken with fear, and Oopi looked horrible as well. The name Escursia seemed to scare them to death.

"Oh, my dear Amora, you . . . you must not upset yourself. We . . . we need to keep our wits about us now. Yes . . . yes, we must," Oopi said, trying to convince himself at the same time. "Matthew, we need to get home, and we *must* find the book. Amora will sleep, and when she awakens, you will take us to the crates."

"Oopi, you said you need to go home. . . . Did you mean Egypt?"

"Yes."

"Well, we are leaving in three days to go to Egypt."

Oopi perked up, and Amora fluttered her droopy wings.

"I take it that's good?" Matthew asked, smiling.

"It is the only way," Oopi said.

"The only way for what?"

"Everything you will learn of after we find that book," Oopi replied.

Matthew knew that he wasn't going to get many answers till the book was found. He decided not to even ask the next million questions he had.

"Do you have nectar?" asked Amora.

"Nectar, what nectar?" asked Matthew.

"I believe in your world it is called golden liquid . . . ah, honey," Oopi replied.

"Yes, we have it downstairs. Do you want me to get you some?"

"Please; it is what Amora needs."

As soon as Matthew left to get the honey, Amora turned to Oopi and said, "He knows not what he is against. Why can we not tell?"

"He will find out soon enough, Amora. You know what we vowed, and we must be obedient."

"Yes, Oopi, her words are still in my heart."

"Don't worry, Amora, Matthew is a fine young man. He will fulfill the prophecy."

"I feel sure he will too. His heart is of the purest I have ever seen. He truly is the awaited heir. They knew too," she added, looking down, shaking her head.

Oopi assured her with a consoling nod.

"He comes," and Amora flew up and went to the door. "Nectar," she cooed as Matthew closed the door.

As soon as he opened the honey bottle, Amora began to sip it wildly with her long, slender tongue, and the more she drank, the darker her purple color became. She finished, and slowly pulled her pointed, cylindrical tongue from the jar and licked clean the few drops of honey that dripped from her pink lips and delicate smile.

"Amora, why didn't you tell me sooner you needed this nectar?"

"It is of no importance now, my purehearted one." She floated up and gently rested in his hand. Her tiny body was hardly noticeable, and all Matthew felt was the tickling flutter of her delicate wings. He raised his hand as she motioned him to do so, and they were eye to eye.

"We shall sleep now. When we awaken, we shall find the answers you seek. Have faith, dear heir, a pure heart will reveal all that is to be."

"Come, Matthew," Oopi said. "Put us to rest for now."

Chapter Twelve

While Amora and Oopi slept, Matthew went for a swim while waiting for Pearle to come home with Daniel. As he swam, he thought over all the extraordinary things that have happened recently.

"Let's see, we've had a robbery, my freaky nightmares, Oopi, and now Amora. Then, of course, there's this mysterious missing book. They say I'm royal, not once, but twice . . . *me an heir* . . . yeah, right!" He began to swim laps as fast as he could to release his frustration. Soon his arms began to ache, and he decided to bask in the nice warm sun for a while. He was almost asleep when he heard footsteps behind him. He turned around, and Daniel was standing behind him with his hands on his hips and with the oddest expression that only he could do.

"I thought you were sick."

"Hi to you too. I was, this morning . . . had a bad migraine. . . . Did you bring my work?"

"Oh . . . really. . . . And yes."

"Thanks, Dan. . . . Did we get a lot to do over vacation?"

"Like, duh . . . . You know Haram; he seeks perfection in us all! I just can't believe he would do that to *us* . . . especially with going to Egypt! I don't know how we will ever get his work and studying for finals done!"

"Dan, right now, that is the least of my problems," he replied, with his mood turning somber.

"Oh . . . what's up, buddy?"

"A lot . . . and I'm not sure, but either I'm losing my mind, or I have a tumor on the brain!"

"Well, spill; tell me what's going on."

"Not here; come on," he said as he picked up his towel and headed to the house.

Matthew spilled his guts about everything to Daniel, even though Robert had him promise not to. For the first time since they've been friends, Daniel was speechless, which, as anybody who knows him knows, is extremely rare.

"Matt, don't get mad at me, but . . . have you been . . . you know . . . sniffing . . . doing drugs?" he asked, looking quite seriously at him.

"Of course not. Are you *crazy?* Geez! Look, I know this all sounds way looney, but have I ever lied to you?"

"No . . . well . . . not that I know of . . . , but come on, a purple talking worm and a flying whatever you call it is a bit much for anybody to believe!"

"You, of all people, I thought I could trust to believe me," he said, looking at his best friend disappointed.

"Hey . . . wait a minute here, I didn't say you were a liar . . . . It's just kinda hard to believe this story. We have been friends for as long as I can remember, and I have *always* trusted and respected you. This is just hard to swallow, Matt. Just put yourself in my place. What would your reaction be if I told you something like this?"

"I'd probably tell your mom to have you committed to Looneyville," Matthew said, laughing.

"See, I told you so," he replied, plopping down on the bed.

"I'll tell you what, after dinner you will see for yourself."

"Brother swear?"

"Yes, I double brother swear, Dan!"

The blazing sun was finally sinking into the horizon, and after a long, hot, tedious day of investigating at the lake, Robert was glad it was over. He had several things the divers uncovered and was anxious to show them to Pearle. He signed off on the items he had in his possession and gave the paperwork back to Addy. The last person to drive out was Brian Kelly. Robert was filthy and exhausted, emotionally and physically. He was looking forward to a long shower and dinner with Pearle. When he got to the house, she was waiting for him by the pool, seemingly deep in her thoughts.

"Well, how are you, Robert?" she asked, looking up when she heard his footsteps.

"Tired and glad that's over," he said as he sat down and placed a brown paper bag on the table.

"What's in the bag?" she asked.

"Some things that the divers found today, and it's strange . . . nobody seemed to know what they were."

"Hey, Robert," Matthew said as he joined them.

"Hi, Matthew. Sorry you couldn't come down there today. It was such a mess!"

"Don't worry about it. So . . . did you find anything?"

"Yes, your grandmother and I were just getting to that."

"Guess I came out just in time, then."

"Matthew, don't you have Daniel here?" Robert asked.

"Yep, but he's inside making pizza dough with Annabelle. I told him not to come out and that I'd be back in a while. He was having way too much fun, I think, to even care, Robert."

"You haven't forgotten about the confidentiality with this case and not sharing any information, I hope?"

"Of course not. I told you, my lips are zipped!"

"Can we get this over with, Robert? I have been on pins and needles all day," Pearle said while rolling her paper napkin between her sweaty palms.

Robert opened the paper bag and removed several small plastic bags, placing them on the glass tabletop. He warned Pearle and Matthew not to remove the items from inside the sealed bags, as they were going to a forensic specialist in Washington.

"Wow, Nana, are those ushabtis?"

"I believe so. Would you look at them? They are beautiful!"

"Hmm . . . . Looks like they were fashioned for females, Nana."

"I would have to agree. Whoever these were made for had to be pretty important. My question is, though . . . what the heck were they doing in our lake?"

"Pearle, can you elaborate on these items for me?" Robert asked, looking queerly at the unfamiliar, small figurines.

"Did you find anything else?" she asked, as if ignoring his request.

He expected an answer, but Pearle held her breath as he reached inside the paper bag again. What Robert put on the table this time caused Matthew to gasp. It wasn't just the *item* that caused Matthew to hold his breath.

"Rob . . . ert, that's . . . the . . . that's the chain from Oona's necklace," Pearle said, looking stunned.

"Are you sure?"

"Absolutely; that chain is the same as the others," she said, staring wide-eyed at the bag.

"May I see that for a minute, Nana?"

Pearle handed him the bag with the broken gold chain. It was covered with green yuck stuff from being in the lake the last eight years. Matthew, though, only noticed one thing: a large orange claw in one of the links. His skin began to crawl. He caught a sweet reeking odor in his nostrils. Were his dreams now becoming a reality? Or, was this the claw from a gator that the police believe killed his mom? He slowly handed it back to Pearle. Matthew knew he had to tell Oopi about this. He promised himself he wasn't going to tell Pearle anything about Oopi and Amora until he fully understood what was going on. She had too many other things on her mind right now. Matthew picked up two ushabtis and tried to read the inscriptions.

"Nana, I think this one says 'Queen Ceraphy' and something else, but I can't quite make it out."

"Hmm, let me see that," she said.

"Robert, may I take some Polaroids of these?"

"Sure, I don't see why not. Just don't tell anyone, okay?"

"Who would I tell?" she murmured softly, still eyeing the ancient figurines.

"Matthew, go to the den, and get me the Polaroid camera. It should be on the bookcase behind my desk, about the third or fourth shelf up. Oh, and bring the box of film for it too; it should be right next to it."

"I didn't know we had one of those old cameras."

"I guess I had forgotten about it. It was your mom's," she said with her pink-tinted lips curling up to a smile. "She was supposed to use it while cataloging all the crates, but I've never found any pictures. . . . Anyway . . . go get it for me, okay?"

"Sure. I'll be right back."

When Matthew got to the den, he realized he's never paid much attention to the hundreds of books in there, particularly those behind Pearle's desk. Well, there was never a reason to . . . Pearle had always chosen the books they would use in his lessons about ancient Egypt. He made his way over to the bookshelf, squeezing behind her desk, and grabbed a folded step stool she kept under the desk. He hated the old contraption and called it a booby trap! No matter how careful he was, Matthew always managed to get his fingers pinched in it! As he began to pull the camera off the dusty shelf, a big book behind it with gold binding began to emit a pulsating, dull purple light in the dark room. He jerked backward, almost falling off the stool, but managed to grab hold of a shelf with his empty hand to steady himself. *I wonder,* he thought to himself. He pushed the strap of the Polaroid over his wrist to free his hand and carefully slid the heavy book out.

Oh, my God! That's . . . that's just like my birthmark . . . and this is exactly like our family medallion, he muttered silently, staring at the old book's cover. *This must be it! This has to be the one Oopi and Amora said we had to find.* He was ecstatic with his find, but knew he better get back to his grandmother before she came looking for him. He carefully eased the book back into the same spot and raced out of the den with the camera and film in hand.

"Nana, where did all those books in the den come from, especially the very old ones behind your desk?"

"To be honest, I'm not really sure. Your mom had put several in there, and I just haven't gotten around to checking them out yet. You are welcome to read them anytime, though."

How could this be happening? he thought. He was sitting there sweating, trying to figure out how he was going to get that book out of there. . . . Now he didn't have to worry. . . .

"Thanks, Nana. Some of them look *really* old. I bet they make for interesting reading," he added.

"I'm sure they will. Just be careful with those old books. Their pages are very delicate. You may need to use gloves. Do you remember what I taught you about reading the old hieroglyphic scrolls? Treat those books the same way."

"Oh, sure, I remember. As a matter of fact, I think I still have a pair of them in my sock drawer. So, did you figure out what those ushabtis say? Do they have a curse, or just the owner's name?"

"I'm impressed that you remember what I taught you about them, but I'm afraid with all this muck, I'm not able to read much more than you did."

"Robert, you sure have been quiet," Matthew said, looking up.

"I'm just admiring the two most important people in my life, who are absolutely brilliant! Pearle, while you two finish looking these things over, I'm gonna go up and shower."

Matthew held his nose. "I think that would be a **great** idea, detective!"

"You're real funny, kid," he chuckled. "I'll be back in about twenty minutes."

"Don't rush, Robert; we have plenty of time before dinner," Pearle yelled to him as she watched him go into the house. Then she turned around and gave Matthew the dreaded eyebrow look.

"So, are you gonna tell your grandmother what's going on?"

"What are you talking about, Nana?"

Pearle looked him straight in the eyes. "Matthew, there is something this family has been gifted with."

"Oh," he said, "what's that?" and he swallowed hard.

"Intuition, my dear grandson. It has been in the family for as long as I know. So what gives, and what aren't you telling me?"

"Nana, I'm not sure what you mean. What makes you think something is going on?"

"Let's just say my intuition is running on high today," she replied in a matter-of-fact tone with her brows raised.

"Maybe it's just from everything going on," he quickly responded.

"Could be, but if something was wrong, you'd tell me, wouldn't you?"

"Of course I would. You should know that," he said with his cheesy grin as his stomach flipped for the second time.

"Just one thing: Don't try to pull the wool over your grandmother's eyes, okay?"

Matthew was relieved. He thought he was going to have a heart attack when she asked what was going on! He knew she wasn't a stupid woman and somehow always knows when things are amiss in his life. He realized that he must be careful from here on with everything he says and does.

"Guess I better get back inside and help Daniel and Annabelle with the pizza-making. Will you be okay till Robert gets back?"

"Do I look like a woman in distress?" she replied jokingly, pulling on her hair.

"Not at all, Nana," he laughed, and then went inside the house.

"Guys, I'm gonna go say good night to Robert and my grand-mother. I'll be right back, and Dan, then we *really* need to go finish our *homework!*"

"What home . . . ?" he started to say, but Matthew cut him off, giving him a weird look and shaking his head.

"Dan, how could you *forget that?* You know we have to get it done before we leave," he said, looking wide-eyed and raising his eyebrows at him.

"Oh . . . ahh . . . sorry, guess I forgot," Dan said, shrugging his shoulders.

"Why don't you get some snacks to take upstairs; I'll be back in a few minutes. Don't forget to get some *grapes,* and I know how much you like to eat *raw broccoli.*"

Annabelle looked at Matthew strangely. "*Since when you eat broccoli, Daniel?*"

"Since his mother told him he better," Matthew said with a nervous laugh. "***Right, Dan?!***"

"Oh, yeah, I promised my mom more healthier choices in my snacks!"

"Well, good for you. Maybe you can get your partner in crime here to do the same," she added as she walked away to get her mop.

Matthew gave Dan a high five. "Good job, buddy," he whispered. "I thought you were gonna blow it there for a minute!"

"What the heck is going on?" he asked, looking at him as if he lost his mind!

"Just get a bunch of grapes and some broccoli to bring to my room. I'll be right back!"

"Okay, my sick and twisted friend," Daniel replied under his breath as he went to the refrigerator.

"Hey, guys, Dan and I are going up to work on our big homework assignment. I wanted to say good night. Did you enjoy the pizza?"

"Absolutely," replied Robert as he leaned back in his chair and proudly rubbed his stuffed belly. "Couldn't you tell? We ate a whole pie ourselves!"

"It was delicious, Matt, and tell Dan he did good," Pearle said approvingly. "Do me a favor before you head up, and put these pictures and camera on my desk for me."

He picked up the pictures and camera, and said good night. He then took the stuff to the den and ran to meet Dan, who was waiting anxiously at the bottom of the stairs.

"Hey, got everything?" he asked.

"Yes, as you requested, oh sick one!"

"You say that now, dorko, but you'll see," Matt said, racing him up to his room.

He locked his bedroom door and went to the closet to get the leather sack.

"Matt, what's with the honey?" Daniel inquired as he put the tray on the dresser.

"Oh, that's for Amora," he said nonchalantly, putting the bag on his bed.

"Amora?"

"Yessss . . . Amora."

"Ooh . . . kay . . . !" Dan said, rolling his eyes.

"Dan, you have got to *brother swear* that you won't say a word to *anybody,* and that goes for my grandmother too!"

"*I swear,*" Daniel said, putting his hand up as if he were taking an oath.

"And promise me you are not going to freak out here."

"Would you just get showing me already?!" he urged loudly. *"The suspense is killing me!"*

"Sshhh . . . not so loud!" Matthew hissed.

Matthew opened the leather bag, and Dan watched as the bag began to move, and he took a big step backward. A moment later,

Oopi wriggled his wrinkled body out, stood on his tail, stretched, and let out a cute, squeaky sound as he exhaled. He turned toward Daniel and, with his eyes bouncing around, stretched his hands over his head and yawned.

"Hmm . . . I see we have company."

"Yes, Oopi, this is my best friend, Daniel."

He wiggled over to him and held out his little purple hand. "Best friend, I am Oopi."

Daniel held out a finger, looking completely shocked, and shook Oopi's tiny hand.

"I . . . I don't believe this, a ta . . . talking worm," he muttered as his head bobbed up and down while gawking at Oopi's three bulging eyes bouncing around.

"Don't you know it's rude to stare?" Oopi snapped.

"You'll get used to the eyes after a while," Matthew replied casually with a chuckle.

"Huh?"

"Well, what's got your tongue, boy? Don't you speak?" Oopi inquired, annoyed.

"Huh! He speaks just fine . . . trust me; just give him a few minutes for the shock to wear off. In the meantime, I've got good news for you."

"Uh . . . ahem . . . by chance, is that for me?" Oopi said coyly, rubbing his hands together while eyeing the tray of food on the dresser. Daniel shook his head. "Well, fetch it for me, then," he ordered. "Oh, my . . . what *have* we got here?" he asked, eagerly scanning the tray with all the assorted goodies on it.

"Brr . . . occoli, grr . . . apes, pizza, chips, soda, and chocolate," Daniel muttered as he pointed to each one. "I . . . ah guess the broccoli and grapes are for you. . . ."

"Who made you an expert as to what I eat?" Oopi roared.

"Well . . . I . . . just fig . . . ured, I thought that's what you ate," Daniel stuttered.

"Don't think, then!" Oopi said with a tsk.

"Geez, you're *a crabby guy*," he growled back at him.

"Back off, friend, or I'll be on you like white on rice!" Oopi sputtered.

"Good Lord," Matthew said, snickering, "where'd you learn that expression?"

"Oh, I have been reading up on . . . oh, yes, your slang."

"Whoa, Oopi, go a little easier on my friend here; he didn't mean anything wrong." But Oopi was too hungry to apologize and only sneered.

"Guess he gets irritable when he hasn't eaten. Well, it's duly noted," Dan said sarcastically with a salute.

"Funny guy, huh . . . . I might get to like you after all," Oopi said as he eyed up the plate put on the bed for him. "I see you have nectar for Amora. She will be awake soon and in much need of it. So . . . what's this good news you have for me?" he asked, popping a juicy grape into his mouth.

"I think I've found the book!"

Oopi gasped, then inhaled. He tried to swallow, but gagged instead, and Oopi thought he was doomed. Absolute fear engrossed his pathetic purple face, and his antennaed eyes shot straight up in the air!

"Holy crap, Matt, I . . . I think he's choking!"

"Oh, my God! Well, do . . . do something. You know first aid?" Matthew yelled, panicked.

"*Are you crazy?*" he yelled back as his eyes bugged out. "I don't know how to perform the . . . the Heimlich maneuver on *a worm*," he screeched!

Thump!

The boys turned around and were horrified. Oopi had fallen back onto the bed and looked like a purple Popsicle! "DO SOMETHING; HE'S GONNA DIE!" Matthew howled.

Daniel snatched Oopi up by the tail and turned him upside down. He gently slapped his wrinkly back, but nothing happened. Again, he slapped him, then again, and this time he gave him a slight shake and jerk. POP . . . BOINK . . . ZIIIPP! Out shot the slimy grape from Oopi's throat like a greased cannonball! It ricocheted off a pillow, bopped Daniel between his eyes, then soared through the air, tumbling toward the door, where it landed with a loud **splat**!

Oopi began to cough, and Daniel looked down. He still had

ahold of him hanging upside down. "Oh, I'm sorry," he said, and placed him gently down on the bed. Dan's hands began to shake, and his legs felt so weak that he sank to the floor with a soft thud. His face turned pale as paste.

"Oh, my God, are you okay?" Matthew asked as he picked Oopi up and looked him over.

"I am . . . thanks to your friend. He saved my life . . . me . . . crabby old Oopi . . . I am indebted," he said, lowering his head, ashamed of how he talked to Daniel earlier.

"It was nothing, no biggie," Daniel assured him. "But you shouldn't have put the whole thing in your mouth in the first place. You could have choked to death!"

"What is all the commotion about?"

Daniel looked up, and his jaw dropped!

"Amora," Oopi whispered with a raspy voice. "Everything is fine . . . just fine."

She fluttered past Matthew, giving him a quick wink, and whirled around the room several times before landing gently on Daniel's shoulder.

"Does this one have a need for a doctor?" she asked, looking at Daniel, slobbering down his shirt.

"Ah, gross!" Matthew said. "Dude, you are drooling all over, yuck!"

"I am Amora. Who are you?" she asked him sweetly.

But Daniel couldn't answer. He was mesmerized by this small, beautiful creature. She appeared amused by his reaction and giggled. Leaning sideways, she looked at him with her alluring, sweet eyes and politely pointed to his chin. He reached up, swiped the drool from his face with the back of his hand, and wiped it onto the leg of his pants while not budging an eye off her for a second. Amora giggled again and motioned for him to close his mouth. When he did and she was sure he wasn't drooling anymore, she turned to Matthew. "I am famished; have you any more nectar?"

"Yes," Matthew replied. He quickly retrieved the jar and set it in front of her. He then joined Daniel on the floor, and they watched as she eagerly sucked the sweet liquid from the jar. When she had her fill, Amora lifted her head, withdrew her slender, long tongue, and smiled contently at everyone.

"Holy crow, I almost forgot," Matthew said. "Dan, I'll be right back."

"What's wrong?"

"Nothing. I've just got to get the book. Keep an eye on them, would ya? I'll be right back!"

Matthew went down to the kitchen and peeked out the window. Pearle and Robert were still outside. He ran to the den, grabbed the pictures off the desk, took the book from its shelf, and took off for his room, racing up the stairs. He closed and locked the door behind him, then slid down to the floor, panting. Amora let out a delighted sigh and zipped quickly across the room, making a delicate landing on the book.

"Oopi, it is the book; it is her words!" she rejoiced. She then shot up into the air, completely overjoyed, and spun around like a twirling top! Matthew, Daniel, and Oopi watched her spectacular flying acrobatics with amazement. But after several minutes, Matthew realized it was time to get to the book. He got up and went to Oopi with an odd gaze in his eyes.

"I have something else to show you." He placed the pictures neatly in a row on the bed, and Oopi inched back and forth, eyeing them carefully for several minutes without a word. He finally turned and looked at Matthew, scratched his wrinkled head, and exhaled.

"Where did you find these?" he asked, pointing at the pictures of the ushabtis.

"I didn't find them . . . the police did. They were in the lake that's in the back of the house."

"Is this where the chain was also found?"

"Yeah, all these things came from there."

Oopi's face turned stony, and Matthew sensed a terrible dread. He felt uncomfortable and backed away several steps from him.

"Matthew, promise me you will cease to visit this lake at all costs!"

"Okay, but why?"

"Do you know what these figurines are used for?"

"What I have read and what my grandmother has taught me is all I know."

"Yes, yes, boy, *but what* do you know of these things?" Oopi snorted impatiently.

"Ushabtis were made in the image of a deceased person, usually someone of great importance. They were to be used to do their manual labor in the afterlife for them."

"Very good; you have been schooled well. But sometimes someone else . . . would use them for spells . . . magic . . . and act out on behalf of the deceased in a very different way. This is of the worst kind of magic that could be. . . . It is very evil magic . . . very evil indeed! Come, Matthew, and open the book. We have much to do. I'm afraid things are not going as planned," Oopi said stoically, shaking his head.

Matthew sat and put the heavy book on his lap. He grabbed the back and front cover and pulled. . . . He picked up the book and looked it over, then laid it down and tried again. This time he pulled so hard to open it that the tips of his fingers burned.

"Well, open it, boy!" Oopi urged.

"I've tried. . . . It . . . it won't open," he said, nearly out of breath, pulling on it with all his might again.

"Oh, let me have a try," he said peevishly.

"*Wait . . . you mustn't!*" cried out Amora. "She specifically said only the *heir* was to open the truth; don't you remember?"

"Then why can he not open it?" Oopi hissed at her.

"I do not know. But he *must* open it and read the prophecy, Oopi!"

"Yes, yes!" he sneered. "Don't you think I know that? But something prevents him from doing so! There is only one who knows what to do, and we must call her forth, Amora."

"Oh . . . do you truly feel that's necessary? She will not be happy with us for failing. . . ."

"Calm yourself, my dear. We have not yet failed," Oopi said, soothing her. But her wings began to droop, and sadness overcame her.

"Why can't we just break it open," Matthew interrupted, quite irritated. "Maybe you are overreacting. After all, it's only a *damn old book!* What's the *difference* how we open it as long as we do?" He was scarlet in the face, and his bright blue eyes darkened. Matthew's rage shocked Daniel. He has never seen his friend so infuriated. But Matthew has; it was the second time that day he'd become indignant.

Oopi stared fiercely at him. His purple, wrinkly skin began to stretch; his whole body was swelling up! **"Noooo!"** he screeched loudly, sounding like a teakettle whistle. ***"We must have Emia tell how to open the book, and that is final!"***

Matthew was startled over Oopi's outburst of anger. His face grimaced as he watched the purple worm expanding like a puffer fish! He began to panic, thinking Oopi was going to blow up and disintegrate any second. He had to quell the situation, and fast . . . but how?

"Daniel, quick . . . go get some cold water!"

He ran to the bathroom, shaking from the awful sight of Oopi's incredible swelling, and wondered what Matthew planned to do with the water. He hoped whatever crazy idea he had would work. *My kids will never believe this story!* he thought to himself as he fled back to the bedroom, spilling water along the way. He handed his friend the half-empty cup with a questionable look. Matthew gave him a wink, turned, and threw the water at Oopi, who was now the size of a basketball. Oopi fell back onto the bed and bounced so high he hit the ceiling. As he started to plummet toward the floor, Daniel made a desperate dive, reaching his long arms out to catch him, but he bounced off his wrist and shot toward the ceiling again. This time Matthew was right under him and caught him. He felt like a giant squishy water balloon in his hands, and Matthew was sure he'd pop at any second! Oopi was exasperated, and they all knew it.

"Put me down this instant!" he shrieked. And Matthew did just that.

Amora planted herself in front of him with a wicked look and crossed her arms, displaying her displeasure in his behavior.

"Oopi, you must cease this right now!" she said hotly. "You know you are to be in control of that anger of yours. How many times has it gotten you into trouble, or have you forgotten? You are a disgrace and should be ashamed of yourself," she said, winded. Her wings were fluttering as fast as her heart, so fast that they hummed. She was completely aghast by his behavior, especially with him knowing very well the condition it put him in. Her tail was flicking back and forth with her fury, something she hardly ever does. With Oopi seeing her disgust, he realized he lost control and was in big trouble. He slowly managed himself to a wobbly upright position, but soon fell over. Again, he attempted to get up, but as he strained to roll over . . . some very loud, extraordinary, weird noises began to resonate from his lower body. ERRRRRRR . . . GRRRUMM . . . BURRRRR . . . Grrr . . . grrrrrrrr . . . ERRR . . . RIPPP . . . .

"HE'S . . . GOING . . . TO BLOW!" yelled Amora, and she zipped in a purple flash out of sight.

What happened next mortified Oopi. His lower half began expelling a loud, continuous tumultuous roar with an extremely offensive odor. It sounded like someone was pinching the opening of a balloon while slowly letting the air out of it. And if that wasn't enough, there were high-pitched notes in between like someone playing bagpipes! Matthew and Daniel looked at each other, horrified, then began to laugh hysterically. They laughed so hard for so long that neither one of them could breathe by the time Oopi was done expelling himself. Amora too had joined in the laughter, and when they stopped long enough to peer up from the floor, there stood Oopi, looking contented as could be and back to his normal self.

"Okay, you two," Matthew sighed while twisting his lips together, attempting not to laugh. "Let's give Oopi some dignity and be serious here and go talk to him."

After expressing how glad they were that he was himself again, Oopi apologized for his moronic behavior and told them it was time to put the night's events behind them. It was time to get ready for Emia.

Chapter Thirteen

"**M**atthew, we will need several items, and Daniel must assist you. Daniel, you will have to obtain a couple of lilies from the lake. Remember, he is strictly forbidden to visit this place! I also require scented oil . . . have you any of this?"

"We have cooking oil."

"That will have to do, then. We have gathered the spices she likes, and the last thing will be of nectar."

"Daniel and I will get more honey, plus the oil and flowers, and be back in a little while."

As the boys went to the door, he called out to them. "I must stress again that you are to go **nowhere** by that lake if you value your life!"

"He won't, I promise you," Daniel assured him.

"All right, then; hurry! Time is wasting, and we must summon her when the moon begins to rise," Oopi said as he pointed and stared out the window.

The boys went quietly down the stairs and out the front door. They knew if they used the back door, chances were Annabelle would wake up. They ran until they were about fifty feet from the lake. Matthew handed a flashlight to Daniel and warned him to be careful, but to hurry. He assured him he'd be okay and would be back in five minutes with the flowers.

Matthew watched Daniel and the flashlight disappear into the darkness. It wasn't but a minute later when he heard a big splash. All sorts of weird thoughts flipped through his mind, and he wondered if Daniel was okay. Matthew paced zigzag in the dewy grass, convinced that he was wrong to get him involved in all this craziness and he should have gone to the lake himself.

I must be out of my freaking mind for letting him go down there, he thought. *What was I thinking? . . . Oopi is nuts; nothing is going to happen if I go by the lake. . . . I've been there a million times! Besides, I couldn't live with myself if anything happened to my best friend.*

"Hey, next time you send me out on a night mission, can you make sure the flashlight works?!"

Matthew whipped around so fast he almost fell over.

"Good Lord; are you okay? . . . What happened?"

"Well," Daniel began, "the flashlight went out just as I was reaching over to grab a flower, and then I . . . uh . . . I thought I saw a gator, and I panicked. . . . Okay! Yes, I fell in and lost the flashlight! No, I'm not hurt. So go ahead, get mad, have a good laugh . . . whatever . . . I don't care," he said as he swiped mud away from his mouth.

"Man, I'm sooo sorry I got you involved. . . . You could have gotten hurt."

"Listen, Matthew, I'm not sure what is going on here or why. But what I do know is that it seems serious . . . far-fetched, but serious. So let's just do what Oopi says, and hopefully everything will turn out okay. We are brothers, and if you have a problem, then so do I . . . got it?" he said with his finger pointing in Matthew's face.

"Yeah, sure, I get you, but not all this crazy stuff."

"Well, hopefully when this Emia thing, person, or whatever it is shows up," he said, throwing his arms wildly up in the air, "she will have some answers for you."

"Let's hope so, because this is getting weirder by the minute!"

"Weird, Matt . . . no . . . this is more like an episode from *The Twilight Zone!* Come on, let's get back to the house. I need a shower and can't wait to see what the purple guy has planned next."

They raced back to the house and carefully made their way into the kitchen. Matthew froze and squeezed Daniel's arm. "Oh, crap!"

"Quick," he said as he took hold of his wet shirt, pulling him into the pantry. "Sshhh . . . be quiet." The boys sat in the back of the dark pantry, holding their breath. Annabelle was up and fumbling around in the kitchen. Matthew thought for sure she'd open the pantry door any second, and they would be dead meat!

"Oh, God, I hope she . . . ."

"Hush . . . would you just keep quiet?" Matthew whispered, smacking his hand over Dan's mouth.

It seemed like hours before the kitchen lights finally went out. Matthew crawled to the door and opened it up just enough to peek out.

"Shhh . . . I think she's gone. Grab a bottle of honey; I got the oil, and let's get out of here!"

When they made it back to the bedroom, Matthew took a good look at Daniel and started to crack up with Oopi and Amora.

"And what's so funny?" Daniel asked, dumbfounded.

"Well . . . har . . . har . . . har, look into the mirror, friend," said Oopi, sounding like a cat with laryngitis.

Daniel marched over to the mirror and let out a throaty snort. His hair was caked with thick gobs of green muck, and toward the back of his head was a tiny frog stuck to a piece of a lily pad. "Hmm . . . looks like I picked up a hitchhiker." And he plucked him gently out of his hair. "Guess I better find a place for you to sleep tonight until I can put you outside tomorrow," he said to the frog while heading for a shower.

"Ah, what will you do with the creature?" Oopi asked. "I'd like to have it for Emia if you wouldn't mind."

Daniel turned around and rolled his eyes, "Oh . . . what for?"

But he didn't answer him, and by the look on his face, he didn't have to. As unsettling as the thought of what was to come of the frog was, he was too tired to argue and handed it over to Oopi before going to shower.

"Oopi, tell me who Emia is."

Oopi stood before him, stretched tall and looking proud. Matthew thought he looked like the president standing in the Rose Garden, getting ready to give a speech. Then he turned, placed the frog inside a flower, and said, "Emia is a creature like us and above all the chosen kind in our kingdom; she was the closest to our mistress. She witnessed horrible abominations of our people and suffered great personal loss for her loyalty to our queen. You are to treat her with the highest regard, for she is one of your greatest allies. The knowledge she possesses will be invaluable to you, as will her magical powers. And there is something else I feel you need to know. . . . However, I forbid you to speak of this to her. Our queen gave her the enormous responsibility of your safety, and she graciously accepted, knowing she may perish in doing so. Our mistress prepared well for you, and although you may be mystified by what I say and our presence here, I promise, things will be revealed to you as she planned."

"So tell me, what must be done for this Emia?"

"I need you to remove your shirt and lie face down on the floor. No matter what else I may ask of you tonight, just do it with no question."

"Ah . . . . Okay. . . ."

"Now lie down, boy, and I want you to clear your mind."

Daniel came out from the bathroom all cleaned up and saw his friend shirtless on the floor. *Now what?* he thought to himself. "What's this all about, Matt?" he asked, looking puzzled.

"Just go sit somewhere, and don't ask any questions, okay?"

"I can do that," he muttered in a matter-of-fact way, rubbing his wet hair with a towel. He watched as Oopi took some honey and carefully made an outline over Matthew's birthmark. Then Oopi placed oil inside of it, sprinkled some scented spices on top, and fixed the two flowers next to the birthmark. He motioned for Amora to join him. They joined hands, exchanged a few words, and began to chant.

"Oh Emia, great one, we call to you from far away. It is not for our own needs but that of our Heir. Please hear us and appear. We need your vast knowledge if we are to succeed. Oh hear us and bring thy self forth in this time of trouble. Emia in all your greatness, we await your presence."

"Now what?" Dan asked, tossing his wet towel behind him.

"Yeah . . . how long is this gonna take?" asked Matthew.

"Be patient, dear heir; she will come," Amora assured him. "Close your eye . . . rest."

Her voice was soothing, but he didn't dare shut his eyes. He was too anxious about meeting Emia and began wondering all sorts of things about her. He wanted to know what she looked like, the powers she had, and what the horrible things were Oopi said she endured. He took a deep breath in and exhaled. Amora let out a giggle, and he felt her tiny body moving on his back. She was nestled in one of the flowers. Oopi had crawled onto Daniel's lap but decided the pillow on the bed was much softer to lie and wait on. Daniel remained on the floor . . . not too far at all from his friend. Everyone's attention seemed drawn to the window over Matthew's bed. The curtains were flapping back and forth from a gentle breeze, and they watched the moon glisten against the ebony sky while the reflection of silvery stars above the golden orb flickered in and out of the dimly lit room. An hour had passed, and everyone was asleep except Daniel, who dozed occasionally.

HUMMMMMMM . . . BUZZZZZZ . . . HMMMMMM . . . HUMMMMMMM . . . BUZZZZ . . . .

The silence in the room came to an abrupt end when Daniel jumped up and froze. He held his breath with his ear cocked toward the window. His stomach knotted, and his cheeks flushed when he heard it again. It was coming from outside. He knew it was a hornet, a *really big* one at that! Daniel's thoughts turned to finding a weapon of mass destruction and quickly! His eyes bounced around the room, and there it was. He grabbed a thick magazine next to the television and rolled it up in his sweaty palm. He stood staring at the window, gripping the magazine so hard his hand throbbed. Swoosh! Phuff! Whoosh! Daniel's arm went flailing in the air while he swatted the magazine wildly about. "I've never seen anything so freaking big in my life!" he screeched, sounding like a hysterical little girl!

"Cease this at once!" Oopi yelled.

Daniel jumped nearly two feet into the air and turned around. He squinted his eyes, focusing on what was hovering near Oopi. He cautiously lowered his hand and dropped the magazine. "Could it be . . . ?"

"Yes, I am Emia," she said with a husky voice, stunning Daniel as he ogled the large, colorful dragonfly.

"But . . . how'd . . . you . . . ?"

"How did I know what you were thinking?"

"Yes, how'd you . . . do . . . that?"

"One of my many gifts," she replied graciously.

"You are the great friend of our heir?"

"Ah . . . yes, yes, I am," he stuttered nervously.

"Good . . . he will need someone like you."

"I'm sa . . . sorry for swinging at you, but I thought you were a giant hornet."

Emia smiled graciously at him and replied, unyielding, "I would have done the same had I anticipated such a nasty creature. I share your sentiments, Daniel, for that vile beast." Then she turned to Matthew.

"Hello, heir," she said with a dignified bow.

Matthew's eyes grew huge. Emia was stunning, and his fear subsided when her eyes pierced him with her kindness. She was over eight inches long. Her body was bright purple and covered in orange bristly hairs. Her midsection had numerous double layers of orange and purple speckled wings on each side, and her large protruding eyes were a deep violet with tar-colored pupils. Her face, muscular legs, and arms were human, like Amora's, but she appeared much older than she.

"I am in need of nectar and food—hast any?"

"I'm afraid I messed things up, Emia. Oopi had everything prepared for you here," he said apologetically, pointing to his back.

Emia buzzed her wings, flew around, and hovered over Matthew's back. Oopi looked at him and motioned for him to lie back down. She landed gently on Matthew's back, and Amora, who hadn't said one word yet, picked up the flowers and placed them next to her. Daniel watched as the elegant creature devoured the delicate flowers. She turned, smiled at him, and in a flash sucked up and swallowed the small frog in a gulp. She went on to the honey, spice, and oil and gently licked it all clean.

"That was satisfying," she sighed contently. "Daniel, you find it offensive that I have eaten the small green creature?" His eyes widened. . . . "We all must do what is necessary to sustain our lives; always remember that," she added.

"Come here, Matthew," she said, motioning him with a delicate wave of her hand. He got up awkwardly off the floor and stretched. He hesitated, looking at the book. Daniel handed him a shirt, and he slid it on. She motioned again, and he sat down on the bed next to where the three creatures eagerly awaited and picked up the book.

"Matthew, I have much to tell of, but first, tell me something. . . . How many years are you?"

"What?"

"The years of your age," she asked gently.

"I'm twelve, but I'll be thirteen soon."

"When is this to be?"

"The fifth of May."

"That is not but a few weeks, then," Oopi said, hardly able to hold in his excitement.

"Yeah, so what does my birthday have to do with anything?"

"Emia will explain, but that may be why you could not open the book."

"It is not," she scolded Oopi. "Hold your tongue, and think before answering with your thoughts," she added. Oopi didn't dare say another word as she raised up and sat herself on top of the book. Matthew looked into her dark eyes and felt uncomfortable with her being that close. He smiled at her, but she knew it was fake. "There is nothing to be frightened by, heir; rest assured I bring no harm against you. Do you find my appearance repulsive?"

"Oh, no, no, Emia; I think you're beautiful. It's just . . . well, I've never seen a dragonfly so big and . . . I . . . ."

She tilted her head back, laughing aloud, and Matthew's face froze. He felt his stomach drop and began to pity the creature as he stared at an ugly, thick, red scar under her neck.

"I understand," she said as her laughter ebbed. "I felt the same when I first met Oopi." She turned to him, and he was nodding and smiling, recalling that first meeting too. Then, as if someone flipped a light switch, her mood turned somber. "Our mistress always said to never judge by what you see, for looks can be deceiving. Let's continue. . . ."

"We creatures come from Rhondra, a place far and isolated in the desert of Egypt. Oopi is the sole survivor of those known as Phules. He's bestowed with a talent for water. Our Amora, one of very few Efamils that exist from our time, has a very important essence for life's embodiment. As for *my* kind, there are numerous . . . but none as I am. We all were just mere creatures until our queen befriended us, making each of us special in some way. She gave us a voice and abilities beyond anyone's imagination. Our queen not only gave us powers but also the precious gift of her love. And because of that, we pledged our loyalty to her forever. And in doing so, we accepted her last wish, and that was to protect you at any cost."

"Now, I'll continue on with our kingdom; that was ruled by King Mattaheus and our mistress Queen Oonaphelia. It was a glorious place, though isolated from many other cities. Our king and especially the queen strongly believed that every creature, human or otherwise, was a precious gift and was to be treated as such. Our Rhondra was truly like no other. As for the royal family, our queen birthed four male children early in her marriage. Surprisingly, many years later, the queen was again with child, and Zara, her high priestess, said it was female. Zara was a very wise and beautiful high official. She and the queen had an extremely close relationship . . . that some would say was even closer than with her husband, the king. But I know that not to be true. You see, they shared powers, wonderful powers that only the two of them understood. And with Zara's loyalty, her powers of insight made her an invaluable part of the queen's life. However, some things were beyond this ability and understanding.

"Now, as for this female child; there was great celebration for this coming day. You see, she would be the first female in the family's long line of male heirs. The king, who was very protective of his wife and children, commissioned the finest goldsmith, Onkyuk, to make six Apotropaic Medallions. He was not a superstitious man, but believed life was a balance of good and evil. Other than his watchful eye, he felt the medallions would aid in averting any evil that might come upon his family. The king gave Onkyuk a drawing his scribes made from his instructions, along with each child's personal stone they were given at birth to protect them. The medallions were five-sided and had five different colored stones, representing each child and their birth month. The queen's would have the same, but a large sea pearl was to be centered in hers representing the undying protection a mother gives her child. It took Onkyuk many months to finish the costly medallions. Nevertheless, and as he promised King Mattaheus, they were the grandest creation he had ever constructed.

"And so, on the fifth *evening* hour, of the fifth month, of its fifth day, Queen Oonaphelia presented King Mattaheus with their beautiful daughter, Lapria. She was born like her mother, with flaxen hair, cream-colored skin, and light blue eye color. She also bore a strange dark mark on her back unlike anything the queen and king ever saw. But it did not matter to them, for they felt it was a sign that their daughter was destined for something great.

"Things were going well for us in Rhondra, until a horrible plague came upon our city. One by one, the royal sons fell ill and died. Then sadly the king became victim to the plague, and Lapria lost her father at the age of four. The entire city of Rhondra mourned greatly for their king. He was a good king and humble man, but alas, his people knew Queen Oonaphelia would be just as good a ruler. So the queen took over Rhondra as its sole ruler and did so successfully. It was not long after that she began to school Lapria about all royal matters. For one day, she would be Rhondra's next queen.

"On Lapria's fifth birthday, she decided it was time to introduce her to the wonders of her creatures. However, she chose only those who she knew could be trusted and would be loyal to her. This is when I met our future queen, and this is when the queen discovered Lapria had many of her special gifts.

"Matthew, are you understanding all of what I speak?" Emia asked.

"Sort of. I'm following your story, but I don't see the connection to me, other than the same birth date we share."

"As long as you are following this story, you will see the connection soon, I promise."

"Okayyyy," Matthew said with a gaping yawn.

"Now, southeast of Rhondra, near a delta of the Nile River, was another small kingdom.

This city's name was Adelann, and it was ruled by King Paul and Queen Ceraphy. They too had a peaceful kingdom and did not bother much outside their walls with others. They also lost their sons to the plague. Queen Ceraphy had a daughter and oddly, on the same day Lapria was born. Her name was Dorundia, and she came on the fifth *morning* hour, of the fifth month, on its fifth day. King Paul, who was very rich with gold, also went to Onkyuk and had him create a rare object, elegant and unique as his precious daughter. It was to represent his five children and the day of Dorundia's birth. Onkyuk took the challenging job with excitement and finished this beautiful crafted item two years later. It was a five-sided pyramid, encrusted with five jewels and hand-carved with intricate designs. It was exquisite, and Onkyuk called it a '**Heptchepak.**'

"Now, while Onkyuk was working on this item, Queen Ceraphy went to him in secret. She asked him to make a chamber so that she could place a large sea pearl into it. Queen Ceraphy had Onkyuk swear to secrecy and that he was to tell no one of the chamber or pearl. He vowed his secrecy by cutting his finger and the queen taking in some of his blood. It was a vow never to be broken, not even in death. However, Onkyuk was a very clever man, and kept a diary of all his creations and whom they were for. Some say he too was a gifted man with unusual powers. I never knew of any of this to be true, nor did our queen, but she never underestimated him or the rumors heard about him.

"Anyway, when Dorundia was about seven years old, Queen Ceraphy was to birth a son. Halfway through the queen's pregnancy, Dorundia began showing disdain for her sibling to be. The king and queen could not understand why, as she seemed to be a very happy, loving child. However, Dorundia had a very dark side to her, and it exemplified her selfishness and jealousy. She was a clever girl, and knowing her brother would inherit the throne of Adelann, she began to plot terrible, unimaginable things against him, while still in his mother's womb. She was going to rule Adelann, no matter what she had to do. When Dorundia was ten years old, her father passed away. Now, word got out about King Paul's death. Lapria, being a sweet and caring person, sent a message to Dorundia and her mother saying how sorry she and Queen Oonaphelia were to hear of the king's passing and offered great condolences to them and the people of Adelann. Now, Dorundia never knew of Lapria, and being a wicked child who envied everyone, Dorundia became enraged!

"'I will be the first female queen, and no other shall be in this land,' Dorundia screamed to her mother.

"'This is not to be, Dorundia. Besides, Lapria has her own kingdom. She wants nothing of *you*, child! What has become of the sweet girl I bore to this world?' she asked, looking horrified at her daughter.

"Dorundia did not dare anger her mother. Nor did she want her to know what evil she plotted. So she soothed her mother with kindness and asked for her forgiveness. Queen Ceraphy, though, was also a gifted seer who had magical powers. As cunning as Dorundia was, Queen Ceraphy knew Dorundia's heart was cold and growing black.

"Therefore, in light of Dorundia's behavior, Queen Ceraphy assigned a person to watch over her daughter in secret. The queen knew that even her life could be in jeopardy. Still, she had hopes her daughter would change her ways and see that her evil thinking was wrong.

"As Dorundia grew, so did her thirst for power. She decided that one day she would empower many kingdoms, and the first would be Rhondra. Her plans also included getting rid of her brother. Dorundia had inherited great magical powers from her mother, and as she mastered these powers, she befriended many creatures that were most feared. She made her creatures wicked in nature and ordered them to do terrible, unthinkable things. She delighted in the fear she brought to others behind her mother's back, and the more she destroyed, the stronger her power grew.

"Now, by the time Dorundia was fourteen, her inherent nature and love for black magic had matured. Her knowledge of evil spells and deadly elixirs became known all through Egypt. Some say she used magic worse than that of the *Book of the Dead*.

"The woman assigned to watch over Dorundia by Queen Ceraphy was one of her high priestesses, but she fell into a dark spell Dorundia cast upon her. She enslaved her with her powers, and she did whatever Dorundia ordered her to do. This woman still reported to the queen, but lied to her about Dorundia's be-havior. Things got so bad that kingdoms near and far kept their distance in fear of her. The once admired and peaceful Kingdom of Adelann was now known as *"City of Evil."* With her power-ful magic and obedient creatures, Dorundia plotted terrible, un-speakable deeds. This time, though, it would be the death of her brother, then of Lapria.

"Now, Queen Ceraphy had a very trusted creature. His name was **Rhabah.** Rhabah was a great, noble, and trusted ally of the queen's. He was a majestic golden falcon with the power of a hun-dred men and vast heavenly knowledge. His only downfall was that Queen Ceraphy made him vow that he was to be a watchful eye over her kingdom, but never was he to bring any harm to her children. Rhabah and I were friends, Matthew. He told me much of what happened in Adelann.

"One day Rhabah came to me and told a story that would change the lives of many. Dorundia had her brother slain and made it look like an accident. She asked her brother to come to her room late in the night, as she had a great secret to reveal to him about the kingdom he would soon rule. But Dorundia's most trusted creature, who guarded her, thought that he was a thief invading her room. This creature, out of all she possessed, was the most feared. No one . . . ever dared to cross Dorundia because of him. Everyone feared his wrath. He was the '**Egyptian Black Jaw Wasp'** *called Rhuckcha!*

"Rhuckcha was the biggest of any wasps ever known. His size was that of a wild jackal, and his appetite, like a herd of fe-ral dogs. The jaws and teeth he possessed had such strength that he could tear apart a man and swallow him in three bats of an eye! His massive red body had thick black stripes with hair as sharp as knives. Rhuckcha's eyes were fiery red, and they would put his victims in a hypnotic state before he ravaged their bodies. However, nothing compared to his large stinger that was as large and sharp as a slaughtering blade. Yes . . . Rhuckcha was a mighty killing creature that all of us feared.

"Soon after her brother's death, Dorundia planned the demise of Lapria and Queen Oonaphelia. When Rhabah came to me with all this information, I quickly informed my mistress of her evil plans. After that day, our queen took to writing, closed up in her room. We were told by Zara not to enter her royal chamber until we were called upon. When she was finished, she gathered the three of us and a few others. She told us she was going to make a trip and be gone for a few weeks. But while she was away, we were to guard Lapria with our lives. I insisted upon accompanying her, fearing for her safety, but she would not have it. She told me I was needed here and that Zara would be traveling with her and a small army. Our queen returned several weeks later looking ill and filled with worry. She ordered us to a meeting the following day, where we were sworn to secrecy and never to speak of what she said. It was on that day we pledged to protect a great heir, said to come in the future. That heir is you, Matthew.

"This is how the prophecy began, Matthew, and all, I'm afraid, that I can reveal to you. The rest of what you seek is in that book. The rest of all you must know will come from reading the words."

Matthew sat up. He took a deep breath, looked at Oopi, Amora, and Emia. Daniel stared at Matthew intently. Somehow Matthew seemed different at that moment. He peered out the window for some time at the bright yellow moon that seemed close enough to touch. He paced a minute or two, then stopped and coldly stared at Emia.

"Tell me, Emia, what is the connection I have to this story and these people from thousands of years ago? **Tell me now!**" he repeated angrily.

"Matthew . . . both families are related to you. In Rhondra, it was King Mattaheus . . . *Nomrahaufa*. In the Kingdom of Adelann, it was . . . King Paul *Sherapha!*"

"You are their heir because you carry the blood of both families," Oopi said softly. "Your grandmother is a Nomrahaufa, and your grandfather was a Sherapha. Your grandmother is the first female heir since Lapria and Dorundia. How or why this happened is irrelevant at this point, but you must accept who you are," Oopi added.

Matthew seemed to just collapse onto the floor. He put his head down into his hands and remained that way.

"I think we all should get some rest . . . and as far as that book is concerned, we can get to it in the morning," Daniel said as he put his hand firmly on Matthew's shoulder.

"Oopi, what about the dreams and Escursia—is there something we can do so I don't have them anymore?"

"**WHAT!**" shrieked Emia. "Why has no one told me of this yet?!" she demanded bitterly.

"This is why we had to call you, Emia; things are not as they should be," Oopi sighed, twisting his stubby fingers together nervously.

"Matthew, please tell Emia of your dreams," Amora said.

"That will not be necessary, Amora! Matthew, you will sleep without her dread, at least for tonight," she assured him.

"Thanks, Emia," Matthew whispered softly to her.

"Daniel, fetch my bags. The three of us must sleep and in the morning will be ready for some hearty eating. Can you oblige us?" Oopi asked.

"Yes, Oopi, I will take care of you all; no need to worry," Daniel assured him.

Daniel put the three creatures in the closet and pulled out a sleeping bag. He unrolled it and placed it next to the bed.

"What are you doing, Dan? My grandmother fixed the room up next door for you."

"Look, Matthew, I am not too sure I want to leave you alone. Just go to sleep knowing I am here for you, okay?"

Matthew watched as Daniel climbed awkwardly into the sleeping bag. He became frustrated and started mumbling under his breath as he struggled getting the zipper to work.

"Ah . . . Dan . . . would you like me to tuck you in?" he laughed.

Daniel flopped around, and then turned so he could see Matthew. The full moon was bright and beamed a thick gold ray through the window onto Daniel's face. The boys started laughing and kidding around about how they were afraid of the dark, even at their age. Then, Daniel got serious and sat up.

"Matt, do you think you could be in any kind of danger? I mean, if all this stuff is true, has that crossed your mind? Don't you think . . . well . . . maybe it might be a good idea if we told your grandmother what was going on?"

"Yes, Daniel, it has, but I am going to have to trust what Oopi told me. He said they were here to help and protect me. As far as me telling Nana, I don't think so, not yet, anyway. Eventually I will, but not until I fully understand what's really going on. Oh, I forgot to tell you . . . Nana said you didn't have to go to school tomorrow if you didn't want to. She figured since we had all our work and school was going to be out the end of the week for vacation that it was no biggie."

"Thanks, buddy. . . . *Now* you tell me! I've been freaking out how I was going to get up in a few hours, geez!"

"Sorry, but I've had other things on my mind the last six hours."

"Ah . . . yes, King Matthew, you sure have!"

Matthew sat up, grabbed his extra pillow, and threw it at Dan. "Careful, I might make you my jester!" he laughed.

"Har . . . har . . . har . . . very funny, your royal hineyness," Daniel said as he turned over and pulled the sleeping bag over his head.

"Thanks, Dan," Matt whispered.

"Huh . . . for what?" Daniel asked, poking his head out from the sleeping bag.

"For being such a good friend, Dan."

"Yeah, yeah, good night, King Matthew. . . . Your jester is tired," he said with a yawn.

Chapter Fourteen

Matthew awoke at 6 a.m., and Daniel was still asleep. He knew Annabelle would be up, and decided to go downstairs and get some breakfast. On his way down, he smiled to himself. There were no nightmares last night, and he didn't have to go to school today! He thought the day was turning out to be very good so far!

"Good morning, Annabelle. How are you today?" he chirped happily.

"Ah, me, I'm doing good; tired, but good."

"What's wrong, Annabelle? No offense, but you look terrible!"

"I wake with terrible headache this morning. Must be some kind of bug going around," she said, holding her head.

"Well, go back to bed. Nana and I can manage around here."

"Oh, I know that, silly, but I will wait till Pearle gets up to see what her plans are today. Maybe I take a nap later. Matthew, I make potato and egg omelet for breakfast. I even put your favorite cheese in too!"

"Oh, yeah; I'm drooling! I swear, Annabelle, you must be psychic!"

"Why you say that, Matt?" she asked in a serious tone.

"Why? . . . Because, I've been craving this for weeks!"

"Okay, so now you no crave; you eat," she said, laughing.

"You know, Annabelle, Daniel loves this too. I hope you made plenty," he said, stuffing his face.

"Me know. I made a triple batch because Daniel has unfillable stomach!"

Annabelle and Matthew were laughing hysterically when Pearle came into the kitchen.

"Oh, you two are enjoying your morning way too much for me," Pearle said, yawning and stretching.

"Morning, Nana!"

"Good morning, Pearle."

"Umm, something smells delicious! What have you made this morning, Annabelle?"

"It's potato and egg omelet, Pearle."

"Gosh, you spoil us, Annabelle!"

"It is my pleasure to do so," she said, chuckling.

"Where's Daniel?" Pearle asked.

"He's asleep. We were up pretty late working on our assignment."

"Well, then, let him sleep," she said, yawning again.

"Gosh, I don't know why I'm so tired this morning. I slept really good last night too. Oh, well, a couple cups of coffee, and I'll be good to go," Pearle said as she buried her head in the morning news and sipped her coffee.

"Nana, what did Robert say about everything yesterday?"

Pearle put her paper down, removed her glasses, and took another sip of her coffee.

"Well, the items he showed us will have to go to the FDLE (Florida Department of Law Enforcement) in Tallahassee. Once they have done all their tests, they are going to have an expert come in to consult on the results, and this expert will give his opinion on their findings. Robert thinks it will take about six weeks before we hear anything. So as far as I know, nothing yesterday brought them any closer to any answers we are looking for."

"Did Robert say if he was coming with us Thursday, or does he have to stay and meet us later?"

"He said he would let me know today what his plans would be, Matt. He's coming for dinner, so we can ask him then."

"All right, Nana, that sounds good. Oh, by the way, Annabelle isn't feeling too well this morning. I told her to go back to bed and that we could handle everything, but you know her. A stubborn mule is easier to coax then Annabelle!"

"I believe you are right," Pearle said, laughing.

"Ah, I see the laughter has caught up to you, Pearle," Annabelle said, smiling, as she came from the laundry room.

"How are you? Matthew said you aren't feeling too good today."

"I'm better now. I had a headache earlier, but I took medicine. Thank God, because I wanted to chop my head off!"

"Are you sure, Annabelle?"

"Of course; you no worry. I would tell you if I no feel good, Pearle."

"You sure . . . because it would be no problem if you wanted to go stay in bed."

"Oye, mamma mia, I'm a feeling just fine! As a matter of fact, I was thinking of going for a swim when I finish putting laundry away."

"You know, that sounds like a great idea!" Pearle said, perking up. "After I am done with the paper, I think I'll join you! Some exercise will do us both good. Then, this afternoon, I had better start packing. We leave in two days, and I haven't given one thought to what I am going to bring for this trip! Which reminds me, have you started to pack your suitcase yet, Matthew?"

"No, Nana, I haven't, but I figured out what I'm going to bring. It won't take me long. Don't worry, I'll make sure I get that done by tomorrow morning."

"That sounds good to me! So what have you and Daniel got planned for the day?"

Matthew hesitated, then said, "We are going to try to finish that report we started and do some more schoolwork. We don't want to take that much with us," he added, knowing he was lying.

Matthew, again, for the umpteenth time, found himself lying to the most important person in his life. He despises liars! He tried to soothe himself and take away his guilty feelings by telling himself Pearle would know everything as soon as he did.

"Do you guys need any help?" she asked.

"Oh . . . no . . . Nana, but thanks anyway. We . . . we can handle this," Matthew said in a nervous, giddy tone.

Pearle looked at her grandson and was sure that her instincts from the other night were correct. *Something is going on*, she thought as she nonchalantly looked over at him. *Hmm* . . . .

"So what is this report you are working on, Matt?" she asked as innocently as possible.

"Oh, ah . . . Daniel and I are to write about Egypt. Mr. Haram picked that for us. He thought with this trip and all that we would enjoy this kind of essay."

"Sounds like Abe knew what he was doing. You and Daniel will be able to give a firsthand review of Egypt! But how can you do this report, Matthew . . . if you've never been to Egypt?" Now she was looking good and hard at him to see his reaction. Matthew had this all figured out, or so he thought!

"Nana, Dan and I will fill in the blanks as we experience Egypt! Right now, we are just getting facts done by doing research on the computer. That's a lot of work! We aren't sure if we will have time or access to a computer in Egypt! It will be a great report, Nana, I'm sure of it!"

"All right, Matt, if you say so. My offer still stands, though. If you need any help, I do know a lot about Egypt."

"Thanks, and we might need your expertise, but for right now, Dan and I have it under control."

"Okay; good luck with it, then," she said, smiling, and picked up her newspaper, again wondering what he was up to.

"Gooooood morning, everyone!"

"Good morning to you, Dan! How'd you sleep?"

"Pretty good, Pearle, thanks!"

"Matthew tells me you boys were up late working on your assignment, gathering some information."

"Ah . . . yeah . . . yeah . . . we have a lot of facts to still gather, **DON'T WE, MATTHEW?!**"

"Yes, I was telling Nana we were up late doing our research on the project."

"I see A-pluses for us on this one, Matt!"

"Heck, yeah! We should get a good mark, Dan. This is going to be *some* project," Matthew said in a sarcastic way, looking at Daniel and rolling his eyes.

"Sooo . . . what's for breakfast?"

"Potato and eggs, Dan—your favorite!"

"Whooo eeee, sounds yummy, Annabelle! I'm starving," Dan said as he sat at the marble breakfast bar with Matthew.

Annabelle had her head in the refrigerator, taking inventory for her grocery list.

"I guess you really like broccoli, Dan," she said, adding it to her grocery list. Matthew kicked Daniel under the breakfast bar, then shot him a look with his blue eyes just as wide as they could be!

"I guess you could say I am acquiring a taste for healthier foods," he said, laughing.

"Oh," Pearle said, "when did this come about, Dan?"

"When Mom said I needed to make better choices in my food. I promised her I would do my best. I'm sorry that I ate all your broccoli, though, Pearle."

"Ha hah, hah," Pearle laughed, "don't be sorry, Daniel; Annabelle and I will pick some more up today when we shop."

"Oh, ah . . . thanks, Pearle." And Dan gave Matthew a hard kick to his shins. Matthew grimaced, then smiled when he noticed Pearle watching them.

"He's such a card, isn't he, Nana?"

"Yeah, a real joker," she replied in a coy, but sarcastic, tone.

"Well, there is cauliflower and still more grapes, Dan, for you in there," Annabelle commented.

"Thanks, Annabelle. I'll have them for my snack today."

"Hey, Dan, maybe you can get your partner in crime there to get on this healthy kick too," Pearle said, raising her eyebrows sharply.

"I'll give it a shot, but I can't make any promises," Dan said jokingly.

"Don't either one of you hold your breath," Matthew said, pointing at them both.

"Now, if no one needs anything else, I go change and put my swimsuit on."

"Yes, I'm gonna change too. . . . I'll see you by the pool in a few minutes, Annabelle," Pearle said. "If you boys need us, you know where we will be."

"I feel like a juvenile delinquent! This is awful," Dan said to Matthew in a hushed voice.

"What are you talking about, Dan?" Matthew asked, trying to keep his voice low too.

"Your grandmother, that's what! I hate having to lie to her, Matt!"

"Oh, so you think I enjoy lying to her? My guts are in an

uproar! I feel like I ate twelve hot dogs and went on that spinning ride at the fair I hate so much! I know she knows something is up. Did you see how she reacted to you eating broccoli? She *never* raises her eyebrows that high!" Dan looked at Matthew, and they both started to crack up.

"It will all be okay," Dan said, trying to be serious. "All of this stuff happening, Matt, is for a reason. Let's hope today we will find out exactly what it is, though."

"Ya think! They had better have some answers today, Dan. Which reminds me, when you're finished, we need to bring them some food. Oh, and you need to get your muddy clothes clean. We will have to wash them out in the bathroom first. Then, when Nana and Annabelle go shopping, we can do a load of laundry. If Nana sees your clothes covered with all that muck, we are dead meat, Dan!"

"Matt, you don't think . . . that . . . she will go in your room while we are down here, do you?"

"Nah . . . . She has no reason to."

PLOP . . . . *"I'd like an explanation!"*

Matthew and Daniel slowly turned around. Their bodies became stiff as a board! Standing behind them, wrapped in a towel over her swimsuit, was Pearle, and not looking too happy either. She dropped Daniel's muck-ridden clothes on the floor behind them. Her eyebrows now arched much higher than at breakfast. Matthew knew he was in big trouble and had better think of something quick. **THINK, THINK, THINK**, he thought to himself as he panicked!

"All right, Nana, I'll tell you what happened," he said.

"This better be good, buddy!" she screeched and was all red in the face.

"It was a dare, Nana."

"What do you mean, a dare?" she said with a ferocious tsk, raising her arms up in the air.

"It's my fault, Pearle," Daniel interrupted.

"Oh? Well, explain yourself, Mr. Fuscilli," she hissed, nearly foaming at the mouth.

"I bet, Matthew . . . errr."

"Yes, go ahead, go on," she urged, with her eyebrows arched high on her forehead.

"Nana, we were betting each other who was more afraid of the dark. Then I double dared Dan to run down to the lake and back since he said I was the bigger chicken."

"Yeah . . . that's it, Pearle!" Dan said, looking wild-eyed, while shaking his head up and down! "He . . . he bet his new Wii game that if I would do that, I was less of a chicken than him!"

"Really!" Pearle responded while tapping her foot with her arms crossed and looking questionably at them both. "Boys, I am disappointed in you both! It's dangerous at night by that lake. There are **gators** and who knows what else creeping around down there at that hour!"

"We are sorry, Nana, *really.*"

"So . . . do I want to know how your clothes got all mucked up, Dan?"

"Oh, that . . . um . . . I . . . kinda . . . tripped, Pearle. I never was a graceful runner. You know me, ha hah ha, Mr. Klutz O!"

"And you boys expect me to buy that story?"

"What are you talking about, Nana?" Matthew asked, trying to look sincere. "We did a stupid thing, but we are sorry!"

"For sure, it was *crazy,* and I apologize for being an idiot!" Daniel added.

"It won't ever happen again, Nana, we promise. Don't *we,* Daniel," Matt said, holding up his right hand as if he were swearing in at court.

"You bet your bottom dollar, young man, that will never happen again, will it?" she said, looking stiff-faced at both of them. She picked up the clothes and went off to the laundry room in a tizzy! Matthew went after her and offered to do the laundry himself.

"No, let Annabelle do this! I'm sure she will have better luck getting all that yuck out!"

"Nana, please . . . don't be mad. I hate when you're upset at me."

"You know . . . I couldn't care less if your shenanigans were in the daytime, but at night! It was a very foolish thing to do only because of the dangers. Can you understand that?"

"Yes, I do."

"Then it's forgotten, as long as you promise you won't do any more midnight runs to the lake!"

"Absolutely; you have my word!"

"Good, now I'm going for a swim and to lie in the sun awhile. . . . Come give your grandmother a hug . . . you stinker!" Matthew gave her a big hug and squeezed her real tight, then kissed her cheek.

"And what was that for?" she asked, surprised.

"Because you are the best, and I love you very much," he said, walking away. Pearle shook her head and thought, *Boys . . . they are full of adventure!*

"So how'd it go?" Daniel asked.

"She's okay, but we definitely have to be careful from now on. Boy, that was a close call!"

"So what's next, breakfast for our visitors?"

"Yeah, gotta bring them food. I just don't know what else Emia eats other than honey," he said, staring into the refrigerator.

"Well, she did a pretty good job on that poor little frog last night," Daniel said with a grimace.

"Ugh . . . yuck, right! She sure did! But we can't go to the lake again. Nana will be fit to be tied!"

"No . . . I don't think so. . . . Remember . . . she said not to go at night. . . ."

"Gosh, little buddy, I'm sorry, but, oh, Matt, I can't do this," Dan said sorrowfully to the chirping frog he caught at the lake.

"Just give him to me! I'll give it to Emia. Just don't look when she eats it," Matt said, swallowing and feeling nauseated about the whole idea himself.

They made a tray of food for Oopi and the girls, and headed back to the bedroom.

Daniel got the leather bag from the closet, and Matthew put out all the food on his bed. Slowly, one by one, Oopi, Amora, and Emia emerged from the bag.

"Good morning, purehearted one," Amora cooed as she batted her long, lush lashes at the boys. "Oh, it is going to be a glorious day." And she zipped around the bedroom, happy as could be.

"My dear, ha, ha, ha . . . . I'm glad to see you so lighthearted today," Emia said to Amora, amused by her giddy mood. "And you, my dear heir, did you rest peacefully last night?" she asked Matthew.

"Yes, I did, thanks. . . ."

"Well, boy, I see you brought a feast for us! My grumbling tummy is going to have some yum, yummies!" Oopi said, bouncing happily over to the food.

While they ate, Matthew retrieved the book from under the bed. He ran his hand along the gold binding, then continued to trace the outline of the family medallion with his fingers. *Two families,* he thought, and wondered what Dorundia had done. She surely sounded like she was evil. *But what could all this have to do with me?* he kept thinking. *So what that I'm related! What does this have to do with anything?* . . . Emia turned from her nectar and looked at him.

"You will learn of all this soon, very soon," she said, and turned to finish her food.

"Matthew," Oopi began, "your medallion is needed to open the book."

"I do not have one yet, Oopi. Nana said I will receive mine on my thirteenth birthday."

"Oh, this is great," Matthew said in disgust. "Now what do we do? Did I mention also that someone took it and two others?"

"I truly am sorry for that," Emia said, "but the female heir's will work too."

"You want me to go take my grandmother's medallion? It's not bad enough that I've been lying to her; now I gotta go steal her necklace! This is what you want me to do, right?" Matthew was all red in the face. His anger was beyond his frustration, and he knew it. But he realized if this was the only way to open the book, he had to get the medallion. He paced his room. Finally, he stopped and looked at Daniel.

"Oh, no . . . no, you don't! I don't want any part of stealing," Dan said quickly! Then Daniel remembered that he promised to help, *no matter what!* "Oh, geez, all right. What do you need me to do, Matt?" Dan said, exhaling and shaking his head.

"Thanks, buddy. Okay, Dan, I need you to go downstairs. I'll sneak into Nana's room and get the medallion. If she comes in, you need to fly up those steps and let me know!"

"What happens if you get caught? Have you thought about that?"

"Dan, we are just going to have to wing it here. I don't know what else to do."

"Matthew, listen, we only need the medallion to open the book. Then you can put it right back," Oopi said, assuring him.

"I was hoping you'd say that, Oopi," Daniel said nervously.

Before Matthew and Daniel left, they decided to do their brotherly ritual. They stood facing each other with their foreheads together. Then they chanted, "Brothers from the beginning, brothers to the end, and always, we will be friends!"

Then they punched their knuckles together, jumped up, and banged their chest together as they gave each other high fives.

"Such *odd* behavior . . . what is this?" asked Oopi.

"I'll explain it to you later. Right now, I just want to get that medallion," Matthew said.

Daniel went downstairs, and Matthew waited for the *okay* sign from Dan. He whistled twice, and Matthew knew it was safe to get the medallion. They were back in less than five minutes.

Matthew held the medallion from the chain, and Oopi seemed mesmerized as he gazed at it with his bouncing eyes.

"Now take the medallion, and place it on the book. Then, in your own words, ask that it open for you," Emia instructed as she, Oopi, and Amora stood back.

"Ah, book. . . . I am Matthew, the heir," he started, and looked at Emia and Oopi for guidance.

"Go on, boy," Oopi prodded, "you are doing fine. Just tell it what you want; go ahead," he said.

"Please, can you open up? . . . I want to read what it is that I must know."

Matthew had his hand on the medallion when he felt the book jerk, and then heard a click. His hand began to tremble. Amora fluttered onto Matthew's hand as if to soothe him and assure him it was okay. Emia flew over quickly to the book and opened the cover.

"Good, now go put the medallion back," Emia ordered Matthew softly.

Matthew carefully put the medallion back in Pearle's room. He made sure that nothing looked disturbed and then got Daniel. When they opened the door, Emia, Amora, and Oopi were sitting by the book, waiting for him. Matthew's hands began to sweat, and his stomach was twisting. He wasn't sure now if he wanted to know what this book had to reveal to him.

"Come on, boy," Oopi said, seeing his hesitation. "You must come and read her words," he said in a bit of a snit.

"Go on, Matthew, you know you need to do this. At least you will have your answers," Dan reminded him.

Matthew slowly sat on the bed, placed the heavy, ornate book in his lap, and turned the old yellowed page. He ran his hand over the thick paper and felt its roughness. *Papyrus*, he thought to himself. Daniel sat on the floor in front of him. "Go on, buddy, read it," he said anxiously.

Your mark allows you my voice
I will reveal much to you true heir
I grow close to death and treason
Heed . . . Beware
Listen closely purehearted one to the reason
Danger grows for my child, Her mark you share
Two seek Her and Her power for the chair
Hast little they know a curse surely grows
For one with powers as I
Creates dark forces under the sky
My child to be cast into the darkness of the sea
Unknown to her destroyer a wrath returned
And on land forever shall she roam
Greed has brought this darkness
On their land and our green sea
You will be the one true heir

To set them free
For one carries the blood of the other
Shared life was to be
So seek the one who spoils the blood
Undo her evil deed
QO

Matthew didn't have to read it. The voice of Queen Oonaphelia spoke to him. Her voice was calm and soothing. He felt her words as if she were there, in the flesh, speaking aloud.

"Oopi, Emia, what does this mean?" Matthew asked in a calm, even tone.

"There is more, Matthew. You must continue to read now and figure this out. We can only then answer what is permitted," Emia replied.

"Daniel, did you hear her?" Matthew asked, looking at his friend for reassurance that this was all really happening.

"Yes, I did. Go ahead; turn the page. See what else she has to say," he encouraged him.

Matthew was reluctant to go on. Her voice was calm, but he sensed an urgency in the message. What if he read everything and still didn't know what all this was about? Could Oopi and Emia really explain the truth to him?

"Matthew," Amora cooed as she flitted on his hand. You have been visited by three strange creatures and been told you are of royalty. The book reveals what seems strange and impossible. We understand this must be difficult for you to accept. You must believe with your pure heart that what is written *is* your destiny. Sometimes we choose not what happens to us, but it chooses us. All that seems impossible is not, dear heir. You are the prophesied one, and we, chosen for you. Be not afraid of what lies ahead. For your pure heart will overcome any evil you will encounter. No matter what happens, learn to trust yourself, for you are your best ally. Read her words and trust, for only then can all be revealed. Open your heart and your mind. Let it all befall the way it is to be." Matthew seemed to understand the little creature's calming words, and he turned the page to go on.

This book hast been opened by the true male heir
Tis past twelve years of laughter and tears
His history is rich and so is he
The womb of his life fades deep within the sea
The fortune of kings lay before thee
A collection better than gold
Your treasure to be
Amongst your riches you shall see
Special pouches that will assist thee
Thou will be befriended by many you meet
Your journey long, with perilous feats
Your pure heart will guide you along the way
Keep strong-minded be it night or day
The enemies shall be plenty you will see
Some who will falsely tempt you
And steer you away from she
A sea of trouble
On land too they seek
Your task with the Heptchepak is yours to complete
Five tasks for the Heptchepak
For it should hold the sea
It is what she waits for
So you must succeed
To the salty bottom this you must deliver for me
Hence then my dear daughter can be set free
QO

Today the dark one cast evil about
Tomorrow her blood will scream and shout

The blood is four thick her knowledge is none
The dark one will live as she cast upon

Her creatures are great
They obey with true faith
Their spells you'll encounter
Oh young heir don't wait

The good one will guide thee
Her creatures will too
You will have many but none are more true
Hast no fear they will provide safety for you

Take heart dear heir
Five quests you will need
Your life to be spared
If you shall succeed
QO

The first female heir will be spared
The second will be brought home to the throne
She will becometh my slave entrapped in the sea
Only one with a pure heart can set her free
There were but two
One light and one dark
They were to rule many
Their life was to start
One to rule by land
The other by sea
But greed took the pleasure of ruling
And a land of beauty that wasn't hers to be
Her greed to have both cast her into empty eternity
Both bloods are cursed so beware
She will falsely tempt oh you true heir
The evil dark one seeks you
The kind one too who is fair
Gather their wishes and your womb will be spared
QC

Now my dear heir both bloods you have heard
There is much importance in all our words
Take what has been giveth to thee
Come to my chamber it faces north to the sea
There you will find all you will need
The five quests await you with dangers to be

Your success will be noted
Her life freed from the greed
Five elements of life you shall seek
Each one to get you mustn't be weak
Their colors are bright but hidden you'll find
Your allies will guide you do not be blind
Seek with a pure heart
Find strength in your love
Don't get discouraged
For though not promised you can rise above
QO

Matthew placed the book on the bed. All eyes were on him. He took Oopi in his hands and began to speak.

"Oopi . . . I think I know what is being asked of me. I am not sure exactly how or where, but I must go on five quests to save someone, and I will have help. There will be danger and evil to face. Is this what she is telling me?" he asked.

"Yes, Matthew, it is what she has asked of you."

"Oopi, tell me why I must do what she is asking. Why is it so important, though?"

"You share the blood of **all** involved. That is the most important reason, dear heir."

"So . . . what you are saying is that there is more to this than you are able to tell me."

"Yes, Matthew, there is truth in what you say. All reasons will be revealed, when it is time . . . she promised that."

"Well, I guess I better get packing," Matthew said as he put Oopi back on the bed.

"You took all this in pretty lightly, Matt," Daniel said.

"No, I didn't, Dan. It is what it is. You want to hear something even stranger? I have a gut feeling my mother is somehow involved in all this!"

"*What!*" Daniel said, in a shrill voice.

"Dan, don't ask; just believe me, and leave it at that!" Matt said angrily.

"Fine, I will not say any more," and Daniel stomped off to the bathroom.

"Matthew, do not be upset with your friend. He is of true heart to you and is worried of your safety," Emia said with a scolding tone.

"Oh, geez, don't you think I know that, Emia?" he said with an icy tone. "You guys have to realize I am only a kid. I just don't know what everyone expects of me! All I wanted to do was go to Egypt, visit the pyramids and some museums. Now I'm gonna be on some sort of wild and dangerous saving adventure! Can you possibly understand how I feel and why, Emia?"

"Yes, yes, we do, Matthew. That is why we are here. Trust, trust us in all we say, and everything will turn out better than you could have ever dreamed, dear heir."

"I guess at this point I have no other choice, now do I?" he said as he faced them.

"Listen to me, boy," Oopi said. "You have greater knowledge than most your age! So do not feel as if you are a mere boy! For you are a young man of great qualities. Qualities that many kings have desired and only few have possessed!"

"Oopi is right, Matthew," Daniel said, standing behind him.

"Oh, Dan, I didn't hear you come out of the shower," he said apologetically.

"Matthew, let's go for a walk or play with the dogs. You need to get away from all this for a while."

"Your good friend is right," Oopi added. "We will sleep and see you this evening. Come, Daniel, help us to get in our bag."

Daniel helped them in their bag and set it in the closet. He decided he wasn't going to mention anything to Matthew unless he wanted to speak about it. Matthew and Daniel then headed downstairs and out the back door.

Chapter Fifteen

"Come on, Dan, or we're going to miss our flight!" urged Robert. "What did that kid eat last night? He's been in there fifteen minutes!"

Matthew laughed and said, "Ask me what he didn't eat!"

Daniel finally came out of the airport's bathroom, shaking his wet hands in the air, his shirt untucked, and his wet backpack hanging off one shoulder . . . looking like he just climbed out of bed. "I couldn't find any paper towels, and that hand-drying, blowing thing wasn't working."

That's my buddy, Matthew thought to himself. "You all right, Dan?" Matthew asked.

"Yeah, I'm fine! Geez, I just had to go, guys!"

"Come on, boys," Robert said as he turned around, laughing to himself. "Pearle is already at the gate, and the flight leaves in twenty minutes."

"This is awesome, isn't it, Detective Green?" Daniel said, all excited.

"Yes, it is, Dan, but *do* me a favor . . . please call me Robert. . . . I'm on vacation," he said, smiling.

When they got to the gate, Pearle looked relieved. The attendants had just started to board the passengers for first class. The boys loved riding in the first-class section. Dan said the seats were roomier than coach and the movies, way better. First class only had two other couples when they boarded, and the flight attendant told them they could choose whatever empty seats they wanted. After they put their bags under the seats, Daniel thought about the security check they went through and was glad he only had to worry about Matthew's electronics in his carry-on bag. But Matthew had Oopi, Amora, and Emia with him. They were a wreck when he had to go through the screening with them, fearing they'd be detected. After his bag passed through the machine with no problems, Matthew plucked it quickly from the gray plastic bin and breathed a sigh of relief.

It was now 7 a.m. in Egypt, and Matthew figured with the non-stop flight, they should arrive about 3 p.m. He decided to enjoy the flight with Dan and not worry about anything until they got to Egypt!

"*Matt* . . . , come on, get up, we are getting ready to land!"

"Huh? . . . What?"

"Come on, Matt, the stewardess said to sit up and put your seat belt on," Dan said, shaking him. Matthew sat up and looked at his watch. It was three o'clock on the dot.

"Awww . . . ," he said as he stretched. "Hey, dude, you get any sleep?" he asked Daniel while rubbing his eyes.

"Yeah, I think we fell asleep the same time. I just got up a few minutes ago myself."

Matthew looked at Daniel and started laughing. "Dude, you need to do something with that hair!"

"What's wrong with the do, bud?"

"It looks like you were electrocuted, man."

"No way, really?"

"No, Dan, I'm lying to you. Here, use my comb, and good luck getting it through that mess," he laughed.

"Good Lord, Dan, what happened to you?" Pearle said as she was passing their seats. "You look like you were electrocuted! Better put a comb through that, if you can," she said, snickering. Daniel's hair was sticking up in all directions! It looked like he really had been electrocuted!

"Maybe I'll just leave it this way," he yelled to Pearle. "I could start a new trend, you know!"

"Ahh . . . not on my watch," Pearle said, shaking her head and laughing.

Robert looked back when Pearle got to their seats. You could hear them laughing all the way in the back. Robert stood up and yelled back to Dan. "Oh, Danny boy, sorry, but that trend is out! It was called punk in the eighties," he snorted.

"Great, now I am the butt of a joke that probably no one will let me live down this whole trip!"

"Look at it this way," and Matt snapped a picture of him; "you always have been the comic in the group. What a way to start a vacation," Matthew said as he took another picture of his friend.

"Thanks, buddy," Dan said.

"Come on, they've opened the door; let's get outta here! I can't wait to stretch my legs on land again," Matthew said.

"Sol said he arranged a ride for us to the hotel, but I forgot to ask him with whom," Pearle said, feeling rather foolish.

"Let's go upstairs to the outside level. Maybe we can find out there. If not, we can always rent a car and drive ourselves, Pearle," Robert said.

They went to the next level, and a tall bearded man dressed in a dark blue suit turned around. He held a sign that read "Sherapha."

"Oh, look, that must be our ride," exclaimed Pearle.

"Hello, excuse me, I'm Ms. Sherapha."

"Indeed. Welcome; I am Sammy. Mr. Nipuk has hired a car for you and your guest. This way, please," he instructed everyone. "I take your trip was pleasurable, everyone?" Sammy asked.

"Yes, yes, it was nice, but long," Robert replied.

"Please do not worry; I will put bags into car. Just leave here," he said, pointing to the sidewalk. "I be right back with car."

"Whoa! No freaking way . . . an H2!" Daniel roared.

"Now *that* is a vehicle, Pearle," Robert said, running his hands over the shiny black Hummer.

"Are we all going to fit, Sammy?" Pearle asked.

"Yes, of course, madam! No problem; come get in. We have long trip ahead of us to hotel."

When Sammy picked up Robert's suitcase, Robert noticed he was carrying. "What ya carrying, Sam?" Robert asked as he helped him put the suitcases in the back.

"Ah, this is 'Baruk,'" he laughed. "He is 9mm friend I go no-where without, especially when I have such important people in my care."

"Nice," Robert replied.

"Oh, you know of these?" Sammy asked.

"Yes, I am very familiar with them. . . . When I was with the FBI, it was my choice of weapon. I'm a detective now and still carry the same. Good piece of protection, in my opinion," Robert added, patting his side.

"You have no problem taking weapon on plane?" he asked Robert.

"No, not at all. I still can do that," he said with a bit of stiffness. "One of my perks for still working with the bureau," Robert added as he smiled smugly and walked away, leaving Sammy to the rest of the luggage, and got into the Hummer.

"So how long of a ride we got, Pearle?"

"Roughly an hour. But if we have to stop for security checks, it will take longer, Robert."

They arrived at the hotel an hour later. There was only one security check to go through, and they were all glad about that.

"Awesome, Nana, this place looks humongous! Hey, Dan, look at the pool. It's got a giant slide!"

"Sol said we would enjoy the place. He also said there would be something for everyone to enjoy. They have several restaurants in here; all are rated four stars . . . open twenty-four hours a day," Pearle added.

"I hope you enjoy your stay here. It is one of the best hotels we have. Oh, Ms. Sherapha, Mr. Sol has arranged for you to have a vehicle like this one while you are here. The front desk has the keys to it, and if you need anything at all, they will accommodate you completely!"

"Thank you, Sammy," Pearle said graciously.

"I must be off, then," Sammy said after he put their luggage on the valet's rack. "It was very nice to meet you all. I hope your stay here is enjoyable."

"Good afternoon, Ms. Sherapha," said the bald, pudgy front desk clerk. "Your suite is ready. These gentlemen will take you and your bags there. If you are in need of anything, please do not hesitate to let us know. I hope you enjoy your stay with us."

"Thank you. I'm sure we will," Pearle replied as the bellmen took them to the elevator.

"Whoa . . . totally cool . . . . This is *way* awesome, Nana," Matthew said as they came off the elevator and stood frozen in the massive marble foyer. The suite was modern with white marble floors, mahogany wood tables, shelving, and dark leather furniture. And to put it over the top, every room had floor-to-ceiling windows that boasted beautiful views of Egypt! The boys were totally blown away by the sunken living room that had an entire wall dedicated to a built-in aquarium with colorful, exotic fish.

"Remind me to thank Sol," Pearle said to Robert as she plopped herself on the fluffy couch.

"Absolutely," Robert responded as he joined her.

"Nana, Dan and I are going to unpack, okay?"

"Sure, that's a good idea, and when you boys are done, we can go get something to eat if you're hungry."

"I don't know about the rest of you, but I am starving," Robert said.

"Yeah, we are hungry too, Nana!"

"All right, then; we will all meet back here in thirty minutes. Then, we can go downstairs."

"This place is awesome, Matt! By the way, did you see the gaming systems in the living room? This is going to be one awesome vacation!"

"Well, I am glad you like it, Dan. Let's hope the rest of this trip goes as well for us. Hey, don't forget to remind me before we come up after dinner that I have to get Oopi and them food."

"Where are we gonna get that from, and how do we explain that to your grandmother?"

"Don't worry, Dan! If there is one thing I have learned from Nana, that is, if there is a will, there is a way! Listen, let's change so we can get going, and please do something about that hair!"

"Ya know, I don't understand what happened to my hair. I used that hair gel you had in the bathroom this morning. Ah, yuck, it feels so funky," he said as he tried to run his hands through it.

"What hair gel?" Matthew asked him, looking at him weirdly.

"The gel you had on the sink."

"Oh, you idiot," he laughed. You know I don't use stuff in my hair! That was hand sanitizer you used, dorko!"

Daniel's face flushed bright red. "I'll be back; I'm gonna de-sanitize my head," he mumbled, and left to wash his hair.

While everyone was unpacking, Pearle telephoned Sol. She

thanked him for the amazing hotel he arranged for them, and they agreed to meet in the morning at the pyramid. When they all met back in the living room, Pearle gave the boys their own room keys and a credit card. She told them they were free to roam the hotel after dinner, but they had to be back by eight so they could get a good night's sleep, because they were heading out at five the next morning for the pyramid. Matthew and Daniel made it back to the suite by seven forty-five, toting a bag of food for Oopi and the girls. After saying good night to Pearle and Robert, the boys decided to clean up and meet back up when they were done. Daniel, deciding he wasn't in the mood to shower, changed into his nightclothes, had a quick snack, and then went to Matt's room.

"How'd you like the shower, Dan? Mine was awesome!"

"I was too tired to mess with that tonight. Gonna do mine in the morning," Daniel replied with a yawn as he plopped down on the bed, where Oopi and the girls were eating.

"Well, you missed out, buddy," Matthew said as he turned away and bent over his suitcase to get his comfy tee shirt to put on.

"Whoa, dude!" Daniel said, startled, as he jumped off the bed.

Matthew turned around, and his eyes grew wide when he saw the frightened look on his friend's face.

"What's wrong? What is it?" Matthew asked as he swallowed hard.

But Dan didn't answer. He grabbed Matthew's arm, pulled him into the bathroom, and turned him around in front of the big mirror.

"Look," Daniel said as he pointed with a shaky finger at Matt's back.

"Holy . . . cr . . . ap . . . . What the heck?" Matthew gasped, grabbing Dan by his shirt.

Dan went and quickly got Oopi.

"Hmm," Oopi said as he gazed at Matthew's birthmark, which seemed to have grown and looked darker. He then called out to Emia to come quickly.

"They know of his presence," Emia replied, keeping her voice calm as she looked stoically over at Oopi and Amora, who were sitting on the sink, looking stunned.

"Matthew, I think it's time you told your grandmother what's going on! We may be in **wayyyyy** over our heads here," Dan said seriously.

"We can't! Not until I know what this is all about. Not one word to her, *you hear me?!*" he barked while pointing his finger in Daniel's face.

"Chill, buddy. . . . What has gotten into you? I'm just concerned about you, that's all! Look, Matt, I promised, gave you my word that I wouldn't say anything to her, but you *really* need to think about what is going on here! This is just getting too weird! Who knows of his presence?" Dan demanded, turning and looking at Emia. "I want to know what kind of danger Matthew is in!"

"Calm yourself, friend. He will be safe," Amora said assuringly.

"That's not what I asked, Amora! You have to be honest with us and tell what exactly you meant by *'they know,'*" Dan said sternly. "Who are you talking about?"

"Come," Emia said, and they followed her as she flew off to the bedroom. "Tomorrow we go to the resting place. It is there that the souls of the cursed and damned are waiting. They seek you, Matthew, because you will be the one to set them free."

"Boy, you must not let them sway your thinking or emotions. The evil one seeks only for her selfish desires. But there are others, good and pure. They are depending on you to make the right decisions and to fulfill the prophecy. Trust in what I say," Oopi added.

"Once we are in the resting place, Matthew, things will be clear in your mind. You, pure one, are our king now. The evil ones will not like this. . . . But trust me when I say that your protection is a hundredfold over them! That is something no one can change. It was written by the two bloods, and *no one* can change that," Amora assured him.

"Yes, yes, Amora speaks the truth," Oopi assured him. "But there are things that we will not be able to protect you from. As you have been told, your pure heart and love will see you through much, dear heir."

"Matthew, much will be revealed to us too that has not been told from the book. We will go together and shall find the answers we all seek," Oopi said in an assuring way, nodding his head.

"Matthew, you must sleep now," Amora said, soothing him with her tiny hand on his face.

"Tomorrow will come, and so will many answers," she assured Daniel.

"I think I will sleep here with you tonight. I know I won't sleep a wink in the other room worrying about you," Daniel said.

"Well, this bed is big enough," Matt assured him with a smile.

"Come on, guys, I'll get you put away so we can hit the hay," Daniel said.

"Emia will sleep here, outside the bag tonight," Oopi informed Daniel.

"Oh, and why is that?" Dan asked with a curious look.

"That is what she must do, friend. It is her job to protect the heir while he sleeps. Do not ask any more questions, boy," Oopi insisted.

"I'm too tired to argue with you, Oopi," Dan said with a big yawn.

"Come on, Matt, let's go to bed and watch some TV. We have to be up at the crack of darkness, and I sure could use the sleep. It has been a *long* day!"

"Yeah, I'm beat too. Let's see what's on the idiot box," Matt said as he picked up the TV control.

Pearle and Robert were sitting on the balcony of the suite, admiring the views. The lights from the city glowed below them like stars upon a snowy valley. Robert still couldn't believe that he was in Egypt, sitting just a few miles from the Mediterranean Sea.

"This is such a beautiful spot, Pearle. I never realized how amazing it could be here."

"Yes, it is quite lovely."

"Something on your mind, Pearle?"

"I was wondering about the medallions, Robert. Have you heard anything promising yet about the robbery? You know, any leads, as you cops say?"

"Actually, I did speak to Brian tonight, and he said he may have a lead. But he would discuss it in full with me tomorrow. When I called him, I forgot about our time difference, and he was half asleep and not making too much sense. I'm hoping by tomorrow, we will hear something positive, Pearle. Which reminds me, Dr. Hadwick should have Zatu's toxicology report by now," he added.

"Then I'll be hopeful that tomorrow will bring good news, but for now, I better hit the sack. Four a.m. will be here before you know it," she said, yawning. "Good night, Robert. I'll see you in the morning," she said as she gave him a kiss on the cheek.

"Night," he answered, seemingly distracted. And he was. His mind was bursting with questions about the robbery, and he still couldn't fathom the discovery of Oona's medallion in Egypt when she died, he believed, by a gator in Pearle's lake. "Oh, hell, I can't even think straight, I'm so tired," he said aloud. *Maybe I'm losing my touch,* he mumbled to himself, disgusted. He drained the last bit of wine from his glass and headed to his room.

BEEP>>>BEEP>>>BEEP.

"Arrgg . . . it can't be! I feel like I just went to sleep," grumbled Matthew as he flipped his covers off and stared up at the ceiling fan. "Come on, sleeping beauty, time to rise and shine in the land of pyramids and mystery!" But Dan didn't move an inch, even with Matthew flicking at his ear.

"RISE, I say to thee!" Matthew yelled as he jumped up and down on the bed as if it were a trampoline. "Your king has ordered you to rise!" he yelled again.

"Your jester is not listening to you, old pain-in-the-butt sire. . . . Go away, shoo, begone!" Dan said, muffled, with his head buried under his pillow.

"Come on, Dan, get your lazy butt up. . . . Nana will be waiting for us!"

"I'm coming, I'm coming; give me a sec to focus here," Dan said, sitting on the edge of the bed, slumped over.

Matthew packed up Oopi, Amora, and Emia with extra food and put them in his backpack. He got dressed and was waiting patiently on Daniel.

"Ready for today?" Dan asked as he picked up his backpack.

"I guess so. . . . You?"

"Well, I will be after I get something to eat. Let's get going; I'm starved!"

Chapter Sixteen

"This is it," Pearle said as they drove up to the pyramid and parked.

Robert and the boys were absolutely captivated by the enormous polished stone monument that sat in front of them.

"That has to be," Robert said as he tilted his head back, looking up, "I'm guessing . . . at least two hundred feet high. I just can't wrap my head around the idea that they could erect something so grand with primitive equipment."

"Actually, Robert," Pearle responded, chuckling to herself from his childlike amazement, "their secret was water and a specially made sled. The ancient Egyptians were very resourceful, and from what I've seen over the years, quite intelligent!"

"Guys, all I can say is, let's get out of the vehicle, and let me touch it!" Daniel shrieked from the backseat.

Robert noticed a tall, good-looking older man coming toward them. He figured it had to be Sol. When Pearle saw Sol, she ran to him, and he picked her up and swung her around as if she were a little girl.

"Oh, my pearl of the sea, it is so good to see you again," Sol said, hugging her tightly.

"It's so good to see you too, my dear friend. How are you?" she said, teary-eyed.

"Not too bad for an old man, I guess." He was rubbing his bearded face and staring at her with his clear-blue eyes. "What's wrong, Pearle?" he asked as he took her chin in his hand.

"Oh, nothing; I'm just so happy to see you, that's all," and she hugged him again.

"Come, come, my dear. You have some introductions to do here, I see. It is with great pleasure that I meet you all, especially you, Matthew," he said, tussling Matthew's hair. "I have heard many wonderful things about you from your grandmother. She tells me you have studied archaeology, hieroglyphics, and have had extensive teaching of the ancient language."

"Well, she has taught me a lot, but I guess I will see today if I was a good student or not," he laughed.

"Okay, we see. Maybe I even quiz you a little too, no?" he asked Matt and chuckled.

"Why not? And I'll try to make ya proud, Nana," he said, turning and winking at Pearle.

"Now, before we start out today, we must go over some safety precautions," Sol said.

"Yammi, come here, please," Sol yelled, waving to a young man who was sorting digging tools. Yammi was one of Sol's protégés. He has worked on this site as well as others with him since he was a young boy. Now, at sixteen, this tall, slender, dark-haired boy is one of Sol's invaluable excavators. Yammi is well-versed in many teachings of ancient Egypt and its culture. But his talent for translating old magic spells and knack for finding the impossible makes him stand out, even amongst the oldest and most experienced diggers.

"Ah, yes, everyone, this is Yammi," Sol said as he joined them. "Yammi, this is Matthew, Mr. Robert, Daniel, and Ms. Sherapha." Yammi didn't say a word and just nodded politely to everyone. "Yammi will take you over to that table and give everyone all the equipment you will need. Then he will go over very important safety issues. Pearle, you will need some equipment also. You can go through my stuff there," Sol said, pointing to several large canvas bags under a big white tent, "and see what you would like, okay? Then as soon as everyone is prepared, we will go in," Sol said, smiling.

Robert, Matthew, and Daniel were getting an education on the dos and don'ts of being inside the pyramid from Rahga. They were informed about emergency survival cabinets that were strategically placed every hundred feet or so inside the pyramid. He explained all its contents and how to use the self-contained breathing apparatus in case of an emergency. Above all, Rahga stressed never to panic. He explained how panic could kill you quicker than anything else. After their safety lesson, Daniel, Robert, and Matthew had to practice using the breathing apparatus correctly. Rahga assured them they had nothing to fear and that they would be completely safe. His job was to make sure of that.

Everyone received a guide map, which showed the layout of the inside of the pyramid. The map marked the locations of each emergency survival area in red. They also got a flashlight with extra batteries. Yammi and two other assistants would carry food, water, and a first aid kit. Yammi, Robert, Sol, and Pearle had special two-way radios to carry.

Fifteen minutes later, Sol was leading everyone into the pyramid. Yammi and the other two men followed closely. There was a group of men stationed outside of the entrance under tents. They were always there, in case Sol needed them for any reason.

"Psst . . . Matt, come here! How are we going to get Oopi and them out and find what we are supposed to do?" Dan whispered.

"Remember what Emia can do," Matt said, smiling and whispering back at him.

"Ahhh . . . that she can sound like a giant bee and eats frogs. . . . What am I missing here, Matt?"

"No, silly, she can communicate without talking! She's already told me not to worry and just pay attention to the writings on the wall."

"Really. . . . And was that some kind of *epiphany* she had, or is there a specific place we have to look at? Duh . . . good grief, Matt! Not for nothing, but did you happen to notice we are in a *pyramid?!* There is writing EVERYWHERE!" Daniel hissed. "Please tell me she told you more than that," he said, glaring at him.

"You know, Dan, you really do need to chill. You could have a heart attack at your age getting that upset," Matt laughed.

"I'm gonna make pretend you didn't say that and just follow your lead, buddy. By the way, if I do have a heart attack," he whispered, "it'll be on *your* conscience!"

"Come on, let's just keep up with everyone. Relax; everything will be okay," Matthew assured him.

They had been going in a downward direction for almost an hour when Matthew sensed something. He looked up and saw a symbol above a small room they were about to enter.

"*Pay heed here, Matthew; it is important. This is the start to many answers,*" was Emia's message.

"Psst . . . Dan, this is the first room. Emia said it starts here," Matt whispered to him.

"Nana," Matthew called out, "I'm gonna take a few notes. We will be right behind you."

"Yammi, stay with the boys," Sol instructed.

"Yes, sir," Yammi replied, and offered Matthew some help reading the walls.

"I understand this section and this pictograph, but what does this wall say, Yammi?"

"That is very old, and I'm afraid with it being partially destroyed that I can't make sense of it. But we can try," he said as he took out his flashlight.

Daniel listened as the two boys read the hieroglyphics on the walls, as they dragged their fingers over the old carved-out writings. Matthew wrote intently in his little notebook for several minutes and then looked at Dan.

"We really should be moving on now," Yammi said. "We mustn't get too far behind everyone."

"Okay, Yammi, lead the way," Matthew said.

Matthew pulled on Daniel's backpack, and he turned around. Matthew gave him a thumb up, and they continued to follow on. Daniel shrugged his shoulders and nodded his head. He was hoping whatever Matthew got off the wall was going to be useful. He doesn't know too much about hieroglyphics, even though he has sat in on some of Matthew's lessons. All he understands is that the walls are like giant pages of open books everywhere you look inside the pyramid, telling stories about people from thousands of years ago.

As he continued to go down lighted passageways, Daniel noticed that the colors in the drawings were getting more vivid and brighter. He was truly in awe of the sights, and Matthew thought his facial expressions were priceless. The elaborate hieroglyphics and exquisite drawings made it hard to believe they carved into marble and limestone using only primitive hand tools.

It was starting to get uncomfortably warm, and the air grew thicker. Although the passages have been open for many years, their depth caused the air to be very heavy. Yammi looked back and noticed Daniel lagging behind. He was pale and breathing heavily. He stopped quickly and told him to put on his oxygen mask. He told Matthew they didn't have much farther to go; however, if Daniel wasn't feeling well after the oxygen, he would take him back up to the outside. But after a few minutes, he felt his light-headedness disappear, and they decided to continue on, and met up with the others.

"Daniel," Sol asked immediately, "are you feeling all right?"

"Yeah, I just got really tired and out of breath for a few minutes. Yammi gave me some oxygen, and I am fine now. . . . Actually, I feel pretty good," Dan said with an assuring smile.

"Sometimes these old places will affect people like that. Let this be a lesson to all of you. No one here is immune to the effects of the air, even if you have been doing this for years."

Sol started to bang on his chest and cough. Everyone looked startled, and he laughed. "Ah," I was just trying to make a funny. . . . Ahh, you are too serious."

"Oh, Sol," Pearle laughed. "You haven't changed!"

"After all these years, my dear, you better believe it! My own sense of humor helps keep me young. Life is always too serious. . . . I want to die laughing, not crying and miserable!" He looked at everyone. "You see, I made another funny, and no one laugh. I said, 'die laughing,' ha, ha . . . . No takers, I see. Okay, we go on."

"Oh, I get it now," said Daniel with a snorted laugh. That *is* a good one, Sol; I appreciated it." And everyone started laughing.

"Ah, Americans, a day late, a dollar short," Sol laughed.

"I heard that, Sol," Pearle said, giggling.

"Good, now keep your sense of humor handy, my dear, for you will need it soon," he said to himself.

But Pearle heard what he seemed to whisper and looked at Robert, then at Matthew. She wondered if Sol was kidding or being serious. Sol stopped in front of a large room with a symbol at the top of the entranceway. Matthew looked up and realized in an instant what it was. Daniel looked at him and raised his eyebrows.

"Sol, what is this, above the entrance here?" Matthew asked as he pointed to the symbol.

"We are not sure. It might be a family mark or something else of significance. Very strange, this mark; we only found it in one other location, deep inside the last chamber. I have not noted it anywhere else in my fifty years of digging here," he said in a mysterious tone.

Matthew shined his flashlight on it. It was indeed the same, and he tried to hide his excitement. . . .

"Well . . . being you're the expert, Sol, what is your opinion of this symbol?" Daniel asked.

Sol looked strangely at Daniel, then Matthew. The boys stared intently at him, waiting for his answer, but he just shrugged his shoulders.

"Maybe our Matthew can figure it out," Sol said in a matter-of-fact way as he walked into the chamber.

Pearle thought that was an odd reply . . . so did Robert.

"Nana, do you have any of that tracing paper with you?" he asked after they entered the chamber.

"I believe there's some in my bag. Why?"

"May I have it? Yammi, would you help me?"

"Speak to me, Matthew," Sol said. "What is it you wish to do?"

"I want to copy that mark," he said as he dragged one ladder, and Yammi, the other, setting them up under the curved entranceway. Yammi held the paper as Matthew rubbed the mark with a special charcoal pencil to transfer it to the paper. It took them fifteen minutes to get the entire symbol, which was nearly two square feet. When they finished, Matthew laid it out onto the ground to have a better look. Sol knelt down next to him, and Pearle peered over them.

"Look at this, Sol. I believe this shows marked tombs and what seems like a divider, a wall, then more tombs," Pearle said, astounded. "But look at the angle. One is pointing in the opposite direction of the other. What does this mean?" she asked, searching Sol's face.

"Well," and Sol hesitated, "I think we will need better light to fully see all . . .. But Pearle . . . this is similar to the layout of this site. . . . Hmm . . . What this symbol is . . . . Well, it just can't . . . . I don't understand," he said, talking very low now, almost to himself.

"It almost looks like two triangles joined and pointing in opposite directions," Matthew said.

"But what is this circle on the top here?" asked Pearle.

"I'm not sure, Ms. Pearle," Yammi said, "but it must represent something." And Yammi went out of the room for several minutes to examine the symbol on his own.

"A large sea pearl perhaps," Yammi announced. "It does have a similarity to one."

Sol went to look, and Pearle followed him.

"Yes, yes, it does," Sol agreed. "If we look closely, there is even an opulence of color to it, even after all these years! Quite odd, though, what would a sea pearl have to do with the pyramid? . . . Hmm . . . ." He came down from the ladder and went to the thin paper copy, laid out on the floor.

"I have seen this somewhere, but not of this place," he remarked. Everyone was kneeling now, looking over the symbol . . . well, everyone except Matthew.

"Nana, I know what it is; look," Matthew said as he removed his backpack and lifted his shirt. Sol quickly got up and went to him.

"What is this?" Sol asked with his eyes wide open and looking shocked.

Matthew turned around, and Pearle gasped!

"Sol, the mark has gotten darker since we got here. What does this mean?" Matthew asked, searching his glaring eyes for an answer.

Sol turned and faced Pearle, who looked mortified. "Pearle, do you know of this?"

"No . . . I mean, yes, I know of the mark. It's his birthmark, but it has gotten . . . bigger and . . . he hasn't said anything. For God's sake, why haven't you, Matthew?"

"I just noticed it this morning, Nana. I didn't think anything of it till now, though."

"Did you rub against something, Matthew, or bang your back on anything?" Robert asked.

"No, not that I can think of," Matthew replied, shaking his head and shrugging his shoulders.

"Sol, what do you suppose this means?" asked Pearle.

"I'm not sure, my dear," he said, staring at the birthmark.

"Well, it must be something," Robert added impatiently. "Wouldn't you say that this is . . . well . . . weird, Sol?"

"Weird, Robert, yes, but I'm sure there must be a logical explanation. However, this place has many mysteries, sir," Sol admitted, looking at Pearle. "As for this symbol, it seems obvious to me that someone in the bloodline must have had it; otherwise, why would it be here? Whoever it was, though . . . was of great importance. This is a magnificent find, and I shall call it '**Matthew's discovery**'!

"Come, Matthew, put your shirt on," Sol ordered. "You will stay close to me for the rest of the day. When we get out of here, you and I are going to have a little talk," Sol whispered to him as he put his arm around his shoulder and gave him a wink.

"Let's finish what I need to show you, Pearle. Then we will discuss everything back at hotel," he said.

"You hear that, Nana? Another 'Matthew's discovery,'" Matthew said, excited.

"Oh, you have had another?" Sol asked, looking at Pearle, then over at Matthew.

Matthew panicked but was quick to respond.

"Oh, it was just some old stuff we found, nothing of importance," Matthew said in a nervous and evasive tone.

"Hmm . . . ," Sol replied, and wondered what it was that Matthew didn't want him to know about.

"Well, let's get going, Sol," Matthew said, trying to change the subject. "I can't wait to see the rest of this place," he said as he started to walk ahead of everyone. Matthew just knew that Sol was on to him. He just sensed something about Sol and wondered if he would be the person to turn to with all that has been going on. Maybe he could help him understand everything. He tried to wipe his mind clear and think of Emia and see what she thought . . . but strangely, she didn't respond to him.

Robert and Pearle followed behind Sol and Matthew. Daniel and Yammi were last in the line.

"How are you feeling, Daniel?" Yammi asked.

"Pretty good now."

They started to chat, and Yammi tried to answer all of Daniel's questions about archaeology and what he did with Sol. Yammi was happy to oblige, and it made him realize how much he enjoyed teaching others.

"You sure do know a lot, Yammi."

"Thank you, Daniel. I have been working here with my father, Rahga, since I was a young boy. It is a passion of mine. Mr. Sol teaches very well, and someday I want to be like him," he said, beaming ear to ear.

"Where is your father?" Daniel asked.

"He is top side with the other men. He's Rahga, the one who gave you your safety training. He is a very famous rescue worker, my father, and has saved many lives in his years. Some, though, he hasn't," Yammi said sadly. "But he is a great man, whom I am very proud of, Daniel. You know, Sol goes nowhere without him on a dig! They have worked together for many, many years. My father could have perished many times. I am so fortunate he is still with me."

"I would say so, Yammi. He sounds like a hero! Wish I felt like that about my father. My dad, he is a good doctor and all . . . but we . . . we just don't get along very well. Ever since Dad and Mom divorced, things are different between us. We aren't as close as a father and son should be, ya know. We never really were, now that I think about it."

"I'm truly very sorry to hear of such a thing, but you still see him, no?"

"Oh, yeah, we spend time together when he feels like it . . . but, well, it's just not the same as having your dad around all the time."

"Ah, yes, now I understand problem. Well, Daniel, just be happy for what time you do get to spend with father. This life brings no promises of tomorrow, you know," Yammi said with his eyes full of knowledge like an aged man. "Do every day like last one here, and it will leave no regrets in your heart."

"Gosh, how old are you, Yammi?" Daniel asked.

"Hah!" he laughed. "I am young in body, but aged in mind. That happens when you work all day around *older people*," he whispered to Dan.

"Sol," Robert said, "where exactly are we going?"

"We are going to where I have found a grand new room. It is not much farther. We will have some lunch and rest first. How is everyone feeling?" Sol asked, looking back at Daniel.

Pearle turned around, and Daniel was busy talking to Yammi still.

"Looks like everyone is good, Sol," she yelled back to him.

"Now we go up," Sol said to Matthew as they went around a tall, bent archway.

"I thought we were going down," Matthew said.

"We were, but now we go up," Sol replied, smiling at him. "It's amazing how these structures were built, isn't it, Matthew?"

"Yes, and very confusing!"

"Ah, here we go," Sol said as they neared a lighted room. They had walked about two hundred feet up an ascending narrow hallway, practically bent over, before reaching this room. The air was much better now. Robert looked up toward the corners of the structure and saw ventilation pipes. He was glad to see that. Although Robert wasn't claustrophobic, being enclosed a hundred feet underground was a little unnerving for anybody. Now, being closer to the surface, Robert breathed a sigh of relief. Sol stood in front of a large metal locked gate and pulled a set of keys out of his dusty jeans. He unlocked the door and placed the keys back into his pants pocket. He slowly swung the door open, and it was so quiet that you could hear everyone breathing.

"Holy cow," Robert said as he entered the room, looking around, stunned.

"This, everyone, is the king's tomb," Sol announced.

"Would you look at all this stuff?" Daniel said as he gawked.

A large dark sarcophagus of smoothed stone was in the center of the room. On top lay an exquisite coffin, layered in gold and precious stones.

"Everyone, this is King Nomrahaufa. All the beautiful articles you see are here for his afterlife," Sol informed them as if he were a tour guide. "This royal tomb has *very* detailed hieroglyphics of this king's life. They are the most beautiful and distinguishable hieroglyphics I have ever seen in my life."

The boys were speechless as they wandered around the chamber, admiring its treasures. Pearle was amazed at the condition of these relics. They were nearly four thousand years old, but so well preserved. There was elaborate personal jewelry, loose emeralds, deep purple amethyst, turquoise, Egyptian jasper, and beautifully handmade ornamental wood tables and chairs. Over in a corner, upon an intricately chiseled pink marble pedestal, sat a gold bust of King Nomrahaufa. Matthew stood in front of the pedestal and stared curiously at the face of his distant relative. The gold head captured what he thought was a strong man, with high cheekbones and a wide forehead. But as he looked closer and studied his noble face more carefully, the king's large, oval, deep-set dark eyes seemed to reflect a man of tenderness who emitted a humble and kind spirit.

Pearle was reading the king's cartouche and its many inscriptions on the wall behind his tomb. She then went over to the coffin and slowly ran her fingers along its deep carved-out writings and colorful pictures. She shook her head slowly, as if in disbelief. Pearle put both hands on the king's coffin and felt every inch of the beautiful work done to it.

"I find it just incredible," Pearle said aloud.

"What do you find incredible?" Robert asked, now standing by her side.

She turned toward him in a slow, mechanical way, as if she were in a trance. "This . . . this is . . . my ancestor. . . . Can you believe that, Robert?" she said in a calm, soft voice. "Now I know why my family worked, lived, and died for this place. They were looking for him and his family. This pyramid . . . King Nomrahaufa . . . is a direct link to my family."

"Wow, it seems so hard to believe, Pearle."

"To think that someone of such importance is part of my heritage, Robert, just blows my mind." She turned toward the hieroglyphics and took Robert's hand for him to follow her.

"He was a very good man; his people adored him. He was gracious to everyone. It says here that he enriched everyone's life with his riches and kindness. He was a fair ruler and true family man. His kingdom's economy was dependent on the sea and here for its farming. See Robert?" she said as she pointed to the pictures of fish and people plowing.

"I see that they wrote in pictures and symbols. So Pearle, tell me, how do you distinguish exactly what they are saying?" Robert asked as he ran his hands over a picture of oxen in what looked like a field of tall grain.

"We study and use what others have taught us, just like anything else you learn in life, Robert," she replied. "It can get complicated, especially with real old symbols, but you know the old saying, 'A picture is worth a thousand words!'"

"I find this so interesting and amazing, Pearle. Interpreting these hieroglyphics is truly an art."

"It's fun too," Sol added as he patted Robert on the shoulder. "Come, everyone; let's eat. We have much to see yet," Sol said.

"Sol," Matthew began, "when did you find this tomb of King Nomrahaufa?"

"Well, let's see," he said as he took a bite of his pork sandwich. "I guess we discovered the opening about seven years ago, but I could not get into the tomb for several years. We had to make sure it was safe first. It was a slow and tedious process to ensure the structural integrity of the area."

"Sol, are you kidding me? You mean to tell me that it has taken all these years just to reach this king's tomb?" Matthew said.

"Matthew, I have worked on this place for fifty years, and your relatives before me. This has been an extremely dangerous and challenging expedition. Many of your ancestors have perished while here, and it left others to reexamine if they should continue to go on. It has been a very slow process to get where we are today. A lot of mystery surrounds this place and why so many have died trying to find the king and his family. But this is what archaeologists do and the risk we take every day when we walk into such a place."

"What kind of mysteries are you talking about, Sol?" Matthew asked, looking keenly at him, as was everyone else.

Sol crumpled up the waxed paper his sandwich was in and put it in a paper bag. He took a long swig of water, wiped his mouth with his sleeve, and then exhaled. He sat down next to Matthew and looked at Pearle.

"Matthew, your Great-Great-Grandfather Mattaheus had discovered something here that he would not share with anyone. At the time of his discovery, he had ordered all digging to stop and that no one should ever enter this place again. He said that this place . . . ," and Sol began rubbing his solemn stubbly face. "He said this place was cursed, and anyone who continued to go on would suffer great consequences. Now, according to your Grandfather Alexander, his father told him that Mattaheus had found a small chamber with secrets of the family. Among his findings were a book and an unusual gold object. No one ever saw these objects, and the stories Mattaheus told everyone, well, everyone just thought that he had gone a little crazy. But Mattaheus was determined that no one would ever enter this place either, and he caused a cave-in that took his life. The day before he died, they say he told his son that if anyone continued to dig here, the first female heir would have great heartache, but a true male heir would come, and a great responsibility would become his. He said many things like this that day, but no one understood his mad words or found anything concrete to back up his allegations."

"Well, has anyone ever figured out what he meant or if he was just crazy?" Matthew asked, seemingly frustrated.

"No one has ever found this marvelous book." Then Sol looked at Pearle. "But we have found a strange gold object with Oona's medallion," he said with a swallow that echoed across the stone room. He knew his grandmother was withholding information about this trip. Now it was clear why she was so preoccupied that morning when she was making his breakfast. But he did not understand why she just did not tell him of Sol finding his mother's medallion.

Matthew's eyes widened. His heart began to throb. Daniel was now staring at Matthew, hoping he would tell them about the book he found and about Oopi, Amora, and Emia and all the things they told him. Daniel knew that what was going on was very dangerous, and it was time for Matthew to tell! Daniel began to stand up. Matthew *knew* exactly what he was intending and gave Daniel an icy stare. Pearle was watching the two boys silently interact, and so were Robert and Sol. But she was more upset that

Matthew heard from Sol about his mother's medallion and not from her.

"Matthew, I think it's time you told me what is going on. No more lies, young man. This is serious stuff here! As much logic as you may try to use to make sense of all this, you will not be able to. Trust me, I have tried for thirty years. So tell me and Sol what you've been hiding."

Matthew looked at Daniel again and looked irate. He thought if only Dan would have kept his composure, he wouldn't be in this predicament and have to tell his grandmother things that she may not even believe. His hands began to sweat and tremble. He tried to think of Emia and see what she thought he should do. Again, there was no communication from her.

He paced for about a minute, trying to figure out a way of telling. *He thought if they were supposed to know, why didn't they already?* There had to be a reason why only he knew about the book. After all, the book said only the true heir would be able to read her words. Even Oopi and Emia said this. If he told his grandmother, would it put her or Sol in danger?

Matthew wrestled with his thoughts until he felt like his head would explode. *Why, why hasn't Emia kept in contact with me?* he thought. *She had promised! Is this maybe her way of telling me I should reveal everything to Pearle?*

"Matthew, you need to tell her," Daniel said as he put his hand gently on Matthew's shoulder. "You know it is the right thing to do. Don't you, buddy?"

"What if I put her or anyone else in danger? I can't chance that, Dan," he said vehemently.

"Well, what about *you* and *your* safety in all this, Matt? Did you once stop to think about that?"

"You heard Emia and Oopi. They said they would protect me. That is why they are here!"

"Yeah . . . oh, really? Well, then, tell me, Matt, why hasn't Emia been in contact?"

"I don't know . . . maybe something is wrong, or she can't."

"Yes, something is wrong, and you need to discuss this with your grandmother. Look, I may be as dumb as a stick when it comes to all this archaeology stuff, but after last week and what I have seen and heard today, you are in way over your head! Yes, I do believe there is something to what you read, and what Oopi and the girls have told you. It's . . . well, this is bigger than you and I! We need to get help from people who might understand this *wayyyy* more than us, buddy," Daniel said, stretching his arms out as far as they could go. "Don't you think you owe that at least to your grandmother . . . to give her and Sol a chance to see if they can help you?"

All eyes were on Matthew. Pearle was standing next to Robert with her mouth wide open, squeezing his hand. Robert shared her shock of the boys' open conversation. Yammi had been sitting next to Sol. He was stunned also by what the boys had discussed. He got up and went over to Matthew.

"Matthew," Yammi softly spoke, "I am sorry you have carried such a heavy burden upon yourself. But Daniel is correct when he says you should tell what it is you hide. I must tell you, although we have just met, I feel very connected to you and your family. So if you have a problem, maybe I too can help with it. Sometimes what we try not to burden others with becomes a load so heavy that even the one with the load cannot do anything with it. I believe this is true to what you are experiencing now. You can tell me to mind my own business, but I sense that something unusual is happening here, and you will not be able to deal with this on your own for too much longer."

Matthew looked at Yammi and saw the sincerity he brought with his words. He also realized the truth in what he said. Daniel and Yammi were right. He had to tell them what has happened. He just hoped that nothing bad would happen. He just couldn't shake a feeling of dread he had. Was it because he felt guilty for not telling sooner, or was it his gut telling him something else? He looked around and searched everyone's face. He decided . . . it was time to tell.

"Okay, Nana, I will tell you everything, but you have to promise me that you do not keep any more secrets from me either. No matter what, we must promise to be honest with each other from now on."

Pearle let go of Robert's hand and began to walk slowly toward Matthew. Matthew felt his temples begin to throb, and the closer his grandmother got, the more nauseated he became. His nostrils burned, and he felt dizzy. There was no mistaking the wretched, sickening odor. It was Escursia! He fell to his knees, grabbed his head from the searing pain he felt, and started to vomit. Pearle grabbed him just before he passed out.

When Matthew came to, he saw a white flapping canvas overhead. He smelled fresh air and could hear people talking quietly in the distance. A strange man with a very large black mustache was standing over him. He couldn't help but notice the strong garlicky smell of salami on the man's breath. He tried to get up, but the man told him to lie still for a bit and asked how he was feeling. Matthew just wanted to hand him a breath mint but instead decided to answer him and try not to inhale the salami odor.

"I . . . I am feeling okay, but who are you?" Matthew asked, looking around for a familiar face.

"I am Dr. Shah. Are you sure you are feeling okay?"

"Yes, yes, sir. May I sit up now, please?"

"Of course, if you feel up to it," Dr. Shah responded with a kind smile.

"Do you remember what happened?" said a familiar voice behind him. Matthew turned around, and it was Sol. "You gave us quite the scare. You feeling better?" Sol asked as he tussled Matthew's hair.

"Yes, but what happened?" Matthew asked, now sitting up, scratching his head, bewildered.

"Well, I thought you could tell me," Sol said as he sat down on the edge of the cot.

"*Escursia,*" Matthew replied in a low voice.

"Oh, and who is Escursia?" asked Sol, almost amused.

"It's not funny, Sol! She is evil."

"I'm sorry, I didn't mean to insult you. So tell me, who is this Escursia person?"

"You know, I'd rather tell you and Nana everything I know at the same time. And I don't know exactly who she is except that . . . she is *evil* and has an awful . . . disgusting . . . odor!"

Sol felt like someone kicked him in the stomach, and the expression on his face scared Matthew. He took a deep breath in, clenched his fist, and turned to look at the pyramid. He watched Sol squint his angry eyes while staring at the stone monument, clenching down forcefully on his jaws. He thought for sure Sol was going to break a tooth any minute, from the way his jaw muscles were bulging!

"You okay, Sol?"

"Yes . . . yes, I am fine," he said as he looked at Matthew. "Come, we go back to hotel and have a rest. Then we will have a long discussion about everything, okay?"

"So, how is my grandson feeling?"

"Way better, Nana. I'm sorry I ruined the day and we didn't get to the rest of the tombs."

"I'm not too worried about that," she said, stroking his cheek. "I'm just glad that you are okay, Matthew."

"Pearle," Dr. Shah called, "would you come here, please?"

Pearle looked up and saw Sol standing next to Dr. Shah.

"He looks like a serious guy," Pearle joked.

"Yeah, and I wouldn't get too close to him," Matthew whispered. "He needs some breath mints big time!"

"Matthew, what ever do you mean?"

He leaned closer to her and whispered, "I think he ate a pound of salami for breakfast."

Pearle broke into laughter. "I'll be right back. I think I have a mint in my backpack," and she gave him a wink.

"Hey, buddy, you sure do look better."

"Thanks, Dan. You okay?" Matthew asked him.

"Yep, I feel great, well, except my legs are a little sore from all the walking, but no biggie! Never mind about me," Dan whispered. "What happened to you in there?"

"Escursia, that's what happened," he replied angrily as he flailed his arms.

"Dan, you . . . ah . . . didn't say anything . . . did you?"

"Nope, and nobody asked me anything. It wasn't my place to say anything, anyway, buddy."

"Thanks, I appreciate that."

"You don't have to thank me. I'm just glad you came to your senses, though, and decided to tell them."

"Okay, everyone," Pearle announced, "let's load up and go get a shower."

"Oh, no, where's my backpack?" Matthew asked, looking around in a panic.

"Chill, buddy; I got it right here," Daniel said as he clumsily pirouetted, ending with a "Ta-da!"

"You idiot," Matthew laughed. "And yours?"

"Yammi's got it. No way was I gonna let anyone carry yours," he whispered, smiling deviously.

Chapter Seventeen

They arrived back at the hotel by four and decided to meet with Sol and Yammi in an hour in Pearle's suite. Since the three boys hit it off so well, Sol brought Yammi with him. He doesn't have many friends, and most of the people he knows are the older men he works with. Besides, Yammi has never been in a hotel like this before. He lives with his parents in a modest home, but it's meager, compared to a luxurious hotel suite. Sol admires Yammi for his simple and generous nature and dedication he has for his job. He thinks Yammi is an extremely talented, growing archaeologist with a brilliant future.

Everyone quickly dispersed to his or her room to shower. Robert, though, went to his room to call Brian Kelly.

"Hello, Brian; it's Robert. You weren't in bed yet, were you?"

"Robert, no, I was just going over the reports before you called. How is everything going there?"

"Good, Brian. We just got back from the pyramid, and it has been an interesting day, to say the least!"

"I hope that's a good thing?"

"Brian," Robert said with a long exhale, "we'll talk about that later. Right now I just want to know what's going on there. Have you heard anything from Dr. Hadwick? Did he call you with the toxicology report on Zatu?"

"Yeah . . . faxed it over this morning. Hang on a sec; let me get that file."

Robert plopped down, exhausted, on the edge of his bed and removed his boots, hurling them into a corner with a loud thud. He slowly peeled his sweaty socks off, revealing big red blisters on his pinky toes, and fell back onto the bed, thinking he should have gotten a half size bigger like the shoe clerk recommended. As he rubbed his sore feet back and forth through the soft, fuzzy pile of carpet, he ran his tongue over his teeth and the inside of his gritty mouth. He now had a greater understanding as to why the workers outside the pyramid had their mouths covered, and grabbed a Kleenex.

"Okay, I'm back," sounded Brian on the other end of the phone. "You still there, DG?"

"Yeah . . . still here . . . just trying to get some of this sand out of my mouth. Two bottles of water, and ya think I would have swallowed it all by now. . . . I'm sorry, Brian, go ahead."

"Hadwick said they found two chemicals in the blood. One was Valium, and the other substance was valproic acid."

"What's this valproic acid?"

"I didn't know what it was either, and I asked him that. He said it's a medication mainly used to control seizures. He said whoever made this cocktail knew what they were doing. If the dose was any stronger, it would have been lethal to Zatu."

"Did he say anything else?"

"No, just that if you needed him to answer any more questions, feel free to call him."

"All right. Did you check to see if we've had any recent incidents pertaining to these two drugs?"

"I asked Addy to run a check, and I should have a report on that tomorrow."

"Good. I'll be anxious to see what she comes up with. So what else you got for me?"

"I had Abe Haram come in for questioning today."

"Oh, good. How'd that go?" Robert asked anxiously.

"Needless to say, he was a little nervous when I read him his Miranda rights and told him we were going to record the interview. But it appears he has an alibi. He alleges to be home at the time, watching a pay-per-view movie he ordered."

"Did you check his story out?"

"Yes and no. I spoke to a couple of supervisors at the cable company, who said they would try to get back to me in a week or so with that information. I figured they wouldn't give us anything without a subpoena, so I spoke to the DA's office today, and they will put a rush on one, and we should have it by Monday."

"They couldn't give you that information right away? Geez, that's weird. Oh, well, just something else to wait on," Robert replied, showing his impatience. "What about Addy—did she get anywhere on the boot print she took?"

"Only that it is a men's size eight, and the boot wasn't made here in the States. She's still researching it and seemed determined to find out where it came from."

"You see, now that's what makes me happy! I love when my crew is working toward a common goal," Robert laughed. "Is there anything else?"

"No, can't think of anything off hand, Robert. Is there anything you can think of that I may have overlooked?"

"Nope, seems like you are covering every base that needs to be. Just stay on top of this movie alibi with the cable company. Oh, and do me a favor; give Annabelle a call, and make a point of dropping by to see her. I just want to make sure she is doing okay. It wouldn't hurt to ask if she has heard from or seen our Mr. Haram lately."

"You sneaky dog," Brian laughed. "Good idea. I'll give her a call in the morning."

"Oh, before I forget, Brian, make sure you get with all the pawn stores to see if anyone is trying to get rid of those medallions. Also, check our local and international connections, and get word out to our other agencies. Those medallions will bring a hefty price. It'll be a heavy hitter interested in them, not your regular trader Joe. Well, then, I guess that covers everything I can think of, so I'll call you again tomorrow night. But if anything solid turns up, call me."

Robert hung up and went to take a shower. He pondered their discussion, and not a damn thing made any sense. Especially if Abe Haram was truly home that night of the robbery, his suspicions were wrong. Frustrated, he turned up the pulsating showerhead to drown out his thoughts. He watched the brown soapy dirt stream down his arms to the shower floor and slowly inch its way to a small whirlpool around the drain. He wondered if they had many plumbing problems due to all the sand from the desert. *Hmm,* he thought, *job security for the plumber,* and laughed to himself. Fifteen minutes later, he was with Pearle out on the balcony. He gave her a quick briefing but wasn't sure she paid any attention to what he had said. Robert didn't mind, though; he knew she was more concerned about Matthew and what was going on with him.

Matthew and Daniel were in the kitchen having their favorite drink, smashed Creamsicles with club soda, when someone knocked on the door. Matthew looked at Dan.

"You ready for this, Matt?" Dan asked.

"I guess so. Like you said, it is probably a good idea to have people who may know something more than we do, right?"

"Well, let's hope so," Dan replied, and gulped down the rest of his drink and got up to answer the door.

Everyone had gathered in the living room, and after much coaxing, Daniel finally got Yammi and Sol to try the Creamsicle drink. Yammi decided on his second one that he was in love with it, and Sol . . . well, he wasn't too sure if he would try it again since it gave him the hiccups. On the other side of the room, Matthew sat alone, thinking about what he had to tell Pearle. Plus, he was concerned about Oopi and the girls, and why they didn't come out of the bag when Daniel retrieved it to feed them. He knew that they would only do that if he was in some kind of danger. How could Pearle be any danger, or Sol, for that matter? They surely wouldn't hurt him. Maybe *he* did something wrong. He went through the day thinking about when Emia didn't answer him. It was way before he decided to tell Pearle what was going on. So it couldn't be his decision to tell that stopped her from communicating. But what was it? What was wrong?

Although Matthew was in a room with people he loved and trusted, he felt very alone and scared. He was also dealing with his guilt. He had lied to Pearle more than once and dreaded having to do that. Matthew had two weaknesses that he hated: his fear of losing or hurting the people he loved, and his fear of the dark. These fears would almost paralyze him.

He had drifted off so far with his thoughts, he was oblivious to the sudden silence in the room.

"Are you ready to talk to us now?" Sol asked as he put his hand on Matthew's shoulder, causing him to jerk and turn around.

Matthew shrugged his shoulders. Sol could see the fearfulness in his eyes and sat down next to him.

"Matthew, what is it that has you so afraid?"

"Ha . . . a lot, Sol," he said, turning and looking out the big picture window.

"Let me explain something to you, Matthew, about fear. Fear can be good. It can serve as a warning, but it also can get the best of us, and worse . . . defeat us before we even know why, or what we are afraid of. Do you know what fear really is? It is the unknown, that's all! If we let fear rule us, then no one would do anything, or, for that fact, would come to know anything outside of our comfort zone. Life is so precious, Matthew; why waste it worrying about something you don't know about? You must face your fears head-on. Only then will you gain the inner confidence you need. You start with baby steps, and the more you face what frightens you, the more you will realize how strong you truly are. Now come, let's go sit with everyone else."

"Sol, but what if no one can help me?" Matthew asked, searching Sol's eyes like a lost child.

"Ah, that may be so, my dear boy, but you won't know that until you tell us what is going on, now, will you?"

"I guess you're right. Well, then let me get the bag."

"What bag?" asked Sol, intrigued.

"Oh, the first 'Matthew's discovery,'" he replied.

Matthew placed the leather bag on the large round mahogany coffee table. Daniel removed the overflowing flower arrangement and magazines to make room. He kneeled down, and Dan sat right behind him on the couch. He turned around, and Dan gave him an assuring nod. Matthew knew he was there for him, and at that moment, he wished he could tell him how great a friend he has been.

"Nana, first I have to apologize for lying to you."

"Wait a minute," Daniel interrupted. "*We* lied to her."

"Okay, we are sorry that we lied to you. It wasn't because we wanted to; it's . . . just that . . . well . . . we just want you to know we are very sorry."

"But why, Matthew? . . . I thought we could trust each other no matter what. I had always hoped I made that clear to you, always," Pearle said gently.

"I guess just like you didn't tell me everything about mom, to protect me, I was doing the same."

"All right, I can understand your reasoning, but if you are in any kind of danger, keeping something like that from me is just wrong, Matthew," she stressed, nearly in tears.

"How about you tell us what it is that you've been hiding, Matthew. Then we can decide on who needs protecting, okay?" Sol calmly urged him.

"Matthew," Robert interrupted, "you know I will not let anything happen to you or your grandmother. Whatever problem you have, we will find a way to fix it."

"I know, Robert, but this is weird and . . . well . . . hard to believe."

"Trust me, I have already come to that conclusion," Robert said earnestly.

"So, my dear boy, what have you got in that bag?" Sol asked.

Matthew looked around the room. Everyone's eyes were on him. He opened the leather bag and sat back. The bag wiggled back and forth for a moment; then Matthew could see eyes bobbing at the top. Oopi crawled out, stretched his purple wrinkles, and stood on his tail.

"Looks like we have company," Oopi said as he inched his way toward Matthew. "Boy, where have you been? I am starved to death!" he exclaimed with his hands in the air.

"Oopi, I tried to get you several times, and no one came out of the bag. I've been worried sick about you guys!"

"Hmm . . . very strange, very strange indeed," Oopi said, scratching his tummy. Then he cocked his head aside, looked past Matthew, and smiled at Daniel.

"Ah, friend, there you are. How about some food for my tummy, and please make sure it is yum, yum, yummy!"

Daniel quickly jumped up and went to Matthew's bedroom, where they had stashed the food.

"Now, are you sure this is what you want to do, Matthew?"

Oopi said, looking at everyone, who still could not see him.

"Yes, Oopi, I think it's probably a good idea."

"Very well. . . . So be it . . . ," and Oopi suddenly became visible to everyone.

"Is everyone just going to stare? How rude! Come, boy, introduce me to these strangers," Oopi prodded.

Matthew first introduced Oopi to Sol, then Yammi and Robert. Then he got to his grandmother.

"Alas . . . you must be the first female heir," Oopi said with a bow to Pearle. "It is with great pleasure, my dear, that I meet you."

Pearle looked at Matthew, then back at Oopi, and everyone sat gawking in complete silence. Daniel rushed back into the room and put the greens, fruit, and honey on the table.

"Ah . . . hem . . . ," Daniel said, clearing his throat. "I see you all met Oopi. It's okay, guys," he said, laughing, as he looked at their shocked faces. "I had the same reaction when I first met him. Actually . . . I think my mouth hung open for quite some time, didn't it, Matt?"

"Give it here!" Oopi commanded. "Can't you see I'm totally famished . . . wasting away to a mere caterpillar?!"

Daniel chuckled and gave Oopi the food. Oopi sat back on his tail and began to devour the broccoli and strawberries.

"So I see the cat's got everyone's tongue," he said in between his chewing, exposing the green and red slurry in his mouth.

"Oopi, where is Amora and Emia?" Matthew asked.

"Oh, dear, foolish me; I'm so hungry I forgot about them!" Oopi said in a panic. He took another bite of his strawberry and then wiggled clumsily over to the bag. He stuck his head in and muttered something, then shimmied his way back to his food.

The bag started to move, and everyone heard what sounded like a swarm of bees buzzing. BZZZZZ . . . ZZZZZ . . . ZAAAPPPP . . . . POOF . . . . Out zoomed Emia, and she flew into the air, stretching her wings. Then, POP . . . ZIP! Out whizzed Amora, who joined Emia, zipping around the room.

"Good day, purehearted one," Amora said to Matthew. "I am in much need of nectar," she cooed as she gently floated down onto the table. Daniel opened up the honey bottle, and Amora wasted no time in dipping her tongue into the gold nectar. Then Emia came to Matthew and hovered in front of him.

"I am sorry I could not stop Escursia today, dear heir. I'm afraid her powers grow. Do not be troubled, though. Now I must eat to gain my strength."

Her words seemed cold and uncaring, nonchalant, and it angered him. She seemed contradictive, and he was confused. After all, he trusted them. . . . They told him they were there to protect him. Then a terrible thought crossed his mind. . . . But Emia quickly turned from the honey jar and looked him in the eye. He cautiously looked back at her with a peevish stare.

Matthew looked over at Pearle. She was watching the girls as they siphoned the honey with their long tongues inside the bottle. So was Robert, who seemed more flabbergasted than anyone. Yammi and Sol were talking quietly amongst themselves, but were keeping their eyes on Oopi.

"Matthew, what is it that you wish for me to do?" asked Oopi.

"I'd like you to tell them why you are here."

"Again, I will ask, do you think this is wise?"

"Are you saying it isn't, Oopi?"

"That is not what I ask," he said, showing his annoyance.

Matthew glanced over at Pearle and Robert and, after a moment, shook his head and turned to Oopi. "Yes, it *is* wise."

"Then I will explain to them why it is we are here." And he sidled his wrinkly mass slowly across the table and stopped in front of Pearle.

"You," Oopi began, pointing a fat, stubby finger at Pearle, "are a Nomrahaufa, royal by blood and the first female heir in over three thousand years. Strangely, quite strangely, I might add, you married a Sherapha, who was also of royal descent. According to the prophecy, Matthew is the true heir of both royal families. It is not only his blood, but also the mark he carries of a Nomrahaufa that speaks his royalty. By a strange coincidence, you married into the family that destroyed not only your ancestor's kingdom of Rhondra, but also their own, of Adelann! The one responsible for this was evil, dangerous, and greedy. Her bitter selfishness and twisted evil doings are what caused the destruction of two great families and their kingdoms. Because of her, blood turned on blood and horrible things fell upon all involved. That is how the prophecy came to be and why Matthew is involved. He is blood of blood, the legal heir who can set things right . . . and that is why we are here, to assist him in fulfilling the prophecy.

"Now if he does *not* fulfill the prophecy, I'm afraid things will worsen for your family. The dark will continue to reach out for him and . . . . Arrgg . . . ," Oopi groaned, frustrated. He clenched his little hands till they shook and stretched his wobbly neck out real long. "I may not speak of all that is to come and, in truth, do not know all that may befall your way and his. But what I can tell you is that if he is successful in what the prophecy asks, many lives will be put to rest, and peace will take over darkness for all involved. Blood is to be shared . . . not spilled." Oopi leaned back into his tail and exhaled, feeling exhausted. He crossed his arms over his potbelly, and Pearle thought he was going to cry. For a moment, she felt sorry for him and leaned back into the sofa with a sigh.

"So you're telling me that a prophecy written over three thousand years ago has to do with my ancestors and Matthew's grandfather?"

"Yes," Oopi replied.

"You are sure that I am the first female heir since then?"

"Of course you are, my dear. Otherwise, I assure you that we creatures would not be here today."

"Let me ask you this, then," Pearle said with a frightened tone to her voice. "Who wrote this prophecy, and what must be done to fulfill it?"

"Have you not been told anything over the years from your blood?" asked Oopi, seemingly surprised.

"My great-grandfather said some sort of gibberish about the first female heir and then something about the second before he died, but I never really understood what he meant. My father said one day he would explain it to me, but that never came about. Is that what you are talking about?"

"What was it, my dear, that he said to you?" Oopi asked cautiously.

Pearle's face grimaced as if she were in pain, and she looked up at Matthew, then down to the table for a moment and paused. "Something about the first female heir would be spared and the second would come home to the throne. I believe it was something like that."

Matthew gasped, and she looked up. "Nana, that's what I read. . . . It's in the prophecy. . . ."

"So he knew of this prophecy, as did your father and all of your shared blood that has perished in the home," Oopi replied.

"What home?" Pearle asked, looking away from Matthew.

"The home you were in today!" Oopi replied impatiently.

"Are you telling me that everyone who has known about this prophecy has died because of it?"

"No, I am telling you that whoever has known and tried to alter it or deny it has perished."

"Good God, Sol, what is going on here?" Pearle shouted. "After all these years, don't tell me you haven't any knowledge of all this! You've been involved with my family and that pyramid for fifty years! You must know something about this prophecy!" she insisted.

"Pearle, please calm down," Sol answered, trying to soothe her.

Matthew was watching his grandmother and seeing her as he never witnessed before. He got up and went to her.

"Sol, what is it that you know of this prophecy? If you are truly the friend you seem to be to my grandmother, then you should tell us what you know."

"I was told this day would come. It has weighed heavily on me for many years. First, I must assure you both . . . well, all of you, that I really do not know much at all. That is why I am still here after all these years. It was the condition of your family's wishes. This secret has been a heavy burden, but one I gladly accepted for your family, Pearle. I am not of your blood but was always treated like so. To me, that was the greatest honor I could have been given."

"Do not be upset with him," Emia interrupted, "for he is a truehearted ally and not your enemy. He too has been protected for your sake."

"Protected from what, Emia?" Matthew asked.

"From the curse," she whispered as she looked around the room.

"May I say something?" Robert interrupted as he cleared his throat.

"Yes, Peacekeeper," Emia replied.

"Thank . . . you," Robert said slowly, looking at Emia strangely. He wondered how she knew he was a police officer.

"I know much, Peacekeeper," she replied to Robert.

"But how'd you . . . ?"

"How did I know what you were thinking?"

"Yes, how did . . . you . . . do that?" Robert asked in amazement.

"I am gifted that way," she hummed.

Robert stared at Emia for a moment, and then he arose from the couch and started to pace the living room. "Sol, you need to tell us everything that you know of this prophecy."

"Of course I will tell you everything I know, but I assure you, it will not be much more than I said today, and surely not enough of what we need to know."

"Sol, any information at this point will help," Robert assured him.

"Well, when I was a young man just starting out at the dig site, Pearle's great-grandfather had found a special room. He would let no one in it, though. Over time, he became obsessed with a book he found and spent many hours reading it there. He also carried around a leather bag. I do not know what was in it, but I knew it was of much importance, because he never let it out of his sight. Slowly, as the months passed, his health started declining, and he began to age very quickly.

"Since I lived with him for many years, not having any family, he was like a father to me, and I tried to speak to him about the changes I saw happening. However, being a stubborn man, he insisted everything would be okay. One night as he slept in his chair by the fireside, I noticed the book he was so obsessed with lying on the kitchen table. Of course, my curiosity was running high, and I just had to read it, I thought. To my dismay, I could not open it. When I went to get up from the table, to my surprise, he was standing there behind me, angry and breathing heavily.

He grabbed me by my shirt, and Sol grabbed the front of his shirt to show everyone. Then he began to yell at me in ancient Arabic. I knew at that moment he was not of himself, but of something evil! He must have realized he was acting like a madman because he slowly let go of my shirt and sank into a chair at the table. He put his weary head into his hands and sobbed like a baby. He truly was not the man I knew and loved. When he stopped crying, he stared at the book on the table for quite some time. Then, he looked up at me and started to speak. I stared into his bloodshot eyes as he spoke, and I saw so much heartache that I too wanted to cry. He told me the book held many secrets to the Nomrahaufa family and that the greed of one had brought the shedding of blood to many. He was not specific as to who this was, just that they shared the Nomrahaufa blood. I asked him to explain everything to me, that maybe I could help. But he said that I would be the one who would never know all the truths, for it would condemn me and all that was to be done. He made me promise that no matter what happened to him, I was never to speak of this book or what he told me!

"So that is exactly what I did. The day before he died, he came to me in my bed and said he had several important things he needed to tell me. So I got up, and he made me a cup of tea, and we spoke of many things. I knew he wanted to tell me something of great importance. I just waited as he made his small talk. Ha," Sol laughed as he remembered the man, "he did like to talk a lot! Anyway, he finally began to tell me that he was going to get rid of the book. I was very happy to hear this and told him so. I told him it would be good to have the man back who was like a papa to me. He didn't seem to share my happiness, though. I just could not understand this. Then he said he wanted to tell me things that I was to hold in strict confidence. He made me vow that I was to uphold my word and promise not to speak of his words to anyone. . . . This is what he said:

"*One day you will meet the true heir of the Nomrahaufas. This heir will carry a mark, and he shall fulfill the prophecy. A book's been written for him, and any who try to deny its words or sway destiny shall be cursed. Your job, my son, is until he arrives to serve the family, be the keeper of the pyramid and the guard to its treasures."*

Sol sat back into the couch. His shoulders slouched, and his head hung down as he stared blankly at the floor.

"The next day, there was a cave-in . . . your Great-Grandfather Mattaheus was in it, Pearle," Sol said sadly.

"Now, this was my father's grandfather, right, Sol?" asked Pearle.

"Yes. Why do you ask?"

"Well, my mother's grandfather I'm sure knew of this book too and the prophecy. He was the one that told me of the first female heir."

"Hmm, so others knew too," Sol said, looking baffled.

"Oh, I thought you meant it was your father's grandfather that told you, Nana!"

"No, it was my mom's honey," Pearle replied. "He was an archaeologist too."

"Sol, have you ever seen this book again, after my great-grandfather died?" asked Pearle.

"I never saw it again, Pearle, but I know it was found when they cleared the cave-in."

"What makes you say that?" asked Robert.

"Because of the similarities in others' behavior, they resembled Mattaheus's, when he possessed the book."

"Do you know where this book is today?" Robert asked.

"It must be in a crate that was given to Pearle. She was given everything that was ever found up to her father's death."

"Sol, what did this book look like?" asked Matthew.

"Matthew, need you really ask that question?" Oopi hissed.

"I just wanted to make sure, Oopi, that's all," he replied as he went to the leather bag.

It's not here, Matthew thought to himself as he searched the bag.

"It will not be visible to anyone but the few who have already seen it, for now, anyway," was the message Emia sent Matthew.

Matthew looked at Emia and nodded, then sat down by Daniel.

"You have seen this book, Matthew, haven't you?" asked Sol.

"Yes . . . but . . . wait a minute here . . . ," Matthew said as he bounced up, catching everyone's attention. "If only the heir can open this book containing the prophecy, then it can't be the same, can it? Sol, you are the only person here that saw the book Mattaheus had. Do you remember what it looked like, and could you give me a description of what it had on the cover?"

"It was a long time ago, I'm not sure of . . . . Wait . . . yes . . . it was brown leather, quite worn and not too big. There were initials on it in hieroglyphics with a few symbols, but that is all I remember."

"Okay, so it isn't the book with the prophecy in it. I wonder, though . . . whose it is and where it is," Matthew muttered.

"Like I said before, it must be in one of those crates. So I take it that the book you read the prophecy from is different?"

"Yes . . . yes, it is, Sol," Matthew answered.

"Pearle, have you seen such a book?" asked Sol.

"No, and I would've remembered if I did. When Robert and I did inventory of the crates, we didn't find a book matching that description either, but there's a multitude of books in my study that Oona put there. Matthew, where did you find this book with the prophecy?"

"In your office; it was right behind the camera I got for you the other night."

"So that's how you found it. Well, that answers that question. As for this other book and its whereabouts, that will have to wait until we get home. But for now, I want you to focus and tell me *everything* you read about this prophecy.

Chapter Eighteen

Daniel awoke out of a deep sleep with his ears ringing from a high-pitched buzzing sound. He rolled over to see Emia zipping back and forth frantically in his room. He was half asleep but knew something was terribly wrong. He jumped up from his bed and went straight to Matthew's room. He switched the light on and stopped dead in his tracks. He looked on, horrified, as he watched Matthew's legs and arms jerking wildly about as if he were having a seizure. He was also speaking in what Daniel guessed was Arabic.

"Matt . . . it's me . . . Dan. Wake up," he said as he shook his friend. But he didn't budge, so Daniel yanked all the covers off of Matthew.

"You better wake up!" he said, shaking him now violently. Daniel began to panic when that didn't work. So he bent down and yelled right into his ear. "WAKE UP, MATTHEW!"

Matthew's body shot up to a sitting position, and he stared blankly at Dan. His eyes were dark and glazed over, like a window covered in winter frost. He was dripping with perspiration, and his face was gray. Matthew's appearance was so frightening that Daniel freaked out, thinking Matthew was possessed.

"Are you . . . ," Daniel gulped as his legs shook. "Are . . . are you all right, Matt . . . th . . . ew?"

"What . . . are . . . are you crazy screaming in my ear like that? What is wrong with you?"

"Good grief, Matthew, don't yell at me. I . . . I was scared to death and ready to call 911!"

"Well, what for?" Matthew sneered as he got out of bed, holding his head.

"You were jerking like you were having a seizure and talking in some other language and . . . well, you were freaking me out! I didn't know what the heck was going on, and I thought maybe you were like . . . you know . . . possessed!"

Matthew looked at him, then over at Oopi and Amora, then stumbled back onto his bed.

"Oh, God, I was . . . I was having an awful nightmare, Dan!"

"Do you know what it was about?" asked Oopi.

"Not exactly. . . . I mean Escursia was there, but someone else was there this time."

"Do you know who it was?" Oopi asked impatiently.

"I think it was . . . a woman . . . in a long purple robe," Matthew said, drifting off with his words, trying to recall his dream. "Yes . . . yes, it was, and she called herself "**Zara**.""

Oopi stood tall and stiff, looking like a frozen purple Popsicle again. Emia and Amora stood close to Oopi, holding hands. Oopi swallowed, and you could hear his belly loudly grumble. Then he looked at the girls, took a deep breath, and wiggled closer to Matthew.

"Who is this, Oopi? Who is Zara?" Matthew asked.

"She is our guardian. She will bring no harm to you, Matthew. On the contrary, she carries the safety of all. You must try, though, to remember what, if anything, she said to you in your dream. Please, it is very important," Oopi stressed.

"She spoke in old tongue, and I am not so good in translating that, Oopi," Matthew said, frustrated.

"Just do the best you can," Amora cooed.

"I think she said something about seeing the truth before the sun rises. Does that make any sense to you, Oopi?"

"It is time," Emia announced. "She has brought him the message, and we must show him."

"Are you sure, Emia?" asked Amora.

"Yes."

"But how are we to do this without the others interfering?"

"We will need help. The one they call Yammi. He can be trusted. We must find him and bring him with us."

"Do you think he is the proper one, though?" Amora asked.

"Yes, yes, he is. This Yammi will be of much assistance to our heir, as will his friend," Emia assured her.

"Are you up to this, though?" asked Oopi.

"That does not matter. . . . But I will need some nectar and spice before our journey."

"Okay . . . ah . . . are one of you going to tell me what's going on? What journey, and where does Yammi come in to all of this?" Matthew asked, looking at them as if they were crazy!

"Friend, please bring the bag and nectar right away," Oopi ordered Dan.

Daniel looked at Matthew, who nodded for him to do it.

"Matthew, where is this boy, Yammi, now?" Oopi asked.

"Being that it is one o'clock in the morning, I would have to say he's asleep in his bed, where I would like to be right now!"

"Listen here, Matthew; this is of the utmost importance. We must get Yammi and go to the home! Where is he now?" Oopi pressed urgently.

"He is in the suite at the other end of this floor with Sol," Matthew said, looking at Oopi as if he had lost his mind.

"Amora, have your nectar, then go to Yammi and get him. Matthew, Daniel, dress yourselves, and get what preparations you will need for a journey to the home," Oopi instructed.

"Oopi, please bring me the '*Aka*,'" Emia requested.

"You are sure of this, then?" Oopi asked her.

"Yes, it is what we must do," she said, assuring Oopi.

"Very well, then," Oopi replied. He went to their bag and retrieved a purple vial. Oopi gave the Aka elixir to Emia, and she began to suck its contents. Matthew and Daniel had gotten dressed. They filled one backpack with water and snacks, and checked to make sure they had their flashlights. Then they filled Matthew's pack with honey and food for Oopi and the girls.

"So I guess we are going to the pyramid?" Daniel asked, raising his eyebrows.

"Yes, that is what the home means, Dan, but *why* is what I don't know," Matthew said, putting his backpack on.

"Don't you think it would be a good idea to know what is going on here, *before* we venture anywhere?" Daniel said in a low whisper.

"Look, Dan, I have come to trust Oopi. Whatever he says, I must do; I'm just going to. If you don't want to come, that is your decision, and I will understand."

"Hah, are you kidding me?! **Me** . . . miss out on this adventure? No way, buddy," Dan laughed sarcastically. "Seriously, like I told you before, we are in this together! Besides, I definitely don't want to be the one left here to tell Pearle where you went!"

"Maybe I should leave her a note," Matthew said.

"She will know where you are, heir," Emia replied.

"Oh . . . . And how is that?" Daniel asked.

"She will know, friend, and that is all I will say."

Daniel tsked under his breath and mumbled to himself, "She will know, huh! Yeah, well, I know her better than they do, and she's still going to have a hissy fit."

"Oopi, Amora has Yammi. We must go. They are awaiting us, and not too far. Matthew, open that door there; we must go now," Emia urged.

Matthew looked oddly at Emia. She looked different and . . . well . . . bigger.

"Emia, ah . . . have you . . . well gro . . . grown?" Matthew asked with a swallow.

"Yes, and once I am outside, I will grow much larger. Now quickly, open that door for us," she insisted.

"Well, open the door, boy," Oopi nudged. "We must get going!"

Matthew and Dan went to the patio door and slid it open.

"Go, Emia; we will follow," Oopi instructed her.

A moment later, a loud droning was coming from the patio, and the boys felt their feet vibrating.

"What is that?" Daniel asked as he peeked outside reluctantly.

"Holy crap, Matt; you are not going to believe this!" he yelled as he jumped back.

"Shush! You are going to wake everyone! What is it?" he said as he pushed him out of the way to see.

"Holy . . . ! *E . . . mi . . . a?"*

"Yes, it is I, Matthew. Do not be afraid. Have you boys got everything?"

Matthew didn't answer. He and Daniel just shook their heads and kept staring at her. Emia had grown to such an enormous size that her tail alone was over ten feet long and sticking out over the marble balcony.

"Now come; get on my back, and hold on tight, boys," she ordered.

"Are you serious . . .? Emia, you mean we are going to ride on . . . on your back?"

"Yes, yes, you are. Now let's go. Hurry, and make sure you hang on tightly to my hairs."

Matthew and Daniel gawked at each other with dumbfounded looks, then, shrugging their shoulders, climbed onto her back. Her body vibrated as her colorful, transparent wings seemed to flap a thousand miles an hour, and with her tail, she pushed off the patio and into the night sky. They circled around the hotel and spotted Yammi in an empty parking lot behind a Dumpster. Emia landed, Amora waved him to get on, and they took off for the pyramid.

The night air was warm and sticky. Matthew looked down upon the city, and the streetlights below looked like tiny amber bubbles as they soared higher toward the silvery stars. The domed buildings with gold steeples glistened, and Matthew thought how ironic it was that he felt so big compared with the enormous over-populated city below him. Daniel tapped Matthew on the shoulder and pointed out ahead of him to a blanket of rust-colored sand that seemed to go on indefinitely into the moonlit horizon.

As they flew over the vast desert, the boys began to shiver from the sudden drop in temperature. Oopi felt it too and popped his head out of Matthew's backpack, yelling, "If anyone cares, I am freezing my wrinkles off in here!" Emia laughed, and so did the boys. A few moments later, her wings glowed with a silvery purple hue, and heat radiated from her body, warming everyone.

"She's brilliant!" Matthew yelled out with a laugh.

As they approached the pyramid, Matthew saw an enormous mound of sand piled in the back of it. He remembered Sol saying that due to the sandstorms they have, and depending on which way they come from, it is not unusual for these mountains of sand to form. Matthew, though, thought there was something odd about the formation, but before he could give it more thought, Emia began to circle the area in front of the pyramid. Although there are no buildings or walls standing today, he could see where excavators dug, exposing the outlines of where the city of Rhondra once existed. As he looked over the empty city, he tried to imagine what the homes looked like, where the children played, and what kids his age did without video games or televisions and computers.

His thoughts were quickly interrupted when his body fell forward as Emia began to descend. They landed in front of the lighted pyramid, and Emia went right in. Yammi had warned her of the security there, but as she promised, no one saw them enter. She kept everyone on her until she reached the ascending hall, where it became too narrow for her wings to pass. She shrunk down in size a bit, then rested upon the floor.

"Emia, why have you not gone to your regular size? Is there a problem?" Matthew asked.

"No, dear heir," she buzzed with a laugh, "quite the contrary; everything is wonderful."

"Have you any nectar in that bag, friend?" she asked Daniel.

"Yes, we brought all we had," he replied as he reached inside the bag.

"Oh, very good because I am in need of some after the journey," she said, exhaling wearily.

Daniel knelt down and opened the large honey bottle. He was glad they decided on buying the bigger size, even though he had complained about having to carry it around.

"Please, friend, bring it closer so I may drink of it."

Daniel picked up the jar and held it for her. He watched as she plunged her purple tongue down into the jar and slowly suckled the honey. He marveled at the way she did this. As he stood there, he could not help but stare. *She's so beautiful,* he thought. Her half-human and half-insect features made her fascinating. Emia finished the whole bottle and licked herself clean. "Let's get Oopi and Amora," she said, looking content.

"Emia, wait . . . I need to know why I couldn't be in contact with you yesterday."

"Oh, I am truly sorry for that, but we are not sure of the reason, Matthew. You must remember, the darkness of her soul will do what she can to have what she wants. I did not want to worry you with this. . . . But her power grows, for some strange reason. However, we hope to learn tonight why this is so. Remember, Matthew, keep your heart pure, no matter what happens. For that is something neither she, nor any blackness can touch, unless you will allow it. You are the true heir, and with this comes great responsibility and danger. I know now, they chose wisely, and you will one day fulfill the prophecy and your destiny. It is difficult for me not having all the answers you seek, but you must know that there are many who have promised their life for your safety and this prophecy, who know very little as well. We will learn much together, Matthew, on this journey. Just remember the most important thing: Keep your heart pure."

They finally got to the locked door that led to King Nomrahaufa's tomb. Amora shrunk herself and flew into the key opening to unlock it. She popped out after hearing its click, returned to her normal size, and landed on Daniel's shoulder.

"Come here, Matthew," Oopi ordered as they all stood in the king's chamber. "You must have of these spices. They will help protect you from Escursia."

"What spices?" Matthew asked, looking around. Emia turned and put her tail into his hand. She then instructed him to make a cup with this palms so he could gather the elixir she would excrete from her tail.

"Oh, gross," Daniel said as a thick purple liquid oozed from Emia's tail into Matthew's hands.

"Now drink of it, boy," Oopi instructed. This will give you the protection of the mind and power of the eyes. Now you, friend, and then Yammi must drink of this also."

"Ummm . . . tastes like pumpkin pie," Matthew said.

"No, I think it tastes like our Creamsicle drink," Daniel replied, licking his lips.

"Well, I believe it tastes like my grandmother's spice cake," Yammi added, wiping his mouth on his sleeve.

"Hah . . . hah," Emia laughed. "It will taste different to everyone. This elixir will protect your mind from her darkness. Come now; we must go to our mistress's resting place."

"Yammi, please lead us on," Oopi said.

They left the king's chamber and continued to go through four others. They were not as grand as the king's, but Matthew thought they were still impressive. They were the tombs of King Nomrahaufa's sons. They continued on to a narrow, low-ceiling corridor and came to the entrance of Queen Oonaphelia's tomb. Matthew felt a warm tingling through his body. Emia came closer to him.

"Do not fear, Matthew; it is the elixir at work. Escursia knows you are here, but you are protected," Emia whispered to him.

"Hey, Matt, do you feel . . . funny?" asked Dan.

"Yes, I too was going to ask that," Yammi said.

"It is what the elixir does; do not worry," Emia assured them.

They entered the queen's unusual large tomb, and amongst her possessions of gold, jewelry, pottery, and furniture, upon a marble pillar, sat her decorative crown, braided in layers of gold. But something next to the crown caught Matthew's eye. He made his way over to an extravagant jewel-encrusted raised table displaying an enormous glittering, gilded dragonfly. It was extraordinary and fascinating. Its body shimmered in gold, and the wings had hundreds of small crystal boxes that acted like prisms, reflecting soft colors of a rainbow. As he admired the creature, he felt a great sense of loss and turned aside to see Emia next to him. She looked upon him with wet eyes, then over to the dragonfly.

"This is Anua. Isn't she grand, Matthew? Our queen had her immortalized," she murmured.

"She's gorgeous. . . . Who was she, Emia?"

"She was the greatest of my kind, the queen's protector and . . . my mother."

"Well, she is very beautiful, Emia, but . . . what happened to her?"

Emia took a deep breath and raised her head proudly, then said, "She died protecting me and the queen from Rhuckcha. He was clever with her murder, as was the one who put him up to it. Zara said he left no mark to prove his guilt, but we knew what he did. . . . He pierced his stinger into her spiracle. His venom paralyzed her, causing her to suffocate and die a painful death. Mark my words, heir, the day comes when I shall return his wrath."

Emia bowed gracefully to Anua, then turned and went to the queen's sarcophagus.

Matthew put his head down. He felt angry and sad for Emia. Then shame filled him for what he thought of Emia back at the hotel. How could he have mistrusted her? But now he knows differently and has a new respect for the creature. Before he walked away from Anua, he thanked her and bowed his head.

Matthew's attention was drawn now to a particular part of a wall with a drawing of a two-headed woman. A little farther from that was a two-headed child. He had seen hieroglyphics with snakes and animals with two heads, but never a human could he recall. He turned to ask Emia what they meant, but Oopi instructed him they were to move on. He felt that there was something of importance to these pictographs and that he must return to find out what it was. As they proceeded to leave the tomb, Matthew caught a glimpse of a small coffin on the floor next to the queen's. *Hmm . . . maybe it wasn't a coffin,* he thought. *Maybe it was holding Queen Oonaphelia's Coptic jars, containing her organs.* He was intrigued and knew he'd be back.

"We go now to Lapria and Zara," Oopi informed them. "Remember, keep your heart pure and your mind open, Matthew."

"Oopi, in the book, Queen Oonaphelia said to come to her chamber. Why are we leaving? Wasn't there something specific for me to find here? I mean . . . what was her reason for telling me to do that?"

"Matthew, I also don't understand why we leave her chamber. But it is her wish, and we must do as told."

They continued to go down a corridor and saw a strange purplish hue coming from up ahead. Matthew began to wonder what would happen when they got to Lapria's tomb. *What was he going to learn? How could dead people tell him anything? Then again, if a worm and dragonfly could talk, anything was possible . . . right?* As if something clicked in his mind, Matthew started to think about what he read in the book and what he had seen in Queen Oonaphelia's tomb. Matthew was finally getting an understanding of what he had to do. He had to gather what information he got, no matter how vague, and put it all together. The box that looked like a small coffin, the two-headed woman, and the picture of the two-headed child were clues. But what were they? *Hmm . . . they called Nana the first one . . . . Where is the throne . . . ? Who is the second? Five elements of life to seek . . . the Heptchepak . . . .*

"MATTHEW!"

"What?"

Matthew blinked his eyes and shivered.

"You okay, buddy?" Dan asked.

"Yeah, fine," he answered, looking annoyed.

"So do you want to share with me whatever had you in deep thought?"

"I'm just trying to put together all the information, Dan, from the book and what has happened. I've decided that no matter what Oopi, Amora, and Emia tell me, I am going to have to figure out what all this means myself."

"No, that's not true . . . you have me," Daniel said as he put a comforting hand on Matthew's shoulder.

"Oh, I know that, Dan, but I realize the burden is mine to figure this all out, I'm afraid. Maybe if I stop looking to everyone else for the answers, they might come from the things right in front of me."

"You're smart, and I have faith in you, Matt."

"I'm scared, Dan," Matthew whispered behind him.

Daniel stopped and turned around. He looked into Matthew's eyes and said, "So am I, Matt . . . so am I."

Matthew then thought about what Sol had said to him about fear. *Let it serve as a warning, but don't let it get the best of you. It is only the unknown. . . .* Matthew inhaled deeply.

"Come on, Dan, let's see what this next room is about."

Chapter Nineteen

Yammi was waiting patiently for the boys at the entrance to Lapria's tomb.

Emia was inside already with Amora and Oopi. They were sitting on Lapria's sarcophagus.

Matthew entered first; then Daniel and Yammi followed. The three boys stood there, not saying a word. *Something is strange about it,* Matthew thought. All the other ones he had seen were very ornate, and as he looked around the room, he didn't see any treasures or belongings like the others had. He scanned the colorful marble walls with their detailed hieroglyphics with the help of the small dim lights around the room. He noticed he felt different inside of Lapria's tomb. He was comfortable being there. His fear was gone . . . for the moment, anyway. Matthew felt a sense of renewed courage. He proceeded to a wall on the far end of the tomb. It was the longest one in there. Matthew figured it to be about twenty-five to thirty feet long. This wall had no color to it. There were, though, magnificent hieroglyphics and pictographs consuming it. Here would be answers to many secrets. These answers, though, would lead to many more questions for him.

Matthew slipped his backpack off and placed it on the ground next to the sarcophagus. He went back over to the long wall and began to read the carved messages left in the stone.

"Yammi, do you know how to use a digital camera?" Matthew asked.

"Yes, of course. Why do you ask?"

"Well, I have an idea," he replied. "Go into my backpack, and the large inside pocket has my digital camera. I would like you to take pictures of this entire wall. Being you know the ancient writings better than me, could you photograph this wall entirely as it should be read?"

"Sure, Matthew; I would be happy to assist you," Yammi replied as he dug through the backpack.

"Then when you are done with that one, I'd like you to photograph all the other walls in here. Oh, and let's get some pictures of the sarcophagus too."

"It will be my pleasure. I think this is a wonderful idea, Matthew," Yammi said, smiling.

"So, what do you want *me* to do?" asked Daniel, feeling a little left out.

"Well, if you wouldn't mind, I'd like you to carefully go around the sarcophagus and see if there are any hidden drawers or openings. They were quite clever in hiding things that were sacred; maybe we might find something useful, Dan."

"I'm on it, Matt," he replied, feeling all excited about being helpful to his friend.

"Great, Dan, thanks! If you do find something, let me know."

But Daniel was already on his knees with his flashlight, and he didn't hear a word that Matthew said. He was running his fingers over the grand carvings on the bottom of the sarcophagus and wondering what it would be like to do this every day for a living. How exciting to explore ancient history and to touch relics that were thousands of years old.

Matthew laughed to himself while he watched him carefully searching every inch of the carvings. He thought all Daniel needed was a magnifying glass and a cape; then Matthew could call him "Sherlock Dan Holmes." Matthew knew that Dan would do a good job. He could always depend on his best friend for anything.

Matthew began to scan every inch of the room slowly. He noticed, over in a far corner, two items sitting on a small ledge under a light. He went directly to them. It was a medallion, similar to the ones at home, and a strange gold object. He immediately realized it was his mother's medallion. Oona's was the only medallion with a pearl in the center of it. He recognized it from her photographs. As he held the chainless medallion, Matthew wondered what happened to his mom. Why was her medallion in Egypt? The divers found her chain in the lake at home. How could the medallion be here in this tomb? Matthew knew there had to be a connection between his mother's medallion and everything going on. He just didn't know what it was. He placed the medallion down and picked up the gold object. It was quite heavy and exceptionally beautiful. He sat on the ground to study it more carefully. As he inspected it, he saw that it was a triangular shape, but with five sides. *How odd,* he thought. He guessed that it weighed nearly six pounds. The intricate filigree designs indicated that an exceptional crafted goldsmith created this piece. He has seen and studied many gold artifacts with Pearle, but nothing compared with this exquisite relic. The very top of the piece seemed to be of solid gold. It didn't have all the fancy filigree work on it, as the rest of the piece. He tapped the top part. It sounded hollow. *Strange,* he thought to himself. *What does this gold object have to do with all this? Could . . . could this possibly be . . . ?* He then picked up the medallion and put both items in his backpack.

"Any luck?" Matthew asked Dan as he kneeled by him.

"To be honest, Matt, I am not sure what it is that I am supposed to be looking for. So far, the only thing that has caught my attention is the beautiful carvings in this magnificent hunk of stone. Do you have any clue as to what we should be looking for?"

"Not really, Dan, but I'm sure we aren't here for nothing."

"Did you find anything?"

"As a matter of fact I did. I got my mom's medallion and a gold object that was next to it!"

"No way! Let me see them," he said, all excited.

"I'll show you later, when we get back to the hotel. Right now, let's keep looking for anything else that might be of some use to me."

"So what's with Oopi and the girls? They have been just sitting there since we got in here, Matt."

"I'm not sure, but did you notice that purple light has faded in the room since we arrived?"

"Well, now that you mention it . . . yeah! Why do you think that is . . . and, for that matter, what the heck was it?"

"Beats me. Let's hope when Oopi and the girls come out of . . . their . . . err . . . coma, we can get an answer to that," Matthew said.

Yammi was nearly finished taking his pictures when he felt the ground beneath him tremble. Then it shook again. This time Matthew and Daniel felt it. The three boys froze and looked at one another. Several minutes passed, and everything seemed okay.

"Ah, Yammi, is this something that happens often?" Matthew asked, trying not to panic.

"Sometimes it does. Sol says it is just some settling in the structure."

"So . . . we should go, then," Daniel said as he was putting on his backpack.

"If we get more movement, then we should, but for now, I think all will be fine."

"I don't know, Matthew; something tells me we should leave. This can't be good, buddy . . . you know what I mean?"

"Dan, I think if Yammi thought we were in any kind of danger, he would tell us. He has been in these ruins for years. I'm sure he knows what he's talking about, aren't you? Try to relax, and let's keep looking around."

"Why did I have a feeling you were going to say that?" he replied while reluctantly removing his backpack."

"No worries, Daniel. If it shook more violently, then we would have had to go. We are just fine," Yammi tried to assure him.

"Okay, but another shake, and I'm out of here!" Daniel assured them with a screech to his voice.

Matthew looked over at Yammi, and they started to crack up laughing.

"Here we go again," said Daniel. "I am the butt of another joke. It's not funny! This cannot be good when the ground moves. I don't care what you guys say! Especially that we are underground with all these heavy stones above us," Daniel said, looking up at the half-ton limestone boulder above his head.

"Daniel, if it will make you feel better, I will tell you that this structure has managed to withstand a violent flood that came through here thousands of years ago. If it were going to fall to pieces, it would have done so already. These marvelous structures were built to last forever. This pyramid was made extremely well. My father has assured everyone of this. I trust him wholeheartedly. He has never been wrong."

"Okay, Yammi, but if it happens again, we are out of here, right?"

"Yes," Yammi chuckled, "we will leave then."

"Thank you, Yammi. So, what's next, Matthew? What do we do?"

"I'm not too sure, really. I was hoping Oopi and the girls would have given us some input by now. Actually, I am a little annoyed. They dragged us out here in the middle of the night, saying *'she'* said it's time, and made such a big deal about getting to her. Okay, so we are here, and they haven't said one thing to us since we got in this room!" Matthew's frustration was growing, and he was tired and hungry.

"Hey, guys, I need a little snack. . . . How about you?"

"Good idea, Matthew. What have you got?" responded a hungry Yammi.

Matthew and Daniel went through their bags and pulled out some high-energy water and fruit bars.

"This is perfect," Yammi said as he chewed the blueberry fruit bar. "What is this? I must get myself some!"

"I have a whole case at the hotel, Yammi," Matthew replied with his mouth full. "I'll give you some when we get back there."

"That would be very nice, Matthew. May I ask where you purchased this?"

"Oh, I am not sure. My grandmother got them. We can ask her later, though."

"Thank you, Matthew."

"No prob, Yammi, but I should be the one saying thank you. I mean, after all, you were dragged out of your nice, cozy bed in the middle of the night and all."

"To be honest, I was not too sure what was going on in the beginning. But after everything tonight and what I heard yesterday, I am very much honored to be with you, Matthew."

"Really . . . wow! Why?"

"You have such incredible courage for a young man your age. There is much being asked of you."

"Well, I don't think I have much of a choice in this situation. Besides, I truly and honestly believe my mom, who disappeared eight years ago, has something to do with all this."

Yammi put his head down. He knew more than he wanted to. He just wasn't sure if he was the one to tell Matthew. . . . Or was he?

"Yammi, what is it?" Matthew asked.

"Yesterday . . . I overheard what you said to your grandmother. I was not intruding . . . I assure you. I was just getting some ice tea when I heard you speak the words."

"What words, Yammi?"

Yammi went silent for several minutes. The only thing heard in the tomb was a low hum coming from the battery-operated lights. Then, Yammi parted his blueberry-stained lips and decided he would tell Matthew what he knew.

"Your womb will be spared."

"Oh, yeah, we did talk about that. It was what I saw written in the book, Yammi. Have you any idea what it means?"

"Well, and you must understand, this would be my own opinion. There is a lot going on here than meets the eye and . . . I do believe it may have something to do with your mother."

Matthew's stomach felt like it just did a 360-degree flip-flop. For the first time since reading that sentence that night in his room, Matthew had hope. He looked at Daniel with such a smile on his face that Dan thought his friend was going to cry.

"If you would, Yammi, please tell me why you think this."

"Yes, Yammi, being that I don't know too much about all this Egyptian stuff, you probably could fill in a lot of gaps Matthew and I can't figure out."

"Since I was a little boy, I was always amazed and fascinated with magic. For some reason, I was able to interpret basic spells then. After some years of studying the different types of magic spells, good and bad, I have become very good in their interpretations. Have you studied such things, Matthew?"

"Not really, but my grandmother has only told me stories about the ushabtis and how people supposedly used them for bad magic."

"There are many myths about ancient times in Egypt. We will talk, though, about the Middle Kingdom. Your ancestors here are from the Middle Kingdom period. Sol has concluded the period was mid-1900 BC. The people of that culture believed in many different gods, with each said to have different powers and effects on people. For some reason, your ancestors did not idolize many gods. The Nomrahaufas believed there was one superior God, and he was responsible for all that existed. At least that's based from what has been found here so far. Sol thinks that this way of faith made life simple and uncomplicated for them. Now, all Egyptians, though, believed in the afterlife. This is why there are such elaborate pyramids with many valuable possessions of the departed buried with them. The more important the deceased person was, the bigger his tomb and treasures were. Now, this is where the ushabtis come in.

"According to legend, the ushabtis (sometimes called shawabtis) were carved in a likened image of the deceased and placed in their tombs. Their purpose was to do any type of manual labor for these important people in their afterlife. Most important people had servants do their manual labor when they were alive. So, of course, the departed didn't expect to do menial chores in the next life. Now, as for the priests, they were of pure quality and character. They attended to people's spiritual needs in their life as well as afterlife. I would imagine it is like today in many religions where spiritual leaders guide their people in life and pray for them after they have passed on. For the most part, the majority of the ancient priests did just that. However, there were some who practiced bad magic and did horrible things. For most of my educational learning, it was stressed that whatever happened to people who were supposedly cursed, the outcome was mostly coincidental, not magic. For example, if someone suddenly became sick or developed a strange disease, they would say it was a curse. But it was merely because they became ill. For those who died suddenly, actually it was just their time to go. For many who lost fortunes, it was simply because the family fell on bad times. These are just a few examples, so you can understand the teachings of today's modern world and the beliefs of the old days.

"Over the years, I may have agreed on most of these teachings. Although, many times, I have questioned these coincidental events. Some do not seem coincidental at all. To me, there is no other explanation. I believe that in some cases, evil magic was to blame for terrible things that happened. Let's look at most recent events, Matthew. Although I see nothing evil with them, how can we explain Oopi, Amora, and Emia? This must be some kind of magic. Do you not think so too? I am sure that as I sit here, there could be no explanation of coincidence with these talking creatures and their story. Pure magic brings them here. I am sure of this! What brought them here, unfortunately, were circumstances from someone who used bad magic.

"As for your mother, Matthew, I think her reference in all this is only because you are her son. You came from her womb, as did she from Pearle's womb, and so on and so on. I sense you feel and are hopeful that your mother, Oona, may still be alive. I do not know, after all this time, if that could even be possible. I completely understand why you would think this. Whoever wrote this prophecy wanted you to believe that. They were very clever! The prophecy was written in a way . . . well . . . to make you believe if you fulfilled it, your mother would be returned in exchange for your success. Am I not correct in my thinking, Matthew?"

Daniel looked at Yammi and could not believe his words. As he heard them roll from his mouth, he realized what Yammi had said was true. This was exactly what Matthew thought to be true. Although he never said anything to Matthew, he thought that was the whole intention of the prophecy too. That is why he had urged Matthew several times to tell Pearle about everything. That is why he fears for Matthew's life.

"So, am I to believe that this prophecy is something to ignore? What about Oopi and the girls? They aren't bad. . . . They have been protecting me from Escursia. Do you think they could be lying to me also, Yammi?"

But he didn't even wait for an answer. He got up and started walking around the room.

Matthew was a lone thinker. He always had to figure things out by himself. Right now, though, he needed Yammi's help. He was not going to get any closer to answers he wanted by struggling on his own.

"I did not mean to upset him, Daniel; I just spoke truth. After all, he did ask me what I thought."

"Oh, Yammi, I know that," Daniel said, assuring him. "He just needs to think about everything right now."

"May I ask you something?"

"Sure, Yammi; what is it?"

"Who is Escursia?"

"As far as I can make out, she is definitely evil! Matthew said that she comes to him in his dreams and that she has an awful smell that makes him sick to his stomach. She has spoken to him in his dreams, but I don't remember what she told him. There has been so much going on that I just don't remember everything," Daniel said, frustrated.

"That is understandable, Daniel. Especially that you and Matthew are such good friends."

"Wait a sec; I do recall when he told Oopi about her! He said she was wearing a long robe and that she was bald and had long, scary orange fingernails. He has had many nightmares about her. Before we left to come here tonight, he had a horrible, violent nightmare. This time, though, he said there was another woman in the dream. This nightmare was awful, Yammi! He was shaking and sweating when I got to his room. I had a hard time waking him up. . . . I was so scared!"

"I cannot even imagine how that must have been for you to experience. Did he say what this other dream was about and who this other woman may be?"

"He said her name was Zara, and he knew she was good and was protecting him from Escursia. She wore a purple robe and told him in the old language that he would see the truth before the sun came up. Then that's when Oopi and Emia said it was time to come here and find more answers. Oh, and I do remember that either Oopi or Emia told Matthew that she was Queen Oonaphelia's and Lapria's guardian."

"You are sure of this, Daniel?"

"Yes, that is what they said, Yammi. They seemed quite excited about it too."

"Hmm . . . . I am going to assume that these two women are priestesses. They would have been guardians of the female heirs. It is apparent that Zara is a good priestess and this Escursia is quite the evil one. Daniel, remember when I spoke of the priest earlier? Well, I think we have an excellent example here of a good priest with good magic and a bad priest who practiced very evil magic. What I assume, then, is that this prophecy is quite important. Even though I have not read it, I am sure now that there is much more to it. Come, Daniel; let's get Matthew and gather the creatures and go. We must get home before everyone awakes."

"It's funny you say that, Yammi. Matthew was going to leave Pearle a note, but Oopi assured him that she would know where we were."

"Really . . . . That is odd, don't you think?"

"Hey, Yammi," Dan said as he picked up his backpack, "with everything I have seen and heard in the last two weeks, I don't think anything is too weird or unbelievable anymore."

"Dan, I have but one more question before we go, if you do not mind."

"Sure, shoot. What is it?"

"Do you know why I was summoned to come with you?"

"Oopi said that you would be of great help. That is all I remember him saying to Matthew, anyway.

"Hey, where is Matthew?" Daniel asked, scanning the room.

Yammi looked around too. Matthew was nowhere in the tomb, and Oopi and the girls were still on top of the sarcophagus in some kind of daze.

"Come; I think I know where he is."

Daniel ran behind Yammi and followed him to Queen Oonaphelia's room. They found him kneeling over the small box he saw earlier. They watched as he opened it and placed the wooden lid carefully on the ground. Matthew pulled out a purple silk sack tied with a braided gold string. As he held the bag with his right hand, he peered down into the box. Matthew gasped and turned around to see Yammi and Daniel standing at the doorway. He fell to the ground on his butt, seemingly shocked.

"Yammi, please come here," Matthew said in a cracked voice. "I need you to see this. . . . You too, Dan."

The boys peered into the box. Daniel had a look of horror on his face, while Yammi had amazement in his eyes. Yammi kneeled down and carefully removed an infant mummy.

"Daniel, please reach into Matthew's bag and retrieve his camera for me. There is an inscription inside this box, and I need to take a picture of it."

Daniel gave the camera to Yammi, and in exchange, he carefully handed the mummy baby to him. Daniel's eyes got as big as half dollars as he held it in his hands. Yammi took many pictures of inside the box and then put the lid on to photograph the writings on the outside.

"Amazing, isn't it, Dan?"

"Matt . . . I'm . . . just blown away. Can you believe I am holding this thing?" Dan replied as he looked at his friend.

Looking amazed himself, Matthew replied, "Can you believe that you are holding the mummy of a three thousand-year-old baby?"

"No, buddy, I can't," he replied in a whisper.

"This baby is really tiny," Matthew said as he continued to check it out. "I wonder what happened to it and whose it is."

"Since it was buried here, next to the queen, it had to be hers, Matthew," Yammi said.

"No, it can't be," replied Daniel.

"Oh, and what makes you say that?" Yammi asked.

"When we first met Emia, she gave us a thorough history of the family. Emia told us that the family only had five children. They had four boys, who ended up dying because of a plague, and then the one daughter. There was no mention of another child or its death, Yammi."

"Truly she must have been mistaken, Daniel. Only royal infant children are buried with their parent."

"Yammi is right, Daniel. But you are also correct that Emia said there was only a total of five children," Matthew added.

"Maybe Emia didn't know about the baby, Matthew. What I am wondering about is why the baby was inside this plain box. Royal children had beautiful, ornate coffins. It is very strange, to say the least. Well, maybe when we get the pictures onto the computer, we will have some more information about the baby. Oh, by the way, what did you find in that purple bag?"

Yammi asked as he put the infant back into the box gently and covered it.

"Gee, with the baby and all, I totally forgot about it."

Matthew carefully untied the gold ribbon. He placed the bag on the ground and reached into it.

"Wow! That has to be the biggest pearl I have ever seen!" Daniel exclaimed.

"It sure is big," replied Matthew as he held his hand out, admiring the large, shiny pearl.

Matthew put the pearl back into its silk bag and then asked Daniel to hold it in his backpack for him.

"We better go get Oopi and the girls. I hope they have come out of their coma or whatever it is that had them in such a daze. It is nearly five o'clock, and everyone will be up soon," Matthew said.

They got back to Lapria's tomb, and the three creatures watched as they walked up to the sarcophagus.

"I want to go home now," Matthew announced to Oopi. "You said I would have some answers tonight. What happened to you? Why have you not spoken to me since we got here?"

Matthew was angry, and Oopi knew it by the tone of his voice.

"Yes, yes, we need to depart quickly," Oopi replied nervously.

"What is wrong, Oopi?" Matthew asked.

"We are all in danger. We must leave at once!"

"I will need some Aka," Emia interrupted in a weak voice.

"Yes, of course, dear," replied Oopi nervously. "Friend!" he yelled out to Dan. "Quickly now, bring me the purple vial you carry. Hurry!"

Daniel quickly dropped his bag and began searching frantically for the vial when he felt the ground under him shake. Again, it shook—this time more violently, and Yammi yelled for everyone to seek the ground and cover their heads. Daniel grabbed Oopi, Amora, and Emia, and shoved them inside their bag. He dashed to the ground, went into a fetal position, and covered his head. It was not a moment too soon when a huge stone fell onto the sarcophagus with a loud, cracking thud! Then another stone, and another came crashing down! The walls and ceiling began to collapse around them. It was becoming too dark to see. The air was getting heavy, and it was hard to breathe. They listened in horror as more stones crashed down around them in the darkness. The ground began moving more furiously beneath their bodies.

Sharp, jagged pieces of stone sheared off in layers, landing within inches of their bodies. The large razor-edged shards penetrated the ground like a hot knife in butter.

Yammi yelled out again to Matthew and Daniel. He told them to stay as close to the sarcophagus as possible. He wasn't sure, though, they could hear him. The cracking thundering of the stones around them was deafening! He could only hope they did not panic and would remember what his father, Rahga, taught them the day before. Yammi, though, was very worried. This was the worst cave-in he ever experienced. He knew he was injured. His left arm was numb, and he could not move it. He began to wonder if he would see his father again.

Minutes passed. How many, he is not sure. Yammi realized the ground beneath his beaten body had become still, and the roaring thunder ceased. The silence was eerie in the pitch-black room.

Daniel began choking, and he coughed until he puked. The dirt was so thick in his mouth that he was afraid to breathe in. He was lucky, though. None of the stones prevented him from moving. He groped around in the dark, searching for his bag. He pulled it from underneath him and reached in, feeling for a bottle of water to rinse his mouth. He then called out to Matthew and Yammi. Neither one answered him. He rinsed his mouth again and called for Matthew this time. Again, he called, but heard nothing. He began to panic and frantically felt around for Matthew in the dark rubble. He felt an arm. He lifted it, but it fell heavily, with a sickening thud, to the ground.

Complete terror filled his soul. He searched madly again in the rubble and found the arm once more. He ran his hand down to the wrist and searched desperately for a pulse. He felt a weak heartbeat against his sandy, trembling fingers. Relief soared through his panic-stricken body.

Daniel searched his bag and found his flashlight. When he turned it on, he saw the black, filthy cloud that consumed the entire room. As he turned his flashlight down toward the ground, he could barely make out the shape next to him, but he knew it was Matthew. Realizing he had to do something quickly, he pointed the light around the room. The black air was starting to settle.

Relief came, but with horror of what he discovered. The room was a disaster. He knew, though, not to concentrate on that. He was the only one not injured, and it was up to him to save his friend and find Yammi.

"*Think . . . come on, think, you jerk,*" he said to himself. Daniel thought how he always seemed like a joke to others, the sniveling fool! He hated when people didn't take him seriously. He just had a laid-back personality and thought everyone else was too serious. He figured if you couldn't laugh at yourself, you were in big trouble in life. Right now, though, two lives were depending on him for their survival. Daniel had to reach deep inside him to find his strength and get serious. He had to find the courage to do what others, like his father, made him feel he was incapable of doing.

"*Okay,*" he said to himself. "*Both my parents are doctors. They have made me take every first aid course there is. Mom's taught me about injuries and the shock people go into.*" But the harder he thought, the more his head swooned. Dan realized the first thing he had to do was get a first aid kit and some . . . .

"THE EMERGENCY SURVIVAL CABINET!"

"That's it!" he said out loud. "I know I saw one not too far from this entrance!"

He slowly got up, as he didn't want to disturb the rubble around him and make more rocks fall on Matthew. He was now in a much better position to see his friend. He was mortified to see a huge chunk of the limestone ceiling covering Matthew's legs, and he was bleeding from his head and nose. Daniel knew Matthew was seriously hurt and he had to act quickly if he was going to save him. He then made his way around the sarcophagus to find Yammi.

He knelt down next to him and called his name. Again; this time he yelled louder. Yammi started to cough and vomit. Daniel grabbed his water bottle and told Yammi to rinse his mouth out. He did, and spit black dirt and blood from it. Once more, he rinsed, and then spoke.

"Daniel . . . you are okay. Where is Matthew? Is he all right? Please, please tell me he is okay."

"Yammi . . . he is alive but hurt real bad. I am going to try and find my way out of here and get to the emergency supplies. Let me look at your arm." Daniel thought he would vomit again. He saw a large, sharp piece of stone piercing Yammi's arm, and he was losing a lot of blood.

"This isn't good, Yammi. . . . We need to get some pressure on that wound of yours." And Daniel took off his shirt, turned it inside out so it would be cleaner, and wrapped it around Yammi's arm. He hoped it would at least slow the bleeding down for now.

"Does anything else hurt you, Yammi? . . . Can you tell me if something else bothers you?"

"No, Daniel, I will be fine. Just get to that emergency box, and bring the breathing apparatus first. This air is toxic right now and could kill us quicker than our injuries," he coughed. "There is also a two-way radio. Bring that back so we may call for help. Can you get out, Daniel? Is the doorway blocked?"

"There are a lot of big pieces of stone in it, but I think I can crawl out through an opening I see."

"Good, then go, Daniel. . . . Be safe."

"I will, Yammi. Just please try to stay awake, and if you can, try to keep talking to Matthew. Maybe he will hear you."

"I will try. Now go . . . quickly . . . . The air is . . . and Yammi lost consciousness."

He knew Yammi was right. If the air they were breathing was toxic, all the first aid in the world would not save them. Daniel took his flashlight and headed carefully to the door. It wasn't as bad as he thought. He knew he had to push some of the stones out to make the hole bigger to pass through. Then he remembered what he learned in his tae kwon do classes. He concentrated all his energies from his body into his legs and kicked at them. After several attempts, he was successful. Numerous rocks broke free and rolled into the hallway.

As he looked down the hallway, his heart sank. That was the only way out, and it had a wall of stone blocking any exit to the outside. He turned around, fearing the worst. He shot the flashlight down the corridor. To his surprise, he saw the cabinet. He ran to it and struggled, but opened it. There was everything in there that Rahga said it would have. Daniel saw heat blankets, nonperishable food, water, and a large first aid kit. More importantly, he noted the breathing apparatuses that he had to bring back for Yammi and Matthew.

He frantically ripped opened a plastic box and found a two-way radio. He turned it on and began to speak. A voice came back over the radio. It was Rahga. Daniel's heart jumped for joy! He quickly related what had happened.

"Daniel, you boys must get those breathing packs on! It is essential to use them until we can get you out," he stressed.

"I know, Rahga; Yammi told me that."

"Ah, my son, is he okay?"

"Rahga . . . I'm sorry, but . . . he is badly hurt, and so is Matthew. Please, you have to get in here as fast as possible! I know if their crushing wounds aren't taken care of right away, they can develop toxins in their body, and their organs will start to shut down."

"Oh, my God, yes, you are right, Daniel, but how do you know this for sure?" Rahga asked.

"My parents . . . they are doctors, Rahga. I have had extensive first aid training. But I'm afraid Matthew's and Yammi's wounds are more serious than I know what to do with. I am not sure how much I will be able to help them. Look, Rahga, I am going back to them now. I'm at the emergency cabinet as we speak and getting everything I can possibly carry. I am going to the last tomb. That is where we are, okay? Hello . . . Rahga . . . can you hear me?"

There was no answer, no voice to listen to, just static. Daniel wanted to panic but knew he had two people depending on him right now. He quickly clipped the phone to his belt and grabbed a few of the silver heat blankets. He found a blue tarp and opened it up on the floor. Then he grabbed the supplies he needed and put them on it. He took two of the breathing apparatuses and closed up the tarp. He swung it over his shoulder as he struggled to hold on to the two most important pieces, the air packs.

When he got back to the tomb's doorway, he dropped the tarp and took the breathing packs in first. He went to Matthew first and managed to get the mask on him, which was difficult. He knew he had to be extremely careful and not move Matthew's head too much. After Daniel cleaned Matthew's mouth and nostrils of dirt, he was breathing clean air. Ten minutes later, Yammi was inhaling cleaner air too. He decided that he should go back and get another air pack for himself. While at the cabinet, he grabbed a few extra things he did not take before . . . some extra batteries for the phone and a couple of electric lanterns. He knew they would come in handy, as he couldn't care for their wounds and hold a flashlight at the same time. Daniel was on automatic control! He just seemed to know what to do.

Daniel brought everything into the tomb and spread it all out neatly on the tarp. He hooked himself up also to breathe in cleaner air. After he sorted everything, he opened up the large first aid kit. There was everything he could possibly need, he thought. He put a lantern by Yammi and one by Matthew, then opened a water bottle and tried to clean his filthy hands as best he could. He found sterile surgical gloves and put them on. Daniel looked over Matthew's injuries and saw why his head was badly bleeding. As best he could, he removed whatever stones he could from Matthew's body. He quickly cleaned a large head gash and dressed it with a pressure bandage. Then he wrapped Matthew up in a heat blanket and went to Yammi. He removed his mask and bent over.

"Yammi, it's Dan. Can you hear me, Yammi?" he called again.

Yammi shook his head.

"I don't want you to talk, okay? Just listen. I spoke with your father; he knows what happened, and he is working to get us out. Isn't that great, Yammi?"

Yammi managed a small smile before losing consciousness again. Daniel noticed that the large shard of stone was not in Yammi's arm. He figured Yammi must have pulled it out.

He undid his shirt he had tied on earlier, cleaned the gaping arm wound, and pressure bandaged it too. Dan carefully checked him for other injuries and tended to what he could. Then he wrapped Yammi in a heat blanket.

Now back at Matthew's side, he began to sob. He cried until he realized he was having trouble breathing. *How stupid!* he thought to himself. He wiped his gritty tears with his bare arm and looked at Matthew, lying lifeless amongst the rubble.

"Matthew, you are going to make it, buddy," he said out loud. Then he placed his mask on and leaned back against the sarcophagus to rest. Daniel realized he must have dozed off, because he jumped when he heard something. There was a voice coming over the radio.

"Hello . . . hello, are you there?"

"Yes, yes, I am here, Daniel. How is everything inside?"

"Well, Matthew still hasn't woke up, and Yammi goes in and out of consciousness. But I have managed to dress their serious wounds and put the air packs on them."

"How are you, Daniel—are you hurt?"

"No, not really, just banged up a bit, but I am okay."

"That is very good to hear, Daniel, very good indeed! Listen, young man, we are working as we speak to get you all out of there. We have helicopters standing by and many doctors too. Everything will be fine, Daniel. I know you don't have your mask on, so please put it on as I speak. You do not have to answer me," the voice instructed him. He put his mask back on and continued to listen to the voice.

"I must tell you that I have never seen such a brave man in all my days. You continue to be brave, Daniel. I promise, it should not be but a couple more hours, and we will see you . . . okay? Daniel . . . Daniel, are you listening?"

But Daniel didn't hear the calming voice this time. He lost consciousness after smashing his head on a rock as he passed out.

Chapter Twenty

Robert and Pearle were pacing under a tent outside of the pyramid. Rahga and his rescue crew were almost through the wall of stones that prevented them from reaching the critically injured boys. They have been working frantically for hours, with no word from Daniel. There had to be fifty men involved in this rescue, and each one, an essential part to its success. Sol was so proud of these men. But he was even more impressed with Rahga. He had prepared for this kind of catastrophic event. Rahga trained his men continually for cave-ins. They were always improving a method in the making. He always told them to train for the worst and expect the best. More importantly, Rahga had the foresight to know that the necessary equipment for such a disaster should be readily available, and it was. Today he hoped all his planning and training would be enough to save three boys. Today he hoped to save his own son's life.

Rahga knew the air packs the boys had were only good for about four hours. He was glad that he inspected all the emergency equipment in the cabinets last week before Pearle came. He knew the boys had everything they needed until they could get to them. Rahga hoped it wouldn't be too late, though, when they did. They were now approaching the seventh hour.

Pearle was gulping down some cold water when she heard a commotion coming from another tent. She dropped the water bottle and ran to see what was going on.

A man shouted; then another. Soon everyone was cheering.

"They have broken through!" a man told Pearle as he hugged her.

Pearle wanted to go too, but Robert reminded her that there were so many people inside as it was, and she would only get in the way. He grabbed and hugged her as she wept.

"It's going to be okay, Pearle. Matthew is a tough kid, and thanks to Daniel and his quick thinking, everything is going to turn out fine." But Robert wasn't too sure himself as he heard those words coming from his mouth. He knew they just had to wait for the doctors to get to Matthew and the boys.

It seemed like an eternity, but the first stretcher was coming out of the pyramid.

It was Yammi, barely awake and covered in blood and dirt. They took him straight into the triage tent, where trauma nurses were waiting.

Pearle thought she was going to vomit as Yammi's stretcher went by. All she could think about was what Daniel relayed about Matthew being seriously hurt and not being conscious. She knew he must have been hurt the worst.

Forty-five minutes later, a second stretcher was emerging. Daniel was on this one. He wasn't conscious, though.

"Oh, my God, Robert, I thought he wasn't hurt badly. That's what they told us . . . wasn't it?"

"They told us he wasn't *seriously* hurt, Pearle. He had neglected his air mask to take care of the boys. I'm sure with some oxygen and fluids, he is going to be cracking jokes before you know it. Come on, Pearle, you need to calm down. You won't be doing yourself or Matthew any good like this. They will be bringing him out soon. Let's go into the triage tent and wait for him. In the meantime, we can see how the two boys are doing."

"Before we go in, are you going to be okay seeing the boys with their injuries, Pearle?"

"Yes, Robert, I should be just fine," she assured him, and walked into the tent.

They went to Daniel first, who was awake now. They were feeding him oxygen and started an IV.

"Well, you don't look like you're having much fun on this vacation," Robert joked to Daniel.

"How are you feeling, Daniel?" Pearle asked as she bent down and gave him a kiss on his dirty forehead.

"Bloody fantastic! And you, Pearle?" he replied with a smile.

"Oh, Daniel," she laughed. "You manage to have the best sense of humor no matter what. You know that's one of the many reasons I love you so much!"

"Yeah, yeah, that's what all the girls tell me," he replied with a laugh. "Hey, where is Matthew?"

"He hasn't come out yet. We are still waiting," replied Robert.

"Pearle, he is hurt pretty bad," Daniel said with tears welling in his eyes. "I did the best I could for him. I . . . I just hope it was enough."

"I'm sure you did more than anybody could expect under the circumstances, Daniel. I want you to know how grateful I am and so very proud of you. I don't know another person who would have kept his cool and done what you had to do. You truly are a hero, Daniel!"

"Oh, you stop that, Miss Pearle, before I start blushing," he said, laughing through his tears.

"Daniel, I'm sure you two will be getting into more mischief sooner than you think," Robert said, smiling. "Well, you rest now. We're going over to see how Yammi is doing."

"Pearle," Daniel said as he grabbed her hand, "please let me know how he is too."

"Absolutely. We'll be back in a few minutes to check on you again."

Yammi was awake but seemed disoriented. His entire upper body was covered in blood, and his left arm was splinted and bandaged. The nurse changed his IV bag to a second. He was in shock, and they were pushing fluids into him.

"Yammi," she called softly. "It's me, Pearle. Can you hear me?"

Yammi slowly turned his head and managed to give her a smile.

"Pearle," he said in a whisper she could hardly hear.

She bent over closer to his face so she could hear what he was trying to say.

"Yes, Yammi, it's me, Pearle. How are you feeling?"

"Ahhh . . . I have . . . been much . . . bet . . . ter. Where . . . is Matthew? Is he . . . okay?"

"We are waiting for him. He hasn't come out yet, but it should be any minute now," she assured him.

"He is such a brave boy. . . . I find it . . . honor knowing . . . him."

"Yammi, I am sure our Matthew feels very much the same way

about you. I think I can speak for all of us that we are so fortunate to know you. You rest, Yammi. Your father should be here soon."

"I . . . saw Father. He rescued us. I . . . am so proud . . . of him."

"We all are, Yammi; we all are," she replied with tears rolling down her cheeks.

"Dr. Shah, is he going to be okay?" Pearle asked.

"He has lost an awful lot of blood, Pearle. We are going to transport him very shortly to the hospital. He also has a very serious injury to his arm. It was nearly amputated from the elbow down. We won't know anything, though, until the surgeons get him in the operating room, replace the blood he's lost, and see what damage there is."

"Dr. Shah, please do whatever it is this young man needs. If you have to bring in special doctors, do it. Whatever Yammi needs, you must make sure he has it. I will take care of all the financial obligations. He is to have the best medical technology has to offer."

"I assure you, Pearle, Yammi will be well taken care of, as will the other two boys," he said, smiling.

"Thank you, thank you very much, Dr. Shah."

"Now, what about Daniel, doc—what is his condition?" Robert asked.

"Well, Daniel isn't as critical, as far as wounds go. What I am more concerned about with him is the toxic air he inhaled. He is pretty banged up, though, so we will check that he doesn't have any hidden broken bones or fractures. Other than the apparent symptoms of a concussion, I do not foresee too many problems. Like I said, his respiratory system is my main concern at the moment."

"Thank you, Dr. Shah. We appreciate everything you are doing," Robert said.

They left Dr. Shah to attend to the two boys, and sat down on some plastic green chairs sitting in the corner of the tent. Pearle realized this was the first time she had sat since arriving there nearly five hours ago.

"Where is he, Robert? . . . Why is he not out yet? Something is terribly wrong. I just know it," she said. Then she got up and left the tent quickly.

Robert ran after Pearle and found her talking to a man on the radio.

"What is going on, Pearle?" asked Robert.

"This gentleman is calling Sol to find out what is going on with Matthew."

The man turned from Pearle and Robert, and walked away as he continued to speak to Sol.

Pearle grabbed Robert's hand when the man returned with a solemn face.

"Ms. Sherapha," he paused, "Matthew is still being extricated."

"What do you mean?" she yelled with horror in her voice.

"Please, stay calm, Ms. Sherapha. It means that Matthew is under some heavy stones, and they must use extreme care removing them. They must proceed cautiously so not to cause more harm to him. Mr. Sol said to tell you the doctors are with Matthew and taking good care of him as we speak. He estimates that it should be about fifteen more minutes for the extrication. Then, the doctors will have to prepare him for the journey out. Oh, Ms. Sherapha, he said he is sending up Rahga so he can accompany his son to the hospital. He relayed also that he does not want you to worry too much. He will be with Matthew every second and bring him up safely to you."

Pearle just looked at the man, whose gentle dark eyes and calming voice tried to soothe her.

"I know the pain you have and how it weighs heavy in you, but these things take time. I too have waited for loved ones after a cave-in. Ms. Sherapha, I assure you that Matthew will be here as soon as he is safely removed."

"Thank you," Pearle said, "but I am sorry, I haven't even asked your name, and you have been so helpful all day."

"That is understandable, given the circumstances. You can call me Paulie," he said, holding his hand out to shake hers.

Pearle shook his hand, then gave him a hug.

"Oh, Ms. Sherapha, I have done nothing but my job here. If you need anything, anything at all, please just see me. I must get back to the men now," he said, smiling, revealing the front tooth he was missing.

"Come on, Pearle, let's go back to see Daniel and wait for Matthew. He should be here soon," Robert assured her.

Daniel was sitting up this time when they entered the triage tent. A nurse with a raised voice was telling him that he must lie still.

"Daniel," Pearle hissed, "what are you doing? They want you to lie still. You have a concussion, and it is important to listen to the nurse."

"Pearle, I want to know where Matthew is, and no one is telling me anything! I just can't lie here doing nothing!"

"Oh, yes, you can," Robert growled. "Now, you lie down and wait, just like the rest of us, young man."

"It's taking too long, Robert. He has been hurt bad, and I know . . . . It's been too long!"

"Listen to me," Pearle said as she hugged him. "We are all very worried about him, but he is in good hands, and the best doctors are with him as we speak. So you just lie down and keep yourself thinking good thoughts about our Matthew, okay?"

Robert went around the other side of the stretcher and helped him to lie down. "Now, you stay there," he warned him with a smile, "or I will . . . well, I haven't decided yet what I'll do," he laughed.

"Okay, detective, but only because you are bigger than me," he said, smiling back at Robert.

Pearle heard someone coming and froze.

Rahga snapped the tent flap back, looked at Pearle, and headed toward Yammi. She could see the exhaustion and worry on his face. He spoke briefly with Dr. Shah and went to Yammi, who was asleep.

Pearle and Robert watched as Rahga, a strong, muscular man, looked pathetic and small as he began to weep over his son. Pearle went to him and hugged him as he continued to cry.

"The doctor . . . he says he may lose his arm, Pearle. He has hopes to save it, but cannot guarantee this."

"Rahga," Pearle said as she stepped back and took hold of his shoulders, "we will make sure that does not happen. You must keep positive and think good thoughts."

"Yes, yes, I must," he said, pulling a wrinkled blue handkerchief from his dirty, torn pants; then he blew his nose. "He must not see me like this. No, he must not," as he shook his head and put the wet hanky back into his pants. "We must keep his mind positive also, right, Pearle?"

"Absolutely, Rahga. We must always be the light in the dark for our children," she replied, trying to smile as tears rolled down her sympathetic face.

Rahga looked deeply into Pearle's eyes and knew she was suffering too.

"Pearle, your Matthew, he . . . he is badly hurt. They will have him here shortly, but the doctors say he has had a crushing blow to his legs."

Pearle felt her legs weakening. Suddenly the flap on the tent opened. The doctors, along with Sol, carried Matthew in. Pearle stood frozen and watched as the doctors and nurses quickly and methodically cut Matthew's clothes off and started an IV.

Robert grabbed her hand, and she squeezed it so tight it went numb as they moved closer to the area where Matthew lay. They couldn't get any closer to him. All of the nurses and doctors were busy tending to him. But Robert and Pearle had a good view of what was going on.

Matthew's lower body was in a pressure suit, so Pearle could not see the extent of his injuries. But his head was wrapped in a large blood-soaked bandage, and she overheard the doctor's comments about how Daniel's first aid was what saved Yammi's and Matthew's lives. They watched anxiously as doctors then carefully removed the bandage.

Above Matthew's forehead was a large gash. The doctors decided that it was best not to stitch it now and to get him moved as quickly as possible to the trauma center. They applied a clean bandage to his head, and the leading trauma doctor then motioned for Pearle to come closer.

Robert didn't know, but his hand was bleeding. Pearle had dug her fingernails into his palm.

"Sir, did you get hurt? I noticed you are bleeding," a nurse said as she tried to reach for his hand.

Robert didn't hear her. He felt nothing. He moved closer to Matthew, and his heart sank.

"Pearle, I'm sorry, but Matthew is in a coma," the doctor said. "Thankfully, he is breathing on his own, but he has not regained consciousness, and there is extensive damage to his lower extremities. We are going to move him immediately to the trauma center."

The doctor continued to speak to Pearle and Robert, but he wasn't sure that either one of them heard a word he was saying. They were staring in horror at Matthew's swollen, bloody face. He was gray and looked lifeless. Then Pearle hit the ground before the doctor could catch her. Robert turned, as if in slow motion, and watched as her head hit the ground. Quickly Robert bent down and scooped up Pearle's limp body.

"Here, sir, put her here," the doctor ordered Robert, patting the cushion on top of a stretcher.

Robert gently placed Pearle onto the stretcher.

Sol rushed over to Robert, panicked.

"What happened, Robert?" Sol gasped.

"She just passed out, Sol. I was afraid this would happen. She has been so upset all day, and when she saw Matthew up close," and Robert swallowed hard, "I guess it just hit her all at once."

"Excuse me," the doctor said as he made his way between Robert and Sol to get to Pearle.

Robert and Sol backed away from the stretcher. Robert turned, looked at Matthew, then back at Pearle. He felt crushed and walked to the far-end corner of the tent, put his hands over his face, and began to sob. He wasn't too sure how long he had been standing there when he felt a hand on his shoulder.

"Come, Robert, they are moving Matthew to the hospital. Pearle is awake now and asking for you. This is a very difficult time for all of us. I understand how you feel, Robert. It pleases me to see such a man of your character in love with my Pearle. It truly does an old man good to see these things. Now come," Sol said, patting Robert's shoulder. "I have another helicopter waiting to take us to the hospital."

"What time is it, Robert?" Pearle asked with a yawn.

"Would you like Egyptian or American time?" he replied with a smile.

"The present here time," she said as she stretched and yawned again.

"It is 4 a.m., Pearle."

"Good. I can go back in to see Matthew again."

Pearle opened the door to the ICU, and across from a nurse's desk was Matthew's bed. She pulled a metal chair sitting in the corner of the room and sat next to his bed. She stroked his arm and began to talk to him.

"Matt, I am not sure if you can hear me, but I am here, honey."

She looked at his body, with all the tubes coming from it, and wondered if he knew what was going on. The doctors operated on his legs and were able to save them. As for him being able to use them, no one knows yet. Everything about the outcome of Matthew's condition depends on his awakening. Then they would know.

"Robert's right outside. He says to hurry up and wake up. He said the plastic chairs here are uncomfortable, and his butt hurts. You know him; he always has to make a joke about everything. Personally, I think he and Daniel are spending too much time together," she laughed. *Nothing,* she thought to herself as she looked at his bruised, swollen face, hoping for some type of reaction, some sign that he heard her.

"I'm sorry, Ms. Sherapha," a nurse softly said. "We have to ask you to leave now. We are going to be taking him down for some more tests, and we have to prepare him."

Pearle smiled back at the petite, dark-haired nurse.

"Okay, Matthew, I am getting kicked out," she said, winking back to the nurse. "I'll be back in just a bit to see you." And she leaned over and kissed him on his bruised cheek. Then she went to the supervisor of the ICU room.

"Nurse, what test is he going for?"

"The doctor wants another CAT scan."

"Why?" Pearle asked. "He's had two already."

"I do not know, Pearle," she said as she grabbed Pearle's hand. "I would assume, though, that they are watching for any swelling on the brain and keeping an eye on his leg swelling. It's a standard practice with his type of injuries. You may accompany him to the test area, if you would like. Hearing your voice is good medicine, Pearle."

"Thank you," Pearle said, and left the room, turning back to catch a glimpse of her grandson. Pearle closed the ICU door and leaned back against the wall. She inhaled, then exhaled deeply. Robert was watching her closely and had been since they arrived at the hospital almost twelve hours ago. Her passing out again was a main concern of his. She had gotten a nice bump on the head from the fall at the triage tent. He told her in the helicopter that passing out was not an option anymore and not on his watch. He enjoyed the chuckle he got out of her.

They both turned around when they heard the clacking of high heels echoing in the quiet hallway. It was Dr. Elizabeth, head of Neurology at the facility.

"Good evening, Pearle. How are you doing?"

"Good. Thank you, doctor."

"How's that bump on your head? It was quite large when you came in here. Please, let me take a look. Hmm . . . looks good. Only three stitches, not bad. The swelling has gone down a lot too. . . . Any pain?"

"No, not really. I had a headache earlier, but the nurse gave me something for it. I'll be fine. Thank you, doctor."

"When was the last time you ate, Pearle?"

She couldn't remember and shrugged her shoulders.

"Just as I suspected," she said with her bushy eyebrows raised and her pink, well-scrubbed hands on her chubby waist. "You need to go get something to eat, or I will be treating both of you for exhaustion. You won't do Matthew any good, either one of you, if you don't take care of yourselves."

"But they said Matthew is going for another CAT scan and I could go along."

"We just had an emergency come in, so it will be probably another hour before he goes. Do me a favor; go to the cafeteria, and ask for Maria. Tell her Dr. Elizabeth sent you down for her sandwich specialty. She will take good care of you. Now go; it's doctor's orders! Matthew is stable, and if anything changes, we will call you. I know where you are," she said with a wink. "Now go, shoo-shoo," she said with her hand waving.

"I guess I could eat something, and I know you must be starving, Robert."

"Funny," he said, "I haven't thought about food all day. Now that you mention it, I could use a little something for this growling stomach."

"Then go," Dr. Elizabeth said. "And don't come back until Maria has stuffed you." She turned, laughing, and went in to see Matthew.

"Well, she is rather weird," Pearle said.

"Pearle, I think anybody is going to seem weird to us after the last two days with no sleep. Let's just go get something to eat so we can get back here, okay?"

They went to the elevator. When the doors opened, Sol was standing there.

"Sol, what are you doing here?" Pearle said, quite shocked.

"Where are you two going?" he quickly asked.

"We are on our way to the cafeteria," Robert replied.

"Wonderful. Come, let's go get something to eat. I can't remember when I last had some food," Sol said, rubbing his stomach.

They found Maria in the cafeteria's kitchen. She was a tiny elderly woman with thin gray hair pulled back tight in a bun, covered in white netting. Robert didn't think she was more than five feet tall! She was dressed in purple hospital scrubs and had the cleanest white work shoes on that Robert ever saw. Her smile and cheery, sweet personality were heartwarming. She gave them a fresh pot of coffee and told them to go sit. She said that three "Dr. Elizabeth Specials" would be out in fifteen minutes.

Pearle eyed the large fluorescent-lit cafeteria. The orange and yellow multi colors of the chairs and tables oddly reminded her of high school. The highly polished white and green floor tiles gave an aesthetic feeling to the immaculate cafeteria, but the brightness hurt her eyes. She saw the hospital phone near a window table and chose to sit there, as Dr. Elizabeth said she would call it if she needed to speak with her.

The humming fluorescent lights seemed too bright for Sol's tired eyes too, and he rubbed them with his rough, yellow, calloused fingers. He was physically exhausted after spending the last ten hours in the pyramid trying to figure out why the cave-in happened. That pyramid was as safe as a new building. He was sure of that!

A bigger question haunted all their minds, though: How and why were the boys in the pyramid during the middle of the night?

Robert sipped his coffee as the three sat in silence. Robert had a burning question and decided it would be a good idea to start a friendly conversation with Sol and Pearle.

"Pearle, may I ask you something?"

"Sure, what is it?"

"Well, why did you become an archaeologist? For that matter, why would anyone want to dig around all day in dirt under extremely dangerous conditions? I mean, why would you do that? Don't get me wrong; finding gold and other treasures seems wonderful, but what drives you to do that with so much at stake?"

Pearle looked at Sol and smiled.

"You want to tell him?" Pearle said with a wink to Sol.

"No, I am going to let you. I'm interested in hearing your answer, Pearle," Sol replied, patting her hand and winking back.

"Well," Pearle said as she undid her barrette and let her long black hair fall to her shoulders. There is some truth about some archaeologists being fortune hunters. You know, going for the gold, fame and fortune. But a very wise man many years ago told me a truth about the profession. That truth, Robert, became my drive to be an archaeologist. A truth that only those who believe in and live it are worthy enough to call themselves an archaeologist."

"Okay, sounds intriguing so far, Pearle. Tell me more," Robert said as he leaned back into his chair.

Pearle wrapped her hands around her warm coffee mug and continued.

"You see, Robert, it's not like you're a kid at the beach with your pail and shovel. You know, digging deep into the sand, looking for shells to take home as souvenirs. It is so much more. It's not about buried treasure. It is a chance in your lifetime to tell the story of someone who can't speak for himself. You become their voice, Robert. Archaeology is an opportunity to reveal their history. It's a humbling experience to be part of that history and not just tell others, but to show the world. Finding the past and being able to bring it to the present and future is a self-made revelation. Nothing, as an archaeologist, is more satisfying. I can remember every backbreaking moment I have spent digging in scorching sand. I've crawled into numerous small, suffocating tunnels, petrified that they could collapse on me at any second. In the end, Robert, it was the satisfaction of being able to put all my findings, the pieces, together, to tell a stranger's wonderful life story, truthfully. That is why I did it and what drove me to be an archaeologist."

"Wow, I guess I never looked at it that way, Pearle."

Sol looked at Pearle and realized he had been a good teacher to a wonderful student.

"Oh, looks like lunch is here," said Robert as he watched Maria and two other helpers come with their food.

"Lunch," Sol snorted, "it looks like a feast!"

They broke into laughter for the first time in days and began to eat Maria's wonderful meal.

Sol moved his empty plate aside and wiped his mouth. He looked at the napkin and tsked,

"Gee, Pearle, why didn't you tell me my face was so dirty" as he laughed.

"I guess I like looking at you that way," she chuckled back.

"Boy, that was good. But I'm not sure I want to know what kind of meat was on that sandwich, though," Robert said, rubbing his full stomach. "Now, if you'll excuse me," he said, standing up, "I'm going to find the little boys room. I'll be back in a few minutes." As he walked away, a terrible thought crossed his mind. Between the grumbling of his stomach and the taste he had on the back of his tongue, he prayed that he did not just eat lamb. It had a habit of finding its way out of his intestines very quickly.

"Pearle, I have some good news for you."

"Really; what is it, Sol?"

"While I was at the pyramid tonight, I discovered it won't take but a few months to clear up the cave-in and reinforce everything."

"That is good news, Sol, but did you figure out what caused it?"

"Well, there is more good news. I am not sure, but several stones fell from a wall, and I believe it leads to more chambers. I will not know for sure until we can get more of the debris cleaned up, though. It is completely a mystery how this could be, Pearle!"

"Sol, I don't know either. I can't understand this. Do you think this is the reason the cave-in occurred?"

"That is something we will find out in time, but I have my suspicions it could have very well been the cause. That room was extremely well-secured, and right now, it is the only logical answer."

"Promise me, though, you will be careful. You know as well as I do, one cave-in increases the odds for more," she stressed.

"Yes, yes, of course we will be extremely careful, Pearle. You know how I am about safety, especially that of my workers."

"I was talking about you, Sol. No offense, but you are not a spring chicken anymore!"

"What is this you say? Shame on you! I am a tasty old bird," he roared.

Pearle laughed so hard with Sol, they both had tears running from their eyes. As Pearle was wiping her eyes, the phone rang on the wall.

Robert was coming out of the restroom when he caught Pearle running by.

"What's wrong, Pearle?" he yelled as he ran toward her and Sol, heading for the elevator.

"It's Matthew; he's had a seizure!"

They ran off the elevator straight into the ICU room.

"We are taking him down now for a scan, Pearle. I just can't understand. . . . His earlier scans showed nothing. I will be better able to see what's going on after the test," the doctor informed them. She grabbed Matthew's bed, along with two other doctors, and took Matthew quickly to the elevator.

"May I go with you, Dr. Elizabeth?" Pearle asked, trembling.

"No. Stay here," she urged as she pushed the first-floor button repeatedly. "It is very busy downstairs. I'm sorry, but there is nothing you can do, anyway." And the elevator door slowly shut in Pearle's face.

"Come, Pearle, let's wait for him back by the room," Robert said as he took hold of her shoulders and turned her around.

No one spoke for nearly two hours as they sat staring at the elevator door.

"Pearle, I'm just going down the hall to check on Yammi and Daniel. I will be back in a while," Sol said.

"That's a good idea, Sol," Pearle replied. "I'll be right here," she assured him.

Moments later, the elevator door opened.

"Oh, my God ... Dr. . . . Elizabeth, what ... what has happened?"

She took Pearle's hand and led her and Robert to a private room.

"Pearle, I am afraid Matthew has taken a turn for the worst. He had several grand mal seizures due to sudden swelling on his brain, and it has become necessary to put him on a ventilator. Matthew needs a very complex surgery, I'm afraid. What's worse is that we do not have anyone here qualified to perform such an operation."

"Well, can we call another hospital? There has to be somebody who can do the surgery!" Pearle said hysterically.

"There are only a handful of skilled surgeons in the world who are capable of performing this difficult surgery. I have called one in Germany to consult with, and he referred me to someone else, who is a brilliant doctor for this situation but extremely difficult to reach. His specialty is severe head trauma cases and epilepsy. I already put a call in to him, but he will not be available, they said, until later today. I explained the urgency of the situation, and, well, hopefully we will hear back from him sooner. Time is Matthew's enemy right now.

"Let's hope this doctor gets back with us right away. Matthew is stable for the moment, but I don't know how long that will last, Pearle. I'm sorry," she said with tears in her eyes. "We . . . ."

Pearle jumped up before the doctor finished her sentence. Robert and the doctor looked at each other.

"I have an idea, Dr. Elizabeth. Robert, please give me your phone," she ordered. Pearle called Annabelle and got the information she needed. She dialed the phone again.

"Hello, Anthony, this is Pearle. I need to speak with you. It's an emergency and concerns Matthew."

"Who is she speaking with?" Dr. Elizabeth asked Robert.

"Dr. Anthony Almondative."

"Are you kidding me?" she asked, looking shocked.

"No, I kid you not, doc," Robert replied.

"Dr. Elizabeth, Anthony needs to speak with you," Pearle said, giving her the phone with a shaky hand. Pearle stood with her hands over her mouth, watching and listening intently to the doctor. They spoke in length about Matthew's injuries and the seizures he had. Dr. Elizabeth also informed him of the numerous tests done, their results, and medications administered.

"Yes, yes, I can keep him stable. Yes, ah hah, do not worry; we will be ready for your arrival. All right, doctor, I look forward to meeting you. Okay, here is Pearle."

"Yes, Anthony, yes I will. Anthony, thank you," Pearle said with tears rolling down her cheeks. "I'll see you soon, then." She pushed the end button on the phone and handed it back to Robert, shaking.

"We are in luck, and God has answered our prayers," Dr. Elizabeth said. "He was in a meeting with his surgical staff when I called him."

"Oh, that's who you called and left a message for?" Robert asked.

"Yes, that is why when you told me who Pearle was speaking to, I got so excited! I'm figuring about three hours to fly to our closest airport, and then we will transport him and his team by helicopter here. Okay," she said excitedly as she stood. "I am going to check in on Matthew and prepare everyone for the surgery."

"May I see Matthew now, Dr. Elizabeth?"

"Yes, Pearle, but only for a few moments. Come, Pearle, sit here by me."

Pearle did as asked and then began to cry.

"Listen to me, Pearle," she said as she held her hands. "We have been given a great miracle, so I do not want you to cry. Matthew is going to be with the best doctors and a highly skilled medical team who perform this type of surgery on a daily basis. So, I want you to go see Matthew for a few minutes. Then you are going to an empty room down the hall, and lie down for a while. If anything at all is to happen, I will personally come get you, I promise."

"You promise, Dr. Elizabeth?"

"Of course; you have my word, Pearle," and with that, she hugged her.

"Oh, Mr. Robert, that nap goes for you and Mr. Sol, wherever he is," she said with a comforting smile. "Now come, let's go check on Matthew."

Eight hours has passed since Anthony Almondative and his five-member team arrived at the hospital. It was late afternoon, and Pearle was asleep, with her head on Robert's shoulder. Sol was with them in the small surgical waiting room. Robert feels like he has been there for weeks. He rubbed his stubbly, greasy face and thought about how he hasn't shaved or showered in three days. He recalled the last time he went that long without either. It was when he had the flu several years ago. He inhaled and gently rested his cheek against Pearle's head. The floral scent of her hair reminded him of the sweet smell of honeysuckle after a summer rain shower. He wondered how she could smell so wonderful after three days with no shower. He closed his eyes and inhaled her comforting aroma.

Earlier, Sol and Robert had talked briefly about the boys. Robert asked Sol how the boys could have gained entrance into the pyramid with so much security there. Sol said it was impossible and could not understand how they managed it. They thought about asking Daniel, but decided to give him another day while he recuperated from his ordeal.

The door opened to the waiting room. Pearle instinctively

jumped as the door's hinges groaned for oiling. It was Rahga, not who she expected or was hoping it would be.

"Rahga, come, sit," Sol said as he motioned him to a seat next to him. "How is Yammi doing? What have the doctors said?"

"First, I want to know how Matthew is. Has there been any word yet?"

"No, nothing yet; we are still waiting."

"It has been a long time, no?"

"Yes, Rahga, but this kind of surgery goes very slowly. He is with the best doctors, and you know what they say, no news is good news, right?"

"Well, then, we shall wait and think good thoughts, everyone," he said as he forced a smile to his exhausted face.

"That is the plan, Rahga. So please, tell us about Yammi. He had a long surgery also. How is he doing?" Pearle asked.

"The doctors said he has an avulsion to the lower arm."

"What is that?" asked Pearle, who was now sitting on the edge of her seat.

"They explained that the stone that pierced Yammi's arm was like a thick, jagged razor blade. It cut away his muscles and other tissues from the bones. His ulna and radius bones were also shattered in many locations. The doctors said they were surprised his lower arm remained attached, with the severity of the injury. He is going to need more surgery, but they are not equipped here to do this kind of surgery, Pearle. They say he may still lose his arm and have done all they could for now." Rahga held a firm face, but Pearle saw in his eyes the hurting man he tried to hide.

"Did they say how soon this other surgery needs to be done, Rahga?"

"I did not ask, and they did not say. I will ask today, though, when I see his surgeon, Pearle."

"Rahga, if they cannot help Yammi here, then he will go where they can. I promise you, Yammi will be taken care of by the best doctors we can find. Whatever must be done, I will make sure of it."

"Thank you, Pearle. I don't know what to say," Rahga replied.

"Rahga, sometimes the look in one's eyes says more than words ever could." Pearle winked at him, and he sat back in his chair, smiling and on the verge of tears.

She looked around the quiet, bright room. She had gone through all of the magazines on the table several times. There was even an article on Sol in one of them. However, she could not recall what it was even about, for it seemed liked ages, instead of the hours ago, since she read it. She noticed the two trash cans in the room, piled with coffee cups and snack wrappers. Pearle strangely wondered when someone would come to empty them.

The day was winding down, and the crimson sun was getting ready to set. The traffic outside the window seemed to crawl along the road. Life was continuing to go on outside, while life inside was struggling to live.

The creaky door then opened. Several doctors entered, still wearing their green surgical outfits. But Pearle was looking for only one familiar face. There he was; she recognized him even behind his surgical mask. She quickly searched his face. He looked tired but managed a small smile. Dr Elizabeth was behind him, and they sat down across from her and Robert.

"Matthew is stable right now," Anthony began. "The surgery went well, but we will not know if he has had any permanent brain damage until he awakes. I will remain here until he is conscious and make sure no further surgery is required. Otherwise, for now, we just wait."

Pearle felt his icy tone and could not understand how a man who just saved his son's life seemed so unemotional. Even Dr. Elizabeth was surprised with his frosty attitude. If looks could kill, Robert had his hands around Anthony's throat for being so cold toward Pearle. Robert now understood why she did not like him.

Pearle stood up. She looked cold and hard into Anthony's eyes. His behavior was typical. She always thought he was a pompous jerk! However, he just saved her grandson's life, and she was grateful. She bent down and gave him a hug.

"Thank you for coming so quickly, Anthony. What you have done for Matthew, well, there are no words I can find to express my gratitude."

That's my Pearle, Robert thought to himself. *She has more class in her pinky than that man could ever have!*

Anthony stood up and asked where he and his staff could rest.

"We have our liaison waiting to accommodate you, Dr. Almondative. You will find her at the end of the hall in room 258."

"Thank you, Dr. Elizabeth. I appreciate the professional courtesy you have extended to us."

"You are welcome, doctor."

"Oh, I will be notified immediately of *any* changes in Matthew's condition, correct?"

"Absolutely. There are orders in place for both of us to be notified, sir."

He opened the door and left, with his team following.

"My," Sol said, shaking his head, "he is *still* an ignoramus ass!"

Chapter Twenty-one

Pearle, Robert, Matthew, Daniel, and Yammi were on their way back to Florida. They were flying home on a special plane Pearle hired because of Matthew's injuries. He was lucky, though. . . . His injuries ten days ago had left him in critical condition, and the doctors then . . . had little hope for his recovery. However, luck had nothing to do with Matthew's awakening several hours after his brain surgery. Only one person knows why Matthew did not die . . . and it is Daniel.

Sol had brought the boys' backpacks to the hospital after Daniel insisted that he would not leave the pyramid after the cave-in without them. He knew how important the contents were to Matthew. Not only did Daniel's quick thinking save Matthew and Yammi that day; he also saved Emia, Amora, and Oopi.

After Daniel had settled in his room and spoken to his mom, he went into the bathroom with his and Matthew's backpacks. He took the creatures out and checked on what Matthew had collected from the pyramid. Everything seemed okay to him. Then he sat up against the door, looking at the dirty, blood-soaked backpack, and began to sob.

"Daniel, please do not be saddened," Amora cooed as she gently stroked his bruised hand.

"Friend, here, take this," Oopi said as he handed Daniel a wad of toilet paper that was still attached to the roll on the wall, and he made Daniel smile under his tear-soaked face.

"Oopi," Daniel said in a low, soft tone, "what happened in the pyramid?"

"It was her," he said in a disgusted tone. "The evil one became enraged when Matthew took possession of the things it desired! She did not want them or him to leave the home. Her wrath, though, proves how evil she is and that she will stop at nothing to get what she wants. I cannot understand this. If Matthew has to break this curse and fulfill the prophecy, why would she seek to destroy him? I am quite puzzled by this and very much troubled," Oopi said, scratching his wrinkled head.

"I do not believe we should worry of these things at the moment. Our heir is gravely injured, and if we do not help him, I am afraid . . . we will lose him," Emia said sadly.

"What do you mean, Emia?!" Daniel shouted.

Emia sighed, then flew around the small bathroom for a moment, then lit on Daniel's leg. She looked tired and frail, not herself. He then looked at Oopi and Amora. Daniel reached into his bag and took out whatever food he could find for them. He gave Emia and Amora honey, and a single carrot and a few strawberries in a plastic bag to Oopi. They ate ravenously, and Daniel watched as the girls' brilliant colors come back to them.

"Thank you, friend," Oopi said as he inched his way up Daniel's chest.

"I'm sorry it is not more, but I will work on that for you, Oopi," Daniel replied, stroking Oopi's purple belly with his bruised fingers.

"Please, Emia, tell me now about Matthew. What is going on? No one has told me much about how he is except that he needed surgery."

"He fades, dear friend. His injuries are slowly taking his life as we speak. If we do not act quickly, I am afraid our heir will . . . die." Amora and Emia then wept for the first time since he had met them. Their tiny tears, a light purple color, rolled down their sad little faces. Then Oopi stood on his tail. His teary orange eyes began glaring brightly.

"No, no, no! We must do something, Emia! I will not let him perish; do you hear me?!" he hissed.

"Emia, please," Daniel begged, "there must be something we can do to save Matthew. He can't die; he just . . . can't!"

"There is but one thing that can be done, dear friend. But I am afraid it will take a great sacrifice on your part. It is a decision not to be made in haste, for it has consequences."

"Well, just tell me Emia! Whatever it is, I will do it!" Daniel assured her.

"You must give of your life."

"What . . . what do you mean, Emia?"

"For Matthew to live, you must give of yourself. It does not mean that you will perish, dear friend. It means you must sacrifice some of your life essence to Matthew. In doing so, you will lose some of your young years you were yet to live through. You will age, but it will not be physically noticeable to anyone, not even you. However, you will change, Daniel. You must weigh this extremely important decision on your part. It's a sacrifice that will only work when one willingly gives of himself, selflessly, and has pure love for another."

"So how do we do this, Emia? Where do we start?" Daniel said as he stood up and wiped his tears. "Matthew is blood to me. He is like my brother, and I will do whatever he needs to survive, so let's get going here before I lose him."

"You are sure of this, friend?" Oopi asked, looking deeply into his eyes.

"Yes, Oopi, of course."

"All right, then retrieve the Bennu Elixir bottle; its contents are of gold and purple," he told Daniel.

Daniel dug through their bag and found it on the bottom. Amora then went into the bag to find the Opika Elixir. To her disappointment, there was none.

"Emia, we have but one problem," she whispered.

"What is it, Amora? What is wrong?"

"We have no Opika. We must have of it if you and Daniel are to save our heir."

"Then *we* must sacrifice also for the heir. Without the Opika, you know what is required of you."

"Yes," replied Amora without any hesitation. "Yes, and I will do that for him."

"Wait a minute, here," Daniel interrupted. "What are you going to do, Amora?"

"It is the only way, friend," Oopi replied.

"What's the only way, Oopi? Is Amora going to . . . to die if she does this?" Daniel asked, swallowing hard.

"No, not exactly. She will sleep, though, and for a very long time. It will only be until we can get her a healing elixir to bring back her strength."

"Are you sure, Amora, that you want to do this?" Daniel said, looking into her beautiful, kind eyes.

"I am more than sure, Daniel. Come, let's get ready. Matthew is back in his room, and we have much preparation to do."

"What do you need me to do, Emia?" Daniel asked.

"We will require a few drops of your blood and an article of Matthew's clothing. Then we will mix the healing Bennu Elixir with a part of Amora's wing and your blood. You will have to drink of this mixture, and when we reach Matthew, you will then breathe your life into him. In a few hours, the injuries that are taking his life will cease, and our heir will live. Although, I must tell you, the elixir will not heal everything. Only what threatens his life will be gone."

"Okay, I can live with that, but oh, my God, you are going to take a part of Amora's wing off?!" he asked in horror. "Won't that hurt her?"

"It is a pain that will cease quickly because I will sleep immediately, Daniel. As for my wing, it will eventually heal. So please, do not worry. Besides, this is our only way to save the heir," Amora replied.

"What is so special about Amora's wings?"

"Her wings possess the ability of time. It will help pass on the sacrifice you give of yourself to Matthew. The Bennu Elixir will not work properly unless we have her wing. It will bring your life to the Bennu Elixir and heal his body. The Opika we were to use does this also. It is made of Amora's essence. Now go get Matthew's shirt. As soon as we take of Amora's wing, you will put her and Oopi in the bag. You will then drink of the elixir, and we will be off to Matthew."

"I have but one question, guys: How do we get in to see Matthew? He is in a special room, and they won't let me in."

"Ah, yes," replied Oopi. With the elixir inside of you, no one will see you, my dear friend. You will be invisible! Quite clever, I might say too!"

Daniel smiled at Oopi, but couldn't help but cringe, as he still thought about Amora and the part of her wing that Emia would remove.

"Amora, Daniel, are you ready?"

Daniel looked at Amora. They knew each other's sacrifice for Matthew was necessary and realized that what they were about to do would be a memory, shared forever in their hearts.

"Okay, we are ready, Emia," they said together.

As Daniel held Amora in his hand, Emia flew down and quickly snapped a piece of her wing off. Amora fell down gently and went to sleep. Daniel then picked up Oopi and carefully placed him and Amora in their bag.

"Okay, Daniel, put on Matthew's shirt, and drink of the elixir."

Daniel did as Emia instructed. He drank the entire bottle, wiped his mouth, and then began to feel sick.

"I don't feel so well, Emia," he said.

"That will wear off, Daniel," she assured him. "Now come, we must go to Matthew quickly while the elixir is strong," she urged.

He slowly opened the bathroom door and looked around. There was a woman cleaning up his room.

"Oh, ah . . . thank you for doing that, miss," Daniel said nervously.

Nevertheless, the woman didn't even bat an eye and kept doing her chores.

"Daniel, she cannot see or hear you. Please, we mustn't waste any time getting to Matthew!"

"Emia, what about the backpacks? They have those important things Matthew collected. I don't want anyone to see them!"

"No one will be able to see their contents, dear friend. To anyone other than us, they are just dirty bags that belong to you. Now come, we must go."

Off they went down the hall and around a corner to the ICU, where Matthew was. Daniel saw Pearle and Robert sitting outside Matthew's room. He noticed how exhausted they looked. He wished he could tell Pearle that Matthew was going to be okay. But he couldn't. He would not be able to tell anyone.

"They will know soon enough," Emia whispered in his ear.

Doctor Elizabeth was coming out of the ICU room, and Daniel walked right in. They went to Matthew's bedside, and Daniel was not prepared for what he saw.

Matthew was pale in places where his swollen face wasn't horribly bruised. He lay lifeless and on a respirator. Tubes were coming out of his frail body everywhere.

"Oh, my God, Emia . . . no one told me he was on a respirator! Are you sure this is going to work?" he asked, panicked.

"Yes, of course it is, dear friend. You will have to get very close to his face and put your mouth near his. Then you will breathe your life into him. Do you think you can manage that with all those strange things he has in his mouth?"

"Emia, I will make sure I do," he answered.

Shaking and frightened, Daniel slowly bent over the bed, facing Matthew. He eyed over Matthew's gray and purple swollen face. He watched in horror as the cold metal machine pumped air in and out of his dear friend's lungs. Emia stared at the rising and sinking of Matthew's chest as it kept perfect rhythm with the machine. Then Daniel got real close to Matthew's mouth. He cupped his hands around his mouth and Matthew's. As he was exhaling his breath into Matthew's mouth, he saw a purple mist rising around Matthew's head. He began to feel weak, but he did not stop. When every last bit of his breath was gone, he raised his head, held onto the bed rail, swooning, waiting with Emia for a sign. He prayed for any sign that Matthew was going to be okay. Considerable time had passed, and with no improvement. Nurses had come and gone every fifteen minutes, checking on Matthew's vital signs. The reality of losing Daniel's best friend was setting in. Daniel was getting more discouraged with every breath the machine pumped into Matthew's beaten body.

"Hey, Emia, how long did you say it would be before we saw a change in him?"

"How long has it been, Daniel?"

"It's been almost two hours now. I thought we would've . . . ."

Daniel heard Matthew's heart rate picking up on the monitor. He turned and smiled at her. Matthew began to move, and several alarms went off. The beeping noise became deafening to Emia. The alarms began a stir of commotion in the room and around Matthew's bed. This was a night no one in this small hospital would ever forget. What happened next was nothing short of a miracle.

Daniel heard a voice on the hospital speaker asking for Dr. Elizabeth in ICU, STAT! The room filled with a flurry of nurses and doctor. Matthew was coughing and pointing to the tube down his throat. Shocked, Dr. Elizabeth told him to calm down, that he needed to relax. She assured him that if he did, she could remove the breathing tube. Matthew lay back and closed his eyes. Daniel and Emia were huddled in the corner. Daniel was so happy, he cried. So did Emia.

Two hours later, Matthew was eating chocolate pudding and talking with Pearle and Robert.

"There they are," yelled Denise as she squeezed Annabelle's hand. "That's their plane coming in!"

Annabelle and Denise ran to the plane once it had taxied to its designated spot. Behind them were an ambulance, its crew, and Matthew's special nurse. Neither one knew what to expect, but they were happy everyone was finally home. The door opened to the plane, and the first person to step out was Robert. It was a beautiful spring day in Florida. The sun was shining, humidity was low, and you could smell the fresh saltwater air from the Gulf of Mexico. Robert took a deep breath in and slowly exhaled. He was so happy to finally be home.

He waved to Annabelle and Denise, then motioned for the ambulance. Denise then assisted with the careful moving of Matthew and Yammi from airplane to ambulance. After a tearful reunion with everyone, Pearle was ready to go home. Robert went in the ambulance with the two boys. Everyone else rode back to the house with Denise.

"Annabelle, did everything come for Matthew that his doctors ordered?"

"Yes, and Denise helped me to make a sure that everything was all set up correctly. Hey, we no amateurs!"

Pearle just gave her a big smile.

"I have the two bedrooms downstairs prepared for Matthew and his nurse. The room upstairs next to Matthew's is ready for Yammi, and I think everything is set up so the boys will be comfortable. If we a need to change a something, we do, that's all!"

"That's great, and I really appreciate everything you two have done. I can't wait until I get Matthew home and settled in."

"Well . . . I . . . just a glad you are all home, Pearle." Then Annabelle began to cry.

"Annabelle, what is wrong, hun?" Pearle asked, turning around to look at her.

"Oh, I'm a sorry, Pearle. It is just that, well . . . ," but Annabelle couldn't answer her.

"I think she's just so happy that you all are home, Pearle. Hey, did she tell you she spoke with her brother?" Denise said excitedly.

"No, she didn't . . . and may I ask why you didn't, missy?" Pearle said.

Annabelle smiled, blew her nose, and wiped her tears.

"Ah, I guess I so worried about my Matthew that I forgot." She replied with a shrug of her shoulders.

"Well . . . tell me! What did he have to say? Did *he* call *you?*" Pearle asked excitedly.

"No, no, *I* call *him*. I asked him if he could say special prayers for Matthew, and I guess it was perfect opportunity to . . . to mend fences, as you say. Things are good now between us. He even says that one day he will come visit me!"

"Oh, Annabelle, that is the best news I have heard in a long time! This is wonderful that you and your brother are speaking again."

"Yes, yes, I am very happy too. It's been too long. . . ."

Although Pearle had arranged special nurses for around-the-clock duty to care for Matthew, she knew that extra help with the house was needed to take some of the burden off Annabelle. She laughed and told Annabelle, though, that didn't mean she was getting off from cooking.

Annabelle called a few different agencies for help that Pearle suggested and had even mentioned to Abe Haram one day that she was looking for a good housekeeper. He told her he did not know of anyone, but that if he came across someone worthy of the job, he would contact her.

Four days and twenty-six applicants later, Annabelle finally got lucky with Nakia, a woman with excellent references and desperate for a job. Nakia fit all the requirements they were looking for. She was educated, young, fit, and very neat in appearance. And after working a week with Annabelle, she fit right in. Nakia was from Egypt and had learned English while studying American and ancient Egyptian history in college. She told Annabelle she had only been in the country for a short time but hoped to continue her education and that one day, she would like to be a history teacher. Nakia promised that she would work very hard at her position and was grateful Annabelle gave her the job.

Nakia was outside gathering fresh flowers when Denise's SUV pulled up. She quickly put the flowers in a basket, brushed the dirt off her slacks, and made sure her ponytail was neat before meeting Pearle.

"Hello, Ms. Sherapha, I am Nakia. It is so wonderful to finally meet you."

"Well, hello to you, Nakia, and welcome to the family," Pearle responded, shaking Nakia's hand.

"Thank you, Ms. Sherapha. I am very excited about my position here and look forward to my duties."

"That's good to hear, but you must call me Pearle, okay?"

"Oh, yes, whatever pleases you," Nakia responded.

"Good, then I think we will get along just fine. Now, if you would, please help Annabelle get the luggage. Just don't hurt yourself, girls," Pearle yelled as Annabelle, Nakia, and Daniel emptied out the back of Denise's SUV. When the last piece of luggage was out of the SUV, the ambulance pulled up with Robert and the boys.

"Hah, perfect timing," Pearle said while grinning.

"Oh, and why is that, lady?" Robert asked, getting out of the ambulance.

"We just finished putting the luggage inside."

"Aye, what can I say? My mama no raise a stupid boy," Robert replied in an Italian accent. "No, serious, Pearle, you should have waited for me."

"Good gracious, Robert; I was only kidding!"

"Hah, yeah, so was I!"

They shared a good laugh—something neither one of them had done much in the last ten days. The time they spent in Egypt didn't go exactly as everyone had expected, especially for Robert. He had planned to ask Pearle to marry him. However, with everything that happened, he put his plans on hold.

"It's good to be home, isn't it, Pearle?"

"You can say that again. I don't want to see another passport for at least ten years."

Annabelle and Nakia made a big dinner to celebrate Pearle and Matthew's homecoming. As everyone gathered around the table to eat, Pearle noticed the only thing missing was Matthew. Robert held up his glass and looked around the table.

"Ahem," and he cleared his throat. "I want to make a toast," he announced as he stood. "I raise my glass with gratitude to honor a very courageous young man. To Daniel, whose courage, quick thinking, and selfless giving helped save the lives of two people."

They all stood holding their glasses up in thankful silence for a moment. Then they all clinked glasses and sat back down.

"Thank you, Robert, but that wasn't necessary. I only did what had to be done. I think if anyone should be thanked, it should be my mom," Daniel said as he looked over at Denise and smiled at her.

"Oh," replied Denise, "why is that, son?"

"Well, it was you who urged me to take all those first aid courses. I acted like a jerk and gave you a real hard time about it too. Mom, I'm sorry and just want to say thanks for insisting I go to those classes. If you didn't push me to . . . we probably wouldn't be sitting here."

Daniel stared at his mother. He was different, and she noticed it. The Daniel she knows is a quick-tongued preteen, who jokes at just about everything. Tonight, he was articulate and grown up.

Denise pushed her chair back, picked up the linen tablecloth, and looked under the table. Everyone was watching her with the oddest expressions.

"Ah, Denise, what are you looking for? Did you lose something?" Pearle asked.

Denise popped her head up and replied amusingly, "My son, I know I saw him here just a few minutes ago. Boy, that must have been some bump on the head!" And she made everyone hysterically laugh.

Then she began to cry, and everyone, including Robert, started to tear up.

"Okay, mom, that's enough," Daniel said as he got up and went around the table to her. He hugged and kissed her head as he wrapped his arms around her from behind.

"Now, mom, don't let that go to your head," he said with a laugh.

Daniel sat back down and winked at his mom. Pearle raised her glass to Daniel and winked at him. At that moment, Pearle felt she could never be prouder of Daniel. She wondered if he really knew how grateful she was for saving her grandson. Then, as if Daniel read her mind, he glanced over at her and winked back.

Yammi was sitting by Robert, taking everything in. He was so happy to be with a family and their friends that cared so much for one another. He was very humbled by Pearle and all she was doing for him. He just wished that Matthew was not confined to his bed.

"Thank you, Miss Annabelle. That was the most delicious ham I have ever eaten," Yammi said.

"You are very welcomed, Yammi, but I hope you left room for dessert," she replied.

"I don't think I could fit a single crumb into my belly," he said. If I eat another drop, I may explode!"

"Well, maybe later, after you have digested," Robert suggested.

"Maybe a snack *much* later, perhaps," he said, rubbing his belly.

"Hey, Daniel," Yammi said, "why don't we take Matthew his dessert and see how he is doing?"

"That's a good idea, Yammi. He is probably miserable lying there, knowing him."

Nakia and Annabelle were cleaning up the kitchen while Robert, Denise, and Pearle had coffee in the living room.

"Annabelle, may I ask what happened to Matthew and the other two boys?"

"Ah, the boys," she replied, and turned off the sink water. "They were in a cave-in." Annabelle turned around and leaned against the sink. "My poor Matthew almost didn't make it."

"Oh, no! Where did this happen?"

"They were on vacation in Egypt."

"What is Matthew's prognosis . . . is he going to be okay?"

"Oh, yes, but he will have to have more surgery. The doctors called him a miracle."

"Will he walk again?"

"That we do not know, Nakia, and won't until after he has this other surgery, I'm afraid."

"Then we will keep our thoughts good and positive. He is young and seems to be getting very good care. I'm sure he will be just fine," Nakia said, assuring Annabelle. "What about the boy, Yammi? Is he going to be all right?"

"That I am not sure of either. He almost lost his arm, poor thing. He will have to have more surgery too. Knowing Pearle, though, she will do whatever it takes to make a sure that boy is okay.

"Okay, enough talk. Nakia, you finish up the pots, and please make Pearle some more coffee. We talk some more tomorrow. Right now, I want to go and spend some time with my Matthew."

"Sure, Annabelle. I can handle everything here. Is there anything else you would like me to do?"

"Ah, yes, please check that the dogs have fresh water, and there is a load of laundry to dry. I see you in a little bit to check on you."

"I think I can manage all that, Annabelle," Nakia replied with a smile.

"Good, I be back in just a while." Annabelle took her apron off, smoothed her hair, and left the kitchen.

"Well, I see your appetite is good."

"Hey, Annabelle, I was just thinking about you."

She went over to Matthew's bed and gave him a long, but gentle, hug.

"So how are you feeling tonight?"

"Pretty good. . . . How about you?"

"Me, oh, I am wonderful, especially now that you are home."

"Yeah, I am glad to be home too, Annabelle. So tell me, did you miss me?" he asked with a devilish grin.

"Of course. What a silly question you ask," she replied with a laugh. "Well, I see Zatu and Bella glad too. They haven't left this room in hours!"

"Guess they missed me, huh?"

"As you and Daniel say, pfffft, ya think?!"

They laughed for some time; then she filled him in about the dogs and their antics. As Matthew giggled from her stories, her heart filled with a humbling grace, hearing his sweet laughter again.

"Well, I guess I better go check on Nakia. I just wanted to come see you and let you know how happy I am that you are home."

"Thanks so much for taking care of the animals while I was gone. By the way, how is Hunter doing?"

"Oh, mamma mia!" she exclaimed as she put her hands in the air. "I forget to tell you what that little stinker did to me. I take him out one night to clean his cage. I put him in his ball, just like you tell me too. Then when I finished cleaning cage, I find ball but no him! I look until three o'clock in the morning for that hairy Twinkie! You no never guess where he was."

"Hard to tell," Matthew said, giggling.

"Well, I come back in your room, and there he was! He was a sleeping on Zatu's back! Can you believe that little stinker?"

Matthew was cracking up now and couldn't even answer her.

"Ah, I glad YOU LAUGH. For me, I was having heart attack! All the time I was so worried that one of the dogs would eat him. Imagine the nerve of him sleeping on my Zatu!"

Matthew laughed so hard now he had tears coming out of his eyes. "Oh, Annabelle, I . . . I am so sorry he put you through that."

"Well, it's okay, but even better I got you to laugh. I have missed that around here. Next time I watch, I am putting a leash on him! And just so you know, he didn't seem hurt or anything, and I had no other problems with him after that."

"Oh, God, you are too funny . . . ," he said, catching his breath. "Well, Daniel checked on him earlier and said he was just fine. Actually, he promised to bring him down for a while so I could see him."

"Yes, he told me that too. He is getting Yammi settled in, and he will be down soon."

"Ah, Annabelle, this lady, Nakia, who is she?"

"Oh, Nakia, she is going to be helping me out here for a while. Why you ask, Matthew?"

"Just curious, that's all. But you know, I don't think Zatu cares much for her."

"Really, why you say that?"

"Well, when she was here earlier to see if I needed anything, he growled at her. He usually isn't like that."

"Yeah, I noticed that too, but it doesn't seem to faze her. If it makes you feel better, I keep an eye when they are around each other, okay?"

"Thanks, Annabelle."

"No problem, Matthew. Now tell me, what would you a like for supper tomorrow, anything special?"

"Hmm . . . now that you mention it," he said with a grin, "I could go for spaghetti and meatballs and your famous cheesecake!"

"Absolutely. . . . You can have anything your heart desires."

"Well, my heart desires to walk, but I'll settle for that dinner first."

"Matthew, you will walk soon; I know you will. You have to be patient, that's all."

"I know, Annabelle, I know," he answered as he put his head down.

"What's this grim look for?" she asked as she picked up his chin. But he didn't answer her.

"You want to talk about something, Matthew? You know that you and I can talk about anything, don't you?"

"Yeah, I know that, Annabelle. You have always been there for me. Maybe tomorrow, after I get a good night's sleep."

"All right, I won't push you. When you are ready, I am here for you, okay?"

Matthew smiled and reached up. He gave her such a loving hug that she felt tears welling in her eyes.

"Now you rest, and I go check how things are in kitchen. If you need anything, just push that buzzer, and it will ring through whole house. Oh, how do you like the nurse? Is she taking good care of you?"

"Yes, she is very nice, but she seems a little protective. She's almost as bad as Nana and Daniel!"

Annabelle let out a big laugh. "That's a good because she is getting paid a lot of money to take very good care of you," she chuckled.

"Anything you need?" she asked as she got to the door.

"No, thanks; I am good now. I'll see you tomorrow."

"Good night, Matthew, and welcome home!"

Matthew looked around the room and all that she had done to it for him. There wasn't anything else he could think of that he would need or want. He knew there was so much to be thankful for until he glanced down at his legs. Matthew wondered if he would ever walk again, or if he would be able to swim anymore. He thought about Yammi, then Daniel and how he wouldn't be there if it were not for him. Yawning, he reached for the remote and decided to watch the idiot box and not think about anything.

In the living room, Pearle, Robert, and Denise were discussing Matthew's and Yammi's medical care. Denise had spoken to the boys' specialist, being she was going to be part of their recovery as their pain management doctor. She told Pearle until they have their surgeries, there wasn't much that could be done for the time being, except to keep them comfortable and to watch their mental status. She explained how depression sets in when pain goes untreated or becomes chronic. Nevertheless, Denise assured her that she and the surgeons had worked out a good treatment plan and she would watch for any changes in the boys.

Although it was only seven-thirty, it had been a long day, and

Denise was ready to go home. "Now, you're sure with Daniel being here it's not too much for you?"

"Oh, listen to you; of course not," Pearle assured her.

"I think Daniel being here is good for him as well as Matthew. They went through a rough situation together, and I know how worried he is. I guess until he knows Matt will be okay, he is going to be apprehensive about leaving him."

"Yes, and as much as I would love to have him home with me, I know mentally it will be better for him here. Pearle, do me a favor, though. If you see anything odd, you know, out of the ordinary odd for Dan, you'll let me know."

Pearle laughed, "Of course I will, Denise. I think I know him well enough by now."

"All right, then, I am going to take off, but I'll be back in the morning to check on the boys. Maybe I had better check on Matthew once more before I leave. Remember, I am only a few minutes away. If there are any problems, just call me, okay, Pearle?"

"I will, Denise. Thanks."

Robert took the last sip of his coffee and stood up.

"I guess I better head out too. I'm sure you must be exhausted and ready for bed yourself."

"Actually, I'm not, Robert. I'd like it if you would stay for a while longer."

"Funny, I'm not tired either," he said as he sat back down. "I bet you, though, tomorrow we will be exhausted."

"So let tomorrow come. For now, let's just relax and enjoy being home."

Pearle and Robert sunk back into the couch. Then Pearle inched herself over to him and curled up next to him, and he put his arm around her.

"Excuse me, you two lovebirds," Denise giggled. "I just wanted to let you know that Matthew is just fine. I spoke with his nurse and told her to watch his leg swelling, but other than that, I don't foresee any problems, Pearle. So I bid you two *buonanotte,* and I'll see you in the morn!"

"Did you get a chance to say good night to Daniel?" asked Robert.

"Yes, as a matter of fact, I did. He and Matthew were playing with his rat."

Robert laughed and said, "Oh, you mean the hairy Twinkie!"

"Oh, come on, you two, you have to admit, he is cute, though," Pearle added.

"Whatever you say," Denise replied.

Pearle got up, giggling, and walked her to the door.

"Thanks, Denise, for everything today," Pearle said as she hugged her.

"Oh, come on, Pearle, you don't have to thank me. I love you like a sister, and if there is anything else I can do, please let me know, okay?"

"I will. Good night. See you tomorrow."

Pearle closed the door behind her and smiled at Robert.

"I'm so lucky to have her."

"Knowing how she feels about you, Pearle, I would say that you are *both* lucky to have each other."

"Yes, we are, Robert. So, tell me, when will you go back to work?"

"I'm going to talk with Brian tonight. As a matter of fact, he should be calling any minute. Then I will know if the office can wait until Monday morning."

"Pearle, I would like to discuss something with . . . ," and Robert's phone rang. "Hello . . . . Yes . . . I was waiting for your call. Yeah, sure, just hang on one sec. I'm sorry, Pearle, just give me a few minutes, okay?"

"Sure, I'll go check my grandson in the meantime. Take your time, Robert," she yelled as she left the room.

"Knock knock . . . are you awake?"

"Nana, what's up?"

"Oh, nothing; was just wondering how you are getting along."

"Actually, pretty good. Dan was here for a while with Hunter, and he just took him upstairs. Other than that, I've been just chilling."

"Well, good, because that's what you will be doing for a while, my dear."

"I know . . . just don't remind me."

"Aw, it won't be that bad, Matt. Daniel has decided to stay with us, and don't forget that Yammi is here too. I'm sure the three of you will entertain yourselves quite well!"

"Nana, I am sorry for everything that happened. I know we haven't talked much about what happened that night of the cave-in."

"There's plenty of time to do that, Matthew. Besides, right now I am only concerned about you recovering. When you are ready to tell me everything, you will. So, for the time being, I just want you to rest and not worry about a thing. Now, is there anything I can get you?"

"Nope. I'm good, thanks."

"All right, then, I'll leave you to rest. But I will check back with you before I go to bed, okay?"

"Nana, I'm fine; go chill."

Pearle laughed and responded, "Okay, I'm a gonna chill, and I'll catch ya later, dude!"

"You could use some practice with your slang, Nana, but ya got potential!"

She bent over and kissed his forehead. As she walked toward the door, she turned and blew him a kiss. Matthew remembers her doing that when he was younger. Every night after Pearle tucked him in, she would blow him a kiss, and he would catch it. As much as he loved Pearle, though, he wished they were his mother's kisses he caught.

Feeling nostalgic, Matthew picked up the silver picture frame next to his bed. It was his favorite picture of him and his mom, and one of the last ones taken of her. Pearle had taken it after Oona and Matthew had been swimming. He wondered what she would be like or look like today, and if he would be as close to her as he is with Pearle. He began wondering about many things, especially the prophecy and everything that has happened. Regardless of what Sol and Yammi have said, Matthew still believes there is a connection between his mother and the prophecy.

Pearle went to the living room and didn't see Robert. She found a note from him on the coffee table.

Pearle,

Had to run to office
I will call you soon
Get some rest

       I Love you
       Robert xoxo

Hmm . . . that's odd, she thought. *Well, it must have been important. I wonder . . . .*

Chapter Twenty-two

With it being the first morning back, Pearle thought it was a little chaotic in the kitchen. However, she knew Annabelle would have a schedule figured out in no time and Nakia trained to how she ran the household with everyone home.

"Good morning, ladies! How is everything going?"

"Uh... good, Pearle. I'm just a trying to teach Nakia everything we do around here. She is catching on, though. How's Matthew?" Annabelle replied, a little flustered.

"Good! I just checked on him, and he's still sleeping. His nurse said he slept through the night and seems to be doing well. I really thought he'd be up by now, though. Well, guess sleep is good, and they say you heal better then too. Oh, have Daniel and Yammi been down for breakfast yet, Annabelle?"

"Oh, yeah, they came down about seven this morning, and starving too! They eat like hungry bears, Pearle; you should a seen them, mamma mia!"

Pearle laughed and said, "Guess we will be doing more grocery shopping, then!"

"You better believe it, lady! I not know how or where they put all that food! If it was a me, I be three hundred pounds in a week!" Annabelle laughed.

"Annabelle, as long as everybody is healthy, I couldn't care less how much or what they eat!"

"You seem a chipper and on top of world this morning, Pearle! It's nice to see you this happy."

"Annabelle, after almost losing Matthew, I promised myself with every day that I get out of bed, I will live life with a grateful heart and be thankful for every moment I breathe."

"Ah, you finally take my advice," Annabelle said with a snicker.

"You bet your bottom dollar, kiddo! Now, we have to talk about a little surprise celebration for next week," Pearle said as she picked up a pen and pad of paper.

"Oh . . . and what are we celebrating?" Annabelle asked, dumbfounded.

"It's Matthew's thirteenth birthday, silly!"

"Oye, mamma mia, and shame on me," Annabelle said as she raised her hands, waving them wildly about, above her head. "How could I not remember my Matthew's birthday?"

"Well . . . . Come sit," Pearle said. "We have some planning to do!"

Nakia was cleaning up breakfast and daydreaming while she stared out the kitchen window. She wondered how it would feel to have a ton of money and do whatever you wanted to with it. She wondered if money would change her, as people say it often does. Nakia thought about someone, someone very close to her who once said, "If money is the root to unhappiness, then why are rich people having the time of their lives?" She only met Pearle yesterday, but has already noticed Pearle doesn't act like a rich snob, nor does she flash her wealth in your face. Pearle seems humble, like a regular person, and she is very kind. Then again, it didn't matter what her opinion was; she had a job to do and knew where her loyalty lay.

Pearle was sipping her second cup of coffee when Matthew's call buzzer went off. Then it echoed again, this time longer. She looked up and shot Annabelle an odd look. Pearle suddenly realized what the noise was and swiftly took off toward Matthew's room. Annabelle zipped right behind her, and Nakia followed. When Pearle got to Matthew's room, she found him and his nurse laughing.

"What's going on, Matt? What's wrong?" Pearle asked.

"Nana, look!" he said, all excited, and pointed to his toes.

"Oh, my God, Matthew . . . what . . . ," but Pearle fell speechless when she saw him wiggle his toes.

"Ahem, and do you notice anything else?" he said with a brimming smile, showing all his teeth.

Pearle shook her head and looked up from his feet. She gasped when she saw he was sitting up on his own.

"Nana, are you okay?" he said, looking at her shocked face while snickering.

"No . . . I mean, yes . . . of course I am, silly, but how . . . what happened?"

"Nana, all I did was stretch out my arms over my head when I woke up and tried to turn on my side a little. Then when I turned just a little bit more, all of a sudden, I heard all these pops go off in my back and neck, like a BB gun! My legs started to feel all tingly, and now . . . now I can feel my legs and move them!"

Pearle fell speechless again, and Annabelle just stood there with her hand over her mouth.

They weren't the only ones in shock, though. Daniel had heard the buzzer go off and raced downstairs to see what was going on.

"Matt, buddy, give me a high five," Daniel said, smiling, as he raised his hand up.

"This is awesome, Dan, isn't it?" he said as he adjusted himself in the bed.

"Nah," Daniel responded, shaking his head. *"It's freaking wonderful!"* he yelled.

Daniel started to dance around the room as if no one else were there. Then Pearle and Annabelle joined in. Matthew was cracking up, as was Nakia, who watched from the doorway.

"What did I miss?" said a voice in the distance.

Pearle turned around, but Annabelle kept dancing. It was Robert, and Pearle ran to him and pulled him over to Matthew's bed.

"Go ahead, Matt, show him . . . *show him* what you can do!" Pearle screeched excitedly.

Matthew began to move his toes for him. Like Pearle, Robert didn't notice that Matthew was sitting up by himself.

"How in the name of . . . . This is absolutely fantastic!" And Robert picked up Pearle and whirled around the room with her.

Matthew looked over and saw Yammi standing in the doorway and waved him in.

"This is wonderful. I am so very happy for you!" Yammi said, smiling at him in amazement.

"Thank you, and just think, Yammi, in a few weeks after your surgery, you'll be almost as good as new too!"

"I do so look forward to that," he said as he tried to keep his smile from showing his doubt and ruining Matthew's excitement.

"Well, you better," said Pearle. "Don't you doubt for one second, Yammi, you won't be as good as new. Besides, I promised your father you would be okay, and my word is as good as gold."

Yammi smiled politely and hoped she was right.

"Well, I hate to be the bad guy here and break up this party," Matthew's day nurse interrupted, "but Mr. Wriggly Toes needs to have some breakfast and rest for a while. It has been a big morning for him already!"

"Yes, you are right, Patty. Come on, everyone," Pearle said as she started shooing them all out of the room. "Annabelle, will you make Matthew his favorite breakfast, unless he wants something else?" Pearle said, looking at Matt, who was nodding with his approval and making his eyebrows go up and down.

"Of course," Annabelle replied as she and Pearle continued to dance their way out of the room, leaving Matthew and his nurse laughing.

"You have a wonderful family," Patty said as she was taking his temperature and feeling his pulse.

Matthew smiled and nodded his head in agreement.

Robert and Annabelle were chatting about the birthday party Pearle was planning, while she prepared bacon and French toast for him and Matthew. Pearle ran upstairs for something, and Daniel had taken Yammi outside to show him the property and play with the dogs. Nakia was upstairs making the beds and collecting dirty laundry. When Nakia got to Matthew's room, where Daniel was staying, she noticed the bloody backpack sitting on the floor next to the closet. Annabelle had offered to clean it, but Daniel told her he was going to empty it out and throw it away. He didn't want Matthew to see it and have it bring back any bad memories. She was sitting on the bed, staring at it, when Pearle leaned into the doorway.

"Is something wrong?"

"Oh, Pearle," Nakia said as she rose from the bed. "I was just thinking about what it must have been like for the boys and everything they have been through with the cave-in. It's a miracle they survived and are doing as well as they are."

"Yes, we are very lucky. It was touch and go there for a while, and I was so afraid I was going to lose my grandson . . . but he and Yammi have been making excellent progress with their recovery."

"That's for sure, especially with what happened this morning with Matthew," she replied while smoothing the bed covers.

"Well, I'll leave you to your chores. Right now I have to get downstairs and bring Matthew his breakfast, but we will talk more later on."

"I would like that very much, Pearle," she replied and went on with cleaning the room when Pearle left.

Daniel took Yammi around outside and then down to the lake. He told him all he knew about the story of Oona's disappearance, after Yammi had asked him.

"This is truly a sad story, Daniel. However, I am troubled and wonder why, with all that the police have done, they have not come up with any definitive answers as to what happened to her. I cannot understand how someone could just disappear like that. There must be a logical reason, do you not think so?" Yammi said, frustrated.

Daniel looked at Yammi. He knew he could trust him and decided to tell him what Matthew thinks happened, as crazy as it may sound.

"Yammi, Matthew . . . well, he has a theory about what happened to his mother. He told me about it while he was in the hospital. I know Matt trusts you as much as I do, so . . . I don't think he will mind if I share with you what he believes."

"Thank you, Daniel, for your trust, and I would never do anything to make you feel differently. Whatever you tell me will stay between us. I won't even tell Matthew, if you wish, of what you share."

"Oh, I don't think Matt will mind, but for now, let's just keep this between us."

"All right, as you wish, Daniel."

"Yammi, are you sure, though, you are okay out here? I mean, does your arm feel okay in that sling sitting here, or would you like to go back to the house and rest for a while?"

"No, Daniel, I am feeling pretty good today, and besides, I took my pain medication before we left the house. Besides, being outside in the fresh air is doing me good. I am not used to being cooped up in a house, only a pyramid," he said with a laugh.

"Oh, Yammi, before I forget, Matthew asked me last night to get his camera out and to download all the pictures we took in the pyramid to his computer. He also wants us to gather everything we got and then go over it all with you."

"Sure, we can do that this afternoon. Oh, by the way, what has happened to the three creatures?"

"Oh, Oopi, Amora, and Emia told me not to disturb them. Oopi said they would be going through some sort of renewal sleep and that I was not to bring them out until the night of Matthew's birthday."

"That is odd—don't you think so, Daniel?"

Daniel laughed, "It sure is, Yammi. This entire thing is odd, don't you agree?"

"Yes, I do, but I will tell you one thing, Daniel . . . I have a feeling this is going to get more bizarre as time goes by. My best advice to you is to keep an open mind with everything that happens. It is the only way to understand the things we may find difficult to believe."

"Hah, that's funny," Daniel said, looking serious.

"Oh, why is that?" Yammi asked.

"Because after I tell you what Matthew has said, you may find it hard to have an open mind!"

Yammi laughed and said, "Try me!"

"Okay, but first I have to tell you something that Oopi told me back at the hospital. Yammi, to tell you the truth, until I had this conversation with Oopi, I really thought Matthew was just hung up on his mother being alive . . . you know what I mean, wishful thinking stuff. But Oopi made me think about this prophecy, and maybe it could very well be true that if Matthew does this quest, he will be rewarded with his mother."

"We have discussed this already, Daniel, and I find it highly unlikely that *his mother* is being held captive in return for him completing this prophecy quest!"

"All right, then think about this . . . that pyramid was extremely safe. Your father even said so, because he had inspected it a few days before we got there. Why the cave-in, then, when we were getting ready to leave? Did you happen to notice that the first tremble of the ground happened after Matthew put his mother's medallion and that gold thing in his backpack? In addition to all that, it wasn't until we found that large pearl and decided to leave the pyramid that the cave-in occurred! Like I told you before, I may not know squat about Egypt and the ancient times, but with God as my witness, I know there is a connection with Oona and everything that is happening!"

Yammi said nothing; he just looked out over the lake and stared motionless as Daniel went on.

"Then Oopi told me the evil one didn't want us to leave because she desired what we had. He also said that the magic she has is very strong and becoming very dangerous. This evil person will stop at nothing to get what she wants, Yammi! We have to figure out why, because if we don't, I fear she is going to try and hurt Matthew again!"

"What is it that this evil one wants, and why, is what I want to know, and for that matter, who is she? Before I make any uneducated guesses, Daniel, I'm going to put those pictures on the computer and see if I can decipher any hidden messages. Maybe that will be the only way to find out if this prophecy holds truth."

"I don't know, Yammi, but whatever you think we can do to help Matthew I will do. I know you are very educated about the good and evil of old Egyptian magic. Sol has said that you possess a rare, special gift—may I ask what this is?"

"Mr. Sol talks too much sometimes," Yammi replied. "This is not something I share with too many people."

"Sorry, I didn't mean to be nosy; I was just wondering what it was," Daniel said.

"No, no, do not apologize, Daniel. It is quite all right to ask, and I will tell you. You must understand that it is not something magical I possess, although the few who know me might say it is. Let's see if I can explain this to you. Daniel, we have five senses we use every day instinctively, without ever thinking about them, because that is just our natural ability. They are to see, hear, smell, taste, and to feel. Our lives depend on those senses to survive. However, if we were to lose one or more, that is when we become more aware of them, and the other senses we have become keener, more noticeable. Now, scientists and scholars say that we only use a very small percentage of our brain, even though there is much more up there available to us. In some other cultures, and let's take the ancient Egyptians, for example, they knew how to access more of their brain and in doing so found more senses and discovered other abilities they did not know they were capable of. I believe that those who held a higher intelligence were trained how to do this, where others found they just had a natural ability to tap into these other senses. Have I lost you yet, Daniel?"

"No, actually, I have heard of this before, Yammi. My mom, who specializes in pain management, truly believes that we have the power to overcome a lot of pain with biofeedback and relaxation. She too believes we don't use enough of our brain and natural abilities that we have."

"Ah, good, this is good, Daniel! Let's see, oh, yes, now, years ago when I first started going to the pyramids with my father, I thought there was something wrong with me. Whenever I was in certain locations of the pyramid or I would find old text, something strange would come over me like a feeling of how you say . . . oh, like déjà vu! I would see visions or actually feel the pain one had at their death and sometimes hear voices of those thousands of years ago. Daniel, the feelings were so strong, and scared me so much, I eventually didn't go back to the pyramid with Father. I made up excuses all the time so that I would not have to go."

"So what happened, Yammi? What did you do?"

"Well, eventually, my dear father felt something was wrong because he knew how much I loved being with him and learning from Mr. Sol. So we had a conversation one day when I had become so reluctant to go and was crying. I told him of what I was experiencing. That is when I met a wonderful person, who helped me understand what . . . what was happening. Her name is Suhama. She is of the old ways and knew very much of what I was going through. Many people, though, believe she practices witchcraft, but she says it is because they do not use all of their brain," he laughed.

"Anyway, my father came to know of Suhama from his father. You see, my grandfather also had this gift, and that is where

Suhama says I may have inherited it. She explained that I have a sixth sense, which everyone calls ESP, but she added that I possess a seventh, an eighth sense, and possibly up to ten! Of course, at first I thought this woman was off her noodle. Then, as I spent more time with her, I began to see and understand my abilities, making me less fearful of them. She made me realize that I was not a freak and that my capabilities were not evil. My abilities are quite contrary to those beliefs. Accepting what I had and who I wasn't took a long time, Daniel. That is why even today, in our modern society, I do not tell many people of my abilities. There is still that stigma people have about someone like me, but I just call it ignorance. You can be very intelligent, Daniel, but if you are ignorant, then you have no intelligence at all! Now, as for what my abilities are, they are many. It just depends on the circumstances and the surroundings, I guess. Would you like me to show you an example, Daniel?"

"Yeah, that would be pretty cool, Yammi. Go ahead; show me!"

"Ah, you say that now, but you may not like what I am about to reveal."

"Really, why is that?"

"Because it is about you, Daniel . . . and what has happened. Yes, I know what you have sacrificed for Matthew and why. Mind you, I did not know right away, but I had sensed something different of you on the plane the other day. I came to this knowledge today, as we were here talking. The elixir you drank of has *given* to your friend, while it has *taken* from you. This is the most unselfish gift a person can give to another. I hope Matthew knows what a special friend he has. Some people go through life knowing hundreds of people, but not are they able to call one of them a true friend. I am honored to know you as such a friend, Daniel."

Daniel was speechless for a few moments, and then he spoke.

"Yammi, you aren't going to tell Matthew, are you?"

"Of course not, Daniel. It is not my duty to inform him of your selfless deed. I trust you will know when to tell him."

"Well, I am not sure I want him to know or if I will ever tell him."

"It is totally your decision as to what you do or do not tell Matthew. I think you need to know something else. Matthew has my abilities, as does Pearle. He just hasn't learned to fully use them yet, but I believe he will someday. When Matthew does, he will then learn what you have done. Do you want him to find out that way? This is something you must think about.

"Now, Pearle, on the other hand, suppresses her powers and is afraid of them. This is what Oopi and Emia were trying to draw from her that night at the hotel, but she fought them. Those who are capable of these higher senses deal with them in their own way. With Pearle, she has let society and its beliefs dictate her abilities, which is clearly understandable. However, I feel it is most unfortunate that she denies herself the gift she has, because in doing so, she has denied Matthew his."

"Perhaps you can talk to her about it, Yammi."

"What would be the purpose, though, Daniel? I cannot make someone choose to use their gift because they have it. I will only add one more thing about Pearle. Her gift can be truly powerful, and if this prophecy turns out to be of truth, she may very well wish she knew how to use her gift. Now come, I think I have gotten my mouth in trouble, and I am feeling tired."

"Yammi, rest assured, I will not tell anyone what we have discussed. You know, I'm tired too; must be jet lag or something. Anyway, I could go for a little something to eat. How about you?"

"Ha, I am always hungry, and I eat all the time!"

"But you are so skinny. How is it you don't gain any weight?"

"Me . . . skinny, please, you should see my mother, Daniel. She can out-eat my father and me, but she is so tiny!" Yammi laughed and added, "My father keeps telling her she is going to wake up one day as big as a pregnant cow!"

Daniel laughed, and Yammi continued with his story as they walked back to the house.

"You know, I am so glad we met, Yammi. We are turning out to be pretty good friends."

"Likewise, Daniel. I think we are becoming very good friends!"

The boys got back to the house and told Annabelle they were hungry.

"Well, it is a little too early for lunch, but I made an apple crumb cake. Would you like that?"

"Ohhh, baby," said Daniel, rubbing his hands together. "Yammi, this cake will knock off your socks!"

"Ah, Daniel, that may be a problem."

"Huh? . . . What do you mean?"

"Well, I am not wearing any socks; should I be?"

Daniel looked at Annabelle; then they both looked at Yammi.

"Oh, come on, guys, I was trying to make you laugh."

"What's so funny?" asked Pearle.

They turned around, laughing, and Yammi replied, "Do you know that Annabelle can knock off my socks?"

"Oh, now, how can she do that?"

"Come, sit and have a piece of this most delicious cake!"

Pearle cracked up, and so did Annabelle. Pearle agreed to have her socks knocked off and sat next to Yammi to enjoy a piece of the cake too.

"So did you boys enjoy your walk?"

"Oh, yeah," Daniel replied. "It was nice, and it's great being back home again. I showed Yammi the property and guesthouse, and he *particularly* enjoyed the lake."

"You have a wonderful home here, Pearle, just lovely!"

"Thanks, Yammi. Just don't forget this is your home too while you are here."

"It is beginning to feel like home, Pearle. Everyone is especially kind, and it's nice being around people who are genuine and loving."

"I don't think you will find it any other way here. By the way, you missed Denise. She wanted to check on you and see how you were. But she said she will be back tonight to have dinner with us and will check on you then."

"Oh, crap. I forgot about Mom coming this morning!" Daniel said, annoyed with himself.

"Gosh, Daniel," Pearle said, "she will be back later."

"Yes, but I had promised her I would spend a little time with her this morning."

"Guess you will have to make up for it tonight," Yammi replied, smiling at Daniel.

"Definitely. . . . Anyway, I think I am going to lie down for a while. Are you going to also, Yammi?"

"Yes, if that is okay with you, Pearle?"

"Absolutely, boys; go ahead. I might take a little nap myself, now that you say that. I'll see you boys later," she said, and Yammi and Daniel went upstairs.

"Pearle, I have to ask you something."

"Sure, Annabelle, what is it?"

"Particularly enjoyed? When did Daniel start using language like that? Is it me, or do you see a difference in him and his behavior?"

"Now that you mentioned it, yes, Annabelle, he does seem . . . well, mature . . . not half-assed about things. But I guess with everything that's happened, it may just be a temporary thing, and knowing Daniel, he'll be back to his old joking self again."

"So you don't think it's anything to be concerned about?"

"Nah, I think he is okay, but let's keep an eye on him anyway."

"I think that is a good idea, Pearle."

"You're really concerned, aren't you, Annabelle?"

"Yes; otherwise, I not say anything to you."

"Maybe I'll mention it to Denise. But gosh, Annabelle, what do I say to her? Oh, Denise, by the way, your son is acting very mature and responsible! She'd probably look at me like I had a screw loose! I don't think we need to make a big deal about this. But I'll speak to Robert and see what he thinks."

"That's good idea, and in the meantime, we keep an eye on him. Now go take nap while Matthew is resting and everything is quiet."

"Sounds good, but if you should need any help, just come get me, Annabelle. You know, Robert has left here twice since last night in a real hurry. I wonder what is going on at work."

"He is coming for supper, no?"

"He said earlier he was, and if anything changed, he would call us."

"Okay, so you will just wait to see. Now go nap!" Annabelle urged Pearle as she flitted her hands in the air.

"Yes, mamma, yes, mamma mia!" Pearle replied lovingly, mocking her Italian friend.

"Oh, my gosh, Annabelle; this was absolutely the best Italian sauce I have ever eaten," Robert said as he wiped spaghetti sauce off his chin.

"Really?" she asked, blushing.

"Oh, yes, I agree with Robert. I have never tasted anything so wonderful in my life," Yammi replied, licking his lips. "What is your secret to such a delicious sauce?"

Annabelle smiled sweetly at Yammi, then said, "Love, Yammi, pure and simple love."

Daniel and Denise insisted on helping Annabelle clean up dinner. Pearle and Robert decided to go out on the patio with their coffee.

"You sure have been doing some quick vanishing acts the last two days, detective. What's up?"

"Oh, just trying to catch up, Pearle, that's all."

"Listen, I would like to get you out of the house for a while. Why don't we go to our favorite ice cream place and take a nice walk on the beach, you know, just you and me? I already asked Denise if she wouldn't mind staying for a while, and she said she had planned to anyway, because she wanted to spend some time with the boys."

"You know, Robert, that sounds great. I think a little time away from the house with you sounds like fun."

"Great, well, go get your jacket; it might be a little cool at the beach. And I'll meet you in the car, okay?"

"All right, I'll just check on Matthew and be out in a few moments."

As Pearle reached the car, Robert looked up and quickly closed his phone. She opened the door and looked at him. Robert looked like a kid who'd just been caught with his hands in the cookie jar.

"Another lady friend?" and she laughed nervously.

"No, silly," he replied, and put his cell phone in his shirt pocket.

Robert started the car, put it in gear, and pulled out of the driveway without saying another word to her. They had been driving for ten minutes when Pearle realized he wasn't going in the direction of the ice cream shop.

"A new route to get ice cream?" she asked nervously.

But he didn't answer her. He just turned and smiled. Five minutes later, he put his blinker on and made a right into the police station. They parked behind the building, not in his usual spot. He got out of the car quickly, opened her door, and led her to the station's back door, where Brian was waiting for them. Brian led them into his office, looked down the hallways, and then closed the door and locked it. Robert went over to the window and closed the blinds. Brian turned on a radio, then sat down next to Pearle.

"Pearle, I am sorry for being secretive, but I had to get you here without anyone else knowing where we were going."

Still not understanding what was going on, she turned and looked at Robert, then Brian.

"Well, Batman and Robin," she said, slightly agitated, "are you going to tell me what in the world is going on here?"

"Hmm . . . ," Robert moaned, smiling at Brian, "we have never been called the 'Caped Crusaders' before, but I like it!"

"Robert Greene, what is going on here? You had me so scared I thought you flipped out and were some sort of serial killer taking me for my last car ride!"

"Pearle, you really do read too many mystery novels," he laughed.

"It's not funny, Robert," she said, almost in tears.

"Oh, God, Pearle, geez . . . . I didn't even think about how this would look or that I would frighten you. I am sorry . . . but Pearle . . . we have some good news for you," Robert said, leaning over to hug her.

"If this is your idea, detective, of giving someone *good* news, I surely would hate to see what *bad* news looked like!"

Robert got up with a smirk on his face and went to a locked file cabinet in the corner of the room. He got on his knees, took a set of keys from his blue linen jacket, and unlocked the bottom drawer. He removed a large brown paper bag from the back of the drawer and put it on Brian's desk.

"So what's in the bag, Batman?" Pearle asked sarcastically.

Robert shook his head, amused, took his jacket off, put it on the back of his chair, and rolled up his yellow shirt sleeves. "Brian, can you turn that air down? It's awfully warm in here."

"Yeah, I made sure when I left earlier tonight that it didn't look like I was coming back."

Robert donned a pair of blue gloves and proceeded to open the bag. He reached in and pulled out a large manila envelope. He sat down next to Pearle and carefully pinched the metal clasps together and opened the envelope's flap. Then he pulled out a smaller paper bag, and its contents made a clanging noise when he placed it on Brian's desk.

Brian put on a pair of gloves too, then carefully and slowly pulled off a thick strip of tape and removed the contents.

"My medallions!" Pearle whispered as Brian handed them to her.

Pearle handled them delicately while she examined the heirlooms for any type of damage. Satisfied, she laid them carefully on Brian's desk and sat back into her chair.

"So which one of you 'Caped Crusaders' is going to tell me what's going on?"

"We are sorry for all the mystery and how we got you here, Pearle," Robert said. "We will explain everything to you, but what we say must not leave this room."

"Robert, I won't, but what's going on?"

"Well, after Brian got the call from Dr. Hadwick about Zatu's lab results, we were at a standstill. Then, by chance, he remembered a big robbery case we worked last year, which turned out to also be a drug bust. It just so happens that there was valproic acid and Valium amongst the drugs seized—the same exact drugs used on Zatu. Now, on a hunch, he went to the evidence room last night, and being the property person wasn't there, he had one heck of a time trying to find the evidence from that case. That's when he called me at your place, Pearle, and why I left in a hurry. Anyway, we eventually found it and took the bag back here to his office. Now, Brian had sealed this bag with evidence tape, as we do with all property, which is our standard operating procedure. He knew what the contents were, as did I. After we had processed the drugs and paraphernalia confiscated from the bust, we had several envelopes of evidence in this bag that were also sealed."

"The *only* things we put in there, I may add," Brian said.

"But when Brian and I opened this bag last night, we discovered an additional evidence bag with your medallions in it!"

"Thank God for your hunch, Brian," Pearle said, "but I still don't understand all the secrecy, Robert."

"That's because we believe someone in this police department is involved with your robbery."

"Because you found my medallions in one of your evidence bags?" she asked.

"Yes, but it goes a little further," Robert said. "You see, Pearle, we seal all evidence with special tape. We sign our name across the tape and include the date, time, and case number. If anyone has to go into the evidence bag again, it's carefully cut open, but in a *different* location from where it was last sealed. Whoever accesses an evidence bag again must go through the same process when they seal it. What we found was disturbing. The drugs we enclosed in an evidence bag were not in the original bag, and someone had forged our signatures on a new one. Also, after examining the contents, the amount of the Valium and valproic acid did not correspond to the original quantity listed on the property sheet."

"So, we met with the chief and discussed everything we had found. Besides the three of us, he is the only one in this entire department who knows about this and what we propose to do," Brian said. "We have his blessing for a plan that Robert and I have come up with, and that is why you are here very secretively, Pearle."

"Wow, I don't know what to say, guys, except . . . what's this plan you have?"

"We want to give you back your medallions, but . . . we need to have three identical ones to replace them with. Then we can put the replicas back in that evidence bag where we found yours. But first, we would install GPS tracking devices in them. This way, when anyone tried to remove them, which we suspect they will, we will find our thieves! The only problem is, Pearle, we don't know who could do that type of work in such a short period of time," Brian said.

"We think," Robert began as he paced the office floor, "whoever put the medallions in the evidence bag will eventually come back for them. We are hoping for some leeway in time, but they could come back at any time for them. That is why we need to quickly get the fake medallions done and put back into the evidence room, outfitted with those devices."

"Maybe I can help," she replied. "I do know of a jeweler who makes great replicas, but he is in New York. I can call Mr. Schmidth in the morning and ask if he would do me this favor. Of course, I could just tell him . . . well, I could tell him I want copies because I am afraid to wear the real ones at certain events, or something like that."

"Good God, Pearle, that is brilliant!" Robert replied.

"It's brilliant, all right," she smiled back, "but we would have to fly there with a medallion so he could copy it from the original, not a picture, Robert."

"So, my dear, what's the problem?" he asked, looking at her concerned expression.

"Have you forgotten about Matthew?"

"No, of course not," he replied, a little agitated. "It's just that he seems to be doing so wonderful, especially after this morning. I thought if we had to fly to New York and come back the next day, he would be okay without you."

"Ah, not to get off track here, guys, but what happened with Matthew this morning?" Brian asked.

"Oh, geez, Brian, I forgot to tell you the great news," Robert said, hitting the side of his head. "Our Matthew can feel his legs and sit up by himself!"

"You're kidding me! Oh, my God, but how . . . what happened, Pearle?"

Pearle smiled and began to tell Brian the story. When she was done, Brian had tears in his eyes.

"This is wonderful! No . . . it's a miracle, Pearle! I am so happy for him . . . for you and, well, for all of us," he said excitedly.

"So, what does this mean now, Pearle, he won't have to have any more surgeries?"

"I don't know anything yet, Brian, not until he sees the specialist."

"Well, keep me posted on everything. This is the best news I have heard in a long time!" Brian said smiling.

"I will, Brian. Now let's get back to the medallions," she said.

"Gosh, ah, right . . . . Okay, so we need to get copies of these medallions, and you are pretty sure this guy in New York can do this?"

"Absolutely, a lot of people who have valuable jewelry go to him for replicas. Mr. Schmidth, by the way, is brilliant, Brian; he really is!"

"I'm sure if he is that brilliant, Pearle, he probably is expensive too. I know our budget can't handle a big expense like that," Robert replied.

"Don't you worry about that, Robert. Whatever the cost, I got it covered. It will be worth every penny once we catch whoever stole the medallions," Pearle assured him. "I think I have his personal phone number at home. I will call him in the morning and find out if he can see us right away. The sooner the better, I take it, right?"

"Yes," replied Robert. "Since we don't know how long this process takes, the sooner we see him, the quicker we will have them."

"What about the GPS—will you have specific instructions for him about that, Brian?"

"Oh, no, no . . . Pearle! Robert and I will install them. Please, *do not* mention anything or say why you are doing this. Just tell him you would like replicas of your medallion just like others you noted do, that's all."

"I can do that," she said. "So what else have you 'Caped Crusaders' come up with about the case?"

Robert laughed, and so did Brian, shaking his head.

"As a matter of fact, we do have more to tell you, Pearle. How about some coffee?" Brian asked.

"Sure, Brian, that would be great!"

Brian put on a fresh pot of coffee, and Pearle called home to see how everything was. She spoke to Denise, who was giggling and having a great time with the boys. Apparently, everyone, including Annabelle, was playing Guitar Hero, Matthew and Daniel's favorite game. Denise told Pearle to enjoy her time out and not to rush home, as everything and everybody was just terrific! She hung up and got herself a cup of coffee.

"Okay. Brian, tell me what's going on so far," Pearle said as she got comfy in her seat.

"Well, we sent off samples of the Valium and valproic acid we have to Dr. Hadwick for analysis, to see if it matches what Zatu had ingested. We will have those results in about a week. Now, you know we are investigating Abe Haram, correct?"

"Yes, I do. Did you find anything incriminating about him?"

"So far his story for the night of the robbery has checked out, Pearle, but he is not completely off the suspect list, I'm afraid. Due to him being one of very few people who could have known about those medallions, he will remain a suspect until proven otherwise.

"Now, if you remember, we found a boot print next to your medallion and since have discovered that the boots were made in Europe and are pretty expensive. We are trying to track down the manufacturer of this particular boot, and hopefully once we do that, we will be able to find out who purchased them."

"This is all good news, Brian. Is there anything else you have found out?"

"Not really, Pearle. Everything that was fingerprinted has come back with no matches from any of the databases we searched. However, there was one smeared print from the lock off that one crate downstairs, and that is still being processed. Maybe we will get lucky with that one. We will have to just wait and see, though. All the employees from your contractors checked out okay, and there is just a handful more to investigate from the security company. They claim that during the time of your job, they were extremely busy and had to hire a few more subcontractors, and the woman in their human resource office is having a problem finding that paperwork. The owner said this was highly unusual, as this woman knows where everything is. However, he did assure me that with some time, they would find those files. Hmm . . . let's see what else there is . . . oh, yeah, we are still waiting for the analysis of the soil from the lake to come back. The chain and the long claw that was found are still being analyzed, as is the ancient shawabtis from an anthropologist and relics specialist at the FBI."

"That sounds like everything, Brian, doesn't it?" she asked him.

"I think so, and we are hoping by next week, more or all test results will be back, and then we can sit down again and go from there."

Robert began pacing again as Pearle and Brian talked further of the evidence. He was weighing telling Brian about the unscientific part of all this, the unbelievable part . . . the "prophecy." *How would he take it?* he thought to himself. Since everything that has happened seemed far-fetched to him, would Brian consider that in this case and the connection Robert felt it played? He knew there was only one way to find out.

"Brian, I need to talk to you about something."

"Oh, what is it, Robert?"

"Good Lord, I don't even know where to start with this, Pearle," he said, looking at her, shaking his head. "There are some things you need to know about this case that I feel is connected to . . . ." Robert stalled for so long that Brian was getting a little nervous.

"What is it, DG? What's on your mind?"

"Remember when this first all went down, how we talked about things being weird and not making sense?"

"Yes, Robert, I do, and I also recall you saying something about it going to get weirder!"

Robert chuckled, "I did, didn't I. It has, Brian, and while we were in Egypt, some information became available to Pearle about her family and particularly . . . about Matthew. I guess why I am so hesitant here is that you may not believe what I have to tell you. And to be honest, at first I thought I was hallucinating, or, well, I was very skeptical about what was revealed."

"Okay, Robert, you have piqued my interest through the roof! Just tell me already," he said, standing and nervously wringing his hands together.

"You can't discuss this with anyone, Brian," Pearle interrupted, looking serious.

"All right already! You two are giving me premature gray hair, and soon I will be bald! Just tell me what's going on, guys!"

Robert started off by telling Brian about the prophecy. He added how it affected Matthew and what it has done over the years to Pearle's family. Robert went on for about a half hour, explaining what he could with every question Brian asked. Then he got to the part of explaining Oopi, Amora, and Emia.

"Now, as far from real as all this may seem, Brian, I'm going to add three mystical creatures, which are involved."

"Creatures . . . *real* mystical creatures," Brian said, blinking his eyes rapidly.

"Yes," Pearle replied. "They are very real, Brian."

"Oh, you guys are pulling my leg here, aren't you?" Brian said, shaking his head and laughing. "This is a joke; I know there aren't such things!"

He looked at Pearle, who had a solemn face, then over at Robert, who had a blank expression. Brian knows that look all too well. He has seen it numerous times before. Robert was indeed being serious.

"Okay, I'll bite. So let's say this prophecy is real, and Matthew is an heir to two ancient kingdoms. What the heck does it all have to do with this case?"

"That's the part I haven't quite figured out, Brian. But with Oona's medallion showing up in Egypt, the theft of the other medallions, the three creatures, and everything that has happened, I just know there is a connection to all of this and the prophecy. Brian . . . I'd bet my career on it."

Now Brian was pacing the room. He stopped momentarily and ran his hand through his short hair. When he got to the back of his tense neck, he rubbed the muscles until they didn't ache anymore. He twisted his head around several times until his neck cracked.

"Uhh . . . much better," Brian sighed as he sat on the edge of his desk.

"For heaven's sake, Brian, sounds like you need a chiropractor for that neck of yours," Pearle commented as she cringed from the popping noise his neck made.

"I'm seeing, uh . . . I mean I saw . . . I'm going to a pain doctor, who is helping with my neck and headaches," Brian sputtered, all flushed.

Pearle began to grow a smile, and she looked over at Robert, who revealed a devilish grin.

"This doctor wouldn't happen to be a she . . . would it?"

"Ahh . . . yes, yes, she is, Robert," he murmured, almost as if he *didn't* want them to hear his reply.

"Oh, okay," Brian responded like a kid who had to admit doing wrong. "It's Denise Fuscilli! Okay, are you happy now, partner? Yes, I am interested in a girl," he added, with his face turning a bright red.

"Well, congratulations. It is about time, Brian. I don't know why you were embarrassed to tell us. She is Pearle's best friend, and from what I know of her, she is a wonderful lady! Good-looking too, I might add," Robert said, winking at Pearle.

"You are adorable," Pearle chuckled. "I couldn't be happier for her or you."

"Well, now, don't go and say anything that I told you guys. Denise and I agreed to keep things quiet for a while. Especially, please don't say anything to Daniel. She is worried how he would take his mother dating again."

"We won't say a word, Brian, I promise," said Robert, raising his hand and twisting his lips as if he locked them.

"Okay, now, let's get back to this prophecy you say is connected to Oona, and this case. How do we know it isn't some kind of hoax to make you think otherwise?"

"All right, at first I thought the same thing, especially when Matthew talked about this old book. However, when I heard Sol talk about the things Matthew read about and what Pearle has heard from her family, I started to think differently. Not to mention these three creatures I saw, who, by the way, talk, Brian!"

"Robert, this case has brought us to a whole new realm that is not what you and I are accustomed to in law enforcement. I mean, we have had our share of unexplained events in the past, but this by far is an exceptional case. Let's look at what we have here. Oona disappears with no trace, the medallion she was wearing on that day shows up in Egypt, and the chain from it we find in Pearle's lake. Pearle has a robbery, and the thief is only interested in her medallions. After all, they had access to hundreds of millions of dollars in jewels and valuables.

"One crate out of, say, sixty or so was broken into, and according to the inventory you did, nothing was missing from it. But you do have missing pages from the inventory list. Now apparently, whoever was in the house was looking for something in particular, and assumed or knew it should have only been in that particular crate. I presume, with everything that has occurred, this person is looking for something specific and for a reason. This person, or persons, I should say, knows what you have, and they want it. What we have to figure out is what it is and why they want it and what, if anything, this *all* has to do with Oona. . . .

"Do you know how I am sure this person knows more about you than we want them to?

This person knew where your medallion was in *your* bedroom, Pearle. That's what bothers me more than anything about this robbery. I think this person is right under our nose and extremely smart. They have put a lot of thought into what they did, and if my gut is right, they aren't finished. Whatever it was they wanted in that crate, *if* they didn't get it . . . they are going to come back for it, I can almost guarantee that! Pearle, I want you to really consider keeping security at the house until we catch whoever this is."

Robert just stared wide-eyed at him. Although Brian had not yet discussed any of this with Robert, every word made absolute sense to him.

"Brian, you really have put a lot of thought into all this, and I have to say thank you," Robert said as he put his hand on Brian's shoulder. "I'm in total agreement with you. Pearle, you do need to keep the security at the house until we catch this person or persons."

"Yes, of course, Robert. After what Brian has said, I am in absolute agreement!"

"Now, if I may," Brian added, "this prophecy is something I would like to know more of, and these creatures. Will it be possible to see them, Pearle?"

"It might be possible, but I'm not sure. They seem deeply connected to Matthew, and according to them, it is his will if someone will be able to see or not see them. May I ask why, though, Brian?"

"Sure, Pearle. I thought maybe being an impartial person, I might be able to get more information from them, and then we could get a better understanding of how this prophecy fits into everything and why."

"I see your point, Brian, but I don't think you will learn anything more than we have already told you. But that doesn't mean we cannot try . . . right?"

"What have we got to lose, Pearle?"

"All right, I will speak to Matthew about them and see if we can arrange a meeting for you.

"Oh, talking about Matthew, I am going to have a small surprise party for him Sunday night, and we want you to come. It's his thirteenth birthday, Brian, and I'm sure he isn't expecting anything. I figured it would be fun for Matthew and give him something else to think about after everything he has been through lately. Oh, and supposedly, the three creatures will make an appearance that night. So maybe that will be your opportunity to talk with them, Brian."

"Denise will be there too, Brian," Robert added with a smirk.

Brian didn't say anything and just smiled.

"So . . . is there anything else, then, Brian, we need to discuss tonight?" Pearle asked.

"No, I don't think so, Pearle, but that call to your man in New York for the medallions needs to be done ASAP."

"Definitely, that is the first thing I'll do in the morning. I will call you as soon as I talk with him."

"**No**, Pearle, do not call me here. Any communications for me, unless it is an emergency, I prefer you call Robert instead. I don't want to raise any suspicion with you calling me here."

"Right, Brian, I agree . . . that's probably a good idea," Pearle responded.

"Well . . . I think I better get this lady home and then my butt to bed," Robert said as he stood and stretched.

"Yeah," and Brian yawned. "I am going to head out too. Oh, Pearle, here, put these in your purse, and *please* get them locked up in a safe place. Remember, whatever you do, don't tell *anyone* you have your medallions back!"

"Don't you worry about that, Brian! I'll put them where no one will be able to find them!"

"Wait a minute," Pearle suddenly said. "I just had a thought.

Robert, Brian, if we suspect that someone in the department is in on all this, do you think it is a good idea to have the guys from the department still doing security? Maybe we should hire a private company."

Robert looked at Brian and shook his head.

"Absolutely, Pearle!" Robert replied. "I'll check into another company from out of the area tomorrow. I want someone on this right away, though. I'm not chancing anyone's safety here or blowing this case giving whoever from the department is involved carte blanche to walk into your house again!"

Chapter Twenty-three

It was the day before Matthew's birthday. Annabelle and Pearle were in the kitchen going over the last few details when the doorbell rang.

"I'll get it, Annabelle," yelled Nakia from the living room.

It was a special delivery with specific instructions for the courier that only Pearle Sherapha could sign for the package, and her ID had to be verified.

"Pearle, there is a package for you," Nakia yelled, "but the delivery man says he can only give it to you."

"Well, aren't you going to open it?" Annabelle asked when Pearle and Nakia returned to the kitchen.

"No, it is a surprise for Matthew, and I don't want anyone slipping and telling him about it," she laughed.

"Okay, you be that way," puffed Annabelle.

Pearle continued to laugh. "Oh, feeling left out, are we?" she kidded Annabelle.

"Oh, you," Annabelle hissed, "you know I hate secrets!"

"Tough. I know how weak you get when it comes to Matthew. I am just keeping you from letting that loose tongue of yours slip!"

"I forget you know me so well," chuckled Annabelle.

"Girls . . . I've got something to do upstairs for a while, but I'll be back to go over everything about the party and make sure we haven't forgotten anything."

Pearle left the kitchen quickly and went up to her bedroom to call Robert. Fifteen minutes later, Robert walked into her bedroom and closed the door.

"Well, that was quick! Did you use your lights and sirens to get here?" she asked, smiling.

"No, just my lead foot," he replied with a hearty laugh, and then kissed her cheek.

"So, how do they look?" he asked anxiously.

"I haven't opened them yet. I was waiting on you."

"Well, have at it," he said, rubbing his hands together nervous-ly. "Or do you want me to do the honors?"

"Okay, you do it," she replied, handing him the box. "I'm a nervous wreck," she laughed.

Robert reached into his khaki pants pocket and pulled out his trusty old pocketknife. She noticed it was inlaid with mother-of-pearl and had his initials carved in it.

"Oh, that's a lovely pocketknife, Robert."

"Thanks, Pearle. It was a gift from my father after I graduated from law school."

Pearle watched as he carefully flicked the blade out and ran its razor tip carefully along the edge of the box. He pulled out a Styrofoam form wrapped in several layers of plastic bubble wrap and cut it off.

"Holy smokes, Pearle, this guy was worth every penny. They look fantastic!" Robert gently picked one out of the molded holes and held it up. "Wow, even the weight seems good, and the chain is nice too. What do you think, Pearle?"

"Very nice. And if I didn't know better, I'd swear they were the real ones. I told you he was good," she added with a smirk. Now, Robert, I told Nakia and Annabelle, who, by the way, was very nosy, as usual, that this was a special birthday gift for Matthew. How are you going to get this box out of the house, detective?"

"Well," and he laughed, "getting the medallions out will be easy. I'll just put them in different pockets of my jacket. But you need to hide this box until we can get rid of it," he said, handing the empty box over to her. "Oh . . . wait a minute, Pearle; give it back a second."

He took the box and tore off the label, scrunched it up, and put it deep inside his pants pocket. Then he took a black Sharpie pen out of his shirt pocket and crossed off all the shipping numbers and anything that could enable someone to trace the package.

"Here ya go, Pearle; now put this box somewhere no one will find it. If someone does, they won't be able to find out anything on the contrary."

She took it and placed it in the back of her enormous closet, under her winter-shoe boxes. It was barely distinguishable from the others.

"Come and take a look, Robert. . . . What do you think?"

Robert peeked in the massive closet. "Holy cow! Do you really wear all these clothes and shoes?"

"Yes, I do, for your information, detective!"

Robert laughed, "You can hardly tell that it's there. Someone would really have to know what to be looking for. Great spot, Pearle! So tell me, did Abe accept your invitation to the party?"

"Yes, he did, and said he was so excited about coming and being able to see Matthew again."

"Wonderful. Now, you remember everything we went over and what you are going to say?"

"Absolutely, detective. Got it all right here," Pearle said as she pointed to her head.

"That's a good spot," he laughed. "So now, tell me what else is going on here."

"Let's see . . . ahh . . . Matthew and his nurse said they have something special planned for tonight and won't tell me what it is. Yammi seems to be adjusting well, and he and Daniel have really hit it off. Nakia has been doing quite well and seems to be happy with her job so far, and other than that, all else is pretty much the same. Oh, you didn't forget you have to be here before three tomorrow, did ya?"

"Don't worry, I'll be here, silly," he replied. "Brian said he'd be here early too, in case we needed any help. Guess he is a little nervous about being around Denise and Daniel at the same time. I told him to just be himself and relax." Robert began to laugh.

"What's so funny, Robert?" Pearle asked, looking at him oddly.

"Brian. . . . He is so clueless about women, and I don't know why. He really is shy, Pearle."

"For your information, I find it refreshing! Most men his age are like wolves. Brian is really a nice guy, and I think Denise and him make a cute couple."

"I definitely agree with you, Pearle. Well, I've got to get these medallions to Brian's office. I'm sure he is chomping at the bit for them. I called him after I spoke to you, and he said he couldn't wait to see them."

"I think this whole robbery case is relying on your plan, isn't it?"

"You could say that, Pearle, but don't forget, we have evidence coming back soon too. I'm an old-fashioned guy who believes that what goes around comes around. The truth will eventually come out, and when it does, I will see that justice is done, I promise you."

"You really are a great detective, Robert, and I trust you more than you could imagine."

"That's nice to hear, Pearle, especially with how hard Oona's case has been for the last eight years. As selfish as this sounds, and I don't want you to take this wrong, but if all this stuff didn't happen with Oona, I would have never met the love of my life. You do know how much you mean to me, don't you, Pearle?"

"Yes, I do, Robert, and you know I feel the same way."

He stood up and kissed the top of her head hastily.

"Okay, my dear, I need to get my butt in gear and get these medallions to Brian. Then I have an important errand to run. I got something special for Matthew a while ago, had it specially made, and I need to pick it up today."

"You didn't have to do that, Robert."

"Pearle, Matthew is very special to me, and I wanted to do this. Besides, it isn't every day you turn thirteen. It is a big event in a guy's life, and I am happy to be able to share it with him," he replied as he put the medallions in different pockets of his jacket. "All right, I'll call you later."

"Good luck, Robert," she said as he walked to the door.

Robert gently patted his medallion-filled pockets and closed the door behind him.

"Well . . . I'm dying of curiosity," Brian said as Robert walked into his office.

"They came out great! Here, take a look," Robert said as he reached into his pockets.

"Nice job; that is one heck of a good copy, if I say so myself!"

"Pearle thought so too. Every detail seems to be there, Brian."

"Ya think! At ten grand a pop, they ought to be," Brian snorted back.

"It wouldn't have been that much, but with him having to bring extra help in to get them done so quickly, he had to charge that, I guess. Pearle thought it was a fair price."

"It was a freaking rip-off, as far as I am concerned," Brian answered, annoyed.

"Well, it is done, and now we have the job of putting the GPS in. So let's get started."

Brian pulled a tube of jewelers glue and some small tools from his jacket pocket. He carefully removed a colored gem from each of the medallions, glued the tiny GPS device in place, then replaced the stone and folded down the prongs that held it into place.

Robert took a small laptop computer from the locked file cabinet and turned it on. He searched a few programs until he found what he was looking for.

"There we go, Brian; we are up and running! Now, walk around the room just to make sure they are working okay."

Brian picked up the medallions, and as he moved, the program picked up his location and immediately showed his coordinates. Then another program gave the address of exactly where he was.

"Boy, ya gotta love modern technology! What did we do before it, Brian?"

"Robert, I am gonna go out to the parking lot and walk around. Then I will drive somewhere with them to make sure the GPS is working full range."

"Good, and I'll watch how it shows your position too. This is some cool stuff!"

"Geez, Robert, you sound like one of the kids," Brian laughed.

"Come on, you mean to tell me this technology stuff doesn't blow your socks off too?"

"It does, but I guess you old-timers have a harder time accepting it!"

"Funny, Brian . . . real funny . . . ha, ha, ha!"

Brian walked around the parking lot and then took off in his car. He traveled about fifteen miles from the department, made numerous random turns, and forty minutes later was back at the station.

"Looks good . . . those are all the streets I turned down and the routes from and to the station. This is great," Brian said as Robert showed him everything the GPS program recorded.

"So who takes the computer home?" Brian asked.

"Since I have figured out how to get alerts on my phone, you can have it, Brian."

"Wow, I am impressed for someone I thought was techno-challenged," Brian kidded.

"You can do it too, Brian. Just go into the settings, put in the information they ask about your phone, answer a few security questions, put this code in that only you and I have, and you should be good to go."

"Excellent; I'll do that right now then. Oh, are you going to put the evidence bags back now?" Brian asked as he handed him the medallions.

"Yes, sir, we both are." Robert picked up his phone and called Chief Duggard. Five minutes later, he knocked on the locked door. Robert let the chief in, showed him the medallions, and informed him about everything they have done since they talked last. The chief doesn't say much, but that's Duggard. He's a great listener with excellent recall. Duggard leads a great police department and has for the last five years. Everyone respects him and his tough leadership. His presence in a room stands out. He exalts integrity and expects that from every one of his employees. There are *never* any exceptions to the contrary. Chief Duggard has been with the department for twenty-six years and worked his way up through the ranks. His six-foot-five stature can be intimidating, especially to new officers, but when they get to know him, they say he is a gentle giant with little words and a big heart. The chief's office exhibits his numerous honored accomplishments over the years. What he is most proud of, though, and will talk about is his wife, Fran, of thirty-one years and his six children.

"I expect you gentlemen will keep me informed about this little operation?"

"Yes, sir," they both replied.

"Good, then I'm going home. My Fran has decided to barbecue today. Hmm . . . guess I better pick up some antacids on the way home," he laughed. He turned before opening the door and cleared his throat.

"Ahem . . . . You fellows be careful," he said in his familiar low, husky voice, and then left the room.

Yammi worked all week downloading the ton of pictures from Matthew's digital camera they took at the pyramid. He knew it would take weeks, maybe even months to figure out all of the hieroglyphics and to put them into some type of order, to see if they would reveal something about the prophecy. However, he and Daniel came up with a brilliant idea late last night, but with another problem . . . supplies.

"Pearle has an office downstairs with tons of paper and ink for the computers. I'll just go and tell her what we need . . . or . . . wait . . . maybe I shouldn't," he said. "Maybe we better go talk to Matthew before we say anything to her. What do you think, Yammi?"

"That's probably a good idea since he hasn't told her yet that he brought home Oona's medallion and those other things."

"Oh, crap, no, he hasn't," Daniel replied. "Yeah, come on, Yammi, let's go downstairs and talk to him."

"Hi, Matt. How are you feeling?"

"I'm good. What are you two up to today?"

"Well, we need to talk to you."

"What's up? Is something wrong?"

"Daniel and I have come up with a most brilliant idea! Well, we think it's brilliant, anyway," he said with a big grin.

"So . . . what's this brilliant idea?" Matthew asked.

The boys filled Matthew in on what they wanted to do, but needed the supplies to do it. He told them their idea was fantastic, and anything they needed would be in the office and that they could help themselves.

"Nana buys everything in bulk, guys, so you should have plenty of what you need. I also have boxes of tape in the office closet, so help yourselves to whatever you want. Just one thing, Yammi

. . . *Do not* tell my grandmother anything yet. I know she wants to know everything about what happened that night and why we went to the pyramid. She just hasn't pushed the issue, and I guess I've been avoiding telling her."

"Are you going to tell her, Matthew?" Daniel asked.

"Yes, but I am not sure if I will tell her everything . . . especially about the things I brought back with us. I'm going to wait and see how much information we come up with first, then go from there. Look, I promised her I wasn't going to keep any more secrets from her, and I'm really not, well kind of, in a sorta way I'm not," he laughed. "Besides, we both agreed when we got home that we have time to talk about the incident. So by the time we get to that conversation, hopefully the three of us will know more of what happened and why that night in the pyramid. Maybe even a better understanding of this prophecy will come about with the pictures!"

"That is my hope, Matthew," Yammi added.

"Okay, buddy, we are going to leave you to rest and go get all this stuff. There's an *awful* lot of pictures yet to print out. But we're going to get started on that and then come back later to let you know how it's all going," Daniel, said.

"Wish I could go upstairs and help you guys. I feel so useless laying here!"

"I promise, as soon as we get them printed, we'll show you. Besides, you better practice your song on Guitar Hero. . . . You and Daniel have a little competition to finish tonight," Yammi reminded him.

"Bring it on, Fuscilli, bring it on," Matthew replied, laughing.

Daniel turned and glared at Matthew. Then his face twisted up as if he bit into something sour, and with a weird look in his eye, growled like a wild animal.

"Yeah, right, you peon crippled heir!"

Matthew was frightened and taken aback, especially by his cruel remark. Daniel looked strange, and his eyes were black. "What you call me?" Matthew snapped back with a nervous swallow.

Yammi looked at Daniel, and his expression went blank. At first he hesitated from fear; then he went over to him and looked at his horrifying face. He took his shoulders and shook him hard. "What is wrong with you, Daniel? Something strange has happened to you." Again, he shook him, this time so hard he fell to the ground. Daniel got up awkwardly. He was breathing heavily. Then he stumbled and fell back and closed his eyes. Yammi and Matthew were in shock and just stared at Daniel lying on the floor. A few minutes passed. Daniel sat up and opened his eyes. He looked down at the ground, then up and into Yammi's horrified eyes. He shook his head, then held it as if he were in great pain.

"Daniel . . . **Dan** . . . are you all right?" Matthew asked.

He looked up again and over at Matthew. "What just happened?"

"I'm not sure, but you weren't yourself, buddy, for a few minutes. You don't remember what you said?"

"No . . . I . . . I don't. All I know is that I felt this intense anger because you took that stuff from the pyramid. Then it felt like someone punched me in my stomach so hard that it took my breath away, and everything went black. . . . **What is going on?**" he shrilled in a shaky voice. He stood up and held his stomach. "I don't feel . . . very well. I think . . . I'm . . . gonna be sick," he said as he ran out of the room with his hand over his mouth.

Matthew knew at that very moment something was wrong, *very wrong* with Daniel. He's noticed his odd behavior since he got home, but blew it off, thinking it was nothing. Now, with this burst of anger, he knows it is something, and he needs to find out what's going on.

"Yammi, what's going on with Daniel? Don't lie to me either; I know you two have been getting close, so he must've told you something," Matthew said as he looked straight into his kind brown eyes.

"Matthew, as for Daniel, I would say that if you want to know, then you will ask of him yourself. I think, though, that if you allowed yourself, you may be able to figure this out on your own."

"Well, I am not *psychic*, and *he* doesn't even know why he just did what he did! So why would I ask him?"

"Oh, my friend . . . but you are," Yammi said with a calm voice and kind expression.

"Huh," Matthew replied looking dumbfounded. "What are you saying?"

"Matthew, all I will say is this: What you have inside of you, the capabilities you possess will only come out if you let them. You need to trust yourself enough to do that. And when you do, you will understand what it is I say right now. You have amazing abilities inside of you yet to discover. But the only way to see them is to open your mind to those thoughts you bury with fear. Do not disregard your instincts and natural abilities that are just waiting inside of you to come forward. Do you remember what Sol told you about fear that day in the hotel? If so, then think about those words, and think about your feelings and everything you just know inside your gut to be true. The more you come in touch with your thoughts and feelings, the more questions you yourself will be able to answer."

"Yammi . . . how'd you know?" asked Matthew in a hushed tone.

"Because, my dear friend, I too have similar abilities."

"Phew," Daniel said as he trotted back into the room. "Talk about tossing your cookies! Boy, do I feel better. So you two geniuses figure out what happened to me?"

Yammi looked at Matthew, who had no idea either, and they both looked at Daniel and shrugged their shoulders.

"Well, *somebody* has to know what happened. That was pretty scary, and I dare to say not normal . . . wouldn't you agree?" Daniel said, looking at both of them for an answer.

"Daniel, I am not sure what or why that happened to you, and neither is Matthew. But somehow we will find the answer."

"Well, if it happens again, just know it's not me doing that. . . . It's . . . well . . . I just haven't got a freakin' clue!" he said, looking flabbergasted. "There's no sense dwelling over what happened; we have a lot of things to do, so we better get upstairs and get started."

"Daniel, it's going to be okay," Matthew said, assuring him.

"I'm sure it will, buddy. Guess you better rest. We'll be back later," Daniel said as he and Yammi left. "Hey, Yammi, I'll meet you upstairs. I have to use the bathroom again."

When Yammi got to Matthew's room, he closed the door and sat at the computer. He felt exhausted after what he and the boys just went through. He rested his head down on the computer desk and jerked up quickly when he heard a strange noise coming from the closet.

"What the . . . ?" he said aloud.

"What's wrong, Yammi? You look like you've seen a ghost," Daniel said, entering the room.

"I . . . I am not sure, but I just heard something weird . . . and it came from inside the closet. I'm not sure I can take much more today," he said, pointing to the closet, shaking his head.

Daniel tiptoed to the closet and opened the door slowly. As he listened, he heard something moving around. He went into the closet and slowly walked toward the noise. It was coming from the large bag Oopi, Amora, and Emia were in. He picked it up and brought it into the bedroom. Sitting on the floor, he untied the heavy cord knotted around its opening. The bag jerked back and forth, and the three orange eyes he hasn't seen in a few weeks poked out. Then the wrinkly purple body of Oopi slithered from the bag.

"Friend!" Oopi said joyously as he stretched so far that his wrinkled body looked smooth.

"Oopi, what are you doing up?"

"Oh, my, Daniel, I could not wait one more hour without something yummy for my tummy! No, indeed, I must have something now to fill it, please!"

"Yes, of course! Are the girls coming out too?" Daniel asked, looking at the bag.

"No, I am afraid not. They will sleep until the night of our heir's birthday."

"Are they okay, though, Oopi? Oh, and how is Amora's wing . . . has it healed yet?"

"They are fine, and as for our dear Amora, we shall see tomorrow how the wing has come healed."

"I'm so happy to hear that," Daniel said as he picked Oopi up and put him by the computer with Yammi.

"Oopi, you remember Yammi?"

"Yes, young man, how are you?"

"Hello, Oopi, sir. My arm is doing well, but I must have more surgery soon."

Oopi inched his way up to Yammi and near his arm. He ran his plump purple little fingers along it and hummed a song neither one of the boys were familiar with.

"You will only need one more surgery, and you will heal," Oopi said.

Yammi smiled back at him. "Thank you, Mr. Oopi. I will hope this is truth, then."

"The truth is only what I am capable of, young man," Oopi said, and then turned to Daniel. "So, how about some food for me, my friend?"

"Sure, I'll go get you some. Yammi, I'll be right back."

Daniel returned with a plate full of grapes and greens.

"Wait just . . . a minute here, Oopi. I will give you this food on *one* condition," he said, holding the plate far from Oopi's reach.

"What *is* it, boy?" he said in a snit.

"You have to promise not to choke this time," Daniel laughed.

"Oh, yes, yes, that was quite an unpleasant situation. Yes, friend, I promise to try and not choke this time," Oopi said, gesturing with his hands for Daniel to give him the food.

Yammi watched in amazement as Oopi used his fat, wrinkled hands and casually placed large green grapes in his mouth.

"You better slow down," Yammi cautioned, "or you will have a tummy ache," he laughed.

Oopi smiled and rubbed his tummy while letting out a most delighted sigh. Ten minutes later, the plate was empty. Oopi leaned back, quite contented with his bulging belly, gurgling.

"Full, are we?" asked Daniel, poking at Oopi's tummy.

"Yes, quite . . . ." *Buurrrpppp!*

"Oh, my," Yammi laughed.

"Aahh . . . that was just wonderful, wonderful indeed," Oopi said, patting his rotund stomach. "So what events have taken place during my sleep, friend?"

"Not too much, Oopi. I am glad, though, to see you today.

Yammi and I were just getting ready to print out the pictures we took in the pyramid."

"Interesting, but what do you mean 'print out,' Daniel?"

"Here, watch," he said as he pointed to the printer next to the desk."

Yammi pushed print on the file that contained the first wall of photos in Queen Oonaphelia's tomb. He made a file for each tomb the pictures were taken in so that nothing would get mixed up. Daniel removed the first picture that printed and showed it to Oopi.

"Is this some kind of *magic?*" Oopi asked cautiously.

"Oh, no," laughed Yammi. "This is what we call modern technology, Oopi. I assure you, it is *not* magic at all!"

"Looks magical," Oopi said stiffly as his three eyes bounced around while watching other pictures slip out of the printer. Oopi turned around and looked at Daniel. He stared at him for a few moments and then spoke.

"How are you, friend, since the hospital last? I know our heir is doing well."

"We are both fine, Oopi."

"This is truth of yourself, Daniel?"

"Yes, as a matter of fact. Matthew can move his legs now; isn't that wonderful?"

Oopi tsked, grinded his baby teeth together, and stiffened. He then sat back and crossed his arms atop his pudgy belly.

"I know the heir is well, but that is not what I asked."

Daniel looked at him, wondering what he wanted to know. He thought he answered his question. Daniel suddenly became very angry and resentful of Oopi's question.

"If you have a direct question, Oopi, then ask me. Otherwise, stop sticking your nose where it shouldn't be," he snapped vehemently.

"Daniel, I am sure Oopi meant no harm in what he asks, and you acting this way is completely wrong! What is the matter with you?" Yammi asked while standing quickly and knocking over his chair.

Daniel managed to catch the chair before it hit the wooden floor. He looked up at Yammi and Oopi and was at a loss for words. Their shocked faces did not need words. What just happened? *Did those words really come out of me?* he thought.

"Oopi, what is happening to me?" Daniel moaned, holding his head.

"Oopi . . . something is wrong! At times, I feel like myself, happy and glad to be alive. Recently, though, I feel angry, resentful, restless and . . . *not me!* Is this from drinking that Bennu Elixir?"

"No, Daniel," he said, shaking his head, looking concerned. "If anything, you should be quite the opposite. I am not sure what has gone wrong, friend."

"Yammi, you are smart—have you any feeling about this or thought of what is happening to Daniel?" Oopi asked.

"I do not know, Oopi, but if you can tell me what this Bennu Elixir is of, I can research it in my book. I have not heard of this name before, but maybe there we can find something."

Yammi quickly got his book of ancient elixirs and spells from his backpack. Oopi then proceeded to tell him what the ingredients were of the elixir. He searched the many pages of different ingredients the elixir contained and after a half hour closed his book.

"I see *nothing* to the contrary of what Oopi has said. The Bennu is very old magic, but it does not have the effects you are experiencing, Daniel. I have another idea, though. Daniel, I need to call home. May I use your cell phone?"

"Of course."

Yammi took out his address book, found the number, and put it into the phone.

"Good evening, Suhama. . . . Yes . . . yes, it is Yammi. I hope I have not called and inconvenienced you this evening. Oh . . . I am fine and doing well here in America. Yes, everyone has been extremely wonderful to me. How are you, though? I have missed seeing you at the market on Sundays. Oh, ha, ha, ha, yes, I miss the egg jugglers too. Listen, Suhama, I need to talk with you about something of great importance. It is something that only you would understand. Yes, no . . . all right, I shall tell you, then."

Yammi had a lengthy conversation with Suhama. In between questions and answers, occasionally he would repeat them aloud so Oopi could help him answer them.

"So . . . you really think this is what I should do, then? Aha, yes, all right, Suhama, then I will call tomorrow, as you asked, and let you know how it goes. Thank you ever so much. I kindly appreciate all this time you have afforded me. What . . . what did you say? Yes, he is a *very* good friend, and if you get to meet him, you will know this too. Yes, all right, Suhama. Good night to you as well."

"So what did Suhama have to say?" Daniel asked anxiously.

"Yes, please do tell. Was she of any help to the answers we seek?" Oopi asked.

"Well, yes and no. First, she wanted to know how I found out about the Bennu Elixir because she said only kings, queens, and their high priests and/or priestesses of ancient Egypt had possession of that potent elixir. I just told her a friend of mine was doing research of an old Egyptian case in school that involved the elixir. Suhama knew differently, but said she would not press me about the situation. Then, of course, she wanted to know if I was in some kind of trouble, which I assured her I wasn't. Anyway, as far as someone having a different personality with the elixir, she said that is a possibility, but not a negative one. Especially she stressed, if a person gave freely of himself with its use. She thinks . . . that maybe . . . someone put a *curse* on the person who suffers the personality change. Can you think of anyone who would want to curse our Daniel?" Yammi asked Oopi.

"I can only think of one, but *how* is the question here, Yammi."

"And who may I ask, then, is responsible?"

"It may be the evil one having Escursia doing her dirty work. But I just cannot understand this or how she would be able to, being Daniel has no ties to their family. He has no blood involved."

"Daniel, if I may ask you a few questions that Suhama brought up, maybe we can figure this out," Yammi said while looking at the notes he took from his conversation with Suhama.

"Sure, Yammi, ask away," Daniel said as he sat down on the bed.

"Very good, then. Daniel, the first thing I need to know is, when did you notice that you were feeling not of yourself, as you said before to Oopi?"

"I think I started to have these angry feelings the day after we got home. I remember on that morning, we had breakfast and went for that walk, Yammi. I was feeling fine until that afternoon, after Nakia gave me a glass of juice. I just figured it was a new kind of fruit juice and my stomach didn't like it. But I haven't felt right since. I thought I was coming down with something because I even mentioned to Nakia that my throat was feeling scratchy. You know when you get sick, you just don't feel like yourself. But since then, Yammi, I swear I feel really *odd* sometimes. . . ."

"Do you remember what kind of juice this was, Daniel, and what it tastes like?"

"Oh, I don't know . . . ahh . . . I think Nakia said it was fruit of the gods or something like that, kidding around, but she said it was *her* special juice that she drank every day to keep healthy. So I figured it had to be okay, ya know? It didn't taste like anything I've ever had before, but it was pretty good, kinda like a sweet but had a tangy sour aftertaste to it."

"Has she offered it to you again?"

"No, Yammi. As a matter of fact, I went to ask Nakia about what was in the juice because of my upset stomach, and she said she couldn't remember and she had thrown out the container it was in. At the time, I didn't think anything of it, but now it does seem odd. I did tell her, though, that when she got more to let me see the container for the ingredients so that I might try to figure out what got my stomach sick. Usually I can eat or drink anything and not have a problem, ever! You know, Yammi, she kind of blew me off, now that I think about this. Hey, you don't think she tried to *poison* me or something, do you?"

Yammi and Oopi looked at each other, then at Daniel.

"She may have poisoned your spirit, Daniel," Oopi replied. "Who is this woman, and what do you know of her?"

"All I know about her, Oopi, is that she works for Pearle. She recently came here from Egypt, and Annabelle hired her a few days before we got home. I mean, other than the juice thing, she seems to be very nice, and everybody . . . well . . . now, wait a minute," Daniel said, rising from the bed. "Matthew did mention to me that Zatu doesn't like her and growls at her whenever she is around him. Come to think of it . . . Matthew said something to me one night about how he isn't sure if *he* likes Nakia. When I asked him why, he said something about her just doesn't sit right with him. But he really hasn't said too much about her since. She does keep her distance from him, though, and you too, Yammi. I have noticed that many times. Have you got any idea why she avoids the two of you?"

Yammi got up, and his face was red. He asked Daniel to get the objects he had hidden that Matthew took from the pyramid. Daniel went to the back of the closet and removed a shelf. Behind it was a small trap door, and inside it, a safe, where Matthew keeps his special possessions. He told Dan to put the items there for safekeeping. Daniel removed the objects and brought them to Yammi.

"Thank goodness! I was so worried they may have been taken," Yammi replied with relief.

"Daniel . . . have you been staying in this room?" asked Oopi.

"Yes, I have. Why?"

"Oh," replied Yammi, "yes, oh, yes! This is making perfect sense to me now," he said.

"She knows they are here, doesn't she, Yammi? She wants these objects," Daniel said angrily. "Well, I got news for that sneaky evil witch . . . she *isn't* going to get them, especially not after all Matthew, you, and I went through to get them!"

"Calm yourself, Daniel. You are correct that she desires these items, but I am not sure she is directly responsible."

"What are you talking about, Yammi? It has to be *her,* and if she is playing around with us, she is responsible!"

"Friend, you need to listen, for what Yammi is telling you may be truth. I think Yammi, as well as myself, believe this Nakia may be under a spell from the evil one. However, she may be working for the evil on her own free will. Did Suhama say anything about this to you?"

"Yes, Oopi, she said a scenario of these possibilities could exist, and she hopes we are dealing with a spell and not the evil one *herself!*"

"How are we to know this, Yammi? How do we find this out?" asked Oopi, who was quite shaken.

"Daniel, please secure those items, and we will talk of a plan. The first thing we must do of importance is to find out if you were poisoned or cursed. Once we find that answer, we can treat you or try to break the curse. Now, get Oopi's bag from the closet, and bring it to him."

Daniel did as asked and put the bag on the floor. Yammi took Oopi off the desk and brought him to it. As Yammi and Daniel sat there, they watched Oopi crawl into the bag and wiggle around inside it. Oopi was carrying on and speaking, but neither knew if it was to himself or someone in the bag.

"Yammi, do you really think we can find out what Nakia is doing and why?"

"I am very much hoping so, Daniel. Whatever is manipulating your behavior involves very strong and evil magic. I trust that Oopi, Suhama, and I will work together to have those answers and rid you of whatever possesses your soul. The more days that go by, the more your soul will disappear from you. It is important for us to discover as quickly as possible exactly what kind of magic is doing this. Do not worry, my friend. I promise we *will* find the answers."

Daniel leaned back onto his elbows. As he lay on the floor, he looked up at the starry ceiling that he and Matthew created. He wished for those days right now, when things were simple, Matthew was walking, and he knew nothing about a prophecy. He wondered if their life would ever be normal again.

"What is he looking for, Yammi?" Daniel asked impatiently.

"He is searching for a special ingredient we will need. He believes he has everything in that magic bag of his," Yammi laughed.

"Well, I'm not *dumb*," he replied sharply. "I want to know what *exactly* it is that he searches for."

"Ancient herbs, Daniel, and by the sound of your voice, he is not finding them quickly enough."

"Tell me how you *two* masterminds are going to tell the difference of a spell or if a curse is on me. Come on, Yammi, I don't think there *is* any difference to this madness! Oh, and how about Nakia—how are you going to figure out if she is cursed or if she is just plain evil?"

"Daniel, there is very much a difference of a curse than a spell, although both bring sorrow and evil intentions. A spell will usually only last for a brief period of time, and they are often *easy* to break. On the other hand, a curse is *very strong, dark magic,* and its wicked intentions can last for someone's *entire life* and even go on to curse this person's family, generation after generation. There are many rituals for both, but a curse will be more difficult to deal with than a simple spell. It is belief, the more powerful the person is who casts a curse, the worse and longer it lasts."

"It sounds confusing to me, Yammi, but I'll have to trust you and Oopi. I guess whatever has been done to me . . . I assume it can be fixed?"

"Don't assume anything, Daniel," he warned, "but yes, that is the plan."

Oopi finally found his way out from his leather bag, dragging behind him a gold velvet sack. He placed it on the floor and went back inside. He returned with yet another sack. This one was much bigger and was purple with gold flecks all over it.

"Geez, Oopi, that bag is almost as big as you!" Daniel said.

"Yes, and quite heavy! I believe, though, I have gathered all of what we will need."

Then he rested on his tail and sat quietly for a few moments. He drummed his fingers on his belly like someone in deep thought. Then he straightened up and cleared his throat.

"Ahem, Yammi, I was thinking about something, and, well . . . we need to consider what the reason is why our friend here was hoaxed. I believe, though, I have come up with a solution to find that very important answer."

"We must think alike, Oopi. I too was wondering the reason of Daniel's involvement after you said he has no blood ties to Matthew. But he *does,* though, Oopi. After the Bennu Elixir and what Daniel has done for Matthew, they will forever be tied like blood. Daniel's essence is within Matthew, and during that exchange, Matthew's essence is now a part of Daniel."

"Even though this may be true, Yammi, what would be desired from Daniel?"

"I think I have something here that can help us find out, Oopi. It seems to be quite a simple procedure if we have the right ingredients. We can, if this is done correctly, find out not only why, but who has made Daniel not of himself."

"Well, this is great, Yammi," Daniel replied, looking hopeful.

"Yes, it is, but the only problem we have is that we must make a special elixir, and it will take several procedures to complete."

"So what does that mean, Yammi?"

"Daniel, it means that this elixir will not be ready for twenty-four hours, at the most twenty-eight!"

"Why is this a problem? I mean . . . is it a problem, Yammi?" Daniel asked, wide-eyed.

Yammi looked at Oopi and shook his head.

"Daniel, there is but something else I must tell you. We will need to have Nakia present when we have the elixir ready, and *she too* must drink of *another* elixir. This must be done at a *precise* time after the elixir is finished, or it will not work."

"Well, let's try to figure this out. Tomorrow is Matthew's birthday, and with the little party Pearle is having, I know she will be here to help Annabelle. I heard them talking this morning about the plans. She will be here the *entire* day to work. We would just have to think of a way to do this without her knowing, though, right?"

"Yes, and we must be careful as to how we get her to drink the elixir, Daniel. If the evil one is responsible, I am *sure* she will have Nakia on her guard all the time."

"Yammi, my friend, I will take care of how she *gets* the elixir. You and Oopi just worry about getting it done and fixing me up," Daniel said with a smirk on his face.

"Oopi reached into the gold bag and pulled out a small gold box.

"Come, Daniel," he said as he opened the lid. I want you to take a pinch of these herbs between your fingers. Then put them to your nose and inhale deeply. These will keep you safe until Yammi and I can complete the elixir."

Daniel bent down and looked at the contents in the small box. He thought the stuff inside looked like gold sand, but did as Oopi instructed him. He felt a hot sensation over his entire body, and then he became very relaxed.

"Wow, Oopi, that made me feel good. I don't feel . . . so angry and, well . . . tense. . . . Gosh, was I really that terrible?" he asked Yammi.

"Yes, your anger's been quite alarming lately. We have much more important things to do now, so do not worry about that, Daniel. Let's plan on what we are doing tomorrow and get started on these elixirs!"

Chapter Twenty-four

Today is Matthew's birthday, and there is a happy and lively buzz in the kitchen this morning. Pearle and Annabelle just checked their list, and everything for Matthew's little surprise party is ready. But what has everybody abuzz all morning is the *big* surprise he sprung on them last night. Matthew, assisted by his nurse, came out of his room in a wheelchair. Apparently, after much coaxing from him, his nurse had a lengthy conversation with his doctor, and he agreed if Matthew felt up to sitting in a wheelchair, he was comfortable with him doing so. Daniel will never forget the look on Matthew's face last night. Everything he has gone through for his friend was worth it. Even every bit of trouble he faces now.

Yammi and Daniel were down early for breakfast. They had a busy morning ahead of them. They still had to add a few more ingredients to the elixirs. Yammi told Dan he had a little tweaking to do to make up for ingredients they used from the garden, because Oopi did not have everything they needed. Daniel had asked Pearle if she could tell Nakia not to worry about cleaning in his room, because Yammi and he were working on a surprise for Matt and did not want anyone to know until tonight. She agreed, but with some curiosity, to his request.

"Good morning!" Matthew yelled as he wheeled himself into the kitchen.

"Well, look who it is. Our own speed racer," laughed Pearle. "How are you today, birthday boy?"

"Actually . . . great, Nana! How are *you doing?*" he giggled. "I mean, last night, I thought you were gonna have a heart attack when you saw me wheel into the dining room," he laughed.

"Oh, so you thought that was funny," she joked back.

"Nana," he said, still laughing, "all I'll say is that everyone's face was priceless!"

"I bet, smarty pants! So what would you like for breakfast?"

"You will never guess what I want, Nana."

"Ahh . . . French toast?"

"Nope, how about some hot cereal the way you make it with butter 'n' sugar. I don't know why, but I woke up with such a craving for it."

"You know, I haven't had breakfast yet either, and that sounds really good. Give me about twenty minutes, and it will be ready, okay?"

"Sure. . . . Have you seen Dan and Yammi?"

"Yes, they are up in your room. Guess they are doing some *secret thing* for your birthday. Daniel asked that they not be disturbed," she laughed.

"*Hmm,*" he muttered, and wondered what it was.

"So Nana, are we doing anything special today?" he asked mischievously.

"Annabelle is making you a special dinner, and of course she will make you a cake, but other than that, there isn't much we really can do with you in a wheelchair."

"Oh, yes, there *is,* Nana. There is one special thing I would like to do today."

"Really. . . . Well, do tell!"

"After dinner, I want to go down to the fire pit, just like we do every year on my birthday, and have s'mores."

"Matthew, I am not sure that's a good idea. Do you really think you are up to that?"

"Of course I am. If I wasn't, I would tell you. The doctor said I could sit in this chair a couple of hours several times a day."

"Well, I will agree to your request, but if I think you don't look up to it later, then no way, kiddo. I don't want you pushing yourself and having a setback."

"I'll be fine, Nana, and I'll rest before we go down, promise."

"All right, birthday boy, s'mores at the fire pit tonight!"

After breakfast, Pearle called Robert and asked him if he could pick up the chocolate and marshmallows for the s'mores and if he would help set up the fire pit when he came. He told Pearle he would be there at one with the supplies and was glad to hear that Matthew felt up to his birthday ritual. He asked if Matthew suspected anything about his party, and she told him she hoped not. As far as she knew, everything was going just as planned, and the day seemed to be perfect! Upstairs, Yammi and Daniel finished the last part of the elixirs and decided to go downstairs and visit Matthew.

"There you guys are," Matt said, greeting them coming down the stairs.

"Hey, Matt, we were just on our way to see ya."

"Dan, we are going to the fire pit tonight like we do every year!"

"No way! Pearle said it was okay? I mean, can you go down there with being in the chair and all?"

"Sure, there's a paved path to the lake and guesthouse. I'll have Robert wheel me down there, and we will be good to go!"

"Oh, dude, this is awesome!" And he gave Matt a high five.

"This sounds exciting, but what happens at the fire pit?" asked Yammi.

"Oh, dude, we build a big fire and sit around telling jokes and stories and roast marshmallows to make s'mores!"

"S'mores?" Yammi said, looking quite baffled.

"No way . . . Yammi! Don't tell me you haven't had s'mores before?"

"I don't think so, Daniel, but I have had marshmallows."

"Do you like chocolate, Yammi?" Daniel asked.

"Yes, very much so," he replied.

"Well, then you will find out tonight what a s'more is, and I promise you it will be another favorite of yours!"

"I will take your word for it, Daniel! The Creamsicle drink was wonderful, so I am sure this will be too."

"Psst, Dan," Matt said in a lowered voice, "how are the pictures coming along?"

"Good. As a matter of fact, we need to talk to you," he whispered as he looked around to see if anybody was nearby.

"Okay, let's go to my room."

"Patty, now that I am settled in, why don't you go take a break. Thanks for making my bed and everything."

"Oh, I see," she laughed, "the boys want some guy time! I guess

I could use a cup of coffee. That's fine, but if you need me, I'll be in the kitchen."

"I'm good. Go enjoy your coffee," Matthew said as he helped her with pulling the bed sheet over his legs.

"So what's up, guys?" Matthew asked eagerly.

"Matthew," Yammi said, "I must ask you something. Please be honest with your answer, for it is important we know the truth."

"Okay, ask away," Matthew said, looking oddly at them.

"Have you been having nightmares?"

"Why?" he quickly answered. Then he put his head down and began to bite his lip nervously.

"Because . . . it is important for me to know."

"Yes . . . I have, Yammi."

"Who is in the dreams, Matthew, and what are they about?"

"It's Zara *and* Escursia. They seem to be fighting each other and trying to win my trust. Zara keeps telling me to trust only those who have been my ally. Then Escursia tells me not to trust who I think I can, and she wants me to know that my injuries came from those who said they would protect me."

"This Escursia *lies* to you, Matthew. She is trying to win your trust, but for the wrong reasons. She only has evil and selfish reasons for what she does. I, well *we,* must tell you of something that has happened. But you must promise me that you will not upset yourself. We have a problem. . . . But Oopi is helping, as is an old friend of mine from back home."

"I've had a feeling that something was wrong, especially with you, Dan. I'm not sure *why* you guys haven't spoke to me about it, though."

"Matthew, you've had a lot to deal with the last few weeks, and your recovery is the most important thing to us. But what's happening we feel you should know about, and so does Oopi."

"Yammi, I'm glad you guys came to me because I am very concerned about this Nakia lady."

Yammi and Daniel looked at each other and knew it was time to tell Matthew everything.

"What is it that concerns you about her?" Yammi asked.

"To put it point blank . . . I *don't* like her or *trust* her, guys. It isn't anything specific, though. I just get the **heebie-jeebies** from her and an overwhelming sense of dread when she is around. Even Zatu doesn't like her! Apparently, you guys are having a problem with her, aren't you?" Matthew said.

"You have no idea, buddy!" Daniel said.

"Oh," Matthew said as he adjusted himself in his bed. "Well, let's hear it, then."

Yammi filled Matthew in on Dan's anger, when it started, and why they think Nakia is involved. He told him about the elixirs they have brewing and a plan they have come up with that must happen tonight.

"We didn't want to ruin your birthday, buddy," Dan said apologetically, "but we have to do this before things get worse, or before she may try to do something to you, Matt! That has been my biggest concern!"

"So what exactly and when did you guys plan all this for?"

"It has to be tonight, Matthew. The elixirs will be finished by then, and Emia and Amora will be awake by then to join us. They have been asleep, Oopi said, healing since right after the cave-in. This fire tonight has worked in our favor. We have special spices that need to burn before the elixirs are to be drunk. In doing so, we hope this will evoke the one responsible for Daniel's anger. I must tell you both something, though. Suhama said that we are to be extremely careful, for the evil one may become dangerous. Matthew, you will have to dig deep inside of you for the strength you possess, should this happen. Do you remember when I spoke of your gift? I think today would be a good time to reexamine what you feel but are so afraid to see."

"I have been, Yammi. . . . I mean I've been truly searching inside of me, my feelings, and mostly my thoughts. And you were right. I have learned that when I keep an open mind with no fear, I seem to have more understanding of what I feel."

"What have you learned?" Yammi asked, smiling.

"It's kind of weird and, well, hard to explain. I find myself seeing things and feeling strange stuff, Yammi."

"Okay, like what, Matthew? Can you be more specific so I may try to help you?"

"First, I have like this strange feeling come over me when Dan is around. It isn't a bad feeling, though. I get like a . . . well, a strong feeling that we have a connection, better than we did before the cave-in. We have always been close, and I know he saved my life in there, but it is something more, Yammi. Can you explain that to me?" Matthew asked.

Yammi stood up and turned to Daniel.

"I think it is time we told Matthew what you have done and why, don't you, Daniel?"

Daniel was sitting on the edge of Matthew's bed and fighting an awful angry feeling that was growing violently in him. He wanted to get up and punch Yammi in the face! *How dare he say something to him!* he thought.

Matthew and Yammi could see the anger that was filling Dan's face. His eyes looked glassed over, and his whole body was tense. They knew this wasn't Dan. It was something or someone else doing this to him. Daniel stood and faced Yammi within inches. His eyes were now glowing with a red haze. Yammi swallowed hard. He knew Daniel was possessed with an evil spirit. However, no way was Yammi going to back down.

"Who are you that possesses my friend with a pure heart?" Yammi asked with a strong voice. "You have no real power here! Be gone, you simple spirit!" Yammi ordered with his hands waving in the air.

Daniel turned and slowly walked toward Matthew and began to laugh with a hideous growling in his throat. "You truly think this pitiful indignant is going to help you with your gift? You're a *fool,* heir, and there is only but one who will make you understand the powers you possess. Why do you listen to such nonsense from creatures who will only betray you once again! You lie in this bed because of their uselessness. Have you no brain of your own to see these things? You will soon come to me, and I will show you the prophecy and what must be done to free me. Once you have done this, you shall be rewarded. We will share the two kingdoms with a power greater than anyone hast seen. You must be loyal to those who promise such wonderful truths, not to the ones who speak false words. You are a *Sherapha,* by blood, and shall rule with me. It was written of this, and so it shall be!"

"Who are you that speaks through my friend?" Matthew asked in an authoritative tone.

"Ha, ha, ha, you ask such stupid questions! Are you truly a fool, heir, with no sense at all of who I am?" Daniel growled.

"I know very well who you are . . . *Escursia,*" Matthew replied calmly. "Your tricks will not work, and neither will using my friend. Your words mean nothing to me! So be gone, you evil force, for I will extinguish the powers you try so hard with to empower. Now, be gone before you *rot* in your world forever!" Matthew ordered.

Daniel slumped to the floor, and Matthew began to smell the putrid odor of Escursia. Yammi pulled Daniel up by his arms and looked into his eyes. They were brown again, and Yammi knew he was okay.

"Come, sit," Yammi said to Daniel as he helped him to a chair.

"How are you feeling, Daniel? Are you okay?"

"Yes . . . yes, I think so. What happened, Yammi?"

"Ahh . . . ," Yammi said as he exhaled in relief and plopped on the floor in front of Daniel. "It wasn't pretty, but we know now who is trying to control you, Daniel. *It is* Escursia. Matthew, though, has made her go away. But I am sure as I sit here . . . she will be back."

The boys sat in silence. Yammi's legs were still shaking, and Daniel, still dazed. Matthew was looking at Daniel, and suddenly he saw a vision of him standing over him at the hospital. He wanted to cry; he wanted to hug his best friend and tell him how he loved him like a brother.

"I know what you did in the hospital, Dan, but why . . . why sacrifice so much for me?"

Dan, feeling exhausted, just shrugged his shoulders and said, "Because I know you would have done it for me, buddy."

Matthew and Daniel exchanged glances. Nothing else had to be said.

"I'm very proud of you, Matthew. You used your powers with Escursia and did it very well, I may add. You see now what I was speaking of when I said to not be afraid?"

"Yes, Yammi. I wasn't sure how she was going to react, but I knew I had to act quickly for Daniel; it . . . well, it just felt natural. I just didn't let my fear get me. Of course, I was scared, though, of what she might have retaliated with. Thank goodness, though, she is gone."

"I am sure it is only for a short time. . . . She will be back. However, we have a fix for that upstairs," Yammi said with a giant grin.

"I just hope it works, this elixir. I don't know if I have the strength to go through that again, Yammi."

"Daniel, I must tell you, when you drink of the elixir tonight, it will evoke her and call her out. I am not sure as to how she will react or if she will choose again to speak through you. Just know that with the creatures, Matthew, and I, you will be safe, I promise this."

"Regardless of what can happen, we have no other choice. This has to be done, Yammi."

"We'll make sure she is gone and can't bother you anymore," Matthew said, convincing his friend with his words.

"Ah, I would not make promises you can't keep," Yammi said cautiously.

"What makes you say that, Yammi?"

"This Escursia is very clever, and her magic, very powerful. You must not think that what we do tonight will be the end of her nonsense, because it won't be," Yammi cautioned again. "She has an agenda, and winning you over is at the top of her list. We must get all the pictures printed and make sense of the writings. Only then will we have a better understanding of the prophecy, including why Escursia is doing these things."

"You guys do realize that one day before this year ends, I will have to go back to the pyramid and fulfill this prophecy. Before I do, though, I will need both of your help in trying to figure out the prophecy and what I must do. You know, it's funny, I am not afraid anymore. Leery, maybe," Matthew laughed, "but not petrified like I was before."

"I don't want this to come out wrong, Matthew, but do not have false courage in all this. You must be honest with yourself and know it is okay to fear the evil you encounter. Only a fool would underestimate what danger can come from Escursia. What is most important to remember is keep that heart of yours pure, regardless of what may happen. Does that make sense to you, my friend?" Yammi asked.

"Yes, Yammi, it does. I don't know what Dan and I would have done without you here."

"Well, Matthew, I am glad to be here and help in any way that I can. We will do this together and hope for the best. Besides, I have met the two best friends I will ever have."

"Knock, knock; may I come in?" Pearle asked as she opened the door.

"Sure," the three boys said in harmony.

As she entered the room, she looked at the boys and noticed how exhausted they all looked.

"What's . . . been going on?" Pearle asked hesitantly while scanning their faces.

"Not much, Nana. What are you up to?" Matthew asked.

"Oh, not much either. Just was checking in on you and seeing if you needed anything," she said.

"I'm good, but getting hungry again," Matthew replied, laughing.

"As if that surprises me," Pearle laughed back.

"Since we are having dinner early, would you like to have lunch now? It is almost eleven thirty."

"Yeah, how 'bout you guys—you hungry too?"

"Like, duh! Of course," Yammi said.

"And you thought *my* appetite was bad," kidded Daniel.

"Annabelle made a homemade cheese and macaroni casserole for lunch. It will be ready in just a few minutes. Do you want to get up, Matt, or hang out here for lunch?"

"I think I'll stay here so I can be okay for later in the wheelchair."

"You mean you actually are going to listen to me, for a change? I think I may have a heart attack," she joked. "All right, I'll bring your lunch in just a few. Would you boys like to eat here with Matthew?"

"Oh, we don't want you to go through any trouble, Pearle. We can go to the kitchen for lunch," Yammi said.

"Oh, don't be silly. Lunch to be served soon," she said, smiling, on her way out.

"You are fortunate, Matthew, in having a grandmother who loves you the way Pearle does."

"I know, Yammi. She is so good to me. I love her very much, and I feel that maybe we need to tell her what is going on. I promised I would not keep any more secrets from her."

"Then you do what you feel is right in your heart, Matthew."

"What if she doesn't believe me, though, or won't let us do what we need to tonight?"

"I will help convince her. She knows much, Matthew, only she chooses to ignore it."

"Huh? What are you talking about, Yammi?"

"Like you, Pearle has much insight to many things, but she chooses not to deal with it. It is as I have told you before. She has your powers but refuses to understand or use them. Maybe she will have a change of heart before the end of the night, though."

"What makes you say that, Yammi?"

"I guess because I truly do not know what will happen this evening at the fire. We may need all the help we can get to find out if Daniel is cursed, or has just a spell upon him. Escursia will not go willingly, and when we give Nakia her elixir, we may face dangers that will call for everyone's power."

"Then I better speak with my grandmother when she comes back. But . . . will you guys help me?"

"Of course, buddy," Daniel replied immediately.

Matthew leaned back into his pillow and exhaled loudly. He then put his arms over his head and locked his fingers before resting his head.

"This is going to be a trip," Matt said, laughing. "She is going to be . . . well, I don't know how she is going to react to this, guys. Well, either way, I am going to be up front with her. No more secrets, like I promised."

"Ahem," they heard and turned around.

Pearle came in the room, followed by Annabelle and then Nakia, who had table trays for Yammi and Daniel to have lunch on. Zatu followed too. He sat right next to Matthew's beds and kept his eyes peeled to Nakia. Pearle was carefully watching Zatu's reaction to Nakia but did not say a thing. Once the girls got the boys settled with their lunch, Pearle thanked them, and they left.

"You do realize, young man, I overheard what you said."

"Ah . . . you heard, huh?"

"Yes, I did, and was very happy to hear you were sticking to our agreement about not keeping secrets. Well, let's have it. What's going on, boys?"

"Nana, I guess I will begin with the night of the cave-in and then . . . to what is going on now," he said, shoving a fork of macaroni and cheese in his mouth.

"Oh, we have a current situation . . . boys?"

"Yes, Pearle, we do," replied Yammi.

"Well, I am all ears."

Matthew started with the night of the cave-in. Then Daniel proceeded to tell Pearle what happened with Emia and his drinking of the Bennu Elixir at the hospital. Pearle hadn't said a word to any of them yet, and Matthew wondered why. Just when Yammi was going to tell Pearle the current situation, Nakia came in to see if everyone was done with lunch.

Zatu began to growl, and his top lip curled back as he slowly stood up. He took a defensive stand as if he were ready to pounce upon prey. He lowered his head and looked straight at Nakia, while all the hair on his back stood up. Pearle seemed frightened by his wolfish behavior and looked at Matthew, who was speechless. Nakia, though, seemed totally unfazed by Zatu.

Pearle was not sure what bothered her more, Nakia's aloofness or how strange his dangerous behavior was toward her.

After Nakia left, Zatu lay back down and went to sleep. Yammi then proceeded to tell Pearle *everything* that was going on and what they suspect of Nakia, and why Zatu probably reacts to her the way he does. He went on to explain what occurred earlier with Daniel and how Matthew accomplished ridding Escursia.

"Pearle," Daniel began, "like I've said before, I'm not too smart, and I only know what is going on from the events since before we left for Egypt. But with God as my witness, I am now a true believer in this prophecy. At first, I just thought it was some sort of scam and something to do with your break-in. I now know differently, though. I mean, I am still learning about all this Egyptian stuff and having a hard time understanding the ancient way, but I do know that just because I don't understand or agree with the ancient ways doesn't mean it isn't true. As far as Matthew having a gift, I saw that today. A regular person could not have done what he did to Escursia otherwise. I truly don't think it is magic, Pearle. I feel inside my gut, it . . . it is a *special gift* and nothing to be afraid of. And . . . it may very well be the only thing that makes him succeed in the prophecy."

Pearle slowly slid off the edge of the bed, where she had sat listening to all three boys and their stories. She looked at all three of them, taking in everything they said. Although they were being honest with her, she wasn't. Pearle has a secret too. She's been having nightmares also.

"Aren't you going to say anything, Nana?" Matthew asked, searching her eyes.

She hesitated to speak and walked around the room. The boys looked at one another and shrugged their shoulders.

"First, I want the three of you to know . . . well . . . I believe everything you have told me. From Emia growing and you flying on her back to Daniel drinking that elixir to save your life and Yammi helping to teach you about your gift and showing what strength you have inside of you. I find myself in *extraordinary* company, with three amazing young men! I just need a few moments, though, to process all this information. This is unreal," she said as she continued pacing. Then Pearle slowly turned around and looked at them.

"Daniel . . . oh . . . my . . . God, Daniel . . . what you have done for Matthew; I'm overwhelmed with gratefulness! How selfless of you, and well, I don't know what to say at the moment."

Pearle went to Dan and hugged him, then Yammi, and lastly Matthew. She sat back down on Matthew's bed and folded her hands in her lap. Matthew wasn't expecting such a calm reaction from her, and watched as she sat there, looking around the room.

"Yammi, please tell me about this woman Suhama and what we must do tonight. If possible, I would like to speak to her. Do you think there's a chance I could?"

"I see no reason why you could not speak with Suhama, Pearle. I trust she will be of valuable information to you. Besides, her knowledge of the old ways has been extremely helpful to us, Pearle."

"Good, then let's go call her now, and you can fill me in some more about the elixirs too. Daniel, I want you to stay here with Matthew until I get back from this phone call. Then we are going to have a meeting of the minds and put a plan into action for tonight. Oh, and keep Zatu in here also. Since we do not know if this Nakia is . . . well, possessed or . . . well, just keep Zatu around you boys, okay? I am first going to tell Annabelle to keep Nakia busy downstairs with something. I don't want her around you boys or poking her nose upstairs either. So does everybody understand what we are doing so far?"

"Yeah, sure, of course," the boys responded.

"Okay, Yammi . . . let's go!" Pearle said as she opened the door, and before she left, she turned and winked at Dan and Matthew.

It was ten minutes after one when Robert arrived at the house. He brought the s'more supplies to Annabelle, who was busy finishing the frosting on Matthew's birthday cake.

"Oh, yum, Annabelle," Robert said. "That cake is beautiful! Matthew hasn't caught on, has he, about the party?"

"I no think so, Robert. Daniel and Yammi have kept Matthew pretty busy all day so he doesn't come in here while I'm finish up everything."

"Is there anything I can do to help? Oh, and where is Pearle?"

"No, there isn't anything here left to do, Robert, but thank you. As for Pearle, she was last seen with Yammi," she replied dryly.

"Annabelle, I may not know you that well, but I *do* know enough to say that something is wrong. What's going on?"

Annabelle looked at Robert, then around the kitchen.

"Ahh . . . I'm not sure, Robert, but something troubles me about Nakia lately."

"Really. Well, tell me, what's the problem?"

"I no sure what it is, just that I get a weird feeling from her lately that I . . . I am . . . well, uncomfortable being around her. It sounds crazy, right?"

"No, it's not. But can you tell me what's happened to make you feel so uncomfortable with her?"

"The big problem I no like is when she is around Zatu. He growls at her, and I'm so afraid he is going to bite her. It's become very stressful having them in the same room. What bothers me more, though, is that she doesn't even *acknowledge* his behavior. I know if it were *anyone* else, they would say something about Zatu and, well . . . be afraid of him, ya know? There is something . . . well . . . *evil* about her. I mean she works very hard and is pleasant to everyone, but Robert, she has something not good of her soul!"

"Have you spoken to Pearle about this?"

"No, I haven't. With everything going on the last few days and her being so happy, I didn't want to ruin Matthew's party."

"Annabelle, I never asked you, but how *did* you find Nakia for the job?"

"You know, I am not too sure. It may have been from the ad I ran in the paper. Why you ask?"

"Just curious, that's all. Did you save her paperwork and references?"

"Sure, I did. I put them all in a folder for Pearle on her desk, but to be honest with you, I don't think Pearle has looked at them yet."

"Oh, really? Why do you think that, Annabelle?"

"Because they are in the same place on her desk where I left them," she laughed.

"Let me ask you one more thing, Annabelle. When you first hired Nakia, did you sense any of this? If not, when *did* you start to notice that Zatu had a problem with her?"

"You know, it's funny, when I hire Nakia, I no sense nothing bad, Robert. If anything, she seemed like the perfect person to work here. She was very eager to work and seemed very sweet. Zatu didn't act this way until . . . well, I would have to say . . . yes, the day after Pearle got home. And as far as me having these feelings about her, I would have to say this last week it became noticeable. Who knows, maybe it might have been sooner, and I just was too busy to catch on. Regardless, Robert, something is very wrong here, and I am worried!"

"Don't worry, Annabelle. I will talk with Pearle about this. I know you would not be so alarmed over nothing, and Matthew did mention to me once how he didn't think Zatu cared much for Nakia. I'll get to the bottom of everything; don't you worry, all right?"

"Good, because this family doesn't need any more problems. We have had our share of bad things, and it's time for good things now . . . right?"

"You bet, Annabelle, it sure is. Ah, could you stand some good news, then?" Robert asked, sounding mischievous.

"Of course, you silly guy, what's up?"

"I'm going to ask Pearle to marry me."

"Well, mamma mia! It's about good time, Robert. I think you two have pussyfooted around long enough!"

"Well, I had planned to do that in Egypt, but . . . well, it didn't go as planned," he laughed.

"So you need any help with this proposal, my dear?" she asked.

"Well, I thought about a romantic dinner, and ya know, all the trimmings to awe her, but then I decided that I want her family to be a part of it. So, I was thinking, maybe tonight at the fire pit. I had a great idea of putting the ring on her marshmallow stick and giving it to her that way. I know it sounds kind of corny, but Pearle and I aren't very traditional, and having everyone around that we both care about and love so much would mean a lot to me."

Annabelle ripped off a piece of paper towel and blew her nose.

"I never hear anything more beautiful in my life, Robert," she sniffed. I think it is a wonderful idea! I am so very happy for you both. I love you like my family and know that you will make Pearle very happy. Now, you just tell me what you need me to do, if anything, okay?"

Robert reached into his pocket and took out a small blue velvet bag with a black silk braided string. He opened it and pulled out a beautiful three-carat, princess-cut sapphire ring with diamonds all around the band.

"Oh, mamma mia, Robert, it is beautiful!" Annabelle gasped. "Where did you find such a lovely ring?"

"Actually, that story is interesting. I had originally bought a ring locally to give her in Egypt. But one day when Pearle went to the hospital early to see Matthew, I went downtown and came upon this jewelry store. To make a long story short, the owner of the store showed me this ring, and I knew it would be the one for Pearle. So I traded the ring I bought here, and I only had to put a few extra dollars toward this one. I priced this ring when I got back here, Annabelle, and I got one hell of a deal. I would never have been able to afford this ring here. Do you really think she will like this, though?"

"You gotta be kidding me. Of course she will love it! I have never seen such a beautiful piece of jewelry!"

Robert put the ring back into the bag and then handed it to Annabelle.

"Why you give me ring, Robert?" Annabelle asked, looking oddly at him.

"If you wouldn't mind holding onto it until tonight, I would appreciate it. I have a few things to do for Pearle outside, and I **do not** want anything to happen to it. Do you mind, Annabelle?"

"Oh, of course not, silly. I put in safe keeping!"

Annabelle turned from Robert and put the bag inside her bra. Then she patted it to make sure it was safe. Robert began to laugh, and Annabelle turned around, all red in the face.

"You say you want nothing to happen to the ring, right? So I put where no one but me will find," she laughed.

Robert hugged her, and she returned his affection, patting his back.

"Okay, I am going to find Pearle and talk to her. But first, I want to discuss this matter with Matthew and make sure he is okay with me asking Pearle to marry me."

"I do not think it is a problem. As a matter of fact, *I know* he will be happy too. But it is very nice to do that, Robert. Go; he is in his room with Daniel. Now I finish cake and put in refrigerator."

Robert was walking out of the kitchen when he turned and bumped into Nakia, who obviously was preoccupied. He noticed she didn't look well and would not keep eye contact with him.

"Mr. Robert, I am sorry."

"It's okay, Nakia, no harm done," he replied coolly and continued on his way to see Matthew, looking back to watch her go into the kitchen. *Hmm . . . maybe Annabelle is on to something about this girl. Like we needed something else to add to all the other mysteries we are dealing with,* he thought. But he put those thoughts aside for the moment and concentrated on the important conversation he wanted to have with Matthew.

Robert knocked, then opened Matthew's door. Zatu had gotten up quickly with a growl, but when he saw Robert, he ran right over to him. Robert bent down and petted him, and Zatu licked him all over his face.

"Looks like he missed you, Robert," Matthew said.

"Yes, it does," Robert said with a laugh, then wiped the drool off his face.

"So how are you guys today, especially you, birthday boy? Happy birthday, Matthew!"

"Thanks, Robert, we are good, and yourself?" Matthew asked.

"Not too bad for an old guy. . . . Ah, listen, Matt, would you mind if we have a little talk? I'd like to discuss something with you."

"Sure, is it okay if Daniel stays, though?"

"I have no problem with Dan being here, but he has to keep mum, as you do, about what we are going to discuss, okay?"

"What's up, Robert? Is something wrong?"

"Oh, no, no, Matthew. Quite the contrary; it is something good!"

"We could always use good news around here. So what's up?"

Robert told Matthew his plans to ask Pearle to marry him and that he was concerned about how he felt about it.

"As Annabelle would say," Matthew snickered, "oye, mamma mia, what a took you so long?!"

"I think it's wonderful, Robert. Congratulations," Daniel added as he shook his hand.

"Robert, I know Nana has had a thing for you for a long time now. You two belong together!"

"A thing . . . Matthew? Oh, my God . . . how lame!" Daniel laughed.

"Oh, be quiet," Matthew said, giving Daniel a slap to the side of his head.

"Rob . . . ert," Matthew began, with hesitation in his voice, "have you seen Nana yet?"

"No . . . why?"

"Well, a lot has gone on here this morning, and . . . let's just say if you are going to propose to her tonight, I advise you to do it as soon as we go down to the fire pit."

"Why am I not getting a good feeling about this, young man?"

"I think I will wait until she comes back with Yammi to tell you *all* about it," he said.

"Matthew, you're scaring me now," Robert laughed.

"Ha . . . you laugh now, but when we tell you everything, you may change your mind about marrying my grandmother, Robert," Matthew said seriously.

"Hmm . . . that bad, huh?" Robert asked, still smiling. Then he added, "I don't think anything would or could ever change my mind, Matthew."

"Oh, so you really believe that for worse or better stuff?" Matthew asked.

"You bet I do, and no matter what it is, we will get through it."

"All right," Matthew chuckled, "we will see."

"So you aren't even going to give me a hint about what is going on? Come on, guys, the suspense is killing me here!"

The three of them broke into laughter, and Zatu got in on the act. He started to howl and jump up and down. Daniel and Robert were roughhousing with Zatu when Pearle and Yammi came in.

"Huh, I knew there was trouble in here when I heard a ruckus," Pearle said, smiling at Robert.

"Hey, you two," Robert said as he patted Zatu, trying to calm him down.

Zatu let out a funny gurgling howl that made everyone laugh. He knew he was the center of attention and repeated his funny howling several times. When everyone finally stopped laughing, the mood in the room became serious. Robert felt it, and he didn't like it or the idea of him not knowing what was going on.

"Pearle, I believe you have something to tell me, according to the guys. I'm not sure what is going on, but I have a feeling it has a lot to do with what happened in Egypt and possibly Nakia." Pearle and the boys were, to say the least, a bit surprised by what Robert said.

"When did you get into mind reading?" Daniel asked with a smirk.

"When I became a cop, and more so, when I got involved with this case. So, who wants to explain?" Robert asked, standing in the middle of the room with his arms crossed.

The boys looked at Pearle as if for a clue as to who should tell Robert. Then Yammi spoke up.

"Robert, you may want to sit down for what I have to tell you."

"Okay," Robert replied, and he took a chair and sat in the middle of the room so he could see all four of them.

Yammi told Robert everything that has happened since the cave-in and what's happened since they got home. He leaned back into the wooden-slated chair when Yammi finished, crossed his arms over his belly, exhaled, and his forehead wrinkled up as he squinted his eyes.

"You boys have been through the mill the last month, haven't you?" Robert said, shaking his head. He leaned forward, planted his elbows on his thighs, and sunk his head into his hands. He rubbed his face up and down as he felt his smooth-shaven cheeks and chin. Then, he looked up into Pearle's eyes, then at Matthew.

"Tell me what we need to do, because I am clearly in unfamiliar territory here, and I assume you have some sort of plan?"

"We do, Robert," Pearle replied. And she told him everything. When she got to the part of the elixirs and spice burning, Robert's eyes grew big with disbelief.

"Are you kidding me? You mean we are going to call on these spirits, and then what?" he said as he stood up, looking at them as if they were all crazy. "Did you want me to use *harsh* language on them?"

Pearle, didn't mean to laugh, but she just couldn't help it.

"My God, this is not funny! How do I protect you and the boys? In case you didn't know it, Pearle, spirits can't be shot! What the hell am I supposed to do?"

Robert got up and went to Matthew at his bed. Matthew put his hand on Robert's.

"Look, Robert, we have to **do** this tonight, with all of us there, and because of our love for each other, *it will work.* There is nothing stronger in this world than that. Nana, Yammi, and I have a special gift that will enable us, along with the elixirs, to rid Escursia and break these spells, or curses, she has evoked upon us. We all have to believe in each other, or this *isn't* going to work, Robert. We all need to trust in each other and what we have to do."

"Well, I am not so sure about all this, Matthew. My only concern is for everyone's safety."

"Come with me, Robert," Pearle said as she got up. "You boys stay here with Matthew, and we will be back in just a little while. I need to fix the wood for tonight."

"Sure, Pearle, we will wait until you come back, but would you like some help?" Daniel asked.

"As a matter of fact, I could use a little extra help. That is, if Yammi doesn't mind staying with Matthew."

"Of course not; Matthew and I will be fine.

Chapter Twenty-five

"Surprise! Happy birthday!" everyone yelled as Matthew wheeled himself into the living room.

"Nana, what did you do?!" Matthew said as his cheeks flushed cherry red.

All the guests, one by one, went over to wish him happy birthday.

"Rachel, wow, it is so good to see you," Matthew said, looking even more surprised.

"How are you, Matt? Everyone at school has been asking about you, ya know. The team misses their captain too! Do you think you will be back this year?" Rachel asked, searching his eyes.

"I'm not sure, Rach. I see my doctor in a few days, and he will let me know what's going to happen, but otherwise, I am doing pretty good. I hear Charlie is doing a great job with the team while Dan and I are out. He really is very talented and one of our best swimmers. So do me a favor, and try to work with him. Oh, and tell the rest of the team to cooperate too. I know if you guys all work together, you may pull off the last meet of the year with a win!"

"You know, Matt, Charlie took the news of your accident really bad, and he asks about you every day at school. Everyone has noticed a big change in him. We just hope he continues to be Charlie instead of Crush."

"I think he will, Rachel, and he really is a nice guy. He has problems, just like the rest of us, and he doesn't have the right friends—ya know what I mean?"

"Yeah . . . I do, Matt. I'll keep ya posted on how things are going with him and the team. So where is Dan? I haven't seen him yet."

"He's here somewhere," he said, looking around the room. "Oh, when you find him, tell him to introduce you to Yammi. He's a friend of ours from Egypt and a really nice guy."

"I will, and it's good to see you again," she said as she walked away, searching for Daniel.

Then Matthew saw Abe Haram. He immediately looked at Robert. Robert looked at Matthew, gave him a nod, then winked.

"Hello, Mr. Haram. It's great to see you. How have you been?"

"Ah, my boy, I think the question is, how are *you* doing?"

"I'm good. So what do you think of my wheels?" Matthew said, rubbing the arms of his chair.

"Pretty impressive, but not as impressive as the young man who occupies them," Abe said as he tried to swallow the lump in his throat.

Matthew thought Abe was going to cry at that moment and suddenly felt sorry for him. He knew Abe was still a suspect in the robbery, but somehow he just could not picture this sweet man poisoning Zatu and stealing from his grandmother.

"Ahem . . . so where is Annabelle today? I haven't seen her around."

"She's probably in the kitchen. Go say hi; I'm sure she would love to see you!"

"I think I'll do that, my boy. We will talk later, yes?"

"Of course, Mr. Haram; I'll be here," Matthew said jokingly and pointing to his legs.

Matthew looked around the room and saw everyone having a good time. Then he heard the doorbell and decided he would answer it. Matthew opened the door, and there stood Charlie Dixon.

"Hey, Charlie. Now this is a nice surprise. Come on in," Matthew said as he backed his wheelchair up while Charlie closed the door.

"Matt . . . er . . . how are you doing?"

"Actually, pretty good, and don't let the chair scare ya. It's just a temporary thing," he assured him. "And you, Charlie, how are things?"

"I'm good too, well, but I . . . I mean, we sure do miss you at school."

"Well, that's nice to know, but I want to hear how the team is doing, Charlie. Do you think they will be ready for the final meet in a couple of weeks?"

"We are working hard at it. I just wish you could come by one day and see us at practice. I mean, after all, you are the captain, and I could use your input."

"I might be able to talk my grandmother into that, Charlie. I'll call you tomorrow and let you know, okay?"

"Sure, that would be great! So how . . . how are you doing, Matthew? I mean you *are* going to be able to walk again, aren't you?" he asked, looking sympathetic.

"That's the plan. It's just going to take some time. The doctor says I am doing better than expected, and I will know more this week after I see him."

"Matthew, I have been praying for you. I'm sure you will be as good as new; I just know it. Besides, we need our captain back!"

"Thanks, Charlie. You know, you really are a good-hearted person. I want to thank you for taking on the swim team and doing everything you are while I've been gone. I knew you would be the right person."

"Matthew, no one has ever believed in me before. I will never forget you for this. I am glad we . . . well . . . I just wanted to say thanks."

"Don't thank me, Charlie, you . . . ."

"Well, hello, Mr. Dixon. How are you?" asked Robert.

"Very good, sir, and you?" Charlie asked, smiling at Robert.

"Not too bad. How's the swim team coming along? I hear you are filling in for Matthew."

"Gosh, I'd know better if our captain could make it to practice this week and check us out."

"Oh, I am sure we can work something out. I think I can sneak him out of here for an hour or so to see you guys," Robert said, bending over, whispering with a devilish grin.

"Fantastic, sir! That would be great!" Charlie said, all excited.

Charlie, Matthew, and Robert continued to talk about the team and were joking around when Pearle announced it was time to eat. When Matthew got to the long table where all the food was spread out, he saw Yammi looking as if he were lost.

"Hey, Yammi, aren't you going to eat?"

"Such a silly question . . . . Of course, but I just do not know where to start. In all my *days*, I have never seen so much food at one time," he said, still looking dazed.

Matthew laughed. "Well, there is a first time for everything. Just start at the beginning, and work your way to the end of the table."

"That is a good idea, Matthew, but would you like me to make you a plate first?"

"Oh, no, Yammi, you go ahead. My grandmother is almost done making mine, but thanks anyway."

"Come on, Yammi," Robert said, handing him a plate. "I don't know about you boys, but I'm starving!" Matthew and Yammi looked at each other and laughed.

"Matthew," Pearle called, "I have your plate; come on and eat. Are you feeling all right?"

"I'm feeling awesome, Nana! By the way, thanks."

"Oh, for what?" she said as she popped a green olive in her mouth.

"Well, for throwing this party. I just want to know one thing. How much did you pay Daniel to not tell me about it," he said, laughing. "I am shocked he didn't let on one bit, though!"

"Not a cent, my dear boy," she said, wiggling her eyebrows up and down. "I just threatened his life," she laughed.

"Oh, no way, you didn't, Nana, did you?"

She just smiled and winked at him.

Everyone raved about the food Annabelle had prepared, but Matthew's birthday cake was the hit of the party! She made a three-layer chocolate sheet cake with rum-flavored Italian sweet ricotta cannoli filling and chocolate whipped cream frosting. Annabelle was glad she made such a big cake because everyone had at least two pieces.

"Okay, everyone," Pearle yelled out to the crowd, "it's time for Matthew to open his presents!"

Daniel and Pearle piled the presents next to Matthew while everyone gathered around.

"So whose should I open first?" Matthew asked, eyeing all the gifts.

"Oh, just close your eyes, and pick one," Daniel said as he held a few presents for him.

Matthew picked a small box wrapped in shiny gold paper with a small white bow. There was a card attached, and he ripped it off and opened it first.

"'To someone very special, a birthday wish for you,'" Matthew read aloud, "'from your friend Abe.' Wow, it is awesome, Abe. I have seen these before, but nothing as beautiful as this. Thank you so much!"

"Well, what is it?" Robert asked.

"It's a tau cross, Robert. It symbolizes enduring life. Holy . . . Abe, this is *a real* antique. Where did you find something like this?"

"It was given to me many, *many*, years ago, Matthew. I never wear it, and . . . well, I want you to have it. I know you will take good care of it. It is as dear to me as you are," Abe said with a swallow.

Matthew looked at Abe and saw the same sad face he had the day they had lunch together in the school courtyard.

"Thank you so much, and I promise you, I will take very good care of it. Are you sure, though, that you want me to have it?"

"Well, of course I am, young man. Happy birthday, Matthew. Wear it in good health."

He unraveled the leather strap the silver cross was on and slid it over his head. He gave Abe a big smile, and he winked back at him. Matthew then went on to open more presents. He got a new watch from Daniel, a backpack and digital camera from Annabelle, two gift certificates from Denise and Brian, two new shirts from Rachel, and a video game he's been wanting from Charlie. There were a few more presents to open, and Pearle handed him Yammi's gift next. Matthew opened the small box and was surprised to see a gold cartouche.

"Holy crap, Yammi! No freakin' way! This is totally cool! Nana, look; it has my name in hieroglyphics!"

"Yammi, this is such an extravagant gift and so beautiful, but where did you find it?" Pearle asked, still admiring the piece.

"I hoped you would like it, Matthew. I had Father pick it up for me back home, and I was praying it would be here in time for his birthday, Pearle."

"Well, thanks, Yammi," Matthew said, and slid the cartouche chain over his head and wore it with Abe's cross.

"Okay, a few more to go," Daniel said as he handed him the next one.

Matthew read the card on the next gift. "To a young man who is like a son to me." He looked up at Robert, knowing it had to be him, then opened the gift bag and reached inside. He pulled out a beautiful pocketknife with mother-of-pearl inlay. In the center of the opaque pearl was a silver plate that glistened with his initials, MS.

"Robert, geez, this is awesome! Thanks!"

"You are very welcome, Matthew. I had hoped you would like it."

"I do. I never had a pocketknife before, and I have *always* wanted one too!"

"Well, enjoy it. Just be careful; that sucker is sharp," Robert laughed.

"Oh, I will be," he replied, still admiring the knife.

"Okay, buddy, here ya go," Dan said as he handed him a very small box.

There was no card on this one, and he looked up at Pearle, but she just smiled and gave him a wink.

"Holy snap, Nana!"

"You like it?" she asked.

"Like it, of course I do! It is incredible and way awesome!"

"It was your Grandfather Paul's ring. He asked that I give it to our first grandson, that is, if we were ever to have one. That ring is a family heirloom, Matt. Your grandfather got it on his thirteenth birthday. I hope you enjoy it as much as he did."

"Oh, I will, Nana."

Matthew put his grandfather's ring on and admired the designs. It had two cobras done in faience, with small emeralds for their eyes. They were wrapped around a turquoise stone, and the gold band had small hieroglyphics engraved all around it.

Matthew looked up and scanned everyone's face slowly with a gracious smile.

"You know, without sounding too cheesy, this has to be the best birthday I have ever had. Thanks, everyone, for all the awesome gifts and for spending this day with me. Ya know . . . I almost forgot . . . I was in this wheelchair," he laughed.

The room became very quiet, and Matthew lowered his head and stared down at his legs.

Suddenly, Charlie stood up and started clapping; then Robert and Daniel. Soon all were on their feet, clapping. It wasn't just for his birthday. It was a heartfelt ovation for a boy whose spirit still soars after coming so close to death, from people who honestly love and care for him.

A lump quickly grew in Matthew's throat, and he could feel the tears welling. He tried to hold them back as he kept his head down, but they flowed anyway. Then he picked up his head as Pearle handed him a bunch of Kleenex. He wiped his nose quickly and smiled at all of them.

An hour later, almost everyone was gone. Matthew was exhausted and wanted to take a nap. Daniel took him to his room and helped his nurse get him in bed.

"There ya go, buddy. Is there anything I can get you?"

"I saw the inscription, Dan," he said, looking up at his best friend.

"Friends from the Beginning, Brothers till the End."

"I think that was the most special gift I got, Dan. Thanks."

"I'm glad you like it, Matt. You know, you *aren't* the easiest person to buy for," he laughed.

"Oh, shut up," Matthew said, laughing, with tears in his eyes. "You know," he said, clearing his throat, "I will never, ever forget what you have done for me, *never*. No matter what happens in our lives, no one will ever mean as much to me as you do."

"Geez," Dan said, staring down, trying not to let him see how choked up he was. "I know that; now stop being a *girl* already, and go to sleep! We have a big night ahead of us, and you need to get your rest." As Daniel walked toward the door, Matthew called him, and he turned around.

"I want you to promise me something, Dan."

"Oh, what is it?"

"You *won't* keep any more secrets from me."

"I won't, buddy . . . promise. Now, before your grandmother has my butt, go to sleep," he laughed. He closed Matthew's door, took a deep breath, and thought about what he and Yammi had to do tonight. He headed upstairs and decided he was going to nap too. It had been a long day already, and he knew he needed to be alert for tonight. Daniel checked in on Yammi; he was already sleeping. They weren't going down to the pit until eight, just before dark, so he set the alarm clock for seven. Yammi and Pearle were going to meet him at seven fifteen to gather up everything they needed at the fire pit. He put his head on his pillow, stretched out, and in a few minutes fell into a deep sleep. Meanwhile, Annabelle and Nakia were almost finished cleaning up from the party. Pearle, Robert, and Brian were out on the patio having coffee. Denise had an emergency and had to go to the hospital. Daniel was relieved that his mother had to go to work. He knew she would be safe there.

"Brian, I need to talk to you about something . . . about tonight," Robert said quietly.

"Tell me, why do I have a feeling there is something wrong?" he replied as his smile disappeared.

"Listen, before you two have your talk, would anyone like something to eat? I have to meet the boys in about an hour, and I'm getting hungry. I was thinking about a small sandwich or piece of birthday cake. Do I have any takers?" Pearle asked.

"That sounds good," Robert said.

Pearle looked at Robert with a smile and said, "Well, which is it?"

Brian looked at Robert and smiled.

"Both," the two men replied together.

"Ya know, I really do know better than to ask that around here," Pearle replied, seemingly amused, while walking away.

Robert told Brian what he found out earlier about Daniel and Nakia and what was going down tonight at the fire pit. He wasn't sure what he would think about everything, but he knew by Brian's face he wasn't too happy.

"Did either one of you even *think* to tell Denise about what is going on with her son?" Brian asked, irritated.

"Brian, I assure you, Pearle was going to discuss this with Denise, but Daniel was very adamant about her not knowing yet. He does not want to upset or involve her. Besides, Pearle and I just found out about Daniel before the party. He promised that he would discuss this with her! We agreed to his request *only* because he assured us he would tell her everything tomorrow."

"Is he in any type of danger, Robert?"

"As far as I understand, everyone is in some kind of danger here. But Pearle is confident that they are taking every precaution tonight. The most important thing she stressed about tonight is that whatever is causing all this turmoil, besides using the elixirs and spices, we all have to stay united and not let this evil spirit thing tear our love or friendship apart. Supposedly, that's what it's trying to do. We have to do whatever is necessary here, Brian."

"This whole thing is off the wall and has totally gotten out of hand, Robert; you do realize that, don't you?"

"No, it hasn't. It's just that we are dealing with unusual circumstances that neither one of us understands! All I'm asking is that you keep an open mind about tonight, that is, if you still want to be a part of this."

"Of course I do, Robert; it's just so freaking weird, and well . . . unnatural!"

"All right, officers, here are your snacks," Pearle announced, arriving with a tray of sandwiches and cake. She looked at Brian, then Robert. Neither one acknowledged her presence. The thick tension between the two men made her feel uneasy.

"You two want to tell me what's going on?" she asked while placing the tray on the table.

"Brian is worried about tonight and upset that no one has spoken to Denise about everything with Daniel."

"So he should be, Robert. How would you feel if it were Matthew, and no one told me what was going on? Look, Brian, what concerns Daniel, as well as me, is making sure we keep everyone safe. It seems that the less who know about what is going on, the better. That is just the way this seems to play out. *Everyone's* safety is, has been, and will continue to be my *main* concern."

"Pearle, I know that, and I am not blaming anyone for what is going on. You have to realize I deal with facts and visible evidence. This is completely off-the-wall here. We are talking about *prophecies, curses, and spirits!* This stuff is in storybooks, movies. There are *no* police manuals to teach you about this type of situation. Look, I am in this *all* the way, to the end. Whatever you need me to do, I will. This case has become just as personal to me as it is to Robert. I don't doubt *anything* you and Robert have told me either. I just wish I could understand what is happening here, ya know?"

"I believe after tonight, we all will have a better understanding as to what is going on, Brian."

"Well, I hope so, Pearle, because this has got to be one of the strangest things I have ever encountered in my life! By the way, talk about strange, did either one of you notice how Nakia reacted when she saw Abe Haram today?"

"No. What happened, Brian?" Robert asked.

"Well, it was like . . . like they went out of their way to avoid each other every time their paths crossed. It seemed *too* obvious to me. Nakia gave me the impression she was annoyed by him, for some reason."

"Maybe they just don't like each other. You know how some people just don't seem to hit it off," Pearle suggested. "Who knows, maybe Abe sensed that something wasn't right about her; that could be the reason too, Brian."

"Could be, Pearle, but I just wanted to bring it to both of your attention. Ya know, I'll bet you my last dollar something is going on between those two!"

"I think tomorrow I will do a little more digging on Nakia. Even Annabelle mentioned something to me today about her. At this point, who knows who else is involved with what! This case and this prophecy are turning out to be a three-ring circus!" Robert said, exasperated.

"Amen to that, and I'm glad we are on the same page," Brian replied.

"We always have been. That's why you and I get along so well," Robert replied as he took a bite of his cake.

"Hey, how come he got the bigger piece?" Brian whined to Pearle.

"Now, now, boys, play nice," Pearle laughed. "Relax, Brian. Annabelle has a large doggie bag packed for you to take home," Pearle replied with a wink. "Okay, you two, I am going to put some jeans on and check in on Matthew. Then I'll see if the two boys are all set."

"Hey, Robert, I forgot to ask you, what happened today when Abe saw Pearle wearing her medallion? Did he react like we thought he would?"

"Ah . . . yes and no. Pearle thought he didn't seem indifferent. He did stare at it for a moment or two, but not a big reaction like we were hoping for. She did, though, talk to him about the robbery a little and the fabricated story we made up of her having to put a claim in to the insurance company for the medallions. He seemed genuinely concerned about the medallions, Brian. However, Abe was really more interested in Matthew and how he was progressing since the accident."

"If you ask me, Robert, I think he is one smooth operator. He has this facade, this nice, caring guy front, with a dark shadow over him."

"To be honest, Brian, I felt the same way when he was introduced to the picture. I just don't know now after everything that has happened, especially since I've been getting to know him more. He seems like a . . . well, a genuinely nice guy."

"Oh, come on, Robert, you really believe that?" he answered in a peevish tone.

"Excuse me," Robert said, annoyed.

"Think about it, DG; you were the one who said Abe was the best suspect, given his history with the family. We don't know *anyone* else who had the knowledge of those medallions or their value, let alone where they would be. I think he pulled off the perfect crime, if you ask me!"

"Look, Brian, I am *not* going to get into a pissing match with you about Abe. Yes, in the beginning, I saw him as the number one suspect. But over the last several weeks, we have learned that Pearle's medallions were known to the public, especially those who knew her and her family in Egypt. Pearle told me she does not recall ever telling Abe she had those medallions. But as I said, they were not some big secret. Given the secured room, where else would she have kept them? I mean, if you were looking for something of value, where would you look, under a bed, or the security vault in a home? Brian, we have the GPS on those other medallions; we set the trap. Now we just wait. I know that whoever put them in that evidence envelope is going to come back for them. We just have to be patient. If Abe is involved, then we will find out eventually. What I want to know is who from the department is involved. There are many possible scenarios here, and I have played them all out in my head, Brian. It comes down to having solid proof as to who broke into Pearle's place, poisoned Zatu, and took the medallions. We have pieces to this puzzle, but not a whole picture yet."

"Yeah, and it seems that every day we keep adding these pieces to the biggest part of this puzzle, Oona! Have we missed the obvious, Robert? Have we done everything that we could've?"

"Well, I hope not, and I believe we have done a thorough job in all our investigations. Heck, we even had soil tested in the lake! Oh, by the way, anything yet from the analyst about that orange claw that was found in Oona's chain?"

"Funny you ask, because the forensic specialist was baffled about it. He said in all his thirty-three years of experience, he has never come across something like that. He sent the claw, chain, and shawabtis to a museum for analyzing, and I don't know when we will get those results!"

"Brian, as much as you and I deal with the here and now, we just can't have a closed mind to this prophecy and all the events we find odd and extremely hard to believe. I am not dismissing any possibility, and I don't think you should either."

"Robert, I really am trying to keep an open mind here about everything. But I want to run something by you that I have been thinking about lately."

"Sure, shoot. What's on your mind?"

"I got to thinking about Oona, the robbery, and what happened in Egypt to the kids and this prophecy. Every one of these circumstances involves the medallions. Either we have an odd coincidence in each case, or maybe they are connected. Do you think that this could be a hoax and that whoever was responsible for Oona's disappearance could be responsible for everything else that has happened?"

"Brian, everything you are thinking about, I have too. With all the variables involved, I don't think we should dismiss anything. Anything is possible at this point. So tonight, I am going to sit, watch, and learn. How everything will unfold, I have no idea, but Pearle seems to know what she is doing, and I trust her."

"Well, that's a relief to hear!"

Brian and Robert turned around. Pearle was standing behind them with Yammi. She was holding a tray with an array of colorful old velvet bags and several glass vials that contained glittering, iridescent liquids, and under Yammi's arm were the ancient scrolls he would recite from tonight.

"How's the arm, Yammi?" Robert asked.

"It is fine, Mr. Robert. I think this sling, though, is more of a nuisance than a help."

"Well, just try to hang in there, Yammi, a few more days, and you see the doctor."

"Yes, and I am very excited about that too. Hopefully, he will have good news for me. But enough of me, we must discuss our plans if we are to be successful."

Yammi took a seat next to Brian and showed him and Robert the old scrolls he got from Oopi. He explained that they contained the words he will use to evoke whatever evil is inflicting Daniel, and hopefully break the spell or curse that is on Nakia.

"As I have told everyone, the most important thing to remember tonight is to keep your heart pure and your mind strong. The evil we are dealing with can take over the mind and play some very nasty tricks on you. Remember, her one goal is to convince Matthew that we are his enemy and that she holds the key to all his desires. I have seen firsthand how manipulative and cunning she can be, and worse, how she will try to steal your soul."

"Yammi, what about the three creatures—are they able to help?" Robert asked.

"Yes, Robert. As a matter of fact, they are eating now and speaking with Matthew. They are very important allies to Matthew. Oopi has been very instrumental in helping us gather everything we needed for tonight. Although I must tell you, there were a few things we had to improvise with," Yammi chuckled.

"Will that make a difference to the outcome of anything, Yammi?" Robert asked, concerned.

"No, it shouldn't, Mr. Robert. We researched everything we used and consulted someone who is an expert in all this. I assure you, we have done our homework and have been very diligent in our work here. All we can do now is pray that everything goes as planned.

"Oh, Mr. Brian, I nearly forgot, you are to go see Matthew now and meet Oopi and the girls. Pearle, would you take him? I just want to go over a few more things here with Mr. Robert."

"Absolutely, Yammi. Come on, detective, time to meet and greet," Pearle chuckled.

"I'm . . . ," and Brian stalled for a moment, then cleared his throat. "Ahem . . . I . . . ah . . . to be honest with you, Pearle, I am a little apprehensive about meeting . . . these . . . these creatures."

"I know, Brian. This whole situation is a bit far-fetched, and . . . well . . . it can be a little nerve-racking. I promise you, though, once you get used to them, they won't seem so out of the ordinary for you. They are very sweet, smart, and I think rather cute," she added, obviously tickled herself by the creatures.

"I'll have to remember that, Pearle, when I check myself into the psych ward at the local institution!"

They got to Matthew's room, and Pearle opened the door. Just like everyone else who has met Oopi, Amora, and Emia for the first time, Brian walked into the room stunned. His mouth hung wide open, which truly was not a pretty sight for a grown man.

"Well, this must be the other peacekeeper you spoke of, am I correct, Matthew?" Oopi asked, smiling.

"Yes, it is. Brian . . . I'd like you to meet . . . Oopi, Amora, and Emia."

"My God . . . you . . . you really do exist!"

Chapter Twenty-six

It was going to be a beautiful sunset shortly. Everyone was staring at the dusky mauve sky, waiting for the brilliant sun to melt into the darkening horizon. They were about twenty-five feet from the water's edge, seated in a horseshoe shape around the blazing fire pit that faced the lake. So far, everything was going as planned. Robert and Brian made sure Nakia sat in between them. Annabelle was two seats away from Robert to his right. Yammi and Daniel were on the far left end, near Matthew and Pearle, who had Oopi, Emia, and Amora. There was a small table set up near Pearle with their drinks and snacks so she could easily mix the elixirs. Everything was set to go.

According to Suhama, the elixirs had to be drunk within fifteen minutes after the sunset. Yammi was then to wait until the elixirs took effect before he began reciting specific incantations from the Maat Papyri. This was very old magic that ancient priestesses would use on spirits with malicious intent. Suhama hoped it would evoke the evil spirits, break the curses, and send Escursia away.

"So Nakia, how do you like living in the States?" Brian asked, trying to make conversation.

"I like it very much. Working with such a wonderful family does not have me as homesick as I thought I would be. I have become very fond of everyone here. They all have made me feel like part of the family. Ms. Pearle is a lovely lady, and I feel like I have known her . . . well . . . almost all my life," she replied with a weird smirk on her face.

Brian shifted his eyes toward Robert, and he gave him a discerning look that told him he heard what she said. Then Robert turned and looked at Pearle as she stood up to watch the sinking orange orb melt into the lake.

"Ms. Pearle, that is a lovely guesthouse. Do you get many visitors?" Nakia asked, breaking the silence.

"No, not really," she laughed, "but it's always ready, if need be. Would you like to see it, Nakia?" she asked.

"Why, yes, I would love to."

"Robert, why don't you and Brian show Nakia the guesthouse while we get this celebration started."

"Sure, I'd like to see what it looks like since you had it remodeled. Come on, Brian, let's give Nakia the five-cent tour!"

With Nakia leaving for a few minutes, it was a perfect opportunity for Yammi and Pearle to mix the *Vendaro Elixir* and the *Enoph Elixir* in her and Daniel's drinks. The Vendaro Elixir contained lavender, poof plant thistle, and cat milk. Its purpose was to cause a euphoric calming, and induce Daniel and Nakia into a deep trance. Neither one would have any recollection of the event. Enoph Elixir is complicated, and it could be lethal, but it's the only thing that could protect them from Escursia . . . if she wished to kill them. Enoph was composed of garlic root juice, crushed blue lotus leaves, honey, linseed oil, and dragonfly blood, just to name a few.

Matthew watched as Yammi and Pearle set out plastic cups. Daniel handed the elixirs to Yammi, and Pearle poured equal amounts of punch into each cup. She made sure they were only half filled so that Nakia would drink the entire cup.

"Psst . . . Nana," Matthew whispered.

"What?" she said softly.

"How are you going to know whose cup is whose?"

"Because your grandmother is brilliant. I have them marked," she whispered with a slight rise to her eyebrows.

Pearle looked around at everyone and put her thumb up, signaling she was ready. Now they just had to wait for Robert, Nakia, and Brian. Suhama was very specific with her instructions, as were the ones in Yammi's old spell book, about timing the drinking of the elixirs.

While Yammi handed everyone a drink, Pearle anxiously looked at her watch. *Five minutes to go. Come on, Robert,* she thought, feeling anxious. Looking toward the guesthouse, she breathed a sigh of relief.

"Okay, guys," she said as she handed them their punch, "let's toast to Matthew on this beautiful night. Raise your glasses, everyone," she instructed. "Matthew, here's to a year of health and wonderful things to come your way. Happy birthday, sweetheart! Bottoms up, everyone."

"So Nakia, have you ever had s'mores?" Pearle asked.

"No, I cannot say that I have, but I am sure they will be delightful because anything with chocolate cannot be bad."

"You can say that again, Nakia. Chocolate is one of my favorite food groups!"

Everyone laughed except Pearle. She was watching Nakia's smiling face go blank as her eyes stood fixed on the fire. Suhama told Pearle she wasn't sure how Nakia would react to the elixir. They just had to wait patiently for it to kick in. . . . But Pearle knew by looking at her that the elixir was already starting to work. She quickly turned around to see how Daniel was. He too was staring blankly at the fire.

"Daniel, can you hear me?" Pearle called to him. But he did not answer her.

"Nakia," Robert uttered loudly as he snapped his fingers in front of her unemotional face. She was unresponsive; her dark eyes were wide and fixed, reflecting the flames in their blackness.

Yammi turned from the fire. He looked at all the familiar faces he has become so fond of lately. Annabelle was holding her Saint Anthony medal tightly in her hand. Robert and Brian were now standing, waiting for the unseen enemy. Matthew and Pearle were side by side; their courage was as obvious as everyone's fearful expression.

The elixirs obviously took effect on Nakia and Daniel, and it was time to call the evil one. Yammi inhaled deeply to calm himself and prayed everything would go as planned, then faced the roaring flames and began to unroll the four thousand-year-old papyrus scroll. Carefully, he opened a purple velvet sack and poured a heaping amount of black opulent *Ephal dust* into his hand, tossed it into the fire, and stood back as brilliant sparks of purple and gold spit out from the blue and yellow roaring flames. The Ephal was to emit a protective barrier around them. The ingredients were of strong magic and contained grounded Black Sea pearls, salt from the east side of the Nile River, and dragonfly blood, taken during the full moon. Yammi then took the tattered, yellowed scroll and moved closer to the fire. He circled it three times while speaking in old Egyptian tongue, reciting the mystical words from the papyrus. He paused, took another handful of the Ephal dust, and threw it carefully into the fire as he muttered again in the ancient language, but this time speaking much louder. He reached into his shirt pocket, opened a blue velvet bag, and poured out the aromatic contents of golden Fafi Spice. It was made of agrimony, anise, clove, and betony. He opened his hand flat, put it up to his mouth, and powerfully blew the protective spirit-calling ash from his palm into the leaping flames. He turned, nodded at Pearle and Matthew, and wrapped a purple silk scarf around his neck, just as priests did thousands of years ago during the same ritual. They knew he was getting ready to call forth the evil one, and they had to prepare themselves. Matthew picked up his scroll as Pearle stood next to his wheelchair, tightly clasping her medallion. The air had become thick and humid with the aroma of clove. Each brilliant spark that ventured out of the fire burst with the pleasant scent of anise. Everyone around the pit deeply inhaled the sweetness of the spices as it calmed their soul, and Yammi began to speak.

"In the world of the dead, may those in peace lay in rest. I summon only the one beyond the darkness who brings harm and wants life for life, who curses the living and those who are pure. I know thee name; I know it well. Listen as I call forth your spirit. . . . For I am pure, I am pure, I am pure. . . . In the name of Sherapha and Nomrahaufa . . . I summon you . . . Escursia . . . Escursia . . . Escursia!"

The lake began to make burbling sounds, and the ground under their feet trembled. Robert and Brian, who almost fell over, managed to hold their ground. The lake's surface began to boil furiously, and large muddy bubbles exploded in the air, giving off a horrible, offensive odor. They all covered their nose, but it was in vain. The smell of raw sewage permeated the thick night air. As Brian gagged, Yammi threw more of the aromatic spices into the fire. The ground rumbled again, shaking harder this time, and an orange glow began to illuminate the ebony-colored lake. It got blindingly brighter as it reached the surface. Then, one by one, four enormous marble pillars abruptly pierced the lake's surface and shot toward the sky. The mysterious golden brilliance broke the surface, and a large oval-shaped orb ascended. It was somewhat translucent, like a jellyfish, and Yammi could see two human images inside. Slowly a figure in a long, flowing, dark-hooded robe rose above the lake and hovered under the mysterious orb. Thick sticky mud dripped from the eerie figure, and slime, like gobs of black grease, slithered down the tall, pointed stone pillars.

Pearle gripped Matthew's shoulder so hard that he bit down on his lip. Robert and Brian took a few steps backward, looking at each other, mortified. Annabelle closed her eyes and continued to pray. They all knew Escursia would appear. Yammi had warned them. Robert began to panic, and a sickening feeling grew in his stomach, knowing there was nothing he could do to stop her. He swallowed hard and prayed for the safety of everyone, and that Pearle truly knew what she was doing.

Matthew knew before anyone that it was the evil from his dreams. The foulness the wind carried of her rotting flesh reeked as it tried to overwhelm his senses. This time, though, he was prepared. Oopi gave him a vial of eucalyptus oil mixed with clove, and he had applied it under his nose to avoid the unsettling experience again.

As Yammi tossed another handful of the Fafi spice into the blaze, Escursia started to slither up and around the thick gelatinous orb like a giant python. Now floating above it, her eyes began to pulse with a red glow. She knew what Yammi possessed and what his intentions were.

"Escursia," he called out, raising the scroll, "you see my hand and what I hold. Heed, and mark these words. The curses you have set forth are broken from these souls. Take your evil, and go! Your power is useless, as are your words, for pure royalty reigns the kingdom now. The truth is inked on holy papyrus, carved deep within the stone of ancient law. I know your past you once held, a priestess who served your queen well. But greed and the sorcery of another chose you to disregard honor and worship her instead. Your deeds have corrupted your soul, and the law of return will bring its punishment you have earned. Your abomination against your queen and her city has cursed you and the one you now serve. Return to your darkness, to yesterday's location, and atone yourself. Return to your priesthood, seize the moment for your freedom, or I shall take this ushabti, cast it into the fire!" Yammi held up the wax ushabti he made and prayed she would be frightened. Burning one during this type of ritual was to rid the spirit forever. Escursia became enraged, letting out a deafening shriek. As she lifted her arms, a dark orange aura began to glow around her. Yammi began to shake and quickly turned toward Matthew and Pearle. They knew it was time for them to step in. Yammi had done all he could.

Suddenly, Pearle sensed someone behind her and turned.

"Abe," she said with a startled jerk, "what are you doing here?"

But before he could answer her, Escursia let out another thunderous shrill, and Abe began to feel sick as he inhaled her decaying flesh. She grabbed Matthew's bottle of eucalyptus mixture and handed it to Abe. He knew what to do with it and quickly applied it to his upper lip. He quickly scanned the scroll Matthew was holding, and it became apparent what was going on.

"I think you could use my help right now. You need to summon the guardian, Pearle, **quickly!**" he shouted to her.

Pearle raised her medallion, and Oopi crawled onto Matthew's shoulder. A white opulent aura began to glow around them. Oopi, Amora, and Emia began to emit a vivid purple light, just like the one the boys had seen in the pyramid coming from Lapria's tomb. They were calling for Zara and the protective power she would bring. With her hand clasped tightly around her medallion, Pearle began to speak.

"Holy priestess, Zara, I am the blood of the blood, who calls to you, oh powerful one. See us here, as I beckon your help with this evil sorceress. Appear, and help us return her and the black magic she brings back to the darkness she comes from. I implore thee, I implore thee, I implore thee!"

Purple flames suddenly burst from the top of the fire, and Zara, the holy priestess, appeared in a glistening white cloud above the pit. She hovered over the blaze with her silky, flowing white robe, untouched by the roaring flames. It glittered almost blindingly with gold and colorful jewels. She drew her arms in front of her, placed her hands on her chest, and looked up. Sparks began to bounce rapidly out of the purple flame, and each one produced numerous large dragonflies. Their magnificent phosphorescent colors were so brilliant they illuminated the night sky and dazzled everyone.

Matthew was astounded by the amount, which was quickly growing. There were thousands of them as they flew around everyone in a circle, creating a protective barrier from Escursia. By now, the mist that appeared with Zara had gotten thicker, and with the dragonflies circling everyone, Robert, Annabelle, and Brian could barely see what was going on with Pearle and Matthew, nor could they move.

"Matthew, I must go to my mistress now," Emia said as she hovered in front of him.

"Remember, you must start reading the old words when I give you my nod. Do not forget, dear heir, your pure heart, above all else, will guide you. You have loyal allies to see you through this. The one who stands behind you, he too is of importance," referring to Abe. "Be brave, my pure one." Then she went to Pearle.

"First one, you will have the power to experience what you hold so deeply in your blood. Do not be afraid, for the heir needs your courage and strength now more than ever. You are the key to the good and powerful magic he is capable of doing. Tonight will test you. It will test us all . . . but forget not . . . this is just the beginning. Our heir faces many battles, according to the prophecy, and should he not succeed tonight, he will never fulfill your family's destiny. . . . Remember . . . the blood of all concerned is shared."

She then flew off to Zara, presented herself with a gracious bow, and touched her glinting robe. Emia's wings began to quiver. As their fluttering sound grew louder, her body transformed to an enormous size. She positioned herself next to Zara, raised her head, and let out a howl that sent a visible, powerful purple vibration toward Escursia. Quickly she turned and nodded to Matthew. His time had come, and he was ready.

"Hear and mark my words, wicked spirit who has no soul. Your feeble curses on the pure are no more. Your black heart has rotted your mind, and you reek of dead flesh that was once pure. You cannot hurt me, for I am the chosen one, the true heir of the prophecy who will destroy you. Your tongue has tried to deceive me, as were your and your evil mistress's intentions to make me believe my truest of allies caused my injuries. Heed my warning, and listen well, sinful one. . . . It shall never happen again. You are a coward to curse the pure, exploiting them for your master's hatred and sinful desires. Heed now the old tongue, and obey these words, Escursia!"

Matthew read aloud the four thousand-year-old ancient ritual used to rid such evil spirits. He had to repeat many of the sentences three times. This was the only way, Suhama stressed, that it would be successful, just as it was in ancient times. The orange glow around Escursia seemed to pulsate like a slow beating heart, and the glaring beacon in her eyes took on the same rhythmical beat. Zara, Emia, and the thousands of dragonflies were still, waiting for any retaliation from her. Her cunning and despicable reputation is well-known, and they were prepared. Yammi was still feeding the fire with the spices, as Suhama had instructed him to do. It was important he continued to do this until Escursia was gone. It was an added defense of protection for everyone.

Matthew began to stutter and stopped reading. Escursia then looked straight into his eyes, and all hell broke loose. She opened her decayed mouth and roared with laughter.

"You fool," she bellowed so loudly that Matthew dropped the scroll to cover his ears. "You spake words of old wisdom, foolish heir, but they hold no power upon me. If thou are the great heir, where is thou *Apothropaic* wand? I have not come to destroy thee. On the contrary, dear heir, I appear because I was summoned. You hold great power, power that together we can fulfill your prophecy. Your allies speak false truths of me. They have made you gullible and blind of the truth. Hast thou not wondered why he sits in a metal chair? *Where were these creatures when you needed them?* I ask. I can be your greatest ally and give you what you so desire. I am very loyal to my mistress, as I can be to you.

I can bestow great fortunes, and the mistress promises you your kingdoms in return of fulfillment of the prophecy. Riches and power can be yours, unforsaken by any, and an eternal life with the wish your heart desires more than anything."

"*STOP.* . . . Your tongue is deceitful; it will not fool me. Your words bring poison from your darkness, but they will not sway me," Matthew responded fiercely. "Tell your mistress that she and her promises are like an asp hiding in gold. She will *never* sway me! I've had enough of you, Escursia! Return to your hole, back to the blackness that possesses your soul. Tell your mistress for me that I *will* succeed in my quest and without her. *Now be gone!*"

Escursia became enraged and began to spin around in the air, faster and faster, creating a violent vortex around her. She rose from its middle with her body engulfed in a fiery blaze. Zara and Emia immediately let out an ear-splitting hum. It was so forceful that Matthew vibrated in his chair, and Pearle, Yammi, and Abe fell to the ground. Abe managed to get up and while doing so picked up the scroll Matthew dropped. Then Escursia began throwing fireballs toward Matthew, but by now, Pearle was on her feet, holding her medallion up. The medallion created a repelling force, returning the fireballs back at Escursia, and she became infuriated! Escursia looked down and howled with anger, then brought her hands up and set her burning eyes on Pearle. She released her wrath into a massive spinning ball of fire, and Matthew knew it was heading for Pearle. But just when it came within inches of Pearle, Matthew pushed himself up from his chair and used his body as a shield, protecting his grandmother. He was stunned and fell back weak into his chair. Pearle was mortified and now as furious as Escursia. Oopi turned around and looked at Abe.

"*You must help him!* The scroll must be read in its entirety to work. Please, friend who shares of the blood . . . read," Oopi pleaded as he squealed from Matthew's shoulder.

Abe put his hand on Matthew's shoulder. But he didn't need the scroll; he knew what it said and what had to be done. He raised his left arm, and in his hand was a small protective amulet he always carried with him. It began to glow a blue hue, and Abe began to speak loudly and forcefully. He told Escursia she was an embarrassment to her god and that she would burn in eternity. He recanted words over and again from the scroll; then came his final warning.

"You are of Mut, your Heka is useless here. We are Maakheru! An army of good and will never fall from that. Now go, but know that the curses you laid upon the pure are gone; their souls are clean. So it shall be in the name of the almighty that created you, but knows you no more. *Be gone, be gone, be gone! MaZetiYeWayia Ka!*"

The lake cracked opened like a giant crater. Silver bolts of lightning shot up from the gaping hole, and an erupting fireball imploded. It quickly consumed Escursia, the billowing orb, and the towering pylons. The abyss that led to the bowels of the earth closed with a thunderous clap, shaking the ground.

Matthew turned and looked at Zara. She put her hand over her heart and bowed her head, and a burst of blinding light exploded over the fire. When he opened his eyes, she was gone, and so were all the dragonflies. And sadly, so was Emia. But he breathed a sigh of relief when he looked over his shoulder, seeing everyone was safe. He leaned back into his chair and smiled at Oopi, who had curled around Amora to protect her. Then he tilted his head back, exhaled, and gave Abe a gracious smile of appreciation.

Chapter Twenty-seven

The summer was unfolding quickly, and the night at the fire pit seems so long ago. Yammi will be going home soon, and Matthew isn't looking forward to that day. The boys developed a strong bond over the summer, and Matthew knows without Yammi, the little bit they discovered about the prophecy, and what they did to Escursia, would have been impossible. He already misses Oopi and Amora. They've been asleep in their bag, inside Matthew's closet, since his birthday. And there they will wait until he is ready to fulfill the prophecy.

Pearle doesn't speak about the night at the fire pit, and it seems almost a distant memory for nearly everyone but Matthew and the boys. Daniel's good, not quite his humorous self, but he hasn't had any abnormal outbursts of anger since. Nakia seems fine too. She and Zatu are getting along and becoming good friends. She even seems to be very friendly now with Abe Haram. As for Annabelle, she took a month off to visit her brother in Italy. It's the first vacation she's had in ten years. Thanks to Yammi and Suhama . . . Daniel, Nakia, and Annabelle have no recollection of what happened that night with Escursia. However, Matthew did tell Daniel all about it.

As for Yammi's arm, it's making progress. After his last surgery, the doctors say he may regain almost total use of it in time. Matthew's recovery, on the other hand, has been dramatic. Although he has a slight limp still and must continue physical therapy, his doctors expect him to make a full recovery.

Robert and Brian, as of yet, have had no luck with their plan and the medallions. They still sit in the evidence room. The results on the soil analysis was inconclusive, due to the fact that Pearle had imported several plants and flowers from Egypt, causing the questionable reason of foreign soil that should not have been in her lake. All the fingerprints were a dead end, and Addy is still trying to track down the boot manufacturer from the print they found. As for the fingernail found in the gold chain, according to the archaeological expert, his findings date them both to be over three thousand years old. But Robert and Brian have a theory about it. Their plausible explanation for it is that it must have come from one of Pearle's crates. What they can't explain, though, is how it got into the lake, let alone stuck in Oona's chain.

Pearle and Robert became engaged on Matthew's birthday, but not as he had planned. They married a few weeks later at City Hall and spent a week on Sanibel Island for their honeymoon.

Sol and Rahga halted work at the pyramid for the time being due to the heat this time of year. But they did manage to work until the end of May, removing many of the rocks and putting in support beams for the ceiling and walls, where most of the damage occurred from the cave-in. Sol has hopes to begin work again in the next few months or maybe sooner if they work at night.

Considering what happened almost three months ago, everyone is doing well and life is going on.

The weeks until Yammi was to leave have passed, and he is going home in a few days. After Annabelle returned from her trip last week, she and Pearle decided to have a little going away party for Yammi. Robert wanted to do something special for him too and took off with the three boys to some area attractions for a couple of days.

"I think they are home," Pearle yelled from the living room when she heard car doors slam. Brian, Denise, Abe, Annabelle, Nakia, and Pearle yelled, "Surprise!" when Yammi walked through the door. His dark eyes got as big and bright as a new half dollar, and his face turned bright red. There were streamers and balloons everywhere. A big sign saying *"We Will Miss You, Yammi"* hung over the arched entrance to the living room, and on it were handwritten sentiments from everyone to him.

"I . . . I don't know what to say except that I will miss you all something terrible. You have all been so good to me and are like my family." Yammi lowered his head to hide the tears running down his cheeks. "I cannot imagine my days not seeing any of you."

Pearle went over to him and hugged him. "We will miss you more than you know, Yammi, but you can come back anytime to see us. All you have to do is call me, and I will get you booked on the next flight here! And don't forget you're coming back in a few months for your checkup. I'm sure your mom and dad are anxious for you to get home. I know how much they have missed you."

"Yes, it will be good to see my parents again. . . . I have missed them terribly too."

"Well, folks, let's get this party started because it will be dark soon. We are going to have a feast of a Southern barbecue, and we have a lot more surprises for you, Yammi," Brian said, smiling and rubbing his hands together deviously as he led Yammi out back.

They went out on the patio, and Yammi was overwhelmed at what he saw. They had balloons floating everywhere, even in the pool, and he thought enough food to feed his small village at home. Annabelle made every type of salad you could think of; Pearle had ribs, steaks, and sausage on the grill; and Denise baked several decadent desserts. There was a pile of presents for him too. He got a digital camera, a set of luggage filled with clothes from Pearle, a Wii gaming system just like Matthew's, and many more gifts. After they ate, he sat back with his belly full and his face full of barbecue sauce.

"Do not tell my mother, but I *do not* look forward to eating her lamb stew twice a week again! I am truly going to miss all this delicious food."

"Well, maybe not," Annabelle said as she handed him a wet towel for his face and a book with a big red bow stuck on the cover. It was a recipe book she made and filled with all his favorite dishes. He was ecstatic and jumped up to hug her. . . .

After they ate and cleaned up, everyone went down to the lake. Robert and Brian arranged for a fireworks display that Yammi would never forget. It lasted about an hour and was so spectacular that he and the boys hardly spoke a word. A short time later, everyone had gone back to the house except the boys, who stayed to play Frisbee with the dogs. Yammi was standing by the lake, and Daniel threw a real high one at him. Yammi jumped as high as he could to catch it, and when he came down, he landed on his butt with his good hand in the water.

"Yammi, are you okay? Holy cow, what a catch!" Matthew yelled out.

"Yes, I am fine," he answered back. "But you better come quick. . . . I have found something, and you are never going to believe this!"

Daniel and Matthew made a mad dash to Yammi and found him still sitting on the ground. He brought his hand up out of the water and handed Matthew what he found buried in the wet sand.

"Oh, my God, it . . . but it can't be." And Matthew babbled on to himself. "Yammi, do you know what this means? You may be right . . . and if so . . . I've been wrong all along. . . . Oh, boy, I *am* in big trouble now."

"Why, Matt?" asked Daniel.

"Well . . . I . . . ahh . . . never got around to telling my grand-mother about the medallion and gold object I took from the pyramid. I'm going to have to show her and Robert this, though. Maybe Brian is right, and I've been wrong all along," he said as he looked at the chainless medallion. "I have assumed so much about this prophecy but know so little still about it, Yammi."

"Matthew, since we didn't find that book Sol told us about, it may be difficult to figure out the rest of the prophecy. According to the few odd messages left in Lapria's tomb, I think that book holds the key to many unanswered questions. Because whoever wrote them, I believe also wrote that book. Whoever it was knew everything and everyone involved in the prophecy. But it doesn't necessarily mean without it, we won't get it figured out. Matthew, I want you to remember this. It is a patient man who will reap the most rewards. It may take us longer without it, but rest assured that even after I get back home, I will continue to help you with this."

"This has been a wild few months, hasn't it, guys?" Daniel said with his arms around their shoulders. It's amazing we survived what we have. Matt, I want you to know that when you *do* figure out this prophecy, I'm here to help, to do whatever we have to."

"And I am sure you know that goes for me too," added Yammi.

As the boys headed toward the house, Matthew stopped and turned around to look at the lake. "Ya know, guys, figuring out this prophecy is only half of my problem. . . . Once that's done, I'll be faced with the other half."

"Yes, this is true," Yammi answered. "And then it will be *Matthew's Quest.*"